Crossing

A Chinese Family
Railroad Novel

Lisa Redfern

Little Mountain
Publishing.biz

Cover design – Donner Summit
Cassandra Raiche

Library of Congress Control Number: 2023924579
ISBN: 978-0-9998591-2-4

Crossing: A Chinese Family Railroad Novel. Copyright © 2024 by Lisa Redfern. All rights reserved. No part of this book may be used or reproduced in any manner whatsoever without written permission except in the case of brief quotations embodied in reviews, articles, and social media posts.
For permissions write to
Little Mountain Publishing
P.O. Box 1038
Nevada City, California, 95959

Dedication

for the ghosts

    First, this book is dedicated to family—the ones we know and the ones we haven't met yet—and to people of differing cultures and genders blending in communities. They make them prosperous, in ways that don't involve money.

    It is dedicated to the State of California, a wild and wondrous place that leaves permanent impressions on those who visit and live there.

    Finally, it is dedicated to bones. Everyone reading this has them. They support and move us from place to place. They're durable. Once water and soft tissues disappear, they lay there just beneath the surface. Sometimes…they return to the world above to retell their stories.

Information & Organization

The story you are about to enter contains a few things you should know about before beginning.

Animal Vignettes are scattered throughout. They are there to remind you that humans are not the only living beings that are part of this story. Each is a mini time snapshot showing body language and thoughts which are communicated in English. (Obviously, this is not how they think!)

Newspaper Article Snippets are mostly, but not always, at the end of the California chapters. They highlight speech styles used at that time as well as topics editors thought were important. Each snippet includes the publication and article title, and the month, day, and year it was published making it easy to find should you wish to read it in its entirety.

The **Spoken Language** in *Crossing* is mostly Cantonese. When English is used, it is noted. Chinese characters also speak a formal language, Mandarin.

Chinese Names are listed with surname first and given name last. Example: Yang (given name) Gee (surname) in Chinese is listed as Gee Yang. Historic Chinese naming conventions are used for all the Chinese characters.

Attitudes in the U.S. during the mid-1860s were bitter. Strong feelings lingered from the Civil War. Hope for uniting the nation focused on completion of the transcontinental railroad.

The Union Pacific Railroad Company (UP), building from the east, employed war veterans and free Blacks.

The Central Pacific Railroad Company (CPRR), building from the west, would cross the Sierra Nevada Mountains, presenting some of the most difficult challenges with steep grades, hard rock, and severe weather. They also struggled to find and keep workers.

To solve the labor problem, Charles Crocker of the CPRR recruited thousands of young men from southern China.

When the newcomers arrived, Anglo-Americans did not understand the function of the Chinese Associations (a social service supporting travelers in foreign countries). They assumed it was another form of slavery and "Celestials" were blamed for taking work from white men.

This **Cultural Scapegoating** set the framework for the for the Chinese Exclusion Act of 1882.

A **Bibliography** at the end contains research resources including books, documentaries, videos, and websites that could keep you busy for years.

LOCKPORT
Early Spring
Sacramento Delta, California
1868
—

Lee squats to scoop up a handful of saturated earth. He spreads it evenly between two palms. "I'm checking to see if my father will speak to me through the soil," he explains to nine-year-old Bing Hap. Lee inhales deeply, closing his eyes to concentrate. He holds his hands out to the girl whose nickname is his shadow, Lǐ de yǐngzi. She brings her nose close, mimicking his actions. With a satisfied smile, she returns his gaze. Lee recognizes the spark of curiosity gleaming there. His delight in the simple moment splinters as thoughts of his children fill his mind. Song, his daughter, would be six and his son, Luck, who he'd never met, would be four. *Have they learned to honor the soil?* He wonders. Another child at his family farm, Ming, makes him wince and turn away.

"Did it work?" Bing Hap asks. "Did he say anything?"

Lee gazes off in the distance while he spreads his fingers, letting the mud drop. He brushes away th e clingy pieces. "Father is content because Mother prepares food for him. He likes the new clothing she sends through the flames." Lee reaches over to rinse his hands in the water of the Sacramento River. As he does, he's acutely aware of its melting headwaters and the snow it comes from—evil stuff. "When I was working on the iron road in the mountains," Lee nods toward the east, "Father sent someone to tell me about your town, Lockport. It shares similarities with my home. It is near the water; families live here. The ancestors knew," he continues, "coming here would help me sort out dilemmas that are too troublesome for a young girl to understand." Lee smiles to take the sting out of his words. He flicks a spray of water in her direction.

Bing Hap giggles, swiping droplets from her arm.

Before reaching for a rope tied to a railroad spike planted in the earth up to its flat head, Lee hesitates. The sight of the cordage, attached to something unseen, makes him think about the most recent tragedy on The Hill. Coburn's Station burned to all but two or three buildings. Was the fire caused by an accidental spark? Or was it set by someone wanting to rid the town of Celestials? While he can't say he loved the place, important parts of his life happened there. When the town was rebuilt, they moved it slightly and gave it a new name, Truckee.

Bing Hap watches him grasp the submerged rope and begin pulling it, hand-over-hand, curving his back. His heels sink into the mud. A fish trap comes into view, emerging like a phantom from the murky green depths. Hauling it onto dry ground, water sieves through the screen. It teems with squirming, potato-sized crawdads. Hap holds a basket steady as Lee opens the door to shake the crustaceans out.

୬୨୧

Signal Crayfish,
Pacifastacus fortis

Falling.

TAIL: Squip…squip. Squip, squip, squip!

Escape moves always worked before. No water.

PINCERS: Waving, snapping.

A crush of squirming hard bodies.

Too many of us together.

NOT good.

୬୨୧

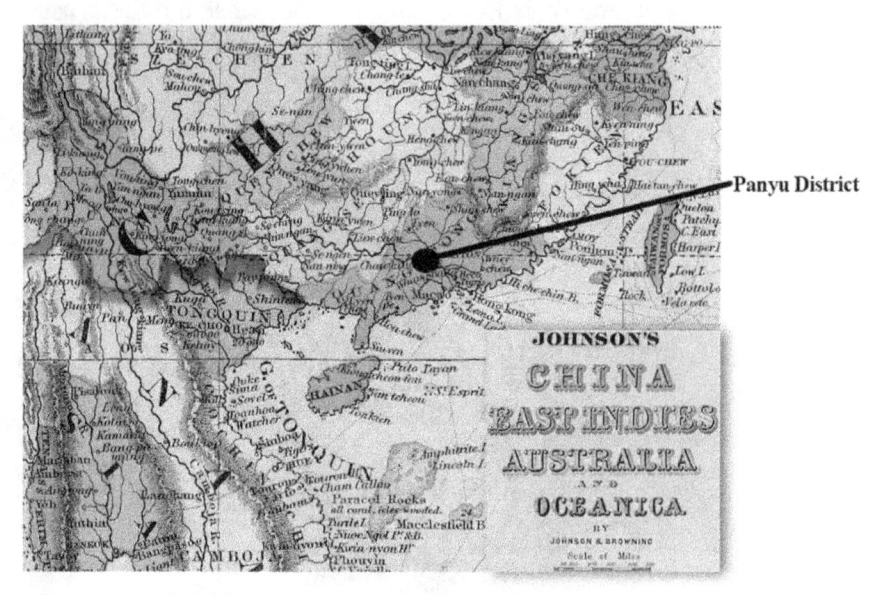

MAP | Southern China, Panyu District

SLEEPWALKER
Panyu District, China
1847
—

"Yang!" Five-year-old Lee, the youngest boy in the family, shouts in the darkness. He was sound asleep but sprang up from bed. His eyes were open, but if anyone saw his face, they'd notice his vacant gaze.

"Yang!" the boy called again.

His brother, Yang, who'd awoken the first time Lee spoke, scooched to the far edge of their bed and tightly pressed a pillow over his head.

The oldest, Fu-chi, who had his own bed alongside his brothers, cracked an eye open to watch their interaction.

Predictably, blankets shuffled, and Lee's bare feet came to the floor. He stood in place while Fu-chi counted five breaths. Holding a corner of his pillow, he backhanded it on top of Yang's.

"Ouch!" Yang complained, uncovering his face.

The front door opened. Fu-chi could see Lee's shape, illuminated by moonlight, moving across the threshold. "Go get him!" he shouted. "You can't let him wander!"

Yang's eyes pooled with tears. "It's scary out there, Fu-chi," he complained.

"If you answered him when he first woke, you wouldn't have to go, would you? You're sharing a bed with him. He's your responsibility."

As Yang went sniffling out the door, Fu-chi groaned and sat up. He scratched his scalp, then combed his fingers through long hair that needed a wash. On his chin, where a few stiff hairs sprouted, there was an inflamed tenderness from a fresh batch of pimples. He'd like nothing better than to scrape away the pus mounds. But the memory of Mother's reaction last time stops him.

She'd narrowed her eyes when she first spotted his handiwork. Stepping close, she pointed. "Phlegm stagnation!" She said it as if she were announcing a crime. He noticed Father unsuccessfully attempting to hide a smile as he left. Fu-chi was further humiliated when Mother made him pull her in the cart to the herbalist, more so when the medicine man, his wife, and their teenage daughter inspected his face. He hated the itchy paste they'd bought. Mother insisted he slather it on the welts and drink the bitter tea they recommended. Thinking about it, Fu-chi's mouth filled with saliva. He swallowed hard to keep himself from gagging.

Making fists, squeezing his fingernails into his palms, Fu-chi forced his attention from his chin back to his little brothers. *I'll give them to the count of ten before I go,* he thought.

Hearing them on their way back, Fu-chi flopped down. "Good boy, Yang. I knew you could do it," he said when the door closed.

MO CHOU & MOTHER GEE
Spring
Panyu District, China
1848
—
*"Success depends upon previous preparation,
and without such preparation,
there is sure to be failure."*
– Confucius
—

Mo Chou slid her fingers under the covers to touch Fu-Chi's bare thigh. It is warm and smooth. By his rhythmic breathing, she could tell he was still asleep. From the time of their marriage, the couple occupied the only private room in the house. Mo Chou knew her husband would gladly respond if she started clouds and rain. But her mother-in-law would know...Rolling out of bed, in complete darkness, she reached for the rough-spun house dress she'd lain out the night before, pulling it over her head. Tiptoeing across the room, she lifted the door handle, putting downward pressure to the left so the hinges wouldn't squeak. Closing it behind her, she slipped her feet into cloth-soled slippers before moving toward the faint candle glow in the kitchen.

Mother Gee was already there, lighting the stove. Mo Chou reached for the empty water pail by the back door. Changing shoes again, she stepped outside, pausing as her chest tightened. A multitude of childhood stories about tiger attacks in predawn hours and roaming hungry ghosts paraded through her mind. The hair at the back of her neck prickled.

At the well, she attached the bucket to a rope and let loose the clamp that held it in place. She bounced up and down on the balls of her feet while waiting for the splash. Once the bucket reached the bottom, she jiggled the rope around, making sure it filled. Assured she'd accomplished her goal, she set to work cranking the shaft. Soon, moisture droplets beaded on her forehead and dripped between her breasts. Mo Chou was relieved that her worries had receded back into the corners of her mind.

Mother raised her eyebrows when she saw splash marks down the front of Mo Chou's dress. She had a cooking pot ready for the water.

This would remain on the stove all day. Mother backed away to the far edge of the workspace, where she filled a teapot with loose leaves, measuring them out with precision.

Mo Chou moved with confidence, adjusting the fire logs to heat another section of the stove top. Adding a mixture of dry grains to a smaller pot, she slid in a heaping spoonful of goose fat before submerging the mixture under water and adjusting its position for maximum heat. She worked on chopping peanuts and pickled vegetables, sliced thin, just the way Mother liked them.

Shao Pei no longer viewed her daughter-in-law as a burden. The girl was fully trained. She'd even accomplished teaching Mo Chou to play the erhu, an instrument like a two-stringed guitar. Pei had learned to play it as part of her girlhood training. Her father had gifted a fine instrument to the Gee family when she married. Grandfather Gee had fashioned a second one, modeled after the first. On special occasions, Shao Pei (Mother Gee) and Mo Chou played together, to the delight of all.

Though she'd never admit it, Mo Chou's work relieved Shao Pei's constant pain. It allowed the cracks in her hands to heal. The ache in her feet that affected the nerves in her legs, causing lower back to spasms, lessened when she sat for longer periods.

Mo Chou's next duty to the Gee family would be to bear Fu-chi a son. If the dandelion root Shao Pei had added to the tea worked as it should, that wouldn't happen for a while. As she poured hot water over the herbs, she thought about her boys.

Fu-chi came early in her marriage. For the next eleven years, with no pregnancies, she wondered if she'd displeased the gods. Her response had been to increase temple visits and offerings. For this, the villagers called her the "Devout One'" For no reason she could explain, the other two arrived almost one after the other.

If Yang were older, Shao Pei thought, *I could have another daughter-in-law trained before a baby hinders Mo Chou.* Shao Pei sipped her tea, nodding at the flavor. Dandelion is also good for digestion and liver cleansing. She poured a cup for Mo Chou, sliding it within reach as the girl stirred their thick morning congee.

FIRST SON LEAVES
Fu-chi, age 20 | Yang, age 9 | Lee, age 6
Panyu District, China
1849

—

Yang sleeps with his mouth open: his putrid breath warmed Lee's face. Lee rubbed the crust from the corners of his eyes. He wondered what woke him. Maybe it was the cat leaving to hunt? Suddenly, he knew! He was full of pee and about to spill!

Lee didn't bother slipping on sandals. From memory rather than sight, he picked his way over floor stones and woven mats, around the mattress where Father slumbered and Mother quietly snored. He crept past the closed door of the only private room in their house, where Fu-chi slept with Mo Chou and their baby.

Lee's dog, Humbug, pushed a wet nose into his hand. Boy and dog trotted a short distance from the family compound to share mutual relief, Lee on a rock and Humbug in a clump of grass. The acrid scent of urine lingered in the surrounding air.

Uncle Lung named Humbug after his Gold Mountain sojourn—a trip across the Pacific Ocean to hunt for gold. The word "humbug" means falsehood. This was Uncle's opinion about the claims of riches that the land would yield. Lee had heard his uncle say that their pronunciation of the word was all wrong, but he never corrected it because it didn't matter to the dog.

Lee heard a flutter in the tree branches above. He froze, looking for shadowy bandits. A calloused hand clamped over his mouth. His parents had warned him about marauders. As his feet lifted from the ground, he kicked and scratched. He was sure he'd feel a knife blade slicing across his throat. *Where's that stupid dog?* he wondered.

"Calm yourself, little brother," a familiar voice hissed in Lee's ear as he was set down.

"Fu-chi!" Lee squawked. He pressed a hand to his chest. "Why are you outside?"

"Shhhh! You'll wake the ancestors in their graves." Fu-chi grabbed Lee's arm, pulling him farther from the compound. "I've come from a meeting."

Lee nodded, matching his brother's steps. Fu-chi was everything he hoped to be when he grew older—strong, handsome, and respected by the elders. His only fault, as far as Lee could tell, was his wife—or their baby daughter, Ngon. Fu-chi wasn't upset about having a girl; he seemed to like her.

Finding a low wall, Fu-chi patted the space next to him. He took off his jacket, holding it so Lee could put his arms through the long sleeves. "I may have to go away for a little while," he said.

"To fight with the rebels?"

Fu-chi shrugged, then picked up a few pebbles.

Comforted by the warmth of the jacket, Lee snuggled into it.

"You are good brother, Lee. If I go, you'll help Mo Chou look after Ngon?"

"If you're not here, it's Yang's job to help look out for the family. He's next oldest."

Fu-chi huffed, "Yang…he'll be lucky if he makes it to manhood. I think someday it will be up to you and me."

"What can I do?"

Tapping the boy's forehead, Fu-chi replied, "You'll use what you have in there."

"No one listens to the youngest son," Lee complained.

Fu-chi tugged on Lee's braid, giving him a wink as they walked back to the house.

※

At sunrise, on the auspicious day of the year when stars aligned and swallows mate under house eaves, Gee Fong took his sons to the fields. They were barefoot and wearing pants that stopped at the knees. Humbug trotted happily after them. Fu-chi carried a long pole, over which hung bundles of rice seedlings. Terraced fields, with their glass-like surface, reflected faint golden light; they resembled silver snakes winding down the mountain slopes. The cool morning water shocked the system when the men first entered, causing forests of goosebumps to roughen their skin.

Fu-chi slogged ahead, with Father walking behind, removing as many seedlings as his grip could carry. He handed some behind to

Yang and Lee. Their footsteps were moiling, pulling each one up through thick, sucking mud. When they stepped down, liquefied earth squeezed through their toes, molding to their ankles.

Father and the younger boys lowered rice starts into the water, nestling them in the mud, saying prayers for fertility. Reap from these plants must be plentiful. Last year, they sold land to pay increased taxes. Emperor Daoguang declared the people must help raise money to support armies fighting the Jesus-loving Taiping rebels. Their land holdings were already smaller than would comfortably feed the family.

Renegades had come through during the last harvest, ransacking villages, ripping up farmland. They'd taken all but a few of the catfish Father had scrimped and saved to buy. Father's plan had been for the fish to eat mosquito larvae, fertilize their plants, and become an additional food source. Now they'd have to wait for the surviving fish to reproduce and pray that cranes didn't eat them all first.

Shao Pei had the difficult responsibility of divvying up food portions. In this, she went against tradition where elders had priority. The boys, Mo Chou, and the baby maintained a healthy weight while the rest of them shrank. The strain showed starkly in their loose skin.

※

Humbug followed on levee tops and napped under shade trees.

While they worked, Lee listened to Fu-chi argue with Father. In front of the women, this disrespectful way of speaking could cause a beating, but Father allowed it out here.

"They've been watching us for over a year," Fu-chi stated. "The only reason they didn't break all our levees is because I've told them I'll join. They won't wait much longer. Either I go or they'll come."

"I can't afford to lose you, First Son," Father said. "Your brothers are too young to be of much help." He glanced over his shoulder, looking back at Yang and Lee. "You must continue putting them off." He lowered his voice. "Your mother has seen bad omens."

Humbug stood. A deep growl sounded in his chest. The hair between his shoulder blades raised. Three-armed Taiping rebels emerged through trees at the end of their planting row, one on horseback, two on foot. The rider held a gun, while the footmen carried a bow and a club.

"You, there!" Yang yelled, "You don't belong here!"

Father and Fu-chi turned to stare at Yang with wide eyes and held their breaths. Humbug charged, barking. For Lee, the next moments moved at half-speed. Father slapped Yang, sending him to his knees.

Lee screamed, "No!" calling after Humbug.

The dog raced towards the intruders, snarling. A rebel on foot stepped forward, aiming his bow. The other squinted and raised his club, gripping it firmly with both hands. Humbug launched at the man, baring sharp teeth. With a mighty swing, the club crushed the dog's skull, making a wet thud. The body fell to the ground, quivering.

Father clamped a hand on Lee's arm, preventing him from running to Humbug, which would have placed him within reach of the strangers. Pushing him back, Father shielded him. Fu-chi threw down his pole, spilling the baskets. He waited in place as Father and Lee came abreast. Father kept a restraining hold on Lee.

The archer pulled his bow string, aiming straight at Father's heart. Fu-chi yelled, "No! It's me you want!"

Lowering the weapon, the archer glanced at the leader. The man on horseback commented to Father, "It works the same on children." He motioned to the dog. "If you want to keep the other two, you won't make trouble." Without saying a word, Fu-chi started walking.

Fong released Lee, who only had eyes for Humbug. Yang stood by Father's side, holding a hand over the red mark on his face.

"He's dead," Lee sobbed.

Fong looked down. His red-rimmed eyes met his son's. "Be grateful it was only the dog," he replied quietly.

The boys watched as their father pressed hands over his face. He shuddered as if he were struggling to keep sound inside when Fu-chi was no longer visible. They knew planting would be impossible without Fu-Chi, and they also knew that the work must continue.

"Mother and Mo Chou must be told what has happened," Fong said. His voice was flat.

Father used his shirt to cover Humbug's fatal wound. He lifted him gently, placing him over Lee's thin shoulders. Father and Yang retrieved the planting implements, hefting each end of the pole, the waterlogged baskets weighing them down. As they walked, Lee noticed Yang sniffling. His stomach churned when he glanced at his father's face, stone-like and fierce. Tears pooled in his eyes when the house came into view. What would happen to Fu-chi?

If the emotions the men carried home felt momentous, they were nothing compared to the storm Mother and Mo Chou made when they heard the news. They screamed and cried, pulling at their hair. Mother begged Father to tell her it was a lie. Mo Chou gathered Ngon in her arms, squeezing until she squalled. Their pain was raw and terrible to witness. Yang ushered Lee to the barn. Neither boy gave any thought to concealing their emotions. Their tears ran freely.

"Are those bad men going to kill Fu-chi?" Lee asked.

"No! He's strong," Yang said. "That's why they want him to fight."

※

Lee and Yang remained in the barn until the adults quieted. Mo Chou appeared; her face as stony as Father's had been earlier. "Ngon is with your mother," she stated. Her tone and words were abrupt, as if she were scolding a merchant in the market for over charging. "You boys are coming with me."

She got fresh baskets and had Yang help her transfer the plant starts into them. Then, she took the boys out to finish planting. She groaned under the weight of the pole, heavy with bundles of grass, balancing the baskets on either side. When her face grew red, the boys asked if they should seek help. In clipped tones, she replied, "The burden will lift as soon as you get the rice in the ground!"

The repetitive work was mind-numbing. Uncle Lung came to help for the last few hours, taking the pole from Auntie. Relieved of her burden, Mo Chou moaned, but she kept going until every plant had its roots married to the earth.

Storm clouds darkened the fading daylight and distant thunder boomed as the bone-weary planters returned, shuffling into the U-shaped courtyard. A center drain served as a corridor, a protected animal keep, and a gathering place when the weather was favorable. Most families kept to their own spaces out of respect and privacy, unless someone needed help.

Auntie Liu, Uncle's wife, motioned for them to come to her house, where she served warm pickled mustard greens and eggs, *Seen Choy Jï Dàn*. It took Mo Chou a few bites and sips of chrysanthemum-infused Oolong tea to revive enough to ask, "Where's Ngon? Is she asleep with her grandparents?"

"She's not!" Auntie surprised them all with her sharp reply. "Baozhai found her a short time ago, almost in the rice fields. You're lucky she didn't drown! Your baby was hysterical and soiled!"

"What!" Mo Chou partially stood, her face pasty, eyes wild.

"You should have known better than to leave her with Pei…" Auntie scolded. "Sit back down," she said, waving a hand as she regarded her nephews, who'd stopped eating to listen. "Baozhai has her asleep in my room." Her voice softened. "Let her be."

When the family finished eating, Mo Chou looked in on her thirteen-month-old daughter. Cousin Baozhai had a protective arm wrapped around Ngon as she slept. Her thumb was in her mouth and her hair was chaotic. *She doesn't know yet, how much her world has changed,* Mo Chou thought.

It was dark in Grandfather's room at the end of the U. The eldest member of the family usually sought slumber before everyone else. Thin light glinted from under the door of Gee Fong's abode. Two candles flickered near the head of each floor mattress in the main room. At the end of one, where Mother and Father had been sleeping, was a pile of clothing. Mo Chou stilled when she recognized them. They belonged to Fu-chi, Ngon, and herself. In the hours they'd been gone, Mother and Father had re-established themselves in the house's private bedroom.

"Why did Mother…" Lee said before Yang halted him with a pinch. He glared at his brother, who pressed a finger tightly against his lips.

Mo Chou sank to her knees on the mattress, not bothering to move the clothes. She pulled Fu-chi's jacket over her as she lay down, turning away from the boys. When Lee blew out the candles, he saw her shoulders quivering.

The monsoon started with fat drops falling sporadically until the skies opened, sending drenching sheets of rain over the roof. Water dripping through the cracks masked the tears the family continued to shed over Fu-chi's absence.

※

The weather broke two-and-a-half weeks later. Grandfather took Lee and Ngon with him into the forest to tend to the charcoal oven.

Yang's status shift disturbed Lee. Even Ngon's singing didn't penetrate his sour mood.

"We're going to make cherry wood charcoal today." Grandfather smiled, revealing dark spaces where teeth had once been.

Lee knew Grandfather was trying to dislodge his temper. He resisted at first, but then, as usual, he couldn't help himself. "Because you like it when you can taste its flavors in the meat."

Grandfather clapped his hands. "And because your mother never suspects."

Lee turned his face away so Grandfather couldn't see it. *Mother knows everything*, he thought, *but she likes keeping that a secret!*

Grandfather's only task was to watch and advise. The round footprint for the support logs was already trenched, and the woodpile was sorted by length and thickness. Lee and Ngon constructed a cone shape with cherry wood at the center. Lee explained to Ngon that the earth oven they were building would look like a beehive when it was complete. They took a brief break for the picnic lunch Mother had sent with them, then started on phase two. This was Lee's favorite part.

Next to the river, they added water to the pre-existing pit where they'd make lots of mud. The mixing of water and soil was fun, as was patting it all around the wood cone. After a while, though, their muscles grew sore from transporting buckets from the mud pit to the oven.

With the completion of the earth oven, Grandfather took a stick and poked holes around the top and smaller ones at the bottom. This would create airflow to keep the fire burning inside.

Evening approached, and they had the oven started by the time Mo Chou, Father, and Yang arrived, pulling Mother on a light-weight farm cart. The women packed food for the evening meal and blankets for Grandfather and Lee. After eating, Yang got to add fresh mud to the cracks that appeared. This sent Lee back to dwelling on angry thoughts.

When it was time for everyone to leave Grandfather and Lee alone, Ngon protested.

"Shhh," Mo Chou soothed. "You're not ready yet to fight night tigers, Little One. You must come home with me."

Lee was looking forward to the camp out…and to being away from Yang. But he wasn't completely sure he was ready to fight night tigers. *If a tiger comes, Grandfather couldn't do anything.* They watched as the family and the cart grew small in the distance.

Grandfather sat for some time on a log, smoking his pipe. He alternated his gaze from the stars to the oven. Eventually, Lee came to sit next to him. Without a word, he offered the pipe to his grandson.

Taken aback, Lee asked, "Really?"

"Go on," Grandfather said.

Lee put the end in his mouth and inhaled like he'd seen Grandfather do. The smoke felt like it burned everything inside that it touched. The need to violently expel the vileness came suddenly. But Grandfather didn't choke and gag, so Lee held it. His eyes watered with the effort, then it all came out with a coughing fit that seemed to last forever.

Grandfather didn't laugh. He gently removed the pipe from Lee's hand, rubbed his back, and smoked.

When he got his breath back, Lee wiped his drool on a sleeve. "Why do you do that?" His expression looked hurt.

"It is interesting, don't you think, that we continue with habits like this when our first experience is so dreadful?" Responding to the question in Lee's eyes, he chuckled and nodded as he said, "Oh yes. My first time was just like that." The pipe lip clicked against his teeth as Grandfather inhaled a deep drag, closing his eyes with pleasure as he did so. He blew out the smoke in a long, thin trail before he turned back to Lee. "You've been mad because you think you are being treated like a child."

Lee's eyes dropped to the dirt between his feet.

"You think it is unjust," Grandfather stated.

Lee nodded.

"You are too young to understand that your approach to manhood is closer than you know. For that, I am truly sorry."

When Grandfather offered him another go, Lee shook his head "no" and crawled under his blankets. He fell asleep watching the fading and glowing of Grandfather's pipe bowl.

WALKING DEAD
Fu-chi, age 23 | Yang, age 12 | Lee, age 9 | Ngon, age 5
Panyu District, China
1852
—

Yang could tell by the angle of the sun; the hour was growing late. He jogged down the ravine carrying a dead goose in a bag. Mother had sent him to their secret hideaway to kill one of their birds. Leaving the cool shade of the canyon, the temperature and humidity generated by the rice fields felt like walking into a hot fog bank. The smell of green plants, water, and fertile soil settled over him, as familiar as the back of his hand, the scents of home. He ran past the two-story village watchtower and to his family compound.

When he saw the windows boarded up, he uttered, "Chrysanthemus! (Anus)" It couldn't mean anything good.

Lee came running in his direction. His eyes were enormous.

"What's going on?" Yang whispered.

"A messenger came right after you left," Lee said. "Priests are coming, escorting the dead. We have to get inside. It's almost dark!" He tugged at his sleeve.

Nodding, Yang shoved the burlap bag in Lee's hands while saying, "I have blood on my clothes. I must wash it off!"

The boys shared wide-eyed looks. Everyone knew the hopping dead were dangerous. As the skin loses color, souls grow angry. They roam nearby looking for energy—qi—to come back to life. Black cats and fresh blood are known attractants for hungry ghosts!

Yang heard the gongs growing closer. Furiously scrubbing at his tunic, he noticed his fingernails. Under each one was a crescent of dirt and dried blood! He could hear the priests chanting! Ripping at his shirt, he pulled it over his head. Crumpling it, he tossed it away.

The sound of marching footsteps grew clear. Glancing up, he saw robed men carrying lanterns walking beside another set of men moving in single file. These men were rigid and had cloth squares covering their faces. One man at the front rang a gong. He called out to Yang, "Is this the home of Gee Fong?"

Yang opened his mouth, but nothing came out. A noxiously sweet, putrid smell like slippery old meat swarming with maggots reached his nose. His stomach clenched. He recoiled as that stink invaded his sinuses. The next thing he knew, his father and uncle were standing in front of him. Uncle caught his eye, directing him to leave. He retreated to the barn, the closest building, but couldn't resist peeking through the gaps in the wood.

Uncle opened the gate for the men. Yang watched Father bow and heard him greet the Taoist priest. After a brief exchange, Father stumbled, then steadied himself. Uncle rested a hand on Father's shoulder.

"What are they doing?" Lee tapped him on the shoulders. Yang, never taking his eyes off the scene, swiped an arm back, pushing him away with an impatient "Shhh!"

The priest, accompanied by a lantern holder, walked along the lines, stopping to examine the writing on the face cloths. He nodded at one, bending over to untie the leather strapping that affixed the man's elbows to his side. At the priest's nod, the men at either end lowered long bamboo poles that had ridden under the arms of the corpses. Two more robed men came forward to lift the body up and over the opposite pole, handing it off to Father and Uncle.

Yang watched as they hefted their awkward burden toward the house. His legs gave out when he heard his mother's high-pitched, agonized scream, "Fu-chi!"

Lee's mind blocked out the meaning of what his uncle and father were doing, as well as the significance of the shouting inside the house. From his position on hands and knees, he watched as the priests redistributed the dead along the carrying poles. He heard them huff as they bent knees and rose to take the weight. They lurched forward, in a stiff shuffle, toward the road. The gong-carrying priest closed the gate behind them, rapping the mallet against the instrument, signaling all within hearing distance to remain in hiding. The dead, suspended on poles, bounced in time with the steps of the priests who carried them home.

Yang's heart felt frozen in his chest. Fu-chi was dead. He was now First Son.

※

There was a moment of indecision inside. Where should they place him? Through her sobs, Mother pointed. "On my bed. Put him in there."

Mo Chou stepped forward, surprising everyone. "I am his wife. No one touches him but me," she declared. Unabashed tears overflowed her eyes; she didn't swipe at them. Holding her chin up and forcing her shoulders back, her gaze dared anyone to challenge her.

After what felt like an eternity, Mother nodded. She leaned forward, whispering, "You'll regret this."

Mo Chou dropped her eyes. She motioned to the men to place her husband on the bed in the room. Speaking quietly, she said, "Bozahai, please see that my mother-in-law rests and light candles. Auntie Liu, would you bring the cleansing supplies and…" her voice broke, "and Fu-chi's good clothes from the chest at the end of my bed?" She turned to Yang and Lee. "Will you boys look after your niece?"

Closing the door behind everyone, Mo Chou gripped the handle with both hands. Leaning her forehead on the wood, she let silent sobs wash over her. If she kept her eyes closed, she could pretend it was still morning, and she was still just a woman with a husband away fighting in a rebellion. She didn't want to be a widow. She didn't want her daughter to grow up without a father. She didn't want to never have a son. When she turned around, she'd have to face the fact that all of those were true. In her mind, she could hear his voice as it had been, deep in the night when they'd last shared a pillow in this bed. *If they come for me, I can't promise I'll return. If I don't make it...* She'd stopped him, placing her fingers over his lips. "Don't even think that way!" she'd said. He'd kissed her hand, then her mouth, and for a while, they lost themselves in marital bliss. *If I don't come back to you in this life, I need to ask you for a promise. Anything,* she'd replied. *You must be the only one preparing this body. If I have a dishonorable death, say nothing. Send me paper money and food and know that I'll wait for you until we meet again in the afterlife.*

She'd agreed, of course, if only to ease his mind, but now she was here, and he was there, she wasn't sure she could follow through. At the soft knock on the door, she opened it for Auntie. Liu handed Mo Chou a stack of cleaning cloths along with Fu-chi's finest set of clothes. From behind her, Auntie's husband handed over a heavy bowl of warm, scented jasmine water. Mo Chou left the door open as she placed it near the head of the bed. "Are you sure?" the older woman asked.

Mo Chou nodded, keeping her gaze downcast. When she was alone again with her husband, she moved to his side. Starting with the cloth face covering, she removed it, tossing the fabric to the floor. His face was unshaven. She'd never seen him with a beard. Her heart ached as she noted the crow's feet lines and streaks of white in his hair. It had been three years since he'd been taken from the fields. She'd had no news for months, but had never faltered in her belief that he would come home walking on his own feet. Frowning and swallowing past the lump in her throat, she reached out to run her fingertip along a scar under his right eye. His temperature and the stiff feel of his skin sent ripples of revulsion up her arms and into her tightened scalp. Holding her breath and biting her tongue, she prepared to wash his hair.

As she scrubbed near his face, she noticed something silver dripping from his ear. Dabbing a finger into it, she brushed it against her palm. It balled up and rolled around when she moved. *What is it?* she wondered. She remembered her mother and grandmother showing her a woman's secret. It was Carinthian Quicksilver! But what was it doing in Fu-chi's ear? She collected the liquid metal, placing it in a teacup. It was in his other ear, too. She added that to the cup. When she went to shave him, she discovered more in his mouth. Trying bravely to not feel afraid of something she didn't understand, she kept her focus on her task.

She cut away the cloth wrapped around his body. As it peeled back, a terrible stench filled the room. Turning her head away, she coughed, barely able to keep from throwing up. Dipping a cloth strip in the water, she wrapped it around her mouth and nose, tying it behind her head. Fu-chi was filthy! Dark lines of grime showed at the base of his neck and where his sleeves ended. *He must not have bathed in months.* Her husband relished cleanliness. His filth was another piece of information that added measures to her sadness. But more terrible discoveries awaited. Bone protruded in places where his feet scraped the ground as the priests transported him. Tough calluses had built up on his palms. He was missing two fingers on his left hand. These injuries must have happened a while ago, because they had healed. More scars were littered across his shoulders and abdomen. A small puncture wound was still open near his navel. *Is this what you didn't want your mother to see?* She circled it lightly with a fingertip.

She discovered she didn't have enough strength to flip him over after the front of him was clean. Crying at her unsuccessful efforts, she briefly thought about asking Father Gee to help. Sinking to the floor, she hung her head between her knees and let the waves of loss carry her. She may have fallen asleep, because the next thing she knew, she jerked awake with an idea.

Taking the top blanket on the bed and folding it over him, she walked to the opposite side. Grabbing the edge, she climbed onto the mattress, then leaned back, using her weight as a counterbalance. She did it! When she saw his back, her feelings of accomplishment deflated. She couldn't stop herself from making a strangled cry.

There was a knocking at the door. "Mo Chou? Is everything alright?" Father Gee asked.

"It's...ok..." She sniffled. "Don't come in."

When she'd turned Fu-chi, the padding packed into his lower back fell away. The material was dark and stiff with blood. Before her was a gaping hole, laying open his insides. He'd been killed by an attack he didn't see coming. Fu-chi was no war hero. He was just a conscripted farmer who died for a doomed ideal. She also knew that with Fu-chi's death, her own value, and Ngon's, plummeted. Wilting to the floor, she pressed her cheek to the stone tile, attempting to keep her own insides from spilling out. She wished Fu-chi's hungry ghost would swoop down and possess her spirit so they could escape this hell—together. But he wasn't moving, and she finally understood why he'd asked for her promise.

Forcing herself to her knees, then to her feet, she avoided looking directly at the wound. She placed several cleaning cloths over it and used the rest of the water to clean his skin. When she was done, she dragged herself over to where Mother kept her sewing box. Her hands shook as she pushed the cloths down into the hole, then tugged ragged pieces of skin across it. Mo Chou sewed.

By the time she struggled through getting fresh clothes on him, turned him to face up, and straightened his pants and shirt fastenings, she could feel exhaustion sucking her toward oblivion. She took a clean bedsheet from the drawer, wrapped the soiled cloths inside, and tied it with twine.

As she regarded her husband, she realized she would never be alone with him again. This was all she had left. She walked to the opposite side of the bed, laid down next to him, and immediately fell into a dreamless sleep.

※

The family had gone into mourning. Ceremonies and rituals were observed. Paper money was burned. First Son would have wealth in the afterlife. Food was set out to appease the ancestors. A hard glint shone in Mother's eyes. She rarely spoke, except to give orders or yell at Father behind the closed door of their room.

※

Two months after Fu-chi's burial, Shao Pei spoke with Gee Fong about an altered plan for the family's future. "A son in the Emperor's service will protect us against tax raises," she began.

Traditionally, Fong's father handled the finances for the entire extended family and made all decisions. But in the last few years, as his mind grew feeble. Fong and his brother Lung had managed their own affairs, sharing expenses such as housing compound repairs and governmental fees. Not long after this change, Fong discovered his wife's skill with numbers. Though they kept her participation quiet, he relied on her assessments and recommendations.

"There's no money for Civil Service school," Fong said. "I need both boys to run the farm! We were struggling before we lost Fu-chi. Now we have to work twice as hard for less."

"Growing things in the dirt isn't working anymore. We have assets to sell," Pei said.

"What assets?" Fong asked, frowning.

"Don't worry, I won't ask you to part with your precious soil!" Pei snapped.

Fong looked at her sharply. Pei lowered her eyes, letting the silence speak for her.

"Why Yang?" Fong asked. "Lee is better suited to studies. Yang is more valuable to me working on the farm."

Pei solemnly regarded her husband. "It is his place," she pronounced each word distinctly, "now that he is First Son."

※

Lee had been working near the house when a tall man wearing city clothes arrived. Mother greeted him. She smiled and bowed as she accepted a wrapped package.

"Daughter, come here."

Wringing out the laundry she was washing, Mo Chou hung it on the line. She wiped her hands on her apron as she answered. "Yes, Mother," she bowed.

"This is Mr. Yet Wah."

Mo Chou bowed to the man.

※

From across the courtyard, Lee couldn't hear the rest of the conversation, but he saw a wide-eyed, stricken expression flushing Mo Chou's face. She straightened her back, following Mother and the stranger inside. Lee trailed them, wondering what was going on. Mo Chou kept her composure as she placed a few of the clothes in a basket. When Ngon came running in, stopping by Lee's side, she asked, "Mama, what are you doing?"

Mo Chou turned to face her daughter. "Ngon…" was all she said before collapsing in a heap, then a deep otherworldly wail came from her. Her dress formed a nest, into which she drew her child. She clutched her too tightly, rocking back and forth.

"Mother! Who is this man?" Lee said, pointing to Yet Wah, who smirked. He made eye contact with Mother, directing his statement to her.

"I'll wait outside. Don't be long. I have a schedule to keep."

Absorbed in her mother's emotions, Ngon sobbed. Mother only allowed this for a moment before reaching down to grab Ngon under the arms. She ripped her out of Mo Chou's embrace. "You dishonor this family," Mother spat at Mo Chou, "and upset your child!" Mother shoved the child at Lee. "Take her out of here."

"Tell me what's happening!" Lee demanded as he squeezed Ngon's hand.

Mother's eyes blazed before slapping him. "You do as I say, or I'll send for your father."

Lee pulled his trembling niece under his arm. They held fast to each other, both quaking and wobbly. With hands still reaching for her child and tears streaking down her face, Mo Chou screamed, "My grief cannot disgrace a family to which I no longer belong! I curse you, old woman, in Fu-chi's name!"

"Leave my house at once, you disrespectful girl!" Mother yelled. "Mr. Yet Wah, she's ready."

Pulling Ngon along with him, Lee retreated out the back door, but not before he saw Mr. Yet Wah grab Mo Chou's hair and drag her to her feet.

Yet Wah began tying her hands.

Mo Chou twisted about, searching for Lee. "Look after Ngon!" she screamed.

Lee couldn't speak. All he could do was watch as the stranger pulled Mo Chou behind him down the lane, leading her like a goat. No one said a word when he carried Ngon away, taking her to a quiet grove where he tried soothing her with song and stories. As was his habit, he touched the scar on her right eyebrow, a forty-five-degree angle with no hair, and swept his fingertips from there around the side of her face to under her chin.

Ngon closed her eyes whenever Lee did this, listening to his whisper. "My poor little duck, duck." This is what he'd said after she'd fallen near the creek when she was first learning to walk. A tumble and a meeting with a sharp rock had created her unique facial feature.

In the days ahead, Ngon developed a habit of speaking out loud with every thought that went through her head. Instinctively, Lee understood it was her way of keeping from thinking about her mother. At night when nightmares woke her, it was Lee who sat with her, stroking her hair, whispering until she went back to sleep.

LESSONS
Yang, age 13 | Lee, age 10 | Ngon, age 6
Panyu District, China
1853
—

Uncle Tie arrived a week after Mo Chou left. He was an Imperial Civil Servant and Mother's brother. He would stay with them for a year-and-a-half to prepare Yang to take the next set of Imperial Exams. His presence created many unwelcome changes for Yang.

Mother and Father returned to sleeping on the mattress in the common room, which meant Yang, after having a bed to himself, had to go back to sharing with Lee and now, Ngon too. Since the family couldn't afford to pay the man for full-time teaching, his morning student was Tung Sun, a boy from Yang's class at the provincial academy. Sun had a habit of pointing out differences—ones emphasizing lack—in other households compared to his own. Having him in their home every day armed the boy with plenty of fuel for his self-satisfied judgments, which he religiously fired off whenever he cornered Yang alone. "We have two horses," Tung Sun proclaimed. "We can go back and forth to the market quickly, making two trips on the same day if we need to."

Another insult was having him in their home under the watchful eyes of the adults. Yang couldn't take care of Tung Sun as he had at school, shoving him against a wall, pinning him there, while stepping on the boy's toes until he squealed like a piglet or forcing him to choose between eating hot peppers or a slug to the gut.

Yang's days started early. He chopped wood, stacked it near the back door, and brought water in from the well. After that, he sharpened tools. When Mother called them in for breakfast, he settled at the table with Father.

Lee worked in the kitchen with Mother, doing tasks Mo Chou used to do. They did their work in silence so Ngon would remain asleep as long as possible. If she remained in bed after Father left, Lee woke her to feed her. He was aware of Mother's short fuse. He gave Ngon chores to do outside, but he couldn't keep her out of harm's way all the time. No matter how many times Mother smacked her and scolded her to stop talking, it didn't change her behavior. Lee kept the little girl supplied with compresses cooled by well water for the swelling and willow bark to chew for the pain. In the afternoons, he worked outside with Father while Yang had his lessons with Uncle Tie.

As it had been at the provincial academy during his younger years, Yang detested sitting, listening, and then being required to repeat what he heard. Confucius Sayings (Analects) were boring beyond belief. Literature and reasoning were not much better. He had no interest in governance. It was only during the infrequent times they worked on building projects he forgot how much he hated school.

Most days, Uncle set them up in separate areas of the family compound. While one student was reading or working on a math assignment, he quizzed the other. He used his walking stick as a correction instrument. Sharp jabs to the forearm or pokes in the back reminded Yang of his frequent failures.

When Yang asked Tung Sun if Uncle used the stick on him, the boy looked perplexed. "He wouldn't dare touch a Tung," Sun said. "My father would report him to his superior." After a few moments, he smiled slowly, adding, "It must be frustrating for Professor Tie to teach a such stupid boy after working with a superior one."

Yang also didn't like Lee listening in when he came in from the fields. It was obvious Lee was hovering close *and* whispering responses to the questions that were correct! An added insult was an accidental discovery. While searching for an escaped pig, Yang had come upon Lee and Ngon down at the creek. They were rinsing roots they'd gathered in a basket. Lee was explaining one of the teacher's lessons to the six-year-old. "In the fable of the ten brothers, they outsmart the executioner and change the judge's ruling. They could do this because they knew their strengths and could work together." The way Lee explained it made perfect sense.

It helped to have Lee available as a target for Yang's frustrations. With his middle finger raised slightly in his fist, he could make bruises on his brother. His favorite place was just under Lee's left arm. Using an elbow to pry up Lee's arm, Yang would jab his knuckle, hard, into the tender spot. Lee would howl and try to retaliate, but Yang would laugh and swat him away like a fly.

※

They had been out in the field repairing a water breach. Yang constructed a wooden structure channeling the water away from their work area while showing Lee how to build up the earth so it would hold against the flow. Upon removing Yang's temporary stopper, both boys smiled widely as they watched it hold. Yang proclaimed, "There are few indeed who fail at something through exercising restraint."

With delighted surprise sparkling in his eyes, Lee turned to Yang, saying, "That's right! You remembered the Confucius quote perfectly!"

As fast as and as stealthy as a night owl, Yang levered Lee's elbow and delivered a painful underarm blow.

MONSOON WEATHER
Yang, age 14 | Lee, age 11
Panyu District, China
1854
—

"Yang!"

At Mother's call, his grip tightened against the rough plank he was nailing. Only one more nail and this outbuilding would be done!

"Making Mother wait," Pei called, "is disrespect!" she added. Her tone was sharp.

Lips tightening, Yang threw his hammer and nails to the ground in a heap, leaving the plank dangling. Stomping back toward Mother, he swiped a hand across his face, wiping at the sweat and pulling stray hair from his mouth. He noted the puffy clouds overhead, tasting the tang of moisture in the air. Father would be upset if he did not complete building repairs before the rains came.

"Yes, Mother?" Yang softened his voice, bowing before her.

"The wood for my cooking fire is low. Fetch more."

"Will you punish Lee for leaving too little wood?"

Mother's spine straightened. Her tone warned him of the danger he was courting. "Don't worry about your brother. Mind your own chores. When you're done stacking, go to the canyon and bring back a goose."

Swallowing past the sudden lump in his throat, Yang bowed a second time before returning to the barn, where he retrieved a straw hat hanging on the wall. Placing it on his head, he lifted a leather-sheathed ax, sliding it into the loop on his belt, and folded a burlap bag, tucking it under his arm before setting out.

Most members of the community didn't have enough food. Theft between neighbors was growing common. The birds, and their hiding place, were insurance the family was careful to guard.

Humming softly, Yang made his way up the ravine. Vegetation along the trail reached into the open space, threatening to obliterate it. Using his ax, he hacked at the encroaching branches of a Gē zǐ shù, dove tree. He pulled the cut limbs away, hiding them in outlying greenery. Spitting on a fingertip and burrowing it into the ground, he brought up a soil clot. Spitting on it again, he crushed it, mixing it with his thumb. Rubbing mud on the amputation spots, he disguised his handiwork. Yang scrubbed his fingers against his pants until his skin was clean. He was confident no one wandering in the hills would notice the fresh cuts or go searching.

The wind was kicking up, making the tree's lower leaves flutter like the birds they resembled. He slid his thumb over the razor-sharp edge of the ax. The swirls of his thumbprint made it bump as texture crossed the blade. Moving his arms into a T-stance, he smiled as he paused, lifting his face to enjoy the fragrance the wind brought. In an exuberant leap, he violently sliced through leaf stems. The swishing, crackling sound the cuts made was deeply satisfying. He stopped to pose and make battle cries like an Imperial warrior.

Once the young fighter axed all his imaginary enemies, he looked around in dismay. The ground was carpeted with leaves. Cursing, he set about gathering and stashing them under a dense bush.

The goose pen, constructed with a combination of found items, bamboo, and twine, was still standing strong after two years! He let those cheery thoughts linger like bubbles floating in a fermented drink. Unfortunately, bubbles always burst once they reach the surface. Inside the pen were two dispirited animals. They had leather straps tied tightly around their necks. That was Mother's idea to keep them quiet so hungry neighbors wouldn't steal them. Instead of honking a greeting or chasing him with flapping wings, they remained nested on the ground, simply lifting their heads to acknowledge him.

"Neih hou, bèndàns. Hello, dumb eggs," Yang said as he picked up a pail to fill with water from the nearby waterfall. He refreshed their drinking water and scattered kitchen scraps. Untying the straps and storing them in his pocket, he rubbed the sore spots on their necks, hoping to get them moving. The first bird to take a drink decided for the other.

Grasping the laggard tightly behind the head, he squeezed while tucking her body under his arm, clamping her wings down with an elbow. He used his foot to open the gate, then closed it behind him. Striding a short distance away, he scurried behind a bush to make quick work of setting the bird down with her neck extended across a chopping block. In one smooth ax motion, he separated the head from the body. Pulling a strap from his pocket, he bound the feet, then hung the body on a tree branch to drain.

Bright red drips spattered, then plopped as they formed a crimson puddle at his feet.

With the survivor's neck retied and the pen secured, Yang placed the butchered bird and its parts in the burlap bag. Using his shirt to polish his blade, he replaced the ax in the sheath and belt loop.

LAND BROKER
Yang, age 18 | Lee, age 15
Panyu District, China
1858
—

Land. When nurtured with care, it brings forth food, joy—and life. Since Lee was tiny, Grandfather began teaching him about their soil, how it smelled compared to mud on the bank of the East River or in nearby Chashanzhen, and how the sweet and tart flavors of their mandarins changed depending on soil additives. Grandfather's favorites were ox dung and compost.

Father had taught him about tending to their crops and how the more land you have, the more things you can grow on it. Their farm was their wealth and sustenance. Lee didn't understand why Father was taking him and Yang to town to talk about selling some of it.

Several nights ago, Lee tried talking with Mother about it. She perched on a bench under the eve of their porch. A light blanket covered her knees. The firelight from inside highlighted age lines around her mouth and grey strands in her hair. She nodded as he settled next to her. From beneath her blanket, Mother revealed a small plate with three Hung Ngon Beang cookies, almond, his favorite.

"Thank you," Lee whispered, taking the plate. When he finished, he set it under the bench. Brushing crumbs from his fingers, he pressed his hands together, tucking them between his knees.

Mother studied Lee's profile. "You look like a grown man," she said. Her voice grew soft and her gaze appeared to wander in the clouds. "Yet in my heart, I still see you as my little boy."

"All my life," Lee began hesitantly, "Grandfather, Father, and Uncles…" He glanced at her. Mother raised her eyebrows, leaning forward.

He took a breath, then continued as if his words were fireflies trapped inside a recently opened glass jar. "Even the Classics say, 'To gain wealth, we must own land, keep land, and get more land.' And Zhuangzi said, 'Life comes from the earth and life returns to the earth.' Mother! We buried our ancestors on our ground. We make offerings to them there. How can we think of selling any of it?"

Exasperated, Mother sat back sighing, "You know why."

"I don't need a wife. Just get one for Yang. We barely have enough land to feed the mouths we have as it is."

Mother compressed her lips. "Before the Taiping war started, our family had been building wealth. My marriage to your father is a good example. But the last decade has brutalized this family, as it has countless others across the countryside. Losing Fu-chi, then Yang throwing away the money we invested in his seat at the exams…" Mother's voice grew thin, tears pooled in her eyes. After an audible swallow, she continued. "If the Taipings continue, they will undo the stability the Empire has known for a thousand years."

"But they've already done this. If we sell, we're adding to it."

"You see?" Mother responded. "The young lack the foresight of the old. Your brother is even worse!"

"Help me understand," Lee pleaded.

She regarded him for a moment. When she spoke, her voice was flat. "If you breed a sow and a boar, what do you get?"

"More pigs," Lee answered quietly.

Mother raised a hand as if she was waiting for his next words to land there.

"Some to sell, some to keep," Lee responded automatically, saying the words she'd taught him by rote. "A hog in the pen means the family eats."

※

Wearing his best clothes—blue cotton pants and a loose overshirt—Lee walked on his father's left while Yang walked on his right. They were on their way through the village to Huanhou Palace, a teahouse, to meet a land broker who would advise Fong about rental, lease, or sale prices.

When they saw people they knew, Father greeted them, bowed, and inquired about the health of mothers, wives, and children as if he didn't have a care in the world. Lee knew his father was not happy about what was coming. He also couldn't help noticing the attention Yang got. And why not? He was taller than most boys his age. He had a powerful jaw, bushy eyebrows, and a hawk-like nose. When he smiled, which he did often, girls twittered like birds.

Father always coaxed Lee into conversations with his elders. "If you develop relationships," Fong instructed, "you can count on help when you need it. If you never speak, people will forget you exist."

"I talk to Ngon all the time," Lee replied testily.

"She's family," Father commented. "That girl opens her mouth when the sun comes up and she doesn't close it until it goes down. Even with Ngon, you do more listening than speaking. You could learn from your brother...he's winsome."

They reached the teahouse, where opaque tobacco and opium smoke twisted near the ceiling like a spectral snake. The land broker, spying his clients, stood and bowed, welcoming them to his table.

Feeling physically ill about the discussion between the broker and Father, Lee tuned it out and focused, instead, on his brother, or what his brother was up to while he should have been giving his close attention to the conversation.

A servant girl with silky hair constrained in a tight bun followed them carrying a tray with tea, plates, and chopsticks. Placing teacups before each of them, she poured the dark, steaming liquid. Already well into regaling them with comparative values from various pieces of land in their prefecture, the broker didn't pause when they sipped. The tea was black with rose petals, a perfect complement of flavors—hearty, yet delicate—to accompany negotiations of this sort. The young woman hurried away, only to return with a platter stacked with diminutive food samplings. Lee watched Yang's eyes follow the girl.

"Selling outright now," the broker concluded as the young woman approached again, "will yield higher profits."

Standing between Yang and Father, the girl placed morsels of chicken liver and cloud ear mushrooms with dates and ginger at the center, reachable by all. As she was lifting the last plate, stacked high with bok choy, Yang scooted closer, knocking the dish from her hands. It clattered to the floor, attracting every eye in the room.

"So sorry!" the girl exclaimed.

"It's my fault," Yang replied, moving away, reaching to the floor.

Lee leaned back, watching under the table.

The serving girl quickly gathered the spilled food, except for the morsel Yang was holding. Instead of dropping it in the dish she held for him, he waited until she came closer. Meeting in the middle, Yang turned his wrist so the back of their hands touched.

Shocked by the contact, her eyes flew to his.

"You're welcome, Bié Kè Qi." Yang smiled and winked.

Lee returned his attention to the table when Yang did. The girl looked flustered, her cheeks were bright red. His brother shoved two shrimp balls in his mouth at once, followed by a noisy slurp of tea as if nothing untoward had happened.

Father sent Yang an annoyed glance. Lee thought Yang looked like a giant black squirrel when he chewed. When he heard Father's comment, "I agree. We should sell. I will confirm with my father," Lee's blood ran cold.

"The superior man understands what is right." Lee murmured under his breath while picking at a hangnail, pulling at it till it stung. "The inferior man understands what will sell," he finished.

"What did you say?" Father asked crossly, angered at another interruption.

Embarrassed, Lee looked everywhere but at Father. "I don't need a wife," he declared bravely. "If you only get one for Yang, we won't have to sell so much land."

"Lee!" Father rebuked, "Apologize for your disobedience. You are here to learn about land management and family finances so you can act as an advisor to First Son."

Lee swallowed the words that sat like broken glass on his tongue. Yang would never be First Son to him. That title would always belong to Fu-chi. Lowering his eyes, he bowed his head, mumbling an apology.

GOAT TO MONKEY YEARS
November through February
Yang, age 20 | Lee, age 18 | Ngon, age 13
Panyu District, China
1860
—

Yang's relationship with his wife, Ting Ai, differed greatly from any Lee had seen before. She behaved appropriately in public; her upbringing was sound. In private with her husband, Ai's snarls and threats added an extra dimension of stress to a household already quaking with his mother's anxiety.

For a few months, Lee complained to Mother about the sounds Ai made when she was alone with her husband. "It sounds as if he's hurting her."

"What happens between a man and his wife is their business," said Mother.

"Shouldn't you or Father talk to Yang?"

"How First Son treats his wife is not to be discussed."

Lee was confused, "But Father told me making a wife happy creates a harmonious home."

Smiling, Mother's voice softened. "Your father is a sentimental fool sometimes."

Yang and Ai's drama calmed down some after they announced her pregnancy. From that point forward, they behaved as if they were cordial strangers.

Noting the differences in how married couples treated one another made Lee worry about what his own marriage would be like.

※

Yang knelt on the tile roof of their compound, methodically working over every inch, replacing broken tiles and scrubbing away lichen and moss. He used tar to patch holes as he went. His wide-brimmed straw hat shaded his face from the bright light, but he allowed the sun free access to his back, chest, and limbs. Sculpted muscles moved powerfully beneath his smooth skin, which glistened with sweat. *I am strong like the Jade Emperor,* he thought, flexing his hands. *These muscles could move mountains!* He clenched a fist and flicked a rock-hard bicep with his opposite hand.

Though Yang was always happy for the company, he was also content working alone. On the roof, he had a view of their family fields, bordered on one side by the East River with green mountains in the distance. Lee and Father were down there spreading fertilizer to prepare for the planting season. Plum blossoms sweetened the spring air while bees whirred by on insect errands. Through the roof, he could hear the voices of the women working in the house. His mother's carried over the others. "Clean out this cupboard, reach in every corner." "Take this bedding out for washing." "Sweep every speck of dirt from the floor!"

Ting Ai came out into the courtyard. His pregnant little wife carried a rug in one hand and a broom in the other. Paper altar decorations spilled out of her apron pockets. He remained silent, observing her. She hung the rug over a laundry line, leaning the broom against its base. Scattering the thin papers cut and folded into shapes representing animals and household items over the smoldering fire pit, she watched them alight. Kneeling, she offered a prayer to the Kitchen God, Zao Jun. "I send these offerings to Heaven. Please give the Jade Emperor a favorable report about the Gee family so he may smile upon us with luck and prosperity."

As she got up, Yang waved down at her and smiled. "All of last year's ill fortune must surely be out of the house by now," he called.

Ai returned the gesture. "Soon we'll put away the brooms and dustpans to keep our good luck in place," she replied, rubbing her belly.

"Good!" Yang grinned. At the conclusion of the Spring Festival, for which all the cleaning was being done, the new Year of the Monkey would begin. Everyone knew that sons born in this year are destined to be clever and competitive.

They'd only been married a year. He had thought little of her when they first met. At seventeen, Ting Ai resembled the year for which she was born—a rat. After an awkward time, while she learned her household duties and how to avoid Mother's wrath, his bride turned feisty across the matrimony pillow. They shared private jokes while she made his cock crow. Vitriol was part of their sex play. She welcomed his attention, meeting them with her own. Even as her belly filled with his son, she continued to be a robust worker.

He felt proud that together he and Ai were establishing their place as family leaders. His rising social status almost made him forget about smiling at the village women. His preoccupation with the pretty fishmonger's wife had been reduced to the size of a speck of sand.

When their work was done, they would have fifteen days of the Spring Festival to look forward to. It was Yang's favorite time of the year, and this would be the best one yet.

Hours later, as dusk dimmed the sky, Yang watched his father and brother approaching. He could tell by the way they walked they were tired and thinking about tea.

Draining the last of his water, Yang stood cautiously, making sure his footing was secure. "Lee!" he called as his brother was about to pass beneath him.

For the moments Lee regarded him, Yang imagined the things going through his mind. He bit on his lip to keep it from turning into a smirk. "I need a refill," he held up his jug, "and I could use a hand up here."

The resistance in Lee's stance broke as his shoulders slumped. Older men, especially one's First Brother, must be treated with respect. Nodding his head in a curt bow, he reached up to catch the pottery.

They worked in silence for another hour, Lee handing Yang clean tiles and Yang replacing them where needed. Holding out a hand for a new tile, Yang was about to snap at his brother for his slowness when he noticed him standing, holding the edge of his hand to his forehead. "I think something's happening," Lee said in a voice laced with concern.

Three tendrils of smoke rose in the distance.

"Should we warn the others?"

Yang stood too. "It's far. Maybe in Qiaotouozhen. The watchman has it." He grasped Lee's arm, pointing to the tower. Inside, a man with binoculars was watching.

"He'll ring the bell if he thinks there will be trouble. Say nothing." Yang pinched his elbow until Lee flinched. "And keep that look off your face!"

Yang couldn't imagine moving the family, especially not now. Mother would slow everyone down and he didn't want Ai to birth his son before it was time.

"What if it's a raid or a pirate attack?"

Releasing his brother, Yang stared at the tower guard, quoting a scholar. "'Arising, I gaze upon the world; chaos is not so distant after all.'"

Cocking his head to the side, Lee stared at him. He rubbed at the spot under his left arm where Yang jabbed the last time Lee had pointed out his correct use of a classic quote. Out of a sense of self-preservation, especially while standing on a roof, he remained silent.

"If the guard signals, we'll respond. But only then," Yang reassured.

※

Several hours later, as the family was preparing for bed, the alarm sounded. Lee met Yang's eyes before they began scurrying to hide valuables and pack whatever they could carry. This time, Lee would remain with the men to defend their home while the women walked to the hidden goose pen. When he was younger, he'd gone with the women. Mo Chou had led the way. She encouraged everyone to keep up a steady pace with her strong, low voice. Now, Ngon didn't have anyone who'd pay attention if she fell behind. Racing to his cousin Bozahai, he grasped her arms, shaking her so she'd focus on what he had to say. "Watch out for Ngon."

"I have my mother and your mother—who can barely walk—to attend to!" Bozahai wailed. "I can't watch a kid also!"

"Please!" Lee urged. "If she's returned safely, I'll give you anything you want."

Bozahai narrowed her eyes, focusing intently on him for a fraction of a second. At her barely perceptible nod, he raced back to help the men ready their defenses.

They lined up every sharp farm implement. Uncle Lung and Father spaced themselves between the two boys, with Lee in the most protected position.

Three youths on foot and two men and a woman on horseback attacked their compound. They appeared to be a raiding party spreading out from the main battalion. Father and Uncle Lung engaged with the men on horseback, holding them back with wide-arcing swings of the farm tools. Yang held his position with the foot soldiers. He had the advantage of size and strength —even with three. The woman on the horse peeled away from the conflict, giving Lee a wide berth. She rode right up to the door of the compound, kicked it in, and ducking, she rode through. Lee chased after her with his heart racing. He gritted his teeth when he heard pottery shattering.

The skirmish ended unexpectedly when a strange roar shook the ground. The fighters assessed the cause. "Flood!" cried the watchman in the tower. "It's mud and coming fast!" Cracking and screams sounded ahead of the East River as it delivered a thick wave of sludge, three feet deep, to blanket their valley. Father, Uncle, and Yang turned the event to their advantage.

Remembering the stories and lessons Father had shared about previous floods, *face what's coming. Keep on top of it. Climb a tree or onto a roof if you have time*, Lee leaped onto their table and then jumped to gain a purchase on a rafter. Below him, he watched the horse panic as mud surrounded it, rising higher on its legs. The woman screamed, commanding the beast to keep its head.

She fell when the horse slipped. In all the thrashing, Lee saw the woman disappear. She resurfaced, looking like a slick, brown thing shaped like a human. Her eyes, the only part of her still recognizable, made him think of lanterns glowing in a moonless midnight forest. The whites showed more surface area than he thought eyes could show. Her gaze locked onto his for the space of a held breath. She opened her mouth as she went down, the gaping hole filled with thick liquid before her eyes could no longer be seen.

In the shock-hazed aftermath, the survivors had difficulty comprehending the damage and loss of life. The few souls who were adaptable enough to make quick assessments and form a plan of action inspired the others to join in search and rescue efforts. Yang was that person for the Gee family. He helped Father down from the barn loft. Together, they found Grandfather and Uncle Lung pinned against the compound wall, crushed to death by a tree.

"Our house," Lee heard the despondent tone of Father's voice as he stood in their doorway, surveying the damage. The only parts of Father not coated in mud were his head and neck. He slogged his way inside, holding on onto the door's headframe to keep from slipping. Yang followed him, steading himself by bracing against a leg of their upended dining table. He cursed before saying, "There's a dead horse in here!"

Lee must have made a sound, because both men looked up. "Thank the gods!" Father exclaimed. He waded over to brace the table while Yang climbed up to help Lee down.

Clenching his jaw, Lee stepped into it. The mud was cold and filled with hard things that scraped against his legs. His skin felt hot and tight. He was sure that if his feet or legs encountered anything that felt like the girl, he'd lose it. The three Gee men clutched each other, weeping.

Sometime later, loaded with the immediate essentials they could scavenge, Yang and Lee headed up into the hills to the goose pen, hoping to find all their women waiting for them.

※

The first thing Fong did after his sons were gone was to coordinate the release of his father and brother from under the tree. Ropes, oxen, and powerful men were required. A similar technique, with the addition of a butcher, was used to remove the horse and its rider from the middle of his living space.

Clean-up efforts lasted weeks. Broken timbers tangled with household debris needed to be cleared and sorted. Rotting flesh created fly swarms. The women, maybe the most resilient of all, scooped the mud from their homes and made clean places for the men to sleep each night when they came in exhausted. Simultaneously, they saw to the lighting of incense and the rituals of honoring the ancestors who joined the ranks of the dead.

It was good luck that most of their rice survived, along with it a few catfish and the new vegetable garden Yang had constructed on a knoll.

Though he wore the mantle of First Son with seriousness, Yang couldn't help feeling unworthy. It frequently kept him up at night. Though his parents and grandfather had never said a word when he failed the Imperial Exams, he could feel the chill of their disappointment. Since the attack, flood, and Uncle and Grandfather's death, it was the first time Yang felt like a First Son.

Yang worked with Father in a Dà liàn ceremony. They dressed Grandfather and Uncle in clean clothes so they would be ready for their journey into the afterlife. Carefully transferring the bodies into the coffins, they stood guard while family members paid respects. They carried the coffins in the chē pí, wagon, to the burial ground, and watched as food and incense were offered. Joss papers were burned.

NEW YEAR
February
Yang, age 21 | Lee, age 18 | Ngon, age 14
Panyu District, China
1861
—

Ready for a lift of spirits, the Gee family dressed in festive red finery and received relatives from other towns. They served a special family reunion dinner that included Laba porridge, long noodles, dumplings, wax-cured duck sausage, soup, lobster, and abalone. An unfinished fish dish symbolized surplus for every year. Late at night, while reacquainted with distant cousins and aunts, the men drank and told stories. Stuffed bellies and communal feelings sent everyone off to sleep in the land of dreams with happy thoughts.

The first duty of the family was to tidy the graves of the ancestors. Vestiges of dirt and recent weed growth were cleared. One might think this would be a somber affair, but it was companionable, in a respectful way. Next, they set out food. Small servings from last night's feast were warmed and artfully placed on the best dishes.

Sumptuous aromas attracted the ancestors. The living sensed them with a delicate touch on a cheek, a remembered laugh that echoed nearby, the imprint of a warm hand placed comfortingly on a back. The space shimmered with sacredness.

Kowtowing with knees and foreheads on the ground, deference was offered to Grandfather by everyone present. When it was time to honor Uncle Lung, a few of the older relatives stepped to the side. Only younger relatives worship elders.

Yang, Ai, Lee, and Ngon were the only ones to kowtow to Fu-chi. They felt the pressure of eyes on them as they made their bows. Mother would have their heads if she felt they did not properly honor her firstborn.

As they rose, Yang held out a hand to steady Ai. He leaned toward Ngon, whispering, "If the gods willed it, your mother is serving a gentle master and knows no hunger."

Lee didn't miss the confused expression crossing her face before she hid it. "Thank you, Uncle," Ngon whispered, bowing.

※

In the next days, Mother went to visit her relatives in Dongguan, a metropolis compared to Qishizhen, the largest town nearest their farm. It was the only time of the year when women visited their birth families.

Ai, Ngon, and the Aunties served food prepared ahead of time to the guests. Days of leisure and catching up were a balm to the soul. Feelings of connection and safety seeped into cells to be carried forward in the coming year.

On the sixth day of the celebration, Mother returned to help take out trash, symbolizing the driving away of the ghost of poverty.

The Jade Emperor receives prayers. Bamboo firecrackers, packed with gunpowder, are set off to frighten the Nian away. This is a formidable creature that is part lion and bull with horns and six-inch-long fangs. It comes down from the mountains at New Year to destroy crops and animals, as well as to terrorize people and kidnap children. Nian does not like loud noises or the color red.

The lantern festival marks the fifteenth day of the lunisolar Chinese calendar. Children are allowed to go out at night carrying paper lanterns that are decorated with riddles. Smiles and laughter are contagious as youngsters race around, greeting one another and problem solving.

Walking beside his wife, Yang watched Lee and Ngon. Too old to carry lanterns, they bent low to read a lantern offered by a neighborhood youngster. He heard Ngon's clear voice as she read, "This lovely maiden eats no meat but eats leaves. She labors each day spinning and weaving for the benefit of others. Who is she?" Lee and Ngon made a great show of trying to sort out the riddle, to the immense delight of the boy.

※

Since Yang's marriage, he noticed that the jealousy he felt about Lee and Ngon's relationship had faded. He wondered how things would change once Lee got married. The bride couldn't be much older than Ngon. That marriage wouldn't take place for at least two years.

Yang felt happy for his father as he watched him assume his place as the head of the family. All honors are directed to Father first. In return, Father greeted everyone, sharing personal stories. He led processions to the ancestral graves, directed ceremonies, led walks into town for gatherings, and delivered gifts to friends.

The conclusion of the festival comes with the giving of red envelopes. Older and married couples pass them out to the youngest members of the clan. Inside are money or small gifts that are kept under one's pillow for seven nights before opening.

When Yang and Ai handed Ngon her envelope, she responded with, "Everlasting peace year after year."

Lee's greeting for his envelope was, "May all your wishes be fulfilled." He took in his brother's relaxed posture and easy laugh, but remembered the times when he was sullen and withdrawn. Having a son born in the Year of the Monkey would be a good sign for Yang and for the entire family. Lee prayed their luck would hold.

LEE'S WEDDING
Yang, age 22 | Lee, age 19
Panyu District, China
1862
—

The sky darkens to purple, and a breeze thick with pungent marsh scent rippled the stray hair escaping their queues. Lights in windows twinkled with a red-golden glow. Crickets tuned up for their nightly concert while fireflies winked in the tall grass near their knees. As he had always done since childhood, Lee crouched low, swinging his arms with fingers extended. When he caught one, he held his hand open to watch the beetle spread its wings for another flight.

Firefly,
Lampyridae delicatula

SMELL: Pheromones detected.

Females!

WINGS: Liftoff. Blink…blink…blink.

Hope on wings.

Lee looked over at Father, taking inventory. They were roughly the same height. Father's muscles were still strong, but ropey. Lee's were smooth; his skin glowed with good health. At times, he felt as if he could move as swiftly as a tiger. He wondered if he could fight as well as the other men in the family.

Since the flood, Father walked with a slight limp. He'd damaged something in his leg when he had to move a tree and a horse. In the quiet moments before Father started speaking, Lee wondered, *Is he satisfied with his life? What was it like for him on his wedding day?*

"The first nights of your marriage will set the tone for the life before you, my son," said Father. If your union is harmonious, your wife will treasure you as her master. If it is forced, she may spend the rest of her days wielding her unhappiness as a weapon."

Father and Mother seem companionable, Lee thought. *Does Mother like Father as a husband?* The idea made him scrunch his face as if he'd bitten into a lemon. *She takes care of him well.*

※

To prepare for the nuptials, they scrubbed the Gee home as if for the Spring Festival. After the flood and grieving period passed, the family reconfigured their living quarters. Auntie Liu and Bozahai moved into a smaller space, giving Yang and Ai private rooms. Lee and his new wife would move into their own set of rooms.

Mother, Ai, Ngon, and the Aunties from the city and had been cooking for days. Food smells mingled lusciously with the warm aromas of grain and summer.

Lee's seventeen-year-old bride arrived in a gold-painted sedan chair. Breeze-ruffled curtains concealed all but the girl's shape and a back as rigid as a fence post. Carried by her brothers and uncles, the conveyance bobbed behind a flock of honking geese, herded by children dressed in red silk. The procession continued with more relatives walking behind the bride's box, while the mother of the bride and several aunties rode in another smaller sedan.

Lee wished he could run down the lane and pull back the curtains to look. Exhilarating mating fantasies occupied most of his thoughts. But his upbringing would not allow him to dishonor his family. He remained standing with his male kin, bland faced.

As the procession drew near, Lee expected the geese to be shooed inside their animal pen. Instead, the children used bamboo poles to avoid vicious snaps while they formed a circle around them.

Stepping forward, the bride's father, Mr. Wèi, declared, "As tradition dictates, a wife must come to her husband with nothing, but my disobedient daughter refused to leave behind one item." Smiling, he bowed deeply. "A messenger bird holds this item. You must decide what to do with it, Gee Lee."

The gander stood in the center of the circle, feathers erect, beak open, hissing, tongue at a full point. Dark eyes locked onto Lee, the enemy. Secured around the messenger's neck was a bright blue ribbon; a yellow purse dangled from it.

Crossing his arms, Lee nodded. This was the first test of the marriage ceremony.

Lee took his time assessing, ignoring the sweat breaking out on his upper lip. The challenge submerged his warm thoughts under the bracing waters of marital responsibility.

He strode forward, dismissing two of the children, accepting their poles as they left. Tapping and swinging the bamboo, Lee separated the messenger from the flock before driving the rest into their pen. Ngon closed the gate behind them, beaming.

Tossing the rods to the ground, he scooped a handful of pebbles while making a cautious advance. The gander raised his wings, honking. The bird lowered its head and charged.

Lee threw stones in the bird's face, deflecting the attack, but not before the infuriated fowl clipped the tender flesh above Lee's knee. It clamped on. The beak was like crab pincers, tearing fabric, drawing blood. Refusing to yell, Lee pulled on the ribbon while jostling with the animal. The purse dropped, landing in the dirt. With a final shake of his leg, the gander released his grip and waddled away to rejoin its gaggle.

Feeling all eyes on him, Lee bit inside his cheek until he tasted blood and salt. He willed himself to walk without limping, to retrieve the purse. As he considered what to do with it—open it, throw it away, or hand it over to his mother, which he thought would have been correct—a Confucian quote floated to the surface of his mind. *When it is obvious that goals cannot be reached, don't adjust the goals, adjust the action steps.*

Lee approached the sedan. After a thoughtful pause, he plunged his hand inside, offering it to the girl. Nothing happened.

As he waited, anger sparked. Time lengthened. The spark turned to a blaze, threatening to incinerate the curtains. It would be within his right to humiliate her, make her kneel before him in the open air.

When cool, trembling hands cupped his, Lee's violent emotions evaporated. A shiver traveled down his spine.

From inside, a breathless, "Xièxiè, *thank you,*" came as the purse lifted away.

Lee forgot what he was supposed to do next. At a word from Father, Yang trotted over, whispering in his ear. They joined the family, gathered by the entrance, waiting for the bride's delivery to their home.

With the clashing of cymbals and monks chanting while swinging smoking incense pots, the bridal entourages approached the front of the house. Mr. Wèi, pulling aside the curtains, held out his hand and waited for his daughter.

Lee's first sight was of her small, pale hand. Next came her elaborate headdress, secured tightly atop bound hair. As she stepped out, Lee glimpsed dark eyes and pleasing features through her translucent veil. Embroidered white cranes decorated her red dress. As he noticed the purse hanging from her wrist, he wondered what treasure was inside.

He moved to take his place standing next to her, feeling his knee wound throbbing. Her father placed her hand on Lee's arm. Nerves urged him to rush forward, but Wèi An's grip tightened when he moved. He realized her costume restricted movement. Steadying her and making a change, he led her through the front door, through the usually dark entryway now illuminated with candles and flowers. Seeing his home with fresh eyes, he felt pleased to welcome this woman into it.

In the center of their family room near the fireplace, Mother and Father sat in finery, ready to receive the couple.

Lee felt like a wooden puppet. He bent sharply at the waist, lowering his head to heaven, then honoring his parents and, finally, his bride. Lee observed Wèi An's movements, matching his bows, so they flowed together as one. Her fingers were long, nails carefully manicured.

Auntie Liu and Bozahai brought in the tea service that the wedding couple would serve to the parents. Wèi An's voice was soft, barely above a whisper. *Is she timid or showing respect?* Lee wondered.

Though he felt as if he had a thousand ants crawling over his skin and his hearing seemed muffled, Lee was relieved to see Wèi An's steady hands as she grasped the teapot handle, lifted it, then poured the tea. *Is she watching me as closely as I'm watching her?*

※

Bozahai brought out the first course, Gau Gay Tong, a Matrimony Vine Soup, while Mother watched her like a hawk, making sure the food, delivery, and presentation were perfect. First to receive food was the married couple, sitting side by side, then the guests. Lee caught a whiff of his bride. Orange blossoms. *Where has she placed her perfume? At the base of her neck? Behind an ear? Lower?*

More courses followed. Musicians from the village arrived to play for the event. Dizi, flute, and Xun, ocarina-like notes danced with the strings of the erhu in *"Running River,"* a song that represents hope for the future. Shark fin and sea cucumber soup, symbols of virility, were served near the end. Wèi An was about to bring a spoonful to her mouth when Lee placed a hand on her thigh under the table. Staring straight ahead, she straightened her spine and carefully set her spoon next to her bowl.

"Are you not hungry?" He leaned close, whispering in her ear.

A slight shake of her head jangled the beads on her headdress. A shift in her body weight sent a message that made Lee remove his hand. Turning his face away, he closed his eyes, mentally cursing his brother for suggesting it…and himself for doing it. He looked at Yang and Ai. *Had Ai been receptive to that move?*

Once the eighth course was complete, the guests made toasts and sang. Lee knew he should take his bride to their wedding chamber before the small servings of rice came out, signaling it was time to depart. As he stood, Wèi An hurried to follow.

"Thank you for attending our wedding and for your wishes of good fortune," Lee addressed the guests. He and Wèi An bowed.

As he turned toward their room, he remembered something Father said. Backtracking, he returned to the table, grabbing two wine goblets. Making eye contact with Father, he was glad to catch his wink.

Entering the matrimony room, he crossed to the window, keeping his back to the door. Although he gazed out over rooftops and trees, every other part of him listened to and smelled…her.

Rustling fabric, orange blossoms, and powder.

"Husband?" she whispered.

The sound of her voice startled him. Turning, he beheld his wife. She'd removed her headdress and wiped the powder from her face. Her dark, wide eyes stared into his. When his gaze dropped, she inhaled, hissing like a boiling pot, pulling a trembling lip between her teeth.

"S-s-shall I assist you with your clothing?" Wèi An asked, bowing.

His chest swelled, and he stood taller. *This woman belongs to me now.* This thought was exhilarating and terrifying. Conflicting wedding night advice from uncles and friends ricocheted through his mind. Mount her like a stallion; poke her with your pole; teach her who is the boss.

As he strode toward Wèi An, she backed away. Her eyes were wide; a drop of blood appeared where she bit her lip. At this moment, he first understood, at least in the bedroom, a wife is not like a dog who responds to a master.

Father's words, forgotten until this instant, rose to slap him across the face like a fishtail, furiously waving to break the fisherman's hold...Forcing a woman to accept you when she is not ready dooms a marriage to unhappiness and opposition.'

When he'd asked, "How do you know when a woman is ready?" Father's reply was, "When she's as soft as a Doufu Hua, tofu flower."

Reaching for her, he took her hand. Her fingers were the temperature of the coldest well water, her movements were wooden. *How do you turn wood into tofu?* he wondered. *This woman will be the mother of my sons. I cannot force her.* When he brought her hand up to warm it with his breath, she yelped.

"What are you doing?"

He stopped, releasing her. She pulled her hand away quickly, hiding it in the folds of her dress.

"No," he said. His voice was curt. "I do not require help." Stepping away, he loosened his sash. Removing layers of cloth, knowing she was watching, made him hesitate. As the last of his wedding attire peeled away, he resisted the urge to cup his male parts when he turned to face her. She made that hissing sound again.

Striding to the bed, he threw the blankets back, using the material to cover his obvious desire. "Now you," he commanded.

Straightening her posture, she looked like she was about to faint.

Heaving a deep sigh, he said, "I don't know how to make Doufu Hua."

She looked at him sharply, then frowned.

"I will not force you, Wèi An. But you will share this bed."

"I don't understand, Husband." She clutched the fabric of her flame-colored qipao in white-knuckled fists and wore an expression like a warrior facing the executioner.

He looked down at the wine glasses where they rested on the bedside table. Hiding a smile, he replied, "Today you have become my wife and a member of my household, and it is also the day when we first met. I make another promise. If it is in my power, I won't harm you." Taking a sip, he warmed the plum liquid in his mouth before sending a scarlet stream arcing into a puddle in the center of the bed. "There," he said, pointing, "is evidence of your deflowering." He turned his chin toward the door. "You have nothing more to worry about tonight," his voice softened.

With a look of surprise still lingering on her face, she used the volumes of cloth in her dress as a shield while she disrobed. The fabric did not conceal the curve of her hip or her naked feet.

Though Mother had said, "Your family cannot afford a bride who wears lotus slippers," he felt a moment of disappointment when he glimpsed his wife's ugly feet. "When you're a wrinkled old man using a cane, you'll be glad for a wife who can walk." Mother had commented while massaging her own foot, with its toes folded flat against the sole.

Kicking at the material, Wèi An concealed herself as she slid under the bedcovers.

He thought she looked like a goddess—one who will carry his seed and bring forth many sturdy sons. His man sword leapt in salute.

Holding blankets up to her chin, she turned to look at him.

Reaching for the other goblet, he handed it to her. He was relieved to see her release the covers to take it. Draining the cup in one gulp, she bowed her head, whispering, "Xièxiè, *thank you.*"

"When you freely offer your hibiscus tent, we will celebrate the Phoenix," he declared with more confidence than he felt. "For now, we'll share this bed as if we were brothers."

Lee was familiar with sexual frustration. Living within a large family, he waited until he could go to private places to seek relief. For the first night of his married life, he shared his bed with a girl who should wish for his attention. But Wèi An wasn't Doufu Hua. She was at the far side of the mattress, pretending to be a stone.

To cool his disappointment, he inhaled deeply. This only clarified her scent, causing more stabbing pains behind his eyes and in his balls. Pressing a thumb into his goose bite, he forced his mind back to last night when his father asked him to walk along the riverbank after the evening meal.

※

Lee couldn't help thinking of Yang and Ai. Once she gave birth to a daughter, their relationship changed again. His brother criticized Ting Ai at every turn. He spent as little time with her as possible and he never intervened when Mother ordered her about like a slave. Yang had lost weight because he claimed she was spitting in his food. Ai, though silent to her husband and mother-in-law, communicated in her own way. Yang's clothes smelled foul. Rips and holes were left untended. She yelled at the baby, making her fussy and fearful.

"Love will grow between you if you respect one another and learn to cooperate," Father advised.

Would Yang and Ting Ai be harmonious if she had birthed a boy? Lee couldn't help wondering.

Father continued, "When you first enter the bedroom, you will want to rush. Your new wife will not. She will do it if you demand, but if you wait for an invitation, she'll be more welcoming."

Lee shook his head, returning his attention fully to Father. "Invite her? How?"

Father smiled, patting Lee's back. "Once you've earned her trust, even after, if you wish for clouds and rain, she will need to be warmed slowly like a Doufu Hua. When she is soft, she will respond as if she were a flower, and you are the sun."

Father could tell by the expression on Lee's face he did not understand. The wrinkles at the edges of his eyes compressed as he grinned. "The great mysteries of a woman must be learned with care," he said. Letting his hand rest at the back of his son's neck, he squeezed companionably. Father motioned it was time for them to return. Almost as an afterthought, he said, "Bring red wine into your room on your wedding night. If conditions are unfavorable, it will save face."

※

Weeks after the wedding, Yang could tell his little brother and the new wife were not behaving like Mandarin Ducks. Wèi An moved like a rabbit, always looking over her shoulder. When she settled into needlework, she curled in upon herself as if she wished she had a shell to hide within.

Last night, Yang had uncharacteristically mentioned this to Ai. "Have you noticed the disharmony between Lee and Wèi An?"

Ai paused while folding diaper cloths. They were in their bedroom after everyone had retired. Ming was asleep in the cradle Yang built along the far wall. "I thought you didn't want to speak once daughter was asleep?"

"It's not that I don't want to speak," he replied testily, then lowered his voice. "It's that I don't want to listen to her crying when she wakes."

Ai puffed up, inhaling, and opening her mouth. But then she stopped, letting her shoulders drop. "How do you mean disharmonious?" she whispered.

"Has he planted his seed?"

Ai rolled her eyes. "No," came her immediate reply.

Frowning, Yang said, "You say that like you know something."

She paused before replying, appearing to weigh her options. Tossing aside the diaper, she closed the gap between them, bringing a hand to rest over his heart.

His gaze flicked to her hand then returned to her face.

"Why do you want to know?" she asked.

Yang's eyes narrowed. "I don't need to tell you," he said, his voice hardening. Tensing, he clutched at her hand.

Before he could move away, Ai leaned in closer, "No," she agreed, "you don't. But neither do I…"

Yang could feel wisps of her breath with every word.

"I can get information you'd find useful, Husband," Ai said, sliding her arms around his neck. She raised up on tiptoes, running her tongue across his lower lip.

Grasping her hips roughly, he pressed himself against her. Their kiss was a hungry thing, a dominance challenge on several levels. Yang pulled away first. "What do you want?"

A light sparkled in her eyes that could have been humor or triumph. "A truce between us…and this," Ai said as she began unbuttoning his shirt.

Sometime later, clean clothes lay mixed with work-worn ones on the floor. Yang and Ai lay side by side, still warm from exertion. Lacing her fingers with his, she commented, "I washed their wedding sheets."

Yang turned to her, raising his eyebrows.

"A stain was there…but it wasn't blood."

※

Lee sought to know Wèi An as a person. He'd ask questions about her home and family that, eventually, she started answering. He'd bring her small gifts from the field, a flower, an unusually shaped stone, a frog, or a cricket. Learning what she liked made her smile.

When Lee noticed the distress caused by his mother and Ting Ai, he made excuses as to why Wèi An needed to join him in the fields. At first, it was to prepare his food, and then it was to help with the animals, planting, or harvesting. They filled their days with sunshine and laughter.

This morning, Wèi An had tugged at his sleeve as he prepared to leave their room. Pleasantly surprised by her boldness, he turned to her.

"When our work is done for the day," she began, lowering her eyes, "may I show you what is in my wedding purse?"

Holding his breath, Lee nodded.

Watching timidly from the corner of her eyes, she smiled. "Good. Before I show you, you must dig a hole at the edge of the garden. Make it deep and wide, then come for me."

That afternoon, Lee and Wèi An knelt side by side next to a pile of dirt, looking down into the hole. A spade stood perpendicular in the soft mound. Lee's tunic was sweat stained. "This is good," Wèi An said, pulling out her wedding purse from her apron pocket.

Yang watched this exchange from across the yard. His sister-in-law poured something into Lee's outstretched hand. Setting the purse aside, Wèi An sandwiched his brother's hands between hers. Curious, Yang crept closer, moving as if he were a cat on the hunt. He noticed Ngon and Ai watching him watch the couple.

"What kind of seeds are they?" Lee's voice carried across the distance.

Yang couldn't make out Wèi An's reply. He knew what was about to happen when he saw his brother pull their folded hands toward him. His stomach clenched. *If Lee produces a son before I do…*

Their lips met in a movement as brief and as light as the wink of a firefly.

※

For weeks since their marriage, Wèi An had been trying to fit in.

"Though your husband is your master," her mother had instructed, "your mother-in-law will control every aspect of your life."

Wèi An understood her place on the Gee family tree: she and Ngon were the lowest branches. She'd wished for female companionship in her new home. Now, she knew if she was quick and efficient about her work, the best she could hope for was to be ignored.

"All men are beasts," her mother told her. "It's best to let them have their way, so you can get on with your chores." It took Wèi An a while to comprehend that Lee was not like the men in her family. Her husband's shy smiles and expressions of gratitude led to short conversations. It surprised her when she realized she looked forward to having them.

In their bedroom, he gave her privacy, turning his back as they prepared for bed. He kept to his side and allowed her to do the same.

Several nights ago, Wèi An braved a comment on his restlessness. "Husband, are you well?"

There was a long pause before he replied. "I am not ill," he stated. Almost as an afterthought, he added, "A wife should call her husband by his name."

"Lee…" she tested it on her tongue. "I'm sorry if I displease you."

He turned to her. Moonlight from outside highlighted the planes of his face and the muscles on his smooth chest in a velvet blue glow. "What makes you think that?"

"Because you haven't made the red string."

He huffed, remaining silent, still looking at her.

"What?" she asked, confused.

"*We* haven't made the red string," he said, emphasizing the first word in his sentence. He turned away and pulled up his covers.

※

After that, Lee seemed to make a point of casually touching her. Their shoulders met when they shared a quiet word, their fingers slid across one another as they passed food at the table, and when he found her alone, he tucked hair behind her ears, then traced a knuckle along her jaw and chin.

Gradually as Wèi An became easy, she initiated contact which thrilled and tortured Lee. He realized that by letting Wèi An approach him, his enjoyment with her continued to build.

She kissed him on the mouth after they'd finished lifting a heavy bag of rice onto the back of a cart. It happened so quickly; Lee was stunned.

His immediate impulse was to jump on top of her, but by then he fully understood what his father meant by Doufu Houa.

"I'd like to be with you now, Husband," Wèi An stated simply.

Lee gulped. "You are with me."

Making meaningful eye contact, she placed her hand over his, saying, "As a wife."

Glancing around to see if anyone overheard, he asked, "Now?" his voice raising.

Wèi An nodded.

Quickly untethering their mule from the cart, Lee tied her under a shade tree where she could graze.

Clutching Wèi An's hand, Lee tugged, encouraging her to run. "I know the perfect place."

Wèi An laughed, squeezing his fingers. She was as eager to consummate their marriage as he was.

Slowing when they reached a stand of tall grass, Lee turned to her, "You are sure?" A frown creased the space between his brows.

Biting her lower lip, Wèi An dropped her gaze, then nodded.

Placing a knuckle under her chin, Lee lifted it so their eyes would meet. "Outside under the sky? Not on our soft bed at home?"

"I'm not afraid of the gods watching...."

When she paused, Lee slid his hand gently along her neck, stroking her earlobe with a thumb. "But?" he encouraged.

Gulping, Wèi An opened her mouth, then, changing her mind, closed it.

"We're in this together," Lee whispered. "You can trust me with your thoughts."

"It's just that..." Wèi An struggled, her eyes growing shiny. "I was taught never to speak ill of my elders."

"I was taught this as well," Lee agreed. "It is correct. But I was also taught that a wife must go to her husband for protection."

"But not from his mother or sister-in-law," Wèi An replied without thinking. Her hand flew to her mouth, her eyes wide.

"I knew it," Lee muttered before a slow smile spread across his face. "If you kiss me again, I'll tell you how to fix it."

Even prepared for the contact, the touch of her lips on his sent shockwaves through Lee's system. As her hands pressed against his chest, fingers splayed, a heat grew, radiating from his heart to all extremities.

Keeping a steady hold on desires that strained for freedom, Lee listened to his wife. He knew the sounds she made at the back of her throat when his strokes brought her pleasure. He recognized the tautness of her muscles and what it meant when they released, leaving her pliant. He registered the instant she realized the effects her touches had on him.

Taking a break before he ruptured, Lee pulled away, swishing a hand through Wèi An's hair. He jumped out of her reach, smiling at her over his shoulder. "Come back, she complained."

"Catch me if you can." Playfully, he led them along a narrow path through shrubbery that concealed a warm spring.

About the size of a small koi pond in the Emperor's garden, the center was crystal clear. Around the edges, green algae congealed into gooey clumps.

Without hesitation, Lee stripped away his clothes and waded in. Waist deep, he turned to Wèi An, holding out his hand.

Standing at the edge, Wèi An clutched her clothes in front of her. Chewing on her lower lip, she dipped a toe into the slime. "Ewww!" she cried, shivering. Looking at Lee, she shook her head, "I don't know how to swim!"

Without a word, he returned to the edge, swiping his arms across the water's surface until the space was clear. Approaching Wèi An, he caught her eyes scanning his body. The hungry look in them gave him confidence. Squaring his shoulders, he gently removed the clothing from her hands, tossing it. Pulling her into his embrace, his rigid desire was cradled between them. With a luscious kiss, he moved backward, pulling her with him. "You don't need to swim," he whispered when he took a breath. "Trust me," he said.

Before Wèi An knew it, she was at the center of the pool. With her upper arms resting on his shoulders and his hand securely on her waist, she felt perfectly safe. As they continued kissing, engaging tongues, Wèi An wrapped her legs around his hips. Lee groaned.

Wèi An could feel the soft tip of his man spear hovering at the edges of her woman's head. Surprised by the heat, she wanted to feel him inside her like she'd never wanted anything in her life.

Squeezing his eyes shut, Lee leaned his forehead against Wèi An's. His fingers pressed into her skin as if he wanted to reach inside her. Speaking each word with great effort, he said, "Use the water to control the pain."

At first, Wèi An was confused, but then, with a knowing expression, she understood. She lowered herself over him until she felt resistance. Her husband had turned into an agonized statue, digging his fingers into her back, his face contorted. As Wèi An raised herself up to relieve a sharp stab, Lee threw his head back, crying out as if he were experiencing it too.

Worried, she placed her hands on either side of his face. "Are you alright?"

"I'm—fine—" he ground out, "but—you're—killing me!"

"What?"

Taking a breath, Lee looked her straight in the eye. "The want to be inside you is killing me."

For a moment of shocked silence, Wèi An regarded him. "Oh—" she said. Biting a lip, Wèi An lowered herself, feeling her womanhood beginning to hurt. When she again hit the pain, instead of pulling back, she gripped her legs tighter around him, pulling herself toward him, crying past the tear-through of her virginity.

Lee cried out, too. For a throbbing moment, they gazed into each other eyes, lost. Breathing heavily, Lee grinned. "How do you feel?"

She nodded, hesitantly. "Alright."

He leaned in to kiss her gently. The gentleness quickly turned to urgency. Against her mouth, he said, "I have to move, Wèi An. I can't hold back anymore."

"OK." Her reply was breathless.

He rode her and once she understood the moves of the dance; she rode him. Together they were like racing wild steppe ponies in love with the wind.

FLOWER OF JOY
Yang, age 22 | Lee, age 19
Panyu District, China
1862
—

On his way back from the Quishizhen market, Yang focused on keeping the ox moving. The animal was always skittish about walking on cobbled roads. Each time the beast stopped, which was frequent, Yang gave his tail a tug. He was pulling on it so much that it felt like sounding the alarm bell in the town's watch tower.

It wasn't a complete surprise to hear his name called as he neared the opium establishment. He knew his school friend, Fun Kee, frequented it. "Gee Yang!" an unkempt man shouted from the open door of 14 Canal Road. Supported by walls covered with peeling aqua-green paint, the building was long and low roofed.

On unsteady feet, Fung Kee squinted against the daylight, holding a hand above his eyes. Yang and Kee were the same age. They'd played together as boys and lived in the same Imperial Exam compound when they thought to enter the Emperor's service. If it weren't for his voice, Yang wouldn't recognize the man. Deep purple crescents hung below sunken, dilated eyes. His skin, an unnatural grey, pulled tightly over sharp bones.

"I'm so hungry, Yang," Kee said, swaying.

Pulling out the coins and smoked duck he had ready for this moment, Yang glanced in both directions before stepping close. Keeping the package concealed, he palmed it to Kee. The sweet, flowery, burnt, syrup scent of opium clung to his clothes. Grasping his friend's upper arm, Yang urged, "Leave this place! Go home!"

Kee focused, attempting to hold Yang's gaze. He gave Yang a beatific smile, resembling the boy he used to be. "There's nothing left." His eyes went glassy. "The flower of joy is all there is now." Stepping back into the darkness, he disappeared inside. "Thank Mama Gee for remembering me."

Yang knew Kee would return to a reclining shelf. A layer of platforms above him would be filled with men in similar states, holding long pipes over small flames, inhaling drugs the British imported from India. It made people stop caring…about anything as they wasted away. Kee's remaining family possessions took up a small space in the corner of his shelf. He'd be tossed out if he lived long enough to run out of items to sell. If he died there, his body would end up in a mass grave. Fung Kee would be condemned to walk the earth as a ghost, the worst imaginable fate.

Gratitude for Mother's persistent warnings about vices washed over Yang. As he prodded the ox to get moving, he thought about the first time Mother discovered his missing market money.

※

Managing family finances, she knew the going prices of produce and calculated the expected return minus the stock that remained in the cart. When she detected the discrepancy, she came after him.

"What have you done?" she screeched, whacking him across the head.

"What do you mean?" he replied, attempting to keep his expression innocent.

Mother stepped back. "Now you lie!" She sucked in wind. "May the gods rain curses on you! Did you gamble it or visit the hundred men's wives?" She stepped closer, sniffing his hair. Her eyes widened. "You're smoking the poppy? You know what it will do to you! As First Son, you risk ruining the entire family?!"

Not able to take the barrage a moment longer, Yang broke down, confiding about Kee.

Listening, Mother's eyes glistened. "No…" her voice sounded raspy. She pressed an unsteady hand to her quivering lips. "It would kill his mother again if she knew what became of her only son." Her eyes returned to Yang. She rested her hands on his shoulders. "It is possible he misses his mother so much he's rushing to meet her in the spirit world."

Yang nodded while keeping his gaze on his feet. He doubted his friend felt that way, but it wasn't worth giving voice to those thoughts.

Since that conversation, Mother packed extra food in his basket whenever he had business in town. Knowing that he delivered the care package to Kee, she still scolded him upon his return.

※

Opening their gate, Yang felt a pang of sadness. Humbug wasn't there to bark a welcome. He parked the cart and unhitched the ox, slapping his rump, letting him have his head. The animal would go straight to the feed trough in the barn.

Yang could feel his tension disbursing. He was very glad to be home.

BIRTH OF SONG
Yang, age 23 | Lee, age 20 | Ngon, age 16
Panyu District, China
1863
—

Ignoring Mother's warnings about going too far from the compound while in her advanced stage of pregnancy, Wèi An thought it was more important to shield Ngon from her grandmother's abuse. Though her pace was slow, they journeyed far afield to deliver the men's mid-day meal.

When Wèi An straightened and her expression changed to alarm, Ngon glanced at her with fright. "Auntie, you peed!" The girl's wide stare regarded a wet spot on Wèi An's slippers. Her mouth formed an "o."

Nodding, Wèi An urged Ngon, "Run ahead, get Uncle Lee. It's nothing to worry about; babies are born every day. But go!" she shouted.

When Ngon was out of sight, Wèi An let loose the groan she'd been holding. Bending forward, she clutched her stomach. She never enjoyed being around Mother Gee, but she wished her mother-in-law were here now. When she could breathe again, Wèi An stood tall to scan her surroundings. Stumbling to the far side of the road, down an embankment, and into the shade, she had lowered herself about halfway to the ground when another pain ripped through her. Dropping onto a hip, she screamed, no longer able to keep it contained. Panting, she turned onto her hands and knees. This position relieved some of the pressure. Her next scream scattered the magpies in the next field over.

After what felt like a year, she heard running feet. "Wèi An!" Lee called. He threw his tools down, racing to her side.

Looking up through tearful eyes, she cried, "Lee! Thank the gods!"

"Your wife is going to drop that baby in the dirt!" Yang's voice chimed in from behind.

"Shut up, Yang!" Lee leaned up to push him. Hard.

Yang sprawled, sending up a dust plume.

"I won't!" Wèi An ground out through gritted teeth, "I will not shame this family!" She screamed again.

Kneeling next to his wife, Lee brushed back her sweaty hair, "Can you stand?" He nodded, looking like he was answering his own question. "I'm here. Lean on me."

Wèi An shook her head. "I can't," she wailed, even as she placed a hand in his.

Lee yelled to Ngon. "Bring your grandmother!"

Yang saw the worried expression on the girl's face, noting the red handprint on her cheek. Removing his shirt, he balled it up, handing it to her. "I'll go. I'm faster." He was gone before they knew it.

Wèi An doubled over with another scream.

"Is she dying?" Ngon asked. Her voice was scratchy and breathless.

"I'm not…dying," Wèi An grunted. Giving Lee an urgent look, she whispered, "Send Ngon to the roadside to watch for help. I can't move—your child is coming!"

"You're sure?" Lee asked, feeling lightheaded.

Nodding, Wèi An returned to her hands and knees. She screamed through another contraction. "She's coming!" Wèi An panted. "Catch your daughter, Lee. Don't let her fall."

"I'll catch her," Lee said. He pushed up his wife's dress, exposing her buttocks and thighs, smeared with blood. A dark patch of hair, resembling seaweed, increasing in size, pushed against the taut opening. A forehead emerged, followed by closed eyes and a tiny nose. "I see it, Wèi An! The head is out!"

So immersed in the wonder of watching the birth of his child, Lee no longer heard his wife's agonized cries.

With Wèi An's last push and a gush of liquid, Lee held his offspring in trembling hands. The birth cord, still pulsing, remained connected to her mother.

"She's beautiful, Wèi An," Lee whispered.

"Why isn't she crying?" Wèi An asked as she slumped to her side. "There should be crying..."

Lee heard his wife's voice as if from a long distance. His daughter was blue. It had been some moments before his wife's worries about their baby's silence cut through his daze.

Ngon had waved down an elderly peddler couple with a cart. As she led them to Wèi An and Lee, she noticed her uncle's stricken expression. The peddler woman must have noticed it too.

With a direct tone that brooked no questions, she shouted, "Turn that baby over! Slap her back! Hard! If you are gentle, she may not live."

As he followed her directives, the woman came in close and bent forward to flick her fingers on the bottoms of the infant's feet.

With enough rough coaxing that went against her father's every instinct, Song turned pink. Her face scrunched, prune-like. She opened her mouth and let out a high-pitched, indignant squall.

Lee leaned back on his heels, letting out a breath he didn't know he was holding.

The woman's smile was warm. She patted his shoulder. "Well done, young man."

With her husband's help, they bundled baby and mother together in the back of the couple's cart and set out for the Gee farmhouse.

※

In the weeks after Song's birth, when Wèi An needed to stay near home with the child. Mother Gee coaxed her into playing their erhus together.

It had been a long time since Pei felt like playing. It astonished her that the desire for music had returned. The new baby must have had something to do with that.

THE BOYS MUST GO
Winter
Yang, age 24 | Lee, age 22
Ting Ai, age 24| Wèi An, age 17
Ngon, age 17 | Ming, age 3 | Song, age 21 months
Panyu District, China
1864
—

With the scarcity of last year's harvest, and skyrocketing taxes, the Gee Family was in dire financial straits. Bozahai was married off with the last of her father's savings. Auntie Liu had gone to live in Dongguan to care for her aging parents.

Yang had been doing odd building jobs in the village to supplement their income while Lee and his wife worked the fields with Fong. Wèi An, the thin waif she'd become, was still nursing her sickly child. She carried Song wrapped next to her heart. Ngon and Ming tended to the house under Pei's supervision. Ting Ai, round again with child, spent much of her time in bed with yùntù, morning sickness. At mealtimes, when no one had enough food to satisfy their hunger, Pei gave extra portions to Ai.

"Yang's son must have enough nourishment," she said, not disguising her glance in Wèi An's direction.

In the quarters they shared with Ngon, Wèi An kept a crock of jook she made with loose kernels of rice she collected in the field and saved in her pocket. The thick, watery gruel helped some, but not enough. When she divided the servings between them before going to bed, Lee and Ngon refused, saying Wèi An should have it all. Their words made her cry.

Lee poured all of his and some of Ngon's into Wèi An's bowl. He patted Ngon's shoulder, nodding his thanks, before leading his wife to their room. He was glad Mother let Ngon live with them in their portion of the family compound. She was a good helper and had become a cherished companion to Wèi An. He worried about not keeping his promise to Fu-chi and Mo Chou. Their daughter, Ngon, was starving too, and the family had no resources to find a husband for her.

Settling Wèi An on the edge of their bed, Lee unwrapped their baby. Marveling as always at her delicate beauty, he also worried about her lethargy. He cradled his sleeping daughter for a few moments, then kissed her forehead before settling her in her crib. Returning to Wèi An, he held the bowl of jook to her mouth, staring her down when she refused. "Just a tiny sip," he coaxed. "We'll share it." After she did as he asked, he pretended to sip from the bowl before setting it aside to help her out of her clothes. He returned it to her between each article he removed. When they were both nude, he poured water from a pitcher and wiped down her face, hands, and feet, then did his own.

A full bath would have to wait for another day. Giving her the last of the porridge, he turned down their covers and pulled her next to him. They held each other, sharing warmth, gentle caresses, and encouraging words of love and gratitude.

※

On the other side of the compound, Fong and Pei worried and strategized. "If Yang takes Ting Ai and Ming to live in the city, he could spend more hours working there." Fong sat at the end of their bed massaging Pei's lotus feet.

"Any place they'd rent," she said, shaking her head, "would take more than what he'd make working extra hours."

"What about your brother? Couldn't they stay with him?"

"His quarters are small. He tutors students there. There's no room for a child, and Ai's in no condition to keep house. Yang is no good at managing money. In Tie's last letter, he wrote that labor brokers are recruiting workers for Gum San."

"Gum San?" Fong seemed confused. "You'd send him to sojourn to hunt for gold? After everything Lung said about that place?"

Pei replied, "Lee would have to go with him, and they wouldn't be prospecting, but working to build an iron road."

"Both my sons?" Fong was incredulous.

"They're paying 170 yuan per month. Think of it, Fong, in one month, they'd earn more than we make on the farm for years!"

Leaning over on both knees, Fong ran his fingers through his thinning hair. "How would they get there?"

"Tie says the Sam Yap Association fronts travel expenses for a loan."

Fong made a heavy sigh. His shoulders rounded as he said, "Lung said the associations require monthly membership fees and there are other expenses as well."

Pei hesitated before saying her next words. "I can write to Mr. Yet Wah about Ngon."

"No!" He stood with eyes blazing.

Pei continued as if he'd said nothing, "It would cover expenses, reduce the dependency on the farm, and now that she's a woman, she'll fetch a higher price."

Fong stormed out. He didn't come back that night or the next morning.

※

"Where's Father?" Yang asked as Ngon placed a warm bowl of jook seasoned with thin strips of dried seaweed and sesame seeds before him.

Lee shrugged his shoulders. He thanked Ngon and gave her an appreciative smile as she served him.

"He had business in town." Mother waved away their questions. "You're grown men. You know what to do."

※

"This is not like Father," Lee mentioned to Wèi An. They were working in the barn on this rainy day, inventorying stores, cleaning out stalls, and grouping implements in need of repair. Since they weren't covering lots of ground, Wèi An spread a blanket atop clean straw and gave Song toys to play with. She'd only recently started sitting up by herself.

"There must be something to celebrate," Wèi An said hopefully. "I heard Mother talking to Ngon about butchering a chicken for tonight's dinner!"

"Something's up," Lee nodded. "Mother had me check the garden; we'll be having garlic and bok choy too. Come here," he said, lowering his voice. "Look what I found. It's not enough for a meal, but it'll make a nice snack."

He handed her a snow pea pod. Wèi An snapped the stem and carefully pulled the side string. With the casing open, they stared at four perfect fresh peas. Lee plucked the first one, popping it in his mouth. Wèi An did the same. They closed their eyes to savor the green sweetness. With the next one, Wèi An held his gaze, challenging him with her expression. She placed a pea on her tongue, holding it there for his regard. Grinning, he followed her lead. After a long kiss that left them breathless, they each had a pea in their mouth with no telling if it was the original. Chewing and smiling,

Wèi An curled each end of the pod in a tight roll. "Let's save this for Ngon."

"Love you, Dove," Lee murmured, pecking her on the cheek.

※

At dinner, Yang was excited to share the news he'd gotten a new job helping to build a house. Everyone couldn't wait to eat. The sumptuous fare had their stomachs growling and mouths salivating. Before they could begin, Father stood at the head of the table. "First, we must thank Mother for this special meal."

They nodded murmuring appreciation. "We're celebrating a change," Father continued. He didn't look well. There were bags under his eyes. His color was sallow.

"On Friday, Lee will be coming with me to visit Mr. Shai's. He'll be showing a new harvesting method."

Lee nodded, knitting his brows together. He always enjoyed learning new farming methods with Father, but they'd never had celebrations about it before.

Father continued, "We should be on the road at the same time as Yang. We'll walk together."

While the brothers and their wives agreed their parents were behaving odd, no one could wrest additional information out of them.

On the appointed day, Lee was excited about the outing. Ngon and Wèi An watched as he loaded a pack with supplies for their long walk.

"Last time they did this," Ngon informed her Aunt, "they learned about a new plow design that worked twice as good as the old one. Grandfather doesn't like change unless increased crop yields can be proven."

The adults nodded, indicating that they heard what she'd said.

"Remember when he started doing the catfish?" Ngon continued, "All the neighbors thought he was possessed, and now almost everyone is doing it too."

"If only you were a boy, Ngon," Lee sighed, "Father would bring you along too."

"I know…" Her face fell.

"Don't worry." He tipped her chin up, giving her a wink. "You know I'll show you everything when I get back."

Ngon's face brightened.

"Mind your Grandmother and stick with Wèi An."

"I always do."

Leaning over to kiss his wife, Lee whispered, "How did I become so fortunate for the gods to gift me with three such lovely females?"

※

Lee's mind was spinning with possibilities on their way home. With the contraption that allowed someone to sit behind an ox while it pulled, one person could do the job of three! He didn't understand why his father was so quiet. "It's revolutionary!" Lee exclaimed. "We should start making one right away."

"There's no need," Father replied, "I ordered one from Mr. Shao two days ago."

"You did?" Lee was confused. "Why didn't you tell me? How can we afford it?"

Distracted, Father nodded ahead, "Look, there's Yang."

Catching up, they walked together for a while. Father was silent as Yang talked about his day and Lee shared what they'd learned. When they reached their land and left the road, Father's pace slowed. "Boys," he drew out the word, "there's something I have to tell you."

Yang and Lee eyed each other, both worried by the tone in their father's voice.

"Your mother and I have decided that you are to sojourn."

After a stunned silence, Father cleared his throat. "Times are hard, as you know. It's what's best for the family."

"Where?" Yang asked.

"Gum San, Gold Mountain, but not to mine gold like Uncle Lung. You will work at building a road for their iron horse. Uncle Tie is already working on the travel arrangements."

"But Father, we can't both go; who's going to help run the farm?" Lee said.

Not willing to see the hurt in his younger son's eyes, or let him view the pain in his own, Fong directed his comment to First Son. "It's already decided. You're both going."

"We can't go. There's no money," Lee claimed, his tone rising.

"Your mother's already taken care of it."

A crushing pain squeezed Lee's chest; his eyes bugged. "How?" he squeaked.

"Ngon," Father whispered.

"No!" Lee screamed, "You wouldn't!" Dropping his pack, he lunged at Father.

Yang intercepted before he could make contact. "Stop, Lee." Yang struggled to contain his brother's flailing arms. "She's only a worthless girl," he ground out.

Like an earthquake, Lee heaved beneath Yang, lifting him up and over. Shoving his brother's head into the dirt, Lee pressed his forearm against Yang's windpipe.

The shock of being overcome flashed across Yang's face before the lack of oxygen began turning it purple.

"Enough!" Father roared, kicking Lee off his brother. "What's done is done."

Lee rolled over to glare at Father. "How can you allow it? After Mo Chou? Do you and Mother have no care for the people Fu-chi loved?"

With that, Fong did something he'd never done before. He struck his son, drawing blood. "You are too young to understand." He pointed a finger in Lee's face. "You WILL NOT disrespect your mother and you will stay here until you can behave as a proper son."

Father stalked off, leaving them both.

Yang groaned, rubbing his throat as he moved into a sitting position. "I always wondered what it would be like to have an adventure. I guess we're going to find out."

Lee glowered at him. "Fuck you."

Yang laughed, "Not you, little brother, but I better get busy with Ting Ai!"

As Yang stood and took his first steps toward their house, another band of chest-crushing pain tightened around Lee. Wèi An!

※

On their last night at home, Mother prepared a feast. She lit candles and incense and said special prayers at the family altar.

Although Wèi An was in no mood to play or sing, Mother insisted they perform. "You must not allow melancholy into the music," she warned. "Long after they've forgotten many things, they will remember the melody. You want that to be sweet for your husband, don't you?"

Wèi An nodded. She tried to comply. Her playing and song may have been the best of her life. The song she composed was this.

―
The dragon and phoenix met in the mists of the clouds and rain.
Inside the hibiscus tent, we sang joyous songs of the peach.
My red leaf found Heaven in your touch.
The need for money takes my husband away.
Now, only dreams can deliver us to the Moon Festival where
we'll meet in the Peony Palace.
Don't forget, my love. Don't forget.
―

As the last note faded, the family sat immobilized by shock. Wèi An expressing such brazen sexual language was unbelievable!

Gathering his thoughts before the others, Lee stood. In several strides, he was across the room. He took the instrument and set it aside while taking hold of her hand. Tugging her to her feet, he urged her to join him as he raced to privacy.

His parents could look after the baby tonight!

CROSSING
Aug. 27th
Yang, age 24 | Lee, age 21
Panyu District & Pacific Ocean
1864
—

In the front of the house, four woven baskets were lined up by the porch. Loaded with traveling supplies, two long bamboo poles attached to the baskets at each end with sturdy twine. Mother had directed the wives to sew special pockets inside of their clothes to carry money. Lee and Yang didn't speak as the family said their goodbyes. Taking turns clasping Father's forearm, they nodded at his wish for a safe crossing. Yang hugged Mother as she cried and petted him. Lee allowed her to do it to him but did not reciprocate. They kissed their wives and children.

Lee had to force himself to remove Wèi An's clutching hands and step away from her. The brothers squatted under the poles, lifting with their legs as the basket weight settled over their shoulders. Father strode ahead to open the gate, keeping his expression composed. As they stepped onto the road, adjusting their gait to their pendulous loads, they began the journey. Yang took the lead. Lee matched his stride.

With each step, Yang felt the tension lift. Troubling emotions had been hanging from him like blood-sucking parasites. Surrounding the burial of his still-born son, he'd been angry at Ting Ai. *Did she do something that caused my son to die?* And he'd been furious with the family. The infant received no name, there was no ceremony, and there was no one to kowtow for him. With Ngon gone, the duty to handle the body fell to Lee, but Yang wouldn't stand for that. Breaking with tradition, he'd taken care of it himself.

Lee bit down on the inside of his cheek, forcing himself to keep his eyes on Yang's feet. It took every ounce of will not throw off the pole and return to his wife. He imagined cupping the new seed of life growing in her belly, kissing her eyelids, wiping her tears, and apologizing for the terrible mistake. "I would never leave you!" he'd say. Snorting up a gob of snot, Lee swallowed it, giving his sour stomach juices something more to work on.

Five miles later, Lee was suffering from a pounding headache and heart palpitations. He wondered if he'd die before leaving. Yang seemed taller and hyperalert. They boarded a riverboat, joining peddlers traveling to market. At each confluence, they turned left, heading south. As the tall peaks of their river valley receded, the landscape grew flatter and more open, and the waterway grew wider than anything the boys had ever seen.

Yang couldn't contain his excitement. "Lee!" He nudged his brother with the back of his hand, "Look at all the boats! Those," he pointed, "are filled with nothing but produce. Did you ever imagine an ox could ride on the water without upending the entire thing?" Lee's gaze followed Yang's direction. He nodded but remained stoic. His body pains had eased but the dark cloud of feeling clung to him still. Yang continued, "Look over there!" He gestured to twenty flat-roofed structures tied together like a floating island. "I've heard of boat people but never thought to see them!"

When they landed at the dock in Hong Kong, they were both overwhelmed by the sheer volume of people and the horizon covered by buildings as far as the eye could see. The unfamiliar caught their attention. The first sighting of armed British soldiers marching in formation was strange. The men wore bright, tight-fitting uniforms. Their voices sounded guttural. Most alarming was their skin and facial structure. If the boys had not grown up hearing stories of the British, they would have taken them for devils.

Horses pulling wagons loaded with cages filled with chickens, turkeys, and monkeys trundled past. The animal calls added to the racket. Men pushing wooden carts and women carrying packages spoke dialects and languages they'd never heard. After becoming separated in the crowd, Yang felt his first pangs of anxiety as he lifted on his toes, scanning for signs of his brother.

Awash with a chill and wondering how he'd find their labor company, Yang began calling, "Lee! Lee!" taking a few hasty steps back in the direction he'd come, all while making sure his pole and baskets didn't get tangled. When a passing ox upended one, spilling the contents, Yang cursed as he scrambled to reclaim his clothing, food, and utensils. Thinking better of his transportation setup, he stacked the baskets, holding the bamboo perpendicular in the crook of his elbow. Still calling, "Lee! Lee!" he pushed his way through.

"Where are you going?"

Yang felt a tug on his sleeve from behind. Spinning around, seeing his brother, he sagged. "Where'd you go? You were right behind me and then you weren't."

The corners of Lee's mouth turned up. He cocked his head to the side. This is new. *Yang never gets rattled.* His tone sounded amused as he replied, pointing a thumb over his shoulder. "I went to read the road sign and then asked for directions."

"Oh," Yang replied.

"We're three blocks from the Sam Yap boarding house." Lee indicated a narrow lane walled in by two and three-story buildings. "Mother said whenever presented with a choice, choose to keep money in our pockets."

"But?" Yang longingly watched a man pass by with an empty cart. Shaking his head, Lee led the way.

※

Lee's physical maladies returned as they crossed the gangway to board the Arracan. The brothers caught a brief glimpse of the first-class accommodations as the crew herded them below deck to steerage, a dark, low-ceiling room, crowded by hundreds of bunks. "Pick one and call it home," the sailor escorting them called in words that held no meaning. A bilingual passenger translated, sending the stalled group into motion.

Yang and Lee chose stacked platforms against a far wall. Yang stowed his baskets next to Lee's. He threw his hat on the top bunk, claiming it for himself. They sat quietly together on the bottom, watching the proceedings. As more men entered, filling the space, the air quickly grew hot and stale. Lee gripped the edge of the platform, attempting to breathe calmness into his body. When he looked over at Yang, watching his eyes dart around, taking in every fresh face with obvious pleasure, it was hard for Lee not to resent him. If Yang had passed his exams, Ngon would still be home and a sojourn would have been unnecessary.

They'd already known of hardships in Gum San from those who returned with stories of wilderness and man devils. They'd also known families whose son's work had increased their wealth. "We are sending you together so you can look out for one another," Father proclaimed. "Yang will find the best opportunities and Lee will make sure Yang is not tempted by vices." Lee was surprised to hear his parents' assessment. Though he agreed with it, it didn't make their decision easier to accept.

As he remembered the days after the announcement, he thought about how it changed his relationship with Wèi An. Every moment crystallized into deep appreciation threaded with sorrow at their impending separation.

Wèi An had an aunt who'd married a man she'd never met. He was already living in Gum San when the wedding took place. They used a rooster as a groom stand-in during the ceremony. Lee could tell by the tension in Wèi An's voice she understood her aunt's plight. Being a young bride and never knowing her husband...or any man, while withering into old age, seemed cruel.

"I don't want to be a Gold Mountain widow!" Wèi An cried.

"You won't be, Dove. I won't be digging for gold." He tried to lighten her intensity.

"We could go with you!" she pleaded.

"I wish you could!" Lee said, feeling his heart in his throat. "The Flowery Flag Nation is no place for a proper woman, and my parents need your help here."

Tears dripped from her eyes when she said, "If your father wasn't here, I'd run away with you."

"I know..." Lee hugged her, tucking her head under his chin.

Every night, Lee savored the sweetness of his Wèi An. He wanted to leave her with memories of love before her husband became a sojourner.

※

Night had fallen aboard the Arracan, cloaking the expansive sea behind a blanket of darkness. Overcast skies played hide-and-seek with the moon.

Lee woke with a start. When he laid down, he was sure he'd never fall asleep. The rolling deck reminded him of his touchy stomach. A dim flicker coming from a lantern, swaying on a beam by the ladder, cast distorted, moving shadows along the wooden floor. He had to look away to keep his stomach down.

Snoring and mumbling men, along with the hum of the giant steam engines, added to his agitation. Pinpricks at his ankles made him jump. More erupted between his shoulder blades. Furiously, he scratched. Moving his spine against the bedpost, he wiggled against it. He dug his fingers into his hair, clawing at his scalp. Lee imagined the entire surface of his skin alive with vermin. Groaning, he threw off his blankets and pulled on his shirt and pants. Slipping on shoes, he took another few moments to work at satisfying scratch cravings.

Carrying his night jar, he took extra care knowing he wasn't all the way awake and hadn't developed what the other men called *sea legs*. As he wobbled toward the foredeck, he nodded to the crew he passed. Lee carefully trundled to the water closet, two open holes hanging over the side of the boat. Dumping his slop, he returned to the deck, selecting a place along the rail to linger, setting the jar near his feet. Leaning over, he caught the flow of air. It shifted his thoughts away from the itch. Reveling in the sensation, he removed his hair tie, loosening the strands so the wind could have her way with them. Across the water, he could make out small white caps that appeared to glow. He briefly considered jumping. *Would Goddess Mazu greet me under the water? Or would she shame me for abandoning my parents, wife, and children?*

Lee picked up the jar. Scraping his nails against his scalp, he shuffled back to his bunk. Fully clothed, he lay on top of the covers. Allowing his eyes to fill without worrying about concealment, he let tears stream freely, pooling in the shells of his ears. With every upward heave, the Arracan crested waves, increasing the distance between him and everyone who was important.

Yang, still asleep, let loose a long fluttering sound. Lee's mouth quirked in a half smile. He waved a hand under his nose. With impatience, he dried his face, then sat up to re-braid his hair. *I did not leave everyone I love behind,* he thought.

※

Yang and Lee had become friendly with Ging Cui, a fifteen-year-old from Guangzhou. The boy's grandfather had visited some of the same places in California that Uncle Lung had mentioned. His was a bottom bunk next to Lee's, and he was traveling alone. Yang and Cui shared enlivening conversations about San Francisco's Chinatown and iron horses. Yang started calling him Bunk Neighbor.

The young man suffered from severe sea sickness almost as soon as they left port. He wasn't alone in this. Unfortunately, the man in the bunk above him shared the same affliction. Doubly cursed, Cui endured living in his own vomit as well as his bunk mate's.

Yang and Lee helped Cui to the water closet and washed his bedding when water was available, which was rare. They brought him tea to sip when he felt up to it. "I'm not going to make it to Gum San," he confided in Yang.

Cui'd seen what happened to others who died on the ship. Authorities confiscated their belongings, riffling through them for valuables before tossing the body overboard.

"Before I left, my sister had incense blessed by monks," Cui whispered. "The smoke will carry me to the afterworld. Promise me, please," he begged, "that you and Lee will burn it. I don't want to be condemned to wander and curse the living!"

※

Yang had been the first to notice when Cui didn't wake up. He said nothing, just nudged Lee and nodded his head in the boy's direction. The crew's disregard for their death rituals had been an affront to every Chinese. It was with this urgency that Yang pretended to talk with Cui while he kept watch to make sure no one noticed Lee searching through his belongings.

Yang wore a brooding expression as he urged Lee to hurry while also saying, "If he's got food or anything else we can use, take it."

Lee's head snapped up. "We can't steal from Cui."

"We're not," Yang spoke out of the corner of his mouth. "He'd give it to us if he could. If there's anything in there naming his parents, you can write to them to let them know what happened to him."

Lee found no written material, only several coins. Less than half of what their parents had given them for the journey. "Take them but leave two for the crew to find," Yang said.

Lee found herbs, medicines, rice, and several sheets of dried seaweed. He was starting to grow worried when he could not locate the incense. He found it inside a small wooden box at the very bottom of Cui's basket.

※

Once they informed the interpreter about Cui, the brothers watched in horror as the scene played out again. Crew members handled the body roughly, wrapping the boy, along with his soiled bedding in burlap, and tying it off around the neck and feet with strings. They searched his baskets, making brutal comments that didn't require translation to understand. As his closest "next-of-kin," Yang and Lee followed the procession to the aft deck. They squinted in the bright light as they watched the crew "make a hole in the water" with all three passengers who'd died that day.

Cui's incense had burned to ash. The last vestiges of its scent were fading as Lee looked through their belongings for spices to contribute to tonight's meal. Holding a small bag of fennel pods that had belonged to Cui, Lee and Yang's sad gaze met and held.

Yang, who usually spent most of his waking hours circulating through the groups of men, had been staying close. "It's been so long since I've been clean; I feel like an animal," he complained.

"It won't be forever," said Lee.

"Why do you always do that?"

"Do what?"

"Look at everything like a Square City puzzle, like there is a solution to every problem." Yang complained.

"Because there is."

"Sometimes I just want you to agree with me!" said Yang, frowning.

"Keep your voice down," Lee urged, glancing over his shoulder. "I choose not to complain about every little thing."

"We've been on this stinking boat seventeen days, stuffed in a dark, airless hole for most of it. And we've watched too many men die," said Yang.

"I know how long it's been! And I haven't forgotten what we've seen!"

"Stop shouting," a man from Guizhou province raised his voice.

"Keep to your own affairs," Lee growled.

"You, filthy, disrespectful Guandongs!"

"Who are you calling filthy? I can smell you from ten feet away!" Yang stood, taking steps in the man's direction.

Lee, balling his hands into fists, followed. "Your stink is far worse than my brother's!" he shouted.

Five or six Haung district men reached for bamboo poles, approaching the brewing clash.

Lee threw the first punch, and the resulting pain felt great! A cabin-wide brawl exploded like a disturbed nest of fire ants. Poles cracked, heads knocked, blood splattered. There was no room for footwork, only pummeling fists, elbows, knees. Pain, though unpleasant, was also energizing like the salt-laced wind whipping over the waves. It dispelled grief, took their minds off indignities, flexed their strength, and above all, got them outside.

White devils descended the ladder, trying to shout above the noise. Tossing buckets of water into the melee, they grabbed hold of those nearest, hauling them up above deck.

When seawater hit Lee, he roared. Swiping at his swollen, stinging eyes, he took a blow to the stomach before his opponent was yanked away.

"Who started it?" Lee heard the whites demanding of the men who could interpret.

Their queries were met with shrugged shoulders. "You lied!" a ship's officer yelled. "You promised the fighting would stop!"

Lee understood their frustration. They wanted targets for punishment.

"If you won't identify the instigator," the officer continued, grabbing hold of two interpreters, "You can spend a few days in irons thinking about it!"

Not understanding why their interpreters were being hauled off, Lee hoped it wasn't because they were protecting him.

※

With peace restored, for the time, the men tended to their wounds and repaired broken items.

Lee inspected Yang's left pinky finger. It bent at an unnatural angle. Pulling on the end, it made grating noises as he straightened it. Yang let loose a high-pitched scream.

"You sound like a male rabbit when Mother chops off his testicles." Lee laughed through his fat lip and groaned at the stabbing pain it triggered in his ribs.

Yang wiped sweat from his upper lip, observing as Lee bound the finger tightly to the one next to it. With a weary smile, he said, "Be nice. It might be me who sets your next broken bone."

"Good fighters have few injuries."

"Right!" Yang laughed, jabbing Lee under the arm.

※

Below Yang, Lee was thrashing…again. Mumbled sentences erupted now and again. "No! This can't be happening!" "I'm alone." "Too much water!"

Like he'd done when he was a boy, Yang tried ignoring his brother's nighttime distress. *Thank the gods he's stopped sleepwalking!* he thought. Unfortunately, since Cui's death, Lee's nightmares had become frequent. Rolling into a ball and clamping his pillow tight against his ears, he couldn't drown out Fu-chi's voice demanding that he be responsible.

Swearing, Yang flung his pillow on the bunk below. By the time he'd climbed down and sat on the edge, Lee was sitting up and blinking. "I woke you again?" he whispered while rubbing his eyes.

"Yep."

"Sorry." Lee handed Yang his pillow.

※

There were those among them who kept fight scores, awarding points based on the type and quantity of injuries. They placed bets on who would win the next one.

Lee did not take part in the betting, but he knew Yang did. He amused himself by joining Mahjong and Arrange in Nine games.

In the afternoon lull between meals, Yang coaxed Lee to retell some of the classic stories. A favorite was the tale of ten identical brothers who outsmarted a judge and death sentence by switching places and utilizing their unique skills.

Yang carved small wooden deities while he listened. His favorite likeness was the Jade Emperor. Being the strongest of all the gods, he had the most power to protect them from the malicious spirits of those who'd been buried at sea. Other men wove baskets or mended clothing. Some listened with their eyes closed while modulating their breath.

Other frequent story requests were *The Journey to the West* and *Romance of the Three Kingdoms*. Lee noticed the men seemed less inclined to fight when they remembered their rich culture, famous military battles, Buddhist pilgrimages, and intrigues of the Chinese bureaucracy. He concluded that his own special skill was remembering and dramatizing material from Uncle Tie's lessons.

※

Yang was in a far corner of the common area, throwing dice. Hearing his brother's snorty laugh and cursing, Lee set his book down. He knew Yang was using Cui's coins to gamble. How dare he act as if he hadn't a care in the world!

Lee began walking in that direction. In his peripheral vision, he could see heads turning, speculative whispers, and money changing hands. His steps were purposeful and direct.

"Yang's in trouble again!" Lee heard comments from behind. "The crew will be below deck in less than ten minutes." "It'll be at least eight." "I'm staying out of this one!" "Lee's going to end up in the brig."

Standing behind Yang, Lee crossed his arms, glaring down at the top of his head. Shui, sitting opposite, eyed Lee before returning to the game. He shook the dice in his fist, tossing them into the circle. Lee tapped a toe. Yang turned to look directly at him. Grinning, he accepted the dice from the man to his left, rolling them in his palm.

With an expletive, Lee kicked Yang's hand, sending the polka-dotted squares flying. As if that were the signal to begin, the room erupted in a boil.

They knew the crew would spray them with high-pressure hoses if they got too loud, disturbing the passengers above, so they refrained from raising their voices.

Perhaps the mean-minded connection served a greater purpose. It was a response to loss growing greater with every knot, fear of the unknown, and the uncertainty of burial with their ancestors.

In a grotesque dance, Yang swiped Lee's legs out from under him. Clutched in a painful grasp, they rolled over each other, contacting soft flesh here and bone there. Grunts turned to shouts, war cries learned in village battles volleyed back and forth, and the men lashed out.

Yang sat on his brother, legs clamped around his hips, attempting to gouge his thumbs into Lee's eyes. Lee bucked, thrashing his head from side to side. "Get off me, cocksucker!"

"Not until you mind your own fucking business," yelled Yang.

"Asshole!" Lee twisted, gaining traction. Knocking Yang off balance, Lee hammer-punched him in the ear.

"I'm going to kill you!" Yang shouted, catching Lee across the mouth with his fist.

Lee blasted his brother's face with spit and blood.

The topside crew, racing above, sounded like thunder cracking. Lightning came as seawater, vigorously cold, directed through hoses, aimed at their faces.

The need to fight for breath deflated the battle-charged atmosphere. There was a long pause as the crew shouted more threats against fighting.

Quiet followed the climax. Combatants helped each other move away from the battlefield, press cloth to bleeding wounds, and heat water for washing. Voices turned warm and cajoling. Laughter was lighter.

Lee's face was darkening and swelling. Yang had a forceful right hook that seemed to contact the same spot on his brother's face each time they went at it. Yang's lower lip had grown twice its size. A torn earlobe oozed blood in a stream down his neck. "Your fighting's getting better," Yang slurred his words.

※

Day Sixty-Seven

Steerage inspections required everyone to move to the top deck. They crowded toward the narrow threshold and further condensed into sets of two as they climbed the stairwell. Hands trailed along metal walls, sensing vibrations of the giant beast within that cranked out steam power to move the ship. Passing first-class level, they glanced down the carpeted walkways lined by wood-paneled walls. Its glossy sheen reflected light from flickering sconces. If they were fortunate, they'd glimpse Gweilo (Americans) standing behind the sailors who stood guard, ensuring below-deck passengers didn't wander. The Gweilo were elaborately wrapped in layers of uncomfortable-looking clothes; their expressions appeared pinched, as if they'd bitten into the flesh of a sour plum.

The day's weather was chilly, with misting rain and low visibility. The brief interlude of fresh air was always welcome, even when they understood the burning torture that was to come.

Captain Kuhlken accompanied several crew members below deck to verify the safety of cooking spaces. Satisfied with what he saw, he took his leave before the fumigation crew started. Wearing eye protection and cloth face coverings, the sailors set alight dried, hot chili peppers inside lantern-like containers. As it produced smoke, another sailor fanned the vapers, directing them into every corner as they walked throughout the space. When the task was complete, they came out of the hold, coughing and wiping red, streaming eyes.

At the beginning of the voyage, through interpreters, the Chinese men were told about the procedure to rid the room of lice and other critters. No one objected to reducing the number of irritating pests, but returning to their cabin after fumigation was dreaded.

Someone spotted dolphins playing in the ship's wake and whales blowing air from giant spouts. Some men reacted with delight while others were frightened. Any animal sighting was cause for much debate and discussion below. If their mother had seen the sea creatures, Yang and Lee knew she'd be quaking on her tiny feet, insisting they pray and make offerings for protection. But both boys had spent enough time with Father and Grandfather, who had taught them to question rather than fear and appreciate opportunities to learn.

After vermin treatment, the burning eyes, nausea, and sore throats took a while to pass. Lee sat cross-legged next to the fire, lighting long wood slivers. He held the flame close to his clothes, moving it close to the surface, using it to burst nits.

Yang stood near Lee, scratching at his own personal lice population, but his eyes were following Law Wing and Sue Kee as they filled a bowl with coins and set it on a table. They were the best of the game masters among the men.

"Why don't you work on cleaning your clothes?" Lee asked, attempting to divert Yang's attention.

"Too lazy," Yang replied, narrowing his eyes. "Besides," he turned his brilliant smile on his brother, "I can pay you to do it with my winnings."

Sue Kee began a chant, "Fan-tan, fan-tan," calling the game to order as he unrolled a mat on the floor. It showed a vertical line, dividing the space into halves with numbers painted across the top.

Lee followed Yang as he went to rummage in their baskets. "Not again!" he admonished. "You were lucky before, but it won't last." He pinched the cloth on Yang's overcoat, urging him to stay.

With firmness, Yang pushed Lee's hand away. "I have a guaranteed method." He winked. "If you come with me and watch closely, you might discover what it is."

Lee scowled. "We can't afford losses," he said crossly.

"And we can't afford inflated prices in California. Best to make money where we can."

Lee dropped his eyes.

"Come with me," Yang said. "If I win, I'll keep playing. At the first loss, I'll stop."

Heaving a deep sigh, Lee delivered his consent with a barely perceptible dip of the chin.

As the players squatted before the gambling table, a commotion from the ladder drew their attention. Law Wing led two white men toward them.

Yang and Lee had seen British soldiers in Hong Kong, but it had been at a distance. Aside from the Arracan crew, these two men, wearing constricting breeches, topcoats, and hard shoes, were the first Ōuzhōurén (Europeans) they'd seen close up.

"Sirs, if you please, show your coin," Sue Kee said. He waited while Law Wing repeated his words so they could understand.

Digging into their pockets, each man held up a fifty-cent piece.

While still regarding the foreigners, the game master addressed the players. "Anyone object to these white devils giving us their money?"

Grunts and head nods showed agreement. Yang bent forward so his mouth was near Lee's ear. "I don't care whose money it is," he whispered. "I'll be glad to have it."

Sue Kee scooped a handful of coins, slapped it onto the table, and immediately covered it with another bowl. Players placed their coins on the mat.

Law Wing explained to the white men that the vertical line indicated an odd or even bet and the numbers across the top were for exact numbers in the pile.

"Double your money if your guess is correct!" Sue Kee smiled.

Yang placed a coin on the even side. He watched as a soldier placed his coin on the odd and the other on an exact number.

Once bets were placed, the overturned bowl was lifted. Sue Kee used a wire with a crooked end to separate the pile into four groups of ten. The players let out groans and cheers when the last pile contained only four coins.

"Even win," the game master announced, paying out coins to correct bettors while claiming all the others.

With many bows and apologies, Law Wing commiserated about the loss with the visitors. "Win some, lose some," he said. "Try again?"

They showed more coins and placed their bets. Lee turned his attention to Yang. Instead of intently eyeing the coins as most players did, Yang studied Sue Kee. His eyes darted between the man's face and hands. Lee noticed a slight movement of Yang's eyebrow once he arrived at a decision. Resolutely, Yang placed a coin to the left of the vertical line.

Player tension ran high as they counted coins. "Even wins again," declared the game master, adding more coins to Yang's winnings. Yang turned to Lee, grinning.

On the third round, Yang bet odd while he and Lee listened to Law Wing as he translated the number markings on the mat. Each player wondered how the whites would react if they lost again. Muscles tightened, preparing for a fight. They knew if violence broke out, the Chinese were guaranteed to lose.

"Oh! So solly sirs," Sue Kee cried dramatically, placing a hand over his heart. "Luck was not with you today," he bowed four times in succession.

Lee didn't need to understand English to know that the white men accepted their loss in good humor.

"Thank you," they bowed stiffly to the other players. The taller of the two made eye contact with Lee, repeating that phrase. Lee acknowledged him, testing out the words, *Th-ank u*, as Law Wing escorted them back to the ladder.

Returning to their bunks, Yang couldn't contain his smug expression as he tucked his winnings into their travel basket.

Choosing not to reinforce his brother's self-satisfied attitude, Lee crawled in, searching for his book.

BEACH & BATH
San Francisco, California
1864
—

Excitement onboard the Arracan hummed like the first notes of an emotion-filled song played on the erhu. Captain Kuhlken had promised to allow steerage passengers on deck at the first sight of land. They could remain there until the ship entered the strait of the Golden Gate.

The tangy taste of fresh air held something more today. Hope. Expectation. Anxiety. Anticipation. As they entered the harbor, the mountains standing guard on either side of the opening drew their gaze. Ahead, they could see ships at anchor and streets lined with buildings, sprawling from the water's edge up into the surrounding sand hills. Nearing the dock, the captain ordered them below to prepare for departure and make way for the crew to tie off.

"What's the first thing you want to do when you set foot on dry land?" Yang asked as they checked and rechecked their baskets, making sure all their belongings were secure. Lee stood, straightening his clothes, and patting the secret pockets, verifying their money was safe.

"I will watch for a temple. We must light incense to thank the gods for seeing us safely to shore."

Yang regarded his brother, wearing a perplexed expression, before nodding. "Yes, that is what we must do. But I was thinking we might bathe before presenting ourselves to the gods."

Timbers creaked and taut lines crackled as the first-class passengers and porters moved trunks and supplies from above. Voices, high and happy, drifted down the ladder hole.

The waiting men, mostly silent, eyed each other. Although they'd battled, formed friendships, and watched some die, they'd also formed a community, one that was about to dismantle.

"Ten minutes!" a crew member shouted down. "Check your space. Make sure you have all your belongings."

At those words, Yang sprang into motion, saying farewell and bowing to the men he considered friends. Lee blinked rapidly, hearing Father's admonitions echoing in his mind. Yang gave no thought to Lee, assuming the watch over their possessions.

Ascending the ladder, a bright, cloudless sky greeted the brothers, a stark change from only hours before. Lee's eyes watered as he turned to grasp the bamboo pole Yang handed him. Adjusting the weight over his shoulders, he blinked to clear his vision. Navigating the gangway took every bit of his concentration. He thought stepping from the gangway to solid ground would come as a relief. Instead, his balance revolted, and his stomach remembered the upset from their first few days at sea.

Hundreds of men wearing clothes similar to the ones who'd played Fan-tan lined the streets. Women in brightly colored gowns stood next to them or watched from inside carriages. Moving with the flow of people, Lee gulped in air, hoping it would settle his insides, which were still moving like the ocean.

At the front of the crowd was a line of men wearing blue pants, matching shirts, and small hats. Each official held a club. Revolvers in holsters at their hips glinted in the afternoon light.

One of the uniformed men shouted. The phrase "immigration inspection" filtered through the crowd. The Chinese shared looks of concern as they surged forward like cattle. Bright sunlight shifted to dark as they entered a warehouse. Unclean human smells assaulted them. Lee's steps faltered. His brother stumbled against his back. When Yang would have made a caustic remark, he noticed the pallor of Lee's skin. "Shit!" he said. "You can't be sick now!"

Nodding, Lee agreed as he continued to move. They waited in line, watching officials paw through baskets while others looked in ears and mouths and directed men to lift their shirts. Yang kept sending worried glances at his brother, whispering, "You're alright. You can do this."

Lee clamped his arms tightly around his shirt, not wanting to reveal his secret pocket. "They're looking for pustules," Yang commented as he leaned close before lifting his arms, allowing the inspectors access to his bare torso.

After awkwardly speaking "Cen-tr-al Pac-if-ic Rail-road" in reply to the employment question, Yang and Lee walked free.

Yang smiled broadly, wearing a look of triumph. Stretching, he squeezed his shoulder blades together, puffing out his chest. He inhaled deeply as if inviting the qi of this place to fill him to his toes.

Lee felt a sense of relief and a deep need for a long, uninterrupted sleep. Sadness over young Cui's absence mingled with his persistent feelings of regret over his separation from Wèi An and Song.

One of the merchants on the street shouted, "Sam Yap House," calling Arracan passengers who were members of the Association. As Yang and Lee approached, the elderly gentleman smiled and bowed, saying, "Greetings. Welcome to San Francisco!" He directed them to set their baskets down to wait for others to arrive. Yang was delighted to see Sue Kee and Law Wing joining their group. Amid their reunion, Yang elbowed Lee in the ribs, directing his attention to five women crossing the gangplank.

Law Yaw whistled. "I didn't know we had Chinese women on the ship!"

"Where were they?" Yang muttered.

They were girls more than women, dressed in bright silk tunics and wearing checkered cotton kerchiefs on their heads, showing their status as prostitutes. Even at a distance, the brothers could see their rouged cheeks and bright-red lips. As they emerged from the immigration area, hordes of Chinese men from the surrounding streets rushed forward. An older woman collecting the females shouted, "Police! Police!"

Some of the armed men from the docks surrounded the group, using clubs on any who dared come too close. They beat back the frenzied crowd as the woman in charge loaded the girls on a wagon and set it in motion. The police held the line until the wagon was too far away to follow.

"What was all that about?" Sue Kee asked.

Their Sam Yap representative approached, smiling. "Chinese women from the homeland are always cause for celebration." He clapped his hands. "The show is over. Pick up your belongings. We have a walk ahead of us. It will be healthful to exercise your muscles after such a long trip. My name is Mr. Loon if you have questions."

Arriving at the Sam Yap house, the brothers noted the building style. It looked like every other two-story building on the street except for a pair of fierce guardian lion statues at the entrance. Their abundant, curly manes and sharp fangs were sure to frighten away all malevolent spirits. The interior was simple and clean, with bare wooden floors and minimal decoration. The familiar aroma of chicken soup and ginger wrapped around them like a well-worn blanket from home. Mr. Loon showed them the altar room and a scroll hanging on the wall. "Your Association fees include record keeping of your whereabouts, and in the unfortunate circumstance of a death, the tracking of remains," he said.

Next, he assigned their sleeping quarters: six men to a room with triple bunks along each wall, not unlike the ship. Mr. Loon showed them where to store their belongings for safekeeping. Lee and Yang would spend three days here before leaving for their work assignment. "While you are here, you should visit Chinese shops and try the street food," he said, smiling. "It is all very authentic. A home away from home."

Seeing Lee's searching glance, Yang said, "I saw a pharmacy a few streets back. I say we seek treatment to rid ourselves of vermin."

Lee nodded, pressing a hand against his stomach. "Maybe the doctor will have something for the queasiness."

Their unencumbered walk was refreshing. A bell above the door tinkled as the brothers entered the pharmacy.

"Ah! Fresh off the boat!" said the herbalist behind the counter, nodding. He used Mandarin. "My name is Hang Coy. Welcome." His accent was slightly difficult to follow, but his meaning was clear.

As they approached, Yang said, "We'd like to purchase an infestation remedy."

The herbalist stared at them blankly. He shook his head, showing that he did not understand.

Yang pointed to his head, making a pinching motion in his hair, and pulling it away.

"Ah, bái shī," the pharmacist replied, pulling out a drawer, and scooping powder onto a flat paper he folded and tied with a string. "Heat water, like make tea, but use Bai Sam instead." He spoke slowly, waiting for their response. Lee and Yang nodded.

"Loose hair, pour all Bai Sam tea, let dry, then wash."

Nodding again, Lee stepped forward, pulling up a sleeve showing inflamed, red patches of skin. Positioning his fingers like claws, Lee made a see-sawing motion.

Pursing his lips, the herbalist tapped a finger on his chin. "Bites while sleeping?"

Lee and Yang nodded.

"Blood on bedding? Smell of rotten raspberries?"

Looking at each other, Yang and Lee exchanged opinions about what was being asked.

Seeing their confusion, the pharmacist picked up a mixing spatula, motioning it across his wrist then repeated the sleeping sign. They nodded.

"Raspberries," he repeated slowly. "Small red fruit." Wrinkling his nose, he waved a hand under it.

Smiling, the boys nodded.

"Bed bugs," he stated, before turning to begin mixing powdered clay with a variety of herbs. "Mix with water into a paste, cover rash overnight."

"Got it!" They said, smiling, feeling relieved and successful.

Before they left the shop, Yang asked the herbalist if he had something for his brother's upset stomach. They walked out with a fragrant package of dried tea ingredients, lemon balm, peppermint, and ginger.

Rather than returning to the house, the brothers continued walking. "We should do the treatments before paying for a proper bath," Lee commented. They stopped at another shop to buy fresh clothes. This merchant spoke in their dialect.

Discovering that the man was from Mother's hometown made them all laugh. "If you need anything while you're in San Francisco, you come to see Mr. Jin. I will look out for you!" He suggested they visit a beach just up the road, pressing thin towels into their hands. "No one goes there," he said, "and the currents are good for swimming."

"Let's go!" Yang enthused. Before they left, the merchant pressed a small package of matches into Lee's hand.

"In case you want to stay awhile," said Mr. Jin, smiling.

They continued in silence. Confidence grew with every step.

Several miles to the north, they found the small beach the merchant had described. It was secluded from road traffic.

"I can't believe we're here," Lee commented while he removed his shoes and shirt. He began collecting driftwood.

"I know what you mean," Yang responded, joining the activity and starting a pile.

Lee added more to it. Yang winked before pulling down his pants. "If you only look at the land and the sea, it could feel as if we never left."

Glancing behind them, assuring himself they were alone, Lee followed Yang's lead. Naked, he trotted to the water's edge. As a small foam-filled wave covered his feet, then pulled away, he sucked in a startled breath. "Except for the cold water!"

Yang walked in until the water was above his knees. "My balls are protesting."

"Mine also," Lee chuckled before lunging all the way in.

The brothers stayed out long enough to acclimate to the water temperature. They sand-scrubbed their skin until it turned red. Starting a fire, they burned their ship clothes while fashioning long spears from driftwood and sharp stones, securing the points with twine.

Wrapping the towels around their hips, they crept over rocks, watching for fish. Yang was the first to spear one. Lee, noticing air bubbles in the sand behind the waves, began digging. It wasn't long before the boys had enough for a hearty meal.

Before preparing their fish and clams, Lee and Yang returned to the sea, splashing until they were damp. Mixing water with the clay, they slicked the herbal remedy over their skin and massaged it into their scalps. "When you were little and when Mother allowed it, you always covered yourself in mud," Yang said. "Remember?"

Lee nodded. "You look like an evil spirit with mischief in mind."

They consumed the fire-roasted meal with grunts of pleasure. With bellies full and the pore-cleansing itch of drying mud flaking from their skin, they lay back on the sand and let languid memories of rice patties and charcoal ovens comfort them.

Lee saw and heard Wèi An playing "The Moon Reflects My Heart" on the long-stringed erhu. When their eyes met, he understood she was sending him her love.

Yang saw his mother holding out her hands, receiving a package. Inside was something from him. She was pleased with the gift, and he was content to have given it.

Daylight was fading as they packed their gear and broke camp. Neither was in the mood to talk, but their steps were in time and their mood companionable.

※

They returned to the boarding house after the day's main meal had been served. The kitchen still had food available: green tea, sweet pickles, and eggs in congee. Since most of the boarders were out for the evening, they had the dining table to themselves. They ate small portions to be polite. Mr. Loon stopped by to chat as they finished. He invited them to his office and went over the details of their work contract, repayment installments, and association fees. He provided their transportation details written on rice paper.

As Yang listened, he sat back in his chair, compressed his lips, and steepled his fingers. He met Lee's gaze when the man finished. At the imperceptible nod Lee gave him, Yang knew his brother agreed with what he was about to propose. "Will you accept a payment today against the principal of our loan?"

Mr. Loon raised his eyebrows. "Certainly!" he replied. He fetched his receipt ledger while the brothers went to their room to discuss how much of Yang's gambling winnings they thought they could part with.

At the conclusion of the deal, Mr. Loon recommended a bathing house. "The one on Pine and Powell Streets is the best value for the money, but you must make reservations, as it fills up quickly."

After the conversation, they returned to their room to talk through their options.

"With the change of clothes and the herbals, we're cleaner than we were when we got off the boat," Lee said, rubbing the stubble on his chin. "I'm too tired to bathe tonight. Will the ancestors be angry if we aren't perfectly clean?"

Yang considered this. It was the first time their parents or elders were not there to guide them when a question such as this came up. Taking a deep breath, Yang proclaimed, "I think they will know our intent was to be clean in their presence. Surely it is more important that we honor them before our first day has passed."

Watching Lee's expressions as he processed this information filled Yang with satisfaction. Together, they lit incense. Holding the base of the fragrant smoking stick between their palms, they bowed before the statue of Mazu, giving thanks for their safe travels. Placing the sticks in a bowl of dry rice to continue burning, they lit new ones and bowed to Nezha, the god of protection, while focusing on the names written on the wall scroll. They prayed for the souls of the dead. Both boys included thoughts of Grandfather and Fu-chi. Yang added a prayer before releasing his incense. *Please do not punish us if we are not clean enough.*

When they reclined in their bunks, both Yang and Lee instantly dropped into a profound and dreamless sleep.

※

The following day, the steep hills, the shops, street vendors, and the mix of Asians and Gweilo kept them fascinated. They soaked in all they could, knowing their time in this city was short.

While they waited for their appointment time at the bathhouse, they looked in shop windows and wandered through a few. In a photography shop, Yang watched customers placing double image cards into a viewer. He startled when a shop worker tried handing him a view. He shook his head, backing away.

"No buy," the young man said, "just try." He held it up to his face, then motioned for Yang to do the same. Once Yang complied, the fellow selected a photo card from the stack and slid it in place. As the image came into focus, Yang jumped.

"Lee! You have to see this!" His voice was loud with excitement. "It's the corner on the street right outside and it floats!"

They bought three cards at eight cents each, but the viewer was too expensive. The cards they chose were one of Powell and Pine Streets, one of ships in the harbor, and one showing the interior of a Chinese restaurant.

"We should find it and have tea or soup there before we leave," Yang said.

※

In the bathhouse, each brother got his own room. Lee gave the attendant the Bai Sam powder. "Please mix this with warm water and divide it between Yang and me."

Deep clawfoot bathtubs filled with steaming water awaited. Lowering into them brought sighs of pleasure. Rubbing their washcloths against the fresh-smelling bars of soap and scrubbing them over their skin elicited feelings of contentment. Leaning back so the attendant could pour the Bai Sam-infused water over hair and scalp was equally soothing, as were the hot towels draped over faces and necks to soften whiskers before a close shave.

Refreshed and well-groomed, the brothers emerged from the bathhouse wearing smiles. "It feels strange to not be itchy!" Yang exclaimed.

Lee agreed. "I almost forgot that feeling."

Sue Kee and Law Yaw, the ship gamers, joined them in front of the lion guardians. Both sets of men would leave town the following day. The brothers would go to work on Donner Mountain. Kee and Yaw were going to El Dorado.

Before leaving the boarding house, Yang showed them the double image photo of the restaurant. "Mr. Loon said this is the Canton Restaurant. He told us how to find it."

After wandering the city, when their feet were aching and they needed tea, they sought the Canton Restaurant. Its yellow silk flag outside made it easy to find. They spent some time watching patrons come and go, wondering if restaurants here operated the same as the ones at home.

Lee nudged Yang and whispered so the others couldn't hear. "We bought the photos. Now you want to buy tea. Why, when we can get tea at the boardinghouse?"

Yang threw his head back with a hearty laugh. "We have to go inside so we can say we were there when we show the picture!"

A waiter wearing a long white apron stepped outside and lit a cigarette. With a friendly wave, he invited them inside.

"Your prices may be too high," Yaw responded.

"There is something for everyone," he responded in formal language. "Even if you are only here a short time, you must not miss the Canton Restaurant!" The waiter smiled and gave them a polite bow.

The real live version of the restaurant exploded with sound, atmosphere, and vitality, something impossible to capture in a still image. Intricate, carved wood panels depicted dragons and willow trees and fish in streams. Chinese lanterns illuminated intimate puddles of low light.

As the waiter settled them, he asked about their Association. He knew Sam Yap well. "Ah! Many members find their gold and make their families rich!" Kee and Yaw smiled broadly at this news.

"These two," Kee said, pointing toward the brothers, "are going to work for the railroad."

"Yes, yes. Very honorable," responded the waiter. "All the railroad bosses eat at The Canton Restaurant. We are very famous."

The young men spent an enjoyable and leisurely afternoon contemplating what to include in their letters home, people-watching, and picking up useful tips from other patrons.

※

Another night at the boardinghouse, infused with rejuvenating sleep, had the brothers alert and ready to take on their next challenge.

STEAMBOAT
November
San Francisco & Auburn, California
1864

—

At the San Francisco Long Wharf, men gathered for transport. Grouped together by destination, Lee and Yang searched the crowd for faces they recognized. Finding none, they boarded a steamer and followed crew directions to the aft deck. They settled next to a wall, using their baskets as seats, as they waited for the journey to begin.

"Where are you from?" Yang asked an older man who squatted next to them. He looked to be in his thirties and wore a mixture of donkey clothes—blue jeans, leather boots, and suspenders over the top of a traditional men's shirt.

"Zhongshan," he replied as his gaze scanned Yang first, then Lee. "You?"

"Shagongbao," Yang replied. "I'm Gee Yang and this is my brother, Gee Lee."

"Pleased to make your acquaintance," the man responded, bowing his head. "I am Tham Kwan. Shagongbao you say? This is to the north of my home."

"We're from the Panyu District," Lee supplied.

"Yes, then definitely to the north," Kwan said. "When did you arrive in San Francisco?"

"Three days ago," Yang said.

"Just three days!" Kwan exclaimed, "I've been here since '57. You must catch me up on news from home."

The three entered an animated conversation that was joined by several others. They exchanged information about political and living conditions.

As the engine boilers roared into high gear, the three men moved to the rail so they could watch the launch and survey the new scenery. They'd barely recovered their land equilibrium as they boarded this watercraft. Yang and Lee wondered about river travel here. The deck shivered slightly as the boat picked up steam and entered the main channel. Other steamboats went by with passengers waving. Pleased by the greeting, the brothers returned the gesture. Kwan, who was closest to Lee, bumped him with an elbow. He gave a slight negative head shake before leaning close to whisper. "Best not to look at them directly." He referred to the Gweilo. Warily, Lee dropped his hand, then nudged his brother to stop.

The banks were thick with trees and other greenery. Beyond birds and butterflies, there wasn't much to see. An hour into the trip, they grew tired of standing. Returning to their baskets, they asked Kwan if he was also traveling to Donner Summit. "No! I'm done with the Sierras. I'm on my way to a delta town south of Sacramento."

"Since we will part ways soon, sir," said Lee, "what do you think is most important for us to know about the Flowery Flag Nation?"

Kwan nodded as he gave this some thought. "Whenever you can, travel with others," he said. "Once you're out of Sacramento Chinatown, lynchings can happen anywhere."

"What is this word?" Yang asked.

"Lynchings," said Kwan, "involve public torture, hangings, and sometimes burning men alive. If you ever see men wearing flour sacks over their heads, run for your life."

"Sacks? Why sacks?" Yang asked.

"I believe it covers their shame. As far as I can tell," Kwan continued, "the magistrates look the other way when there's mob 'justice.'"

"We should carry weapons," Lee stated.

Kwan shook his head. "If you do, keep it hidden," he warned, "any offense or perceived threat can set them off. If they attack, you must be prepared to fight to the death. Never get caught. If something happens, run to the nearest town and blend in with the other Asians. We all look alike to them." He winked as he gave them a wry smile.

Seeing the stricken look on the brother's faces, Kwan chuckled. "I've been here for seven years and traveled to mining towns all over. I'm still breathing," he reassured. "From what you said, your uncle did the same. Keep your wits about you and be watchful. You'll be alright. The railroad has its own security. They don't want anyone but themselves killing Chinamen," Kwan laughed.

Yang and Lee shared a glance. Neither knew what to make of that comment.

Yang started a game of Arrange in Nine, which calmed them and took their minds off the time. As the boat was approaching the dock, Kwan said, "It gets frightfully cold in the high country. If you haven't brought coats and gloves, you'll want to get some. Prices go up the farther away from Sacramento you get."

Nodding, Lee and Yang thanked him before separating.

"We might have enough to buy coats," Yang said as he thought about the conflict they'd had about how much money to pay toward their loan versus how much to send home before leaving San Francisco. Mother would like the amount they'd settled upon.

"We only have an hour to find the iron horse station." Lee checked over the handwritten note Mr. Loon had given him. "It's not cold now. Surely we can wait to spend more money."

With motions, gestures, and a few scattered words, the group going to railroad work navigated six blocks over dirt roads, on boardwalks, giving way to long-skirted women and people of wealth, all the while feeling eyes watching their every move. At the crowded train platform, they held tight to their belongings as they wove through the throng, looking for where to board.

At last, Yang, taller than all of them, heard a familiar call. "This way," he motioned with a smile, clearing a path for the others. Approaching the train, Lee marveled at the sight. Rectangular wooden rooms sat atop platforms. Beneath them, small metal wheels with indented grooves fit perfectly over metal rails secured to a track below. The box rooms connected, one in front of the other, in a long line as far as the eye could see. He knew an iron horse pulled this line of rooms. It was a disappointment to not be able to look upon such a magnificent beast.

Gathered next to the last car were many Chinese and several men Lee was startled to see. Their clothing was the same as the Anglos, but their skin was the deep rich color of hongmu, a dark wood used to make furniture for prominent officials. Lee couldn't stop admiring them. They were tall and thickly muscled, closer to Yang's size. Their hair was tight like a closely-knit sea sponge.

One man noticed Lee's regard. Raising a hand to the brim of his hat, he tipped it, giving a nod before disappearing into the crowd. Pleased with this exchange, Lee smiled.

"Time to go." Yang reached for Lee. "We're headed for camp twenty."

As they found seats and stowed baskets, Lee watched for the dark men. Not finding them, he settled in. The iron horse whistled.

As they picked up speed, Yang decided he liked the click-it-y-clacking sound the wheels made. Past stockyards and factories, the engine belched cloudy particulates into an atmosphere that barely noticed. They sped through residential districts where people tended gardens and hammered limber into house walls. Further on, he saw golden fields with swaying grass while catching hints of the earthy-smelling grain.

Moving at high speed across the land was exhilarating. If Lee closed his eyes, he could imagine riding on the back of a great dragon.

The train slowed as it reached an incline, making a long sweeping turn. It clacked away like a millipede crawling over a mandarin. The boys stood, craning their necks to take in the view behind. Rounded mounds, the color and shape of sand dunes, were punctuated by deep green, expansive oaks. A high-pitched, breathy whistle sounded twice as they approached a small settlement huddled near the tracks. On a station platform, fruit crates, brimming to their tops and filled with apples and pears, looked like colorful children's blocks. Lee grinned at the boys, racing them while several barking dogs chased after the children. As they continued climbing, the soil turned from brown to red, and vegetation grew dense. Sharp pointed trees dominated this landscape, and the air was filled with the crisp freshness of newly cut fir. Cords of wood, stacked like vertebrae, waited on the outer edges of the grade to feed ravenous iron boilers. As they traversed across a very tall wooden trestle bridge, they gasped. The earth disappeared beneath them, revealing a muddied torrent at the bottom. "To think," Yang said, "we'll be helping to build this!"

Yang's tone held a reverence and excitement Lee had never heard before.

"It is remarkable," he agreed.

They heard murmurs of "Auburn" and "Bloomer Cut" a moment before the train entered a mountain, a steep embankment with earth close enough to touch outside the car windows. The interior light shifted abruptly. It went by so fast; they wondered if they'd really seen it.

Passengers around them were picking up bags and moving to stand in the aisle. Doing likewise, the brothers made ready.

The conductor called, "End of the line," as he entered their car.

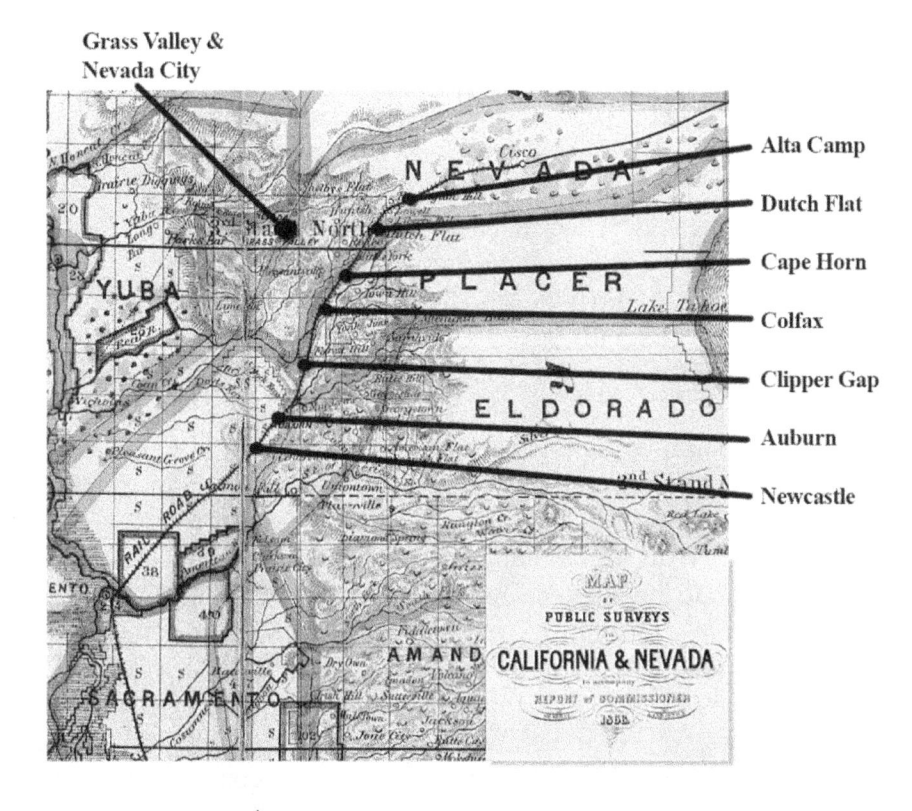

MAP | The Hill (Lower) Railroad Camps
Newcastle | Auburn | Clipper Gap | Colfax | Cape Horn | Dutch Flat
Alta Camp

GRADING
Above Auburn & Bloomer Cut, California
1864
—

They stepped down onto a platform that was merely a flat surface unembellished with a ticket office or handrails, into a startling cacophony. Fully loaded wagons carrying wooden barrels, timber, and rail irons passed by, stirring up dust clouds, hazing the air like a drought-year dust storm. The sound of hooves, horse tackle, and snorts mingled with animal-dropping aromas.

"Sam Yap! Sam Yap Association!" Lee picked out the holler from the others, going off like alarm bells. "That direction." Lee elbowed Yang, pointing. Yang, rising up on his toes, looked to where Lee indicated.

"I see him." He moved toward the speaker.

Once the new arrivals were sorted into company groups, their leaders addressed them. Lee noticed the speakers used different dialects. With Dongguan slang, their sturdy director introduced himself. He looked to be about the same age as Yang and was at least as tall, but with a stringy build. He wore a wide-brimmed straw hat, and his long braid hung to the right side of his neck and came to his waistline. "I am your work boss. I will show you where you will sleep, assign your tools, direct you to construction sites, and deliver your pay at the end of every month. This," he continued in Mandarin, "is Hung Woh." He pointed to an older, short, stocky man who had stepped up onto a wooden box and waited for the other company leaders to finish speaking.

Hung Woh bowed to the assembly. "I know most of you are new arrivals." His Mandarin was flawless. Lee guessed he'd achieved a high-level education. "Thank you for making the long journey. Welcome also to those of you who have left mining and other employment. I am the liaison between the Chinese Companies and the Central Pacific Railroad. I work with the road engineers and Supervisor Strobridge to coordinate your crews—which we call gangs. Work assignments and payment are delivered to you through your company representative, whom you have just met. Americans are only just beginning to know the Chinese. In everything you do, you must bring honor to your ancestors, parents, and your country."

He ended with a bow, which the listeners mirrored before picking up their baskets to follow their company leader.

The leader wove his way through the busy traffic, with his workers carrying their baskets and waddling after him like anxious ducklings. Stopping next to a wagon, he chose two men, saying, "Put your belongings in the back," he pointed, "then load the wagon with those." He showed a pile of grain sacks that had just come off the train. "Mr. Milligan," the work boss nodded to the driver while speaking, "will take you to where you will offload them. He will let you off near our tents. Find an empty bunk, unpack, and be at the canteen at 6:00 p.m. for the evening meal, where you'll receive your work assignment for tomorrow."

The rest of the group continued. At the next wagon, the work boss chose Yang and another fellow. Lee watched his brother step forward and speak urgently to the Company leader. The boss stepped back, cocking his head, frowning at Yang. Giving him a long up-and-down glance, he nodded, then clipped out, "Gee Lee, goes here." He waved the other man back, who made eye contact with Lee as they exchanged places.

"Pedmore's the name." The wagon driver hopped down, nodding to the brothers while gesturing to the area behind the driver's seat for their baskets. "Do ya'll speak any English?" At their blank stares, he responded, "Thought not, damn Chinamen hardly ever do." With elaborate hand gestures, he motioned to a stack of lumber they needed to move.

They knew immediately what was required. When Lee would have moved to comply, something in Yang's body language caused him to pause. Yang wore the expression he used when Mother berated him for something he'd chosen to do, despite knowing it would upset her. His eyes were wide; his thoughts appeared absent. Stiffening a grin, Lee attempted to mirror his brother.

The driver's movements became slow and overly large. When his face turned red, and he started shouting, Yang gave a nod and they got to work. With Lee at one end and Yang at the other end of the eight-foot expanse, they lifted the first one. Surprised by the weight of the thing, Lee let out an "oomph." Straining, they shuffle-walked it over to the wagon, where they laid one end and slid the rest lengthwise.

Pedmore laughed. "You probably seen nothin' like that before." Stuffing his gloves in his back pocket, he searched through his jacket, bringing out a pipe. He monitored them, loading the second piece as he touched a flame to his tobacco and sucked. "That's Redwood. Grows on the north coast, up in the fog." He puffed out plumes, ignoring the sheen of sweat on their skin. "Each one of those weighs about 200 pounds. That'll build muscles on you fast."

Forty minutes later, they were riding in the back of the buckboard as Pedmore guided his horses along the road. "Any idea what he was talking about?" asked Yang.

"None," replied Lee, picking at the slivers in his hands.

Pedmore glanced back at them. "You'll need gloves."

At their blank stares, he raised a hand, still holding reins, and pointed to his own while saying, "Moo."

The boys smiled, nodded, and bowed from sitting positions, "mooing" softly in return.

The driver stopped at the outskirts of the make-shift city, pointing to rows and rows of canvas tents. Hearing familiar language sounds, seeing men with queues, and smelling soy sauce and chicken, they knew this was their stop.

"Xièxiè," Yang said, reaching up for his basket that Pedmore handed down.

"Thank you," Lee spoke the only English words he knew.

Pedmore looked surprised. He made an awkward half-bow, saying, "Welcome."

Walking toward the tents, Lee asked, "What did you say to boss leader?"

"Only that we are brothers."

"I never thought about us being separated. Mother made it sound like she thought we'd stay together."

"Mother's not here."

They laughed.

"I'm glad we're together, Lee."

"Me too."

As they continued walking, the sun was disappearing behind the tree line. Yang commented, "The drop in temperature is notable."

Lee nodded, shivering.

※

The crew detail boss carried a heavy jacket pinned under his arm as he walked toward them. "You are on my crew," he said. Leading the way across the road to the third tent in a long row, he showed them where they could leave their belongings. "This is your temporary home for now."

Yang could tell by the man's coloring and short, stalky build that he was from a tribe of hill people. "Follow me." The crew boss addressed them in Mandarin. He led them to a low-roofed shed where he extracted a pick and a shovel with new metal heads and freshly oiled shafts. From his pants pocket, the boss pulled out a notebook, where he made a few scratches with a short pencil. Showing it to Yang, he asked that he verify the information. Yang gave a curt nod.

Approaching a large tent, the boys smelled fish and lemongrass. With everything going on, they'd forgotten they were famished! Hing pointed to a scattering of shovels leaning against a woodblock near the door. "Cook doesn't allow them inside. Leave them there while you eat."

Several men seated at tables inside called out to the crew boss when they walked in. He offered a brief wave in response. In the kitchen, behind a wooden serving counter, the cook ladled out two steaming bowls of noodle soup.

Yang and Lee gratefully accepted the food with deep, considerate bows. The dishwasher set out two oblong soup spoons. Nodding to him too, the brothers gathered the utensils and headed to the nearest open table to slurp the flavorful broth.

The crew boss arrived carrying two brimming teacups. He set them near their places. "Tea station is over there." He nodded in the direction opposite the food counter. "Most of the men are already asleep. I recommend you do the same as soon as you're done here. Work begins at dawn. Listen for the wake-up bell." Noticing Lee's hands cupping his teacup, he asked, "Do you have coats?"

At their blank stares, the crew boss grinned. "You are fortunate to have arrived when you did! You will only have one workday before Sunday, which is a day off," he said as he thrust one arm, then the other, into his jacket made of a sturdy blue fabric. "You'll need it to buy what you need. There's a company store at the end of the road." He arched a thumb to his left, "Or you can catch a ride back to Auburn where the merchants are slightly less ruthless." The crew boss patted his jacket as if searching for something, pulling out a small pipe. "If you need to borrow money, Hung Woh has reasonable interest rates," he said, patting his jacket once again. He pulled out a small matchbox. "I've started your accounting." Pinching and rolling his fingers, Hing separated the note he made earlier from behind the box. "Sleep well," he said, taking his leave.

Once the crew boss left, Lee noted what he was eating: smooth mushrooms, soft noodles, and chewy bites of seaweed.

With full bellies, their eyes couldn't wait to close.

※

The black of night shifted into purple hues when Yang heard the bell ring. He'd been awake for hours, listening to Lee snoring. The other six men in the tent hadn't complained.

"Good morning, new man," came a soft voice from across the tent.

Yang sat up, surprised to see the other pallets empty. Had he slept, after all? Making eye contact with the fellow, Yang said, "Morning. Where are the others?"

A second bell sounded just then, causing the stranger to scramble out of his blankets. "They're outside finishing Qi Gong. The second bell means the mess tent is open." The boy rushed to pull on his boots. He was through the door before Yang could reply. From outside Yang heard him call, "Hurry or you'll miss breakfast!"

Jostling Lee, Yang said, "Wake up! We've got to go!" Shoving his legs into his pants, he grinned as he watched his brother fling covers back. Lee always had morning difficulties. Their mother called him a snail sleeper, someone who emerged slowly from his shell. The way Lee glanced around the tent in confusion confirmed Yang's assessment. "We're on the mountain, dummy," he chided. "We start work on the iron road today."

In the crisp morning air, their breath made steam plumes. They tugged at sleeves to cover their fingers and stomped their feet as they crossed the compound. Arriving at the mess tent, Yang noticed the woodblock was obscured by picks and shovels. He compressed his lips.

This morning, the sound of spoons clanking against pottery filled the spacious eating area. By the time they joined the food line and received their morning bowls of jook—warm, thick, watered-down rice topped with seaweed, sesame seeds, and a type of meat neither of the brothers recognized—Lee had made eye contact and nodded to a few of the men nearby.

Conversation was minimal. Focus was turned to moving forearms between bowls and mouths, getting as much food inside as fast as possible. Yang and Lee followed suit. Before they knew it, they were on the move. Outside, the men took up tools while eying Hung Woh, who was listening to a tall red devil. He nodded while making notes. Spotting the crew boss, who was waving them over, Yang elbowed Lee. "You should have known that we needed to bring the pick and shovel. Run to get them. I'll find out where we'll be working."

Lee turned his face away so his brother couldn't see his eyes roll. As he ran, he was glad for the exertion as the qi stirring through his limbs warmed him. The distance back to their tent wasn't far, but when Lee returned, he could see groups of men moving off on the road to the east. Searching for familiar faces, his grip on the tools tightened. A high-pitched whistle brought his attention to the crew boss, leading a mule cart harnessed to a small wagon. Two additional men were in their group. Letting out a pent-up breath, Lee jogged over, tossing the tools in the back of the cart with the others. Yang was already in deep conversation with one man. Lee fell in at the end of the procession.

A dust cloud from the teams ahead took shape high in the blue sky. Lee watched men pull brightly colored clothes from their pockets and tie them around their noses and mouths. Most of the workers wore wide-brimmed woven hats and carried gloves. Many of them rolled up their queues, securing their dark-haired braids as they walked. At least half wore the light-weight pants and shirts Lee was used to seeing his people wear, but others dressed in clothing made from the same thick fabric that matched the crew boss's jacket. As they progressed, the end of the road became visible. Beyond it was a deep chasm. They'd been walking on top of a giant fill embankment!

Teams were breaking away, trekking down switchback trails along the steep incline. At the bottom, the crew boss said, "Yang and Gim, start pick testing. Be swift. We've one hour to fill this cart and dump it at the top." A cacophony of ringing sounded as metal stuck against the rock. Lee followed the man closest to him to the cart, where they collected their shovels. The hand grip on his shovel was sun-warmed and slippery.

"For the new boys," the crew boss raised his voice, "this is Wildcat Summit. When finished, it will be nine hundred feet long and forty-one feet deep. As we excavate, we will be moving thirty thousand cubic yards of earth and rock! The soil is so thin here," the crew boss grumbled, shaking his head. "Scrape as much as you can off the top. The farther we have to go for loose dirt, the longer it will take us. Shangpu!" he cried.

"Shangpu!" the men responded as their sharp tools assailed the land.

Until now, the hat had obscured the face of the man nearest Lee. He hadn't spoken a word beyond the start-to-work cry. When Lee got a look at him, he saw rough scars covering half his face and running down his neck. Rigid knots, colored white and deep red, stretched the skin near an eye and his nose, distorting their shapes. Lee faltered.

The man chuckled as he took in Lee's response. "Since it happened, my nickname is Scarred Eye."

Mortified by his own rudeness, Lee stopped, stood ramrod straight, and bowed his head. Words of apology stuck in his throat. The crew boss noticed Lee's hesitation. "Keep moving!" he directed.

"It's nothing." Scarred Eye spoke softly. "Big boss man and I were the only ones who lived to tell this story."

Lee didn't know who the big boss man was, but it registered that this person was the first one he'd come across since leaving home who spoke in Panyu dialect!

※

On their twelfth load, after ten endless hours, they followed as the cart mule named Jumpin plodded up the steep trail. The crew walked with drooping shoulders. They looked like bags of brown flour had sprinkled over them. Scarred Eye stumbled, dropping to a knee. When Lee offered a hand, the man waved him away.

Lee swiped at a trail of sweat dripping down his neck. His hand came away smeared with mud. His palms, where the skin contacted the shovel handle, were raw. His face stung. High-altitude Sierra Sun is brutal on fair skin. Their tea man had taken pity on him when he'd first stopped to deliver refreshment, loaning him his straw hat. Yang was wearing one now, too.

※

Sunday, after the morning meal, Yang and Lee set out to shop for supplies in Newcastle. They grabbed a ride on the back of a supply buckboard and hopped off an hour later when they got to town. The team driver merely nodded at their exit. Tham Kwan, from the steamboat, had been truthful when he'd said the town merchants were ruthless. Coats and hats, of any kind, were four times more costly than they should be!

They simply could not afford them. Outside, the brothers walked along the street as they debated what to do. "At home, twenty-six dollars a month sounded like great wealth!" Lee complained.

"It is, if we were earning it there," said Yang.

"This isn't going the way our parents planned," Lee said, dismayed.

"I have an idea..." Yang said, dropping his voice.

Lee's stomach twisted. He knew he should worry when Yang said that.

"Of all that we need, gloves are the highest priority. Everything else can wait until payday. I think we have enough for two pairs."

Lee nodded but waited for what was coming.

"We buy the gloves today. Did you say that Scarred Eye is from Panyu?"

Lee nodded.

"We need to get back so I can talk to him."

※

After lunch, Lee watched the other men in camp doing laundry and taking baths. Empty pickle barrels functioned as wash tubs. Since he and Yang had only worked one day, they opted for wash cloth wipe-downs this time. Not buying soap would save money.

He was realizing how silly worrying about cleanliness was when making offerings at the makeshift altars. The gods were probably glad to be remembered at all. Surely, if cleanliness were vitally important to them, terrible luck would have rained down on all the railroaders. *Maybe being clean matters more in China?*

He'd taken a brief nap and had woken to see Chy Fey staring at him. Fey was the youngest person in their tent. "Do you want to see something amazing?" His long, wet queue made a damp circle on the front of his shirt.

"What?" Lee threw an arm over his eyes.

"A bird's nest! I found it last week. The babies are getting feathers." There was such enthusiasm in his gap-toothed smile that Lee couldn't help but respond.

He sat up, eyeing the boy. "How far is it?"

"Not far. Just down the hill." He smiled. "My friends call me Animal Boy. You can call me that too."

On the walk, Animal Boy happily regaled Lee with a list of creatures he'd seen that one does not encounter in China. "Grizzlies are exciting because they are big and they run fast. Then there are the tiny red newts." Animal Boy held his fingers out to show the size. "So cute! Nothing at all like the giant salamanders near my village."

At the nest, three blue fledglings enchanted Lee. The mother screeched loudly at them from branches far above. Animal Boy collected bits of speckled shells and feathers from around the base of the tree.

On their way back, they stopped by a ditch to splash water on their faces and necks. Farther down the trail, Lee recognized Yang's voice. As he called out, Animal Boy whipped an arm out across Lee's chest, stopping him in midstride. Alarmed, Lee looked at the young man. Animal Boy raised a finger to his lips, then pointed to a serpent on the rocks where they would have trod. It was gray and almost blended in with its surroundings. Slowly, it lifted its triangular-shaped head.

"Shhhh," Animal Boy whispered. "That's a rattlesnake. Its bite can be deadly."

Just then, Scarred Eye and Yang came over the trail crest, talking excitedly, not watching where they stepped.

Rattlesnake,
Crotalus oreganus

TONGUE: In and out. She gathered taste notes, sampling them inside her mouth. *Musky and sour.*

They have ceased moving and are too far to strike.

Her attention swiveled as two more lumbered near.

Their movements sent ground waves rippling through her coiled body.

TAIL: She raised it, afraid.

It is always so with the need to defend.

BODY: Tenseness spiraled through her.

RATTLE: She jittered her tail tip.

"Stop!" Lee shouted.

Scarred Eye instantly assessed the scene. He raised a booted foot high just as the snake launched. Fangs struck his heel. For a man with impaired sight, his aim was true. He brought his foot down on top of the snake's head, pinning it. Unsheathing a knife with a swift motion, he made quick work of separating the writhing body from the head.

※

Her awareness dimmed
to the sound of whoops and hollers
of the large ones.

This is where I end.
※

Elated, Yang exclaimed, "This has been such a day! First Scarred Eye helped us with clothes, and now he's killed a serpent."

"I've had too many tangles with those things." Scarred Eye squatted to cut off the tail tip. "Look," he wiggled it, "for every button, the animal has lived two or three years." He offered it to Yang, who shook his head, then to Lee who also declined, then he offered it to Animal Boy.

"Thanks!" he extended his arm while stepping sideways to avoid body contact with the still-writhing animal. He counted seven rows.

"Run along, now. Take it to the cook," Scarred Eye said. "That's good meat we should not waste."

"Isn't it poisonous?" asked Lee.

Shaking his head, Scarred Eye gripped the area where the neck would have been between his thumb and forefinger. The jaws were still opening and closing. Using the tip of his knife, he pointed. "The poison comes from a little sack behind the jaws. These are hollow. The meat's perfectly fine. Healthful, I'm told."

Yang shook himself out of his snake fascination. "Lee! Scarred Eye knows Uncle Sum."

They watched as Scarred Eye squatted to pick up an egg-sized rock. He used it to dig a small hole, then dropped the head into it. Standing, he kicked loose dirt over it and dropped the rock on top.

In his mind, Lee went through what he knew about Uncle Sum, his mother's brother. Scarred Eye's accent seemed to match that region.

"With his help, we now have coats and work boots," Yang said, clapping a hand on the man's shoulder.

"For how much?" Lee frowned.

"That's the best part." Yang smiled widely. "For nothing!"

Lee felt like his seasickness had returned.

※

Since Lee first met him, Scarred Eye had left railroad work. The crew boss, observing his stumble, transferred him to another railroad gang, where more of those happened. Eventually, he fell and didn't get up. Thinking he was a goner, his gang loaded him onto a body wagon, where he didn't stir until the unloading.

The fright of finding a "live one" had sent the undertaker into a faint. Once they both recovered, they shared a few stiff drinks. The hunch-backed undertaker was frail looking. He asked, "How old do you think I am?"

Scarred Eye shrugged. "Don't know—fifty, maybe?"

"Thirty-nine. Iron road work up Arcata way chewed me up and spit me out." He smiled, showing several missing teeth. "Now I care for the dead who weren't as lucky as me." His gaze assessed Scarred Eye. "I think you're a lucky one too. How about you come work with me?"

Scarred Eye's blast injuries and the bone-draining exhaustion had delivered him to death's door. In this moment, he felt lucky. *I may be uglied up but I'm in better shape than this guy! And I'm only thirty-six,* he thought.

Becoming the undertaker's assistant was how Scarred Eye had come by free clothes. As a side job, he decided to hunt. It was something he was good at, and he could always count on the camp cooks to buy fresh kills.

※

At the evening meal, the brothers sat with Animal Boy and listened as he explained how he'd traded the snake rattles for a pair of dice. They'd just started on the main course when a small bowl clattered at the center of the table. Started, all eyes flew to the man who'd tossed it there, Scarred Eye. In a grimace that was a grin, he nodded to the bowl. "Special treat."

"Oh, boy!" said Animal Boy, opening his chopsticks and reaching toward the bowl. Scarred Eye knocked him on the shoulder.

"Newbies first."

Nodding and lowering his face, Animal Boy retracted his arm and made room on the bench for the older man.

"Go on, then," Scarred Eye said. "Cook made it special."

Yang and Lee shared a look before regarding the chunks of cylindrical white meat. Both were thinking there wasn't much there. Yang was the first to pop a section into his mouth. He chewed, frowning. He nodded before swallowing. "It tastes like chicken."

"Now you." Scarred Eye slid the bowl toward Lee.

Animal Boy met his gaze from across the table and gave him a slightly encouraging nod. Mimicking his brother, Lee chopsticked a morsel. Its contour and size intimidated him. He remembered all too well the way the creature sprang forth to meet its foe. Lee's throat constricted as he forced his mouth to open. Once it was inside, his tongue rolled it around. The taste wasn't repugnant, but the shape… Before he could gag, Lee chewed twice, then swallowed it almost whole. Immediately after the grist was gone, he chased it down with tea, hoping it would stay. When his regard met Scarred Eye's, something in the man's gaze gave him pause.

EXTRA PAY
January
Clipper Gap & Colfax Camps
1865
—

As the weeks turned to months, the Gee brothers changed like the topography they worked to alter. Their bodies shifted from rice-farming strength to earth-moving and hard-rock-manipulation strength. With youth on their side, they acclimated to the backbreaking work and long hours. The landscape shifted from thin soil, to sandstone, and shale, to granite the farther uphill the crews moved.

It became apparent early on that Yang had an aptitude for building. The work bosses moved him to trestle bridge construction. Lee knew his brother had always been happiest when he was building.

On the day Lee happened upon Yang packing up his gear inside their tent, he asked, "Are you going somewhere?" His tone was sharp and tinged with alarm.

Yang straightened, turning to face his brother. He couldn't contain his grin, but he also couldn't look Lee directly in the eye. "Yes, I'm moving over to the loggers' camp. When I told you about the new work assignment, I assumed you knew I'd move?"

Lee frowned, placing his hands on his hips. "Were you going to leave me and not say goodbye?"

Laughing, Yang said, "I'm not leaving you. I'm just going a little way up the road. You can find me any time."

"But I…" Lee's mouth hung open. He didn't know what to say.

Gathering his gear, Yang shuffled by, nudging Lee on the shoulder. "This'll be good for you. It'll force you to be more outgoing."

※

There was another man in Yang's bunk before nightfall. Lee forced himself not to look in that direction and pushed thoughts of his brother out of his mind.

On the Arracan, he'd had nightmares about the ship sinking. Floating on debris in an endless ocean, he was the sole survivor. Until now, that had been the loneliest feeling in the world.

※

Lee and Animal Boy seemed consistently paired with Jumpin as they continued grading and brush clearing. Jumpin began behaving oddly on the day Mr. Strobridge first appeared. She usually gave them no trouble, obediently hauling heavy loads up and down the hills to the loading and dumping sites. On this day, her ears twitched, and she kept looking around like she was expecting something. Both Lee and Animal Boy spoke to her as if she were a person.

"Come on, girl," Animal Boy urged while tugging the lead. "You haven't forgotten how to do your job, have you?"

"We can't do this without you, dear." Lee scratched between her eyes. "Crew Boss says we'll have to trade you for a new partner if you keep this up."

Mule,
Equus mulus

NOSE & SKIN: Her nostrils flare and her hide twitches.

"What is the matter?" Lee asked.

Just then, two men rode into the work zone. Like the mule, the energy of the entire workforce shifted with their arrival. Tool sounds became quieter, and conversation ceased. Everyone was trying to hear the discussion that was about to happen.

I wish these people would call me by my name, Jane.

I smell my stallion. He is close!

TAIL & FEET: She waved her tail in high arcs and made little front-foot hops.

The stallion responded to her message with a low-huffing acknowledgment.

ఎఖఏ

The white men dismounted. Both had beards, one wore a patch over an eye. Mr. Hung Woh stood closest to them, with the crew boss a step behind. Animal Boy hurried toward them.

"Soldier needs a drink." Mr. Strobridge thrust the horse's reins at him.

The other man did likewise, "So does Apolo."

As Animal Boy led the horses back toward camp, Lee noticed Apolo, the large white mule, eyeing Jumpin and making sounds.

"If you were free to do as you please," Lee whispered into her ear, "I think you'd be chasing after that one."

Later, Lee would learn that the meeting he'd witnessed was between Mr. Strobridge —the big one-eyed boss man—and L.M. Metzler, a civil engineer. The plans they made would directly affect the work that the crews would do next.

For a week after the bosses left, Lee heard the men telling stories about the white mule. It had a mind of its own. It was faster and more daring than any mule in anyone's recent memory. He'd slide down steep inclines if he couldn't walk and never dump his rider. There were people he liked and people he did not. If you were of the latter and anywhere near him, you could count on being bitten or stomped on. Jumpin always acted up when he was near.

※

With Yang's adjusted work assignments, Lee didn't see his brother much. Sundays were when they'd catch up. Today, while their clothes were drying, they walked the short distance to the Auburn Chinese store, where they'd post their combined earnings to the family.

"You'll see it when your camp moves farther uphill," Yang commented about the bridge he'd been working on in Wild Cat Canyon. "It's just like the first one we saw on the train."

"That's good," Lee responded, feeling pleased for Yang. He wasn't paying full attention to the conversation. It was the same every week. What he was thinking about was if there would be letters waiting for them at the store.

After their first few months of getting used to the payment system and their expenses, the brothers had agreed on sending $30 regularly. It didn't take long for the letters to come saying that the money had been received and was a tremendous help.

"I hear there's extra pay for explosive work and tunnel crews," Yang posited.

"What?" This got Lee's full attention. "Have they asked you to join?"

"Not yet, but I think they will soon. What do you think? Wait! I already know what you're thinking. You are calculating how much less time it will take to pay off our travel debt."

"No, I wasn't. I was thinking about how dangerous it might be."

"It is really only dangerous if you are unfocused when you light the charges. If you watch the way the seams in the rocks go, you can send them flying in the right direction."

"What about Scarred Eye and Boss Stro? Do you think they were being careless?"

"I don't know, maybe."

"We should ask Father," Lee said, already knowing Yang would disregard anything that went against what he wanted to do.

※

Outside the camp, they avoided congregating in public squares unless they were heavily occupied by the Chinese. Instead, they enjoyed the forest and the animals they could observe there.

Seated on a log, they finished the salted peanuts they'd bought in town. Yang watched as Lee reverently untied the string on the package that had been waiting for them. He unfolded the paper and handed over a letter from Ting Ai. Lee slipped the one from Wèi An inside his breast pocket. Inside small, folded squares of paper, Mother had included sliced and dried ginger and fennel seeds. They took turns smelling them. Lee was already mentally combining them with other ingredients to make a flavorful tea.

They sat while savoring the moment. "Ok! I am ready to hear their splendiferous news," said Yang.

While Lee refused to incorporate local slang into his language, he thought it amusing to listen to Yang do it. Lee would be the one to read their parents' correspondence aloud.

To our dear sons Yang and Lee,

You are doing well on your sojourn. Our rice bowls are full. We are all beginning to forget the hunger from the last few years. I hope they are feeding you well where you are.

The money you sent is now helping the farm. Father has purchased an ox.

With the tax payments we've made, the Imperial District Officer has stopped threatening to seize more property.

Your wives and children are healthy. They've been helping Father in the fields. When he can spare her, Ting Ai works with me in the house and garden. Our green beans were very good this year! Gee Luck loves gardening. If I let him, he'd pick every bean and eat it raw. He reminds me of you and your grandfather, Lee.

Father and I are especially pleased with Yang for advancing with his work.

May Guan Gong and Guan Yin watch over you and keep you safe until your return.

Mother and Father, Shao Pei and Gee Fong

—

They were silent as they walked the rest of the way back to camp. They'd grown accustomed to the unsettling feelings that came after contact with the family. Mother's words brought back the familiar sights, sounds, and memories of home, and yet everything they saw and touched now reminded them that those things weren't as real as they used to be.

Reaching the camp, Yang patted his brother's shoulder. "It was good seeing you." Before peeling away for a game with his friends, he said, "Father's already answered the question you posed to him."

Without a word, Lee nodded. He was going directly to his tent to read Wèi An's correspondence. Yang would catch a ride back to his own camp before dinner started there. Lee knew he wouldn't see his brother again before he left. "Have a good week, Yang. I'll see you next week."

※

Wèi An was a good writer. She provided such details about their children that Lee felt he could almost see them. She always sent words of love that warmed his heart and inflamed his loins. But he also knew that she was filtering distressing information. He'd learned to read between her words and ask pointed questions.

The tax collector, Mr. Yum, had done more than seize portions of their property for late tax payments. He'd been physically harassing Father and Ting Ai. Father had developed a cough that wouldn't go away, no matter what herbal cure the doctor prescribed. Mother had developed another troubling foot infection, which is why Ting Ai had been working more around the house.

Lee had a special tin under his bed where he stored his letters.

※

It was late, and he was still a little drunk when Yang tumbled into his cot. In the dim candlelight, he fished in his pocket for the letter from his wife.

—

Dear Yang,
Thank you for sojourning and working for your family. You bring us great honor.
Gee Ming, your daughter, is growing fast. She's much less fussy now that she's eating regular meals. Wèi An and Father Fong take her to the fields with them so Mother Pei can direct me about without distraction.
I hope you remain well, Husband.

—

Yang leaned forward to set the corner of the letter alight in the candle flame. He held it steady as it caught hold and watched as it turned from white to curly black. He dropped the delicate transformation on a plate at his bedside and watched the last of the flames sputter out. *Is it odd that I only think of Ai when her letters come? When I am eating, pissing, or pleasuring my package, she's not there.* Even now, as he rolled over and closed his eyes, he was thinking about tomorrow's bridge building tasks.

In his dreams, Yang processed things that rarely surfaced during the day. The sound of blasting triggered thoughts of his older brother going off to war and returning dead.

When he was small, Fu-chi had been like a favorite uncle. Someone who rarely scolded or punished, but who was a protector and playmate. His night mind remembered when Mo Chou first came. Yang had followed on her heels like a lovesick puppy. So much so that Father started taking him along on every trip into town.

This was where he first noticed the funny looks he was getting. It had taken some time to work out the reason behind this. It was because he was so handsome.

A gloominess lingered inside with the realization that he didn't share a bond of affection with his wife like Fu-chi and Lee seemed to have with theirs. Beyond Mo Chou, the only other woman who'd pulled at his heartstrings was the pretty wife of the fish peddler in their village. *Did the gods offer me a choice before birth?* You can find love, or you can be beautiful, but you cannot have both. Apparently, he'd chosen the latter.

News:
Birmingham [Alabama] Daily Post | January 19, 1865
"…it is equally the duty of the Americans to free their four millions of slaves, and they will do it. It is three-parts done already. Nothing stands in the way of its full accomplishment but Lee's army at Richmond." – S.A. Goddard

San Francisco Business Directory | March 4, 1865
The fall of Savannah, Charleston, and Wilmington, and the second inauguration of Abraham Lincoln were celebrated by military parades and salutes during the day and illumination and torch-light procession in the evening.

Grass Valley Union | April 16, 1865
But yesterday we were rejoicing over victories that gave promise of an early restoration of our country to peace and tranquility. Today our hearts are sad and gloom has settled upon every countenance. ABRAHAM LINCOLN, the good, the noble President of our Republic, is dead; dead, too by the hand of the assassin.

BLACK GOOSE
May
Dutch Flat Donner Lake Wagon Road
1865
—

Spring rains were abundant, turning sections of the wagon road into veritable swamps and mud pits.

This Sunday, word spread through the camps that a spectacle was arriving. Scarred Eye, knowing the area well, offered to guide Yang, Lee, and a dozen of their peers to one of the best viewing locations. The young men glanced at each other uneasily as they tramped through the damp forest. They'd only been told that something big and monstrous was making its way slowly up the grade.

Enjoying his role as a storyteller, Scarred Eye made the most of his platform. "It's a colossus, the likes of which you've never seen."

"Is it alive or dead?" someone asked.

"You'll have to wait and see." Scarred Eye guffawed.

Yang, noticing his brother's worried expression, knocked him on the shoulder. "If it was an actual monster, he wouldn't take us there. Every one of us can outrun him!"

"I heard that," Scarred Eye called back, "and I wouldn't count on it."

Yang rolled his eyes and shook his head.

They heard it before they saw it. The shouts and profanity were much worse than Strobridge's. "That'll be Missouri Bill, the infamous muleskinner," Scarred Eye said.

"Forget this!" Lee complained. "I will not watch mules being skinned." His stomach soured at the thought.

The brothers had moved up to a position directly behind their leader.

"It's not that," Scarred Eye replied. "A mule skinner is an expert animal handler, someone intelligent enough to outsmart mules. And that is not easy!"

They rounded a corner and came out on a hill above a dip in the road. What they saw was a spectacle, indeed. It took a moment of silence to make sense of it. "That, my friends, is the Black Goose."

Strapped to a flatbed wagon, fortified with wheels that were two feet wide, was a behemoth chunk of rounded metal, studded with rivet points. It was secured atop an extra-wide freight wagon. A shaggy man with a long whip screamed at a team of ten oxen straining to crest the hill.

The audience climbed up on a rock outcropping for a better view. Behind them came another group, led by Hung Woh. "Move it, boys," Scarred Eye told them as he bent down to lend a hand. Following Hung Woh were the crew boss, their paymaster, multiple cooks, and several Six Company representatives.

As everyone resettled, Hung Woh took up the narrative. "You may not recognize it, but that is a disassembled steam locomotive. It left Sacramento weeks ago and is going up to the summit."

One cook pointed. "There's a long way to go. Will they make it before winter sets in?"

Crew Boss shrugged his shoulders. "It doesn't matter. If they don't make it this year, they can start again when the roads dry out."

"What's it for? There are no tracks up there," someone said.

"Crocker would not like a delay," Hung Woh replied. "They are planning to use it as a hoist. The most formidable challenge ahead of us will be the tunnel at the top." His eyes took on a faraway look. "Many people say it is an impossible task."

"Is it?" Yang dared to ask.

Hung Woh regarded Yang, taking his measure. After a time, he said, "I believe we Chinese will succeed."

The conveyance didn't look like it moved at all when another man shouted for the ox team to halt. Then he called out additional instructions.

Multiple teamsters trotted into view from somewhere behind the Goose. Some began attaching heavy chains to trees. Several more brought out blocks they wedged under the thick wagon wheels, while yet another set began laying thin logs perpendicular across soggy spots in the road. Just as the chain men were attaching them to the back of the wagons, Hung Woh said, "Hold up. Listen behind us."

The group on the rock heard the rattling chains before the teamsters. Cresting the hill was a stagecoach. Lee saw when Missouri Bill noticed the oncoming vehicle. Immediately his arms waved and he yelled, but it was too late.

The coach horses went wild when they saw the fearful thing on the road. Their eyes rolled and they bucked, broke out of their harnesses, and nearly flipped the coach. It was pandemonium for a while until the men below could calm the commotion.

A teamster approached the coachmen carrying a burlap sack. From it, he pulled out what looked like large dark pillowcases. It soon became apparent what he was instructing them to do. Once the hoods were over the horses' heads, they settled enough to be re-harnessed. The coach masters walked the team past the Goose. Once they reached a safe distance, they removed the hoods.

The next phase of the operation moved at a snail's pace. Chains were let out slightly before being ratcheted into place. The wheel chocks were removed, and Missouri Bill urged his oxen forward by only two steps. At this rate, it would take them the rest of the day to make it down the incline.

By twos and threes, the railroad men left to resume their Sunday tasks.

A BLASTER & A CHEF
June
Clipper Gap Camp
1865
—

It had only been a few days since Yang had been moved to a blasting crew. The work wasn't all about explosions. Barrels of black powder had to be moved off the mountain schooners, wagons pulled by twelve mules wearing bells. Yang's camp was the first stop for this shipment coming from Santa Cruz. There, the bosses divvied it up between the sites. Wagons lined up to deliver it to their destinations. He knew that the material was expensive. The sheer number of them coming through assured him that road construction money was flowing.

Another change was a nickname. Big Buck, his tent mate, explained that if he stayed on their crew, the men would give him a new name. Blasters believed the Gods would protect them better if they didn't know their real names. They gave him the name, Manly. It pleased him.

His work schedule was agreeable, too. Granite, one of the hardest known rocks, required extraordinary power. The closer they got to Donner Summit, the more granite needed to be moved. Three times a day, he and his charge setter teammates would be called thirty minutes ahead of time to study their subjects. Each man had his own rituals and methods of rock study. Yang's involved a distance view from every side, running his hands across the areas where the seams were situated and then spitting on his fingertips and rubbing them over the zones he thought best for charge setting. Once the ideal seam was identified, he measured and packed the powder, not too tight, but tight enough to make the blast most effective. Ignition lines were run. The bosses would ring a bell and call, "All clear!" as the blasters lit the fuses. Making sure the sparks were traveling steadily, they ran for cover.

What happened next was the highlight of Yang's day—stillness, followed by the flash, then the bone-rattling boom. A dust cloud rained particles while he waited for the foreman to call it good. Rock movers would be busy for the next few hours. With black hands and smudges on his face, Manly returned to the supply lines until it was time for the next round.

※

Lee's camp was about to move to Clipper Gap. The rails were down, and the first train was expected. As thousands of new Chinese came on the line, Lee's tent mates, including Animal Boy, were transferred. The work crew boss had kept Lee in place to help organize new arrivals. For the last week, he'd been the first greeter at the station, leading the newbies to the central area where they were sorted and given their first assignments.

Dealing with so many people was mind-numbing, but it was infinitely better than grading. Unfortunately, Jumpin had to continue doing her hauling job. She also had new coworkers, but Lee made a point of visiting her in her corral. He thought she looked forward to seeing him. He knew, without a doubt, that she enjoyed the fruit and vegetables he brought for her to eat!

Before bedtime, after a grueling day, Lee sat near the fire pit in the common area brewing a pot of tea. A man approached from the opposite direction, clearly on a mission. It was too dark to make out his face, but Lee watched him pause and raise his nose in the air. He turned toward Lee and quickly crossed the space. "What is that I smell? Liquorish?"

Smiling, Lee chuckled. "It's anise from my mother's garden. Would you like to try it?"

"I would," said the fellow.

Lee recognized him as one of their camp cooks— a heavyset man who always looked stern. Having only one cup, Lee took it over to the barrel of fresh water and rinsed it before pouring tea for his unexpected guest.

Offering the steaming cup with both hands, Lee inclined his head. The man received it the same way, making similar gestures. He brought it to his face, inhaling deeply. "This is lovely!" he exclaimed, cracking a smile. "Ginger? You stimulate before sleep?"

"I find it improves digestion." Lee's eyes grew wide. "I have only compliments for the fine meals you serve, sir, but my stomach likes a little help before sleep. Plus, I've had a sore tooth and thought the ginger might help."

"Exactly right," he said before taking a sip. "Marvelous combination. I thank you for this unforeseen treat. My name is Quong Toy."

"It is a pleasure to meet you formally, Mr. Quong. I am Gee Lee from Panyu District."

"Hong Kong."

Lee nodded. Sometimes tea is best enjoyed in companionable silence.

When Mr. Quong finished, Lee asked, "Would you like more?"

"No, thank you. You must have yours now." He rose up, returning the cup with two hands and a bow. "If you'd like company next time, bring it round to the kitchen. I'm always there and I have many cups."

※

They mobilized. While mule teams pulled many flatbeds along the wagon road, the train passed. Lee was riding with the work crew boss near the end, in the dust's thick cloud. The caboose came first in the string of cars. Through the windows, Lee caught sight of plush red curtains and furniture. It surprised him to see a white woman and children inside, along with the unmistakable Strobridge. Multiple double-decker cars came next, maybe seven or eight. That would be the bunk housing for the white workers. Flatbeds carried telegraph poles and lines, as well as machinery and other parts. Two office cars followed a kitchen and blacksmith shop, all being pushed by a great steam engine.

The new site was less spacious than Auburn. It had more sun because the lumbermen had already felled the trees. There were rocks in and on the ground, which made tent setup a challenge. As the crew boss held some men back to work on camp construction, Hung Woh and Mr. Strobridge started gangs dumping roadbed gravel and moving iron rails. The Chinese got rock and cross tie laying work, and the Irish got the rail and tie spiking jobs. A steady beat of hammers hitting metal blended into the background as Lee worked, setting up tents for the workers. Infused within the noise were Strobridge's curses at men who worked too slow.

Lee was glad to be out of the line of fire on that count. He'd suffered several of those harsh reprimands, which caused Hing to move him to another work team. On the last one, he'd broken the little finger on his left hand. Although their Chinese doctor had attempted to set it, it healed at an angle that made it practically useless.

When the Chinese tent city was complete, Quong Toy hailed Lee to the large mess tent. "I've got fresh barrels of hot tea that need to be delivered to the linemen. Foshan is nowhere in sight. Can you take them?"

"Yes, Sir!" Lee answered, searching for the long balancing pole.

Even though Lee was tired, he enjoyed these types of tasks. Moving barrels filled with liquid would be impossible without physics and a steady mind. Two helpers spotted the ends of the pole as Lee squatted, squaring himself in the center. Proper body alignment made an impossible-seeming task almost effortless if one moved slowly and carefully, which Lee did. He crossed the dusty work zone, avoiding stones that could turn an ankle. As he approached the line, he called out, "Tea Man! A little help."

The closest workers dropped their shovels and hurried over to help lower the weight. Workers often forgot to use Mandarin to communicate when they were exhausted, but Lee knew what they meant in their own dialects as they thanked him for the delivery.

No help was needed to attach his pole to the empties and haul them back for Mr. Quong. On his way, he had an opportunity to admire a trestle Yang had worked on. It was nearly sixty feet high and forty feet long. *Impressive! I must remember the details for Mother and Father.*

※

On Yang's blasting team, She Bang and Dust Biter struck up an instant friendship. Like their day job, they liked to play hard when they had free time. They pressured Yang to join them.

"Manly, your brother can't scratch your itch like the girls in town. You've got to come with us."

"Sorry, we've got a deal worked out. My mother would have my head if she knew I was spending time with a lot like you."

"Yea, yea," Bang slapped his back, raising a dust puff of dirt. "I understand."

The two walked ahead, making bets for how long it would take for him to change his mind.

Yang had been feeling great about his pay increase. He was looking forward to watching Lee's face when he counted the increase. However, Bang and Biter's comments irritated like a sliver jammed under a fingernail.

He'd stopped at the Chinese blacksmith to have his drill head sharpened. While he waited, he overheard a conversation between the boss and his apprentice. "I get $1.34 per day and McGrath over there gets $2.75." He referred to the white blacksmith.

Not interrupting his lifting and lowering of the bellow, the apprentice glanced at Yang and shrugged his shoulders.

"The railroad feeds them! Their food is crap, and it makes them sick, but still...How is that fair?"

Yang pinched his upper lip as he mulled this over. He calculated what a white worker would make doing his job. The amount sounded enormous! But only the Chinese did blasting. *The bosses don't care if we get body parts blown off,* he thought.

FIRST SON HAS SPOKEN
July
Colfax Camp
1865
—

The Blaster Crew grew in status along the line, especially as the managers struggled with labor shortages, namely with the Irish workers. On Mondays, it was common to hear the bosses loudly bemoaning their whereabouts.

Every Chinese knew overindulgent Sunday drinking was the cause. It made the Irish more careless and mean. It also ensured that they slept away the next workday. Their diet and poor hygiene contributed to other problems in their camps. Fever and diarrhea running through them further delayed progress.

No matter, the Chinese kept to themselves and did not begrudge additional countrymen arriving to pick up the slack. Esteem gained for favorable behavior opened ears to requests for protection against violence.

When rumors of a planned attack circulated, armed patrols appeared, as if by providence, near the Chinese camps.

※

After they bathed and finished hanging laundry, Lee put the finishing touches on his latest letter home and asked Yang to turn over his earnings.

Yang shrugged his shoulders, not making eye contact. "I-ah-had some extra expenses this month."

"Wait! What is going on?" Lee exclaimed. "What expenses?"

"I...can't exactly say."

"You can't say? You don't KNOW?"

"I know..." Yang said, glancing away.

"Where did you spend it?"

"The Blasters, we have things we do..."

"What things?" Lee wanted to know.

"We have a code of silence."

Lee crossed his arms, glaring at his brother. "Is it just for this time, or...?"

"I am tired of this shit, Lee! I am First Son! You disrespect me when you needle like a woman," Yang shouted. "Rip Snorter says—"

"Who is Rip Snorter? Who makes up these ridiculous names? Manly? Why would you let anyone call you that?"

Yang turned and stomped away. After a moment, he came back, breathing deeply through his nose. "We will send our postage today," he said calmly, "and that is the last time we will do this together."

"But—"

"No." Yang held up a hand. "First Son has spoken."

※

News from their parents was encouraging. Lee keenly felt the betrayal they would feel when they received their most recent package. He was deeply concerned about future postings. Already he was worried about how he would explain the shift that had occurred.

※

Since Mr. Quong, the camp cook, had a subscription to the Chinese Newspaper, the men made a weekly ritual of gathering to listen to him read snippets of news. Yang usually remained in camp until Mr. Quong had finished.

Yang and Lee were still feeling prickly toward each other after their fight.

News:
Sacramento Daily Union | July 14, 1865
CENTRAL PACIFIC RAILROAD COMPANY.
Over 150,000 acres have been listed to the company by the United States Land Office. As the railroad progresses the lands will become more valuable ... The Pacific coast will feel its exhilarating influence—the arts, commerce, and agriculture will flourish, population will be increased, and there will be numerous, powerful, and prosperous people on this extreme west of our country, bound to the Union by Interest and the strongest fraternal and patriotic ties.

Sacramento Daily Union | July 15, 1865
The Freedmen's Bureau has charge of between thirty and forty thousand acres of abandoned land in Virginia. This would furnish farms of forty acres each for about a thousand families.

The CPRR has purchased additional land near Colfax and is laying out plans for a new town. Tracks will soon follow.

Placer Herald | July 29, 1865
Highway Robbers—Mr. Predmore, a teamster, while returning from Dutch Flat to Clipper Gap, on Tuesday, was stopped by a couple of Highwaymen, between Gold Run and Madden's Toll House, and relieved of $52. On the same day, near the same place, at an earlier hour, several Chinamen were robbed.

"Predmore?" Lee said, leaning back to look at Yang. "Don't we know him?"

"He's the teamster we rode with when we first arrived."

"Aren't you working close to there?"

"Yes, we're starting tunnel work near Applegate."

"Maybe it's best if you aren't carrying money while you're on the wagon road." Lee dropped his eyes and made a small bow.

"Before we finish this evening," Mr. Quong addressed the group, "I want to announce that, starting tomorrow, Mr. Gee Lee will join my kitchen crew."

"What's this?" Yang looked surprised as the assemblage began cheering. "You didn't say..." He wasn't able to finish his sentence as men crowded around to congratulate Lee.

Letters from home.

—

Dear Yang,
Thank you for sojourning and working for your family. You bring us great honor.
I am in good health, your daughter is well, and your parents are also fine. Your father is planning to hire farmhands for the fall harvest season.
Mother let me buy a piece of special cloth to sew something for Ming's birthday. It will be a gift from both her parents.
The tax collector has been back lately. He's paying close attention to Wèi An. I would hate it if she brought shame on this family.
I hope you remain well, Husband.
Ting Ai

—

The fate of this letter was the same as the previous ones.

—

My dear husband, Lee
I miss you! My skin aches for your touch. My ears wish to hear your voice. In my dreams, I think you are here. I have a work shirt of yours that I've been hiding. I knew I would need it to remember your smell.
No one knows I feel like this. Song, Luck, and even Ming see me as their mother and aunt. Your parents know me as a dutiful daughter. I protect the honor of this family.
I know you are doing important work. Your parents are so pleased whenever a package arrives from California.
I worry you won't recognize me when you return. Sometimes I barely recognize myself. Is our youth expendable and of no value? Am I the only one who cares that we are not living our married life together?
Your Wèi An
P.S. Is Yang alright? I worry about Ting Ai. She's more angry than usual and she's too welcoming to Mr. Yum, who has been plaguing us again.

—

It was pitch black outside when Lee finished reading. Crumpling the paper into a ball, he shoved it in a pocket as he left the tent.

Feeling ready to explode, he needed distance from camp. More than anything, he needed to speak with his wife. Grandfather had spoken of legends where some believed water could carry messages. Uppermost in his mind was finding a place to vent.

Not wanting to get lost in the forest, he headed for the closest waterway, a miner's ditch. It wasn't ideal because of its uniformity. A creek gained qui, life, from rocks and switchbacks. Approaching it, he stood where he could see the moon's reflection on its surface. Swiping at the tears coursing down his face, he began to talk.

"Wèi An, how could you say that, think that, or write that? You are not the only one who cares! YOU KNOW I share the same feelings! It is an evil thing that you do writing those words where the gods could see them! You risk bringing bad luck upon us!"

"I live for the day when I return and can once again hold you in my arms. I want to make more babies with you. I want to see your smile, smell your breath, and make love to you so many times we can no longer walk!"

"If only you could hear me, woman."

Kneeling before the water, Lee held the ball of paper in the palm of both hands as he kowtowed, "Please, Guanyin, forgive Wèi An for her impertinence." After three touches of his forehead on the ground, Lee sat back on his heels and uncrumpled the paper. He tore it into small pieces. Sprinkling some on the water, he watched the current sweep them away. "We obediently follow the wishes of our parents," he said as he bowed three more times, then released more. "Hearts suffer sometimes when we do." He tossed more. "It is only love that brings such suffering." He stood and bowed deeply one last time, opening his hand to set the last ones free. "I have nothing but gratitude for the love you allowed to come into my life."

For a moment, he stood with his eyes closed, imagining he could hear the non-existent burble of water over stones. *I hope you are not angry, and I promise to light incense for you at the altar to accompany this important message. My desire is to please you!*

While Lee was moving through the forest, and especially as he stopped near the reflected moonlight—

Owl,
Bubo virginianus

Another lunar worshiper observes the land creature.

WINGS: Extended and gliding in the nearly silent night.

FACE and EARS: Dish-like, funneling prey sounds and their location to the hunter.

Terrible cries coming from it, sounds like grief.

His mate had been lost to a sharp-taloned predator.

Sorrowful, watching our fledglings fall to the forest floor where creatures consumed them.

He flew closer to the land animal,
wishing he could tell it,
Keep eating and communicating with the moon.
Fall will come again, and with it will be another chance to try.

If the god Guanyin and the owl noticed each other, they gave no sign.

CLOUDS & RAIN
August
Panyu District, China
1865
—

After their family rounded a curve in the road, Gee Fong and Shao Pei stood at their gate and looked at each other. They'd sent their daughters-in-law and grandchildren into town for the festival day.

"This feels strange," Fong said. "Have we ever been here alone?"

His wife shook her head. "I don't think so."

He could tell by her expression that their situation was disorienting. "I asked Ting Ai to heat bath water before she left," Fong said.

Pei nodded; her composure returned as a need arose for her to meet. Her mind was already racing ahead to wondering if they had enough of the soap he liked. His next comment surprised her back to uncertainty.

"Let's bathe together." Fong dropped a kiss on her lips, then turned and squatted down. "Jump on," he glanced at her over his shoulder.

Pei's hands flew up to her mouth to stifle a laugh. "What are you doing?" She looked left and right. "Someone might see."

"If you walk, the bathwater will grow cold, and I know how you like your water."

Trying, and failing, to suppress a grin, Pei leaned over her husband's back and wrapped her arms around his neck. She hiked her legs around his waist as he lifted.

He patted her bottom as he set out, making her giggle.

Sometime later, when they were very clean, Fong helped Pei step out of the bath. He held a towel for her to wrap around herself. "I am an old woman now," she said simply, lowering her head.

With a finger under her chin, he raised her face so she could see the sincerity in his eyes. "I will always see you as the beautiful girl I first met on our wedding day."

"I can't see myself that way anymore." She covered his hand with hers while tracing lines around his mouth with the thumb of the opposite hand. "When I look at your face, I see it reflected in all of our boys."

"Our family is OK right now."

"Yes, what's left of it," she commented sadly.

"What's done is done, Pei. We only have this moment and the pleasure it contains." He leaned in to kiss her softly. When he pulled back, he whispered, "Will you find joy with me, my lovely girl?"

She nodded, shifting her weight toward him.

※

In their afterglow, Fong used his toes to grab the sheet and pull it away from her. Looking down, he said, "I still love your lotus feet."

She sighed as she laced her fingers through his. "I know."

"I am so sorry for the pain it has caused."

She nodded.

"I am glad we decided not to bind our granddaughters' feet." Fong could have bitten his tongue for letting that slip. Any mention of their granddaughters brought Mo Chou and Ngon to mind, a wound that would never properly heal. Attempting to brush it away, he pulled Pei close, nuzzled into her neck, and soon began to snore.

BONE JARS
Summer
Cape Horn Camp
1865
—

At Cape Horn Camp, on the outskirts of Colfax, meal preparation had become fully integrated into Lee's routine. With his job change to the kitchen, he'd also gotten a pay raise, for which he was extremely pleased.

The Ning Yeong Company had invited camp cook, Quong Toy, to go to San Francisco to plan and prepare an elaborate meal for a visiting dignitary. No one knew if he would return to The Hill.

Foshan, his assistant, was not happy. Lee overheard their heated exchange.

"You are a little too slow, you're not always where I want you to be, and you don't think ahead well enough to be head cook," Quong Toy explained.

"That shouldn't matter. I've been in the kitchen longer. He should work for me!" Yow Foshan raised his voice. His face reddened, and he lowered his eyes, but he didn't back down.

"I promise you; this is a kindness. If you fail, tired and hungry men will turn on you like the fierce Imperial warriors."

"You cannot shame me like this," Foshan entreated.

Quong Toy sighed. "My decision to make Lee head cook is final. After I leave, you may take it up with Mr. Hung Woh. But if you do so, be prepared to be reassigned. He's well known for giving complainers something worse to complain about."

Mr. Quong spent the next three days training Lee, alternating between resentment and exhaustion. Lee asked many questions about quantities, recipes, and supply ordering while taking notes. Quong provided many opportunities for Lee to practice directing Foshan, who followed orders, but glared and slammed things around as he did.

When it was time to say farewell, Quong Toy took Lee aside. "I have confidence in you, Gee Lee. I'm sorry Foshan is being an ass. Eventually, you will make a good team. In the meantime, if you have questions or problems, go visit Cook Jan or Shuck. They know the situation and they've said they will support you if you need help."

"I thank you for your confidence, Mr. Quong." Lee bowed deeply. "I will endeavor to make you proud."

"I believe you will." Quong Toy bowed and then rose to pat Lee's shoulder. "There are still a few months left on my newspaper subscription. I'd recommend keeping it going and to continue being a news source for the men."

※

Many more crews and work camps were added. Seeing familiar faces became a rarity. The swarm of men was about to take up-side hill rock cutting.

Lee's first meal as the head cook was jook with chicken and scallions, nothing fancy or different. Foshan already knew to prepare the tea.

After touring through the work zone with the crew supervisor the night before, Lee directed Foshan to double the amount of tea they would deliver throughout the day. Different from the grading he'd done, men would slice through slate on steep inclines in order to blast their way down to create a level shelf a thousand feet above the floor of the American River Canyon.

Instead of shovels and mule carts, these crews would rely on sharp picks to scrape dirt out from seams. Massive amounts of blasting powder would propel debris off the cliff edge; no further hauling would be required.

Planning, Lee already had meals mapped out for the week. They had a schedule for precooking and prepping portions of each meal so that delivery at mealtimes would be efficient. He intended to stick with the basics until it became second nature, or until the men complained.

When the blasting started, Lee developed a headache and felt scattered. The nearness of the noise was jarring his nerves. *If I am feeling this way, the linemen must be more so. What can I add to tea or soup that will soothe?*

They'd already made two tea deliveries to their crews and were prepping the midday meal when one of their Chinese teamsters rushed up. "Mr. Gee, you must come."

"What?" Lee didn't know this man and wasn't considering what his presence could mean.

Foshan understood. Laying down his spoon, he approached Lee. "Something's wrong."

Taking a stumbling step back from the U-shaped stove, the color in Lee's face dropped. Foshan grabbed his arm to keep him away from the flames. "It might not be what you are thinking," Foshan said earnestly, almost nose-to-nose with Lee. "I can handle this; you need to go with..." Foshan glanced over his shoulder.

"Ah Get," the man replied.

Nodding, Lee followed and mounted the second mule that Ah Get already had ready to go.

It was an understanding in the camp that when an accident occurred, if there was family nearby, they could drop what they were doing to attend to their relative. The Irish, other whites, the Negroes, and the bosses and managers did not follow this practice. But in this, the Chinese were rock solid and did not negotiate. Perhaps this was because the others did not work with their family. The only relatives Lee had seen were Mr. Strobridge's. For the harsh task manager that he was, it said something about the man that he wanted his wife and children close at hand.

Lee often daydreamed about what it would be like if Wèi An and the children had their own boarding car here. Right now, with all of his focus on Yang, their marital conflict didn't matter.

They were moving too fast for Lee to question Ah Get. He knew that Yang's blasting crew was working on an advance tunnel site near Blue Canyon. They'd be there within the hour.

Lee could see the camp as they approached. It was much smaller than Cape Horn. They gathered near the tunnel mouth. Men were frantically moving rock. "Do you know what happened?" Lee asked as he dismounted, handing the reins to the teamster.

"Only that there was a collapse." Ah Get wore a resigned expression. "Go ask." He nodded toward the group. "I'll wait for you, whatever happens."

"Thanks," Lee said, setting off for the group.

Near to the edge, he recognized Rip Snorter covered in dust, his arm in a makeshift sling. He was sitting on a rock looking dazed. Approaching him, Lee said, "Rip." It felt so wrong to address the injured man by that absurd name, but he didn't know any other way to greet him.

With a haggard look, he met Lee's eyes, recognizing him. "We thought it was clear and went in, then it all caved in on top of us."

"How many?" Lee asked, his voice sounding hoarse.

"Six."

"Yang?"

"Yeah, Manly was in there."

Lee squatted beside him, both hands grasping his knee. Lee bit his lower lip. He realized he was shaking. Rip laid a hand on Lee's shoulder.

After about forty minutes, Lee heard the search crew shouting. He stood up. "I have to go," he said, looking down. "Will you be alright?"

The man nodded. "Yes, go!"

Shouldering his way through the tight knot of people, Lee heard murmurs. "This one's alive."

Tian Hou, don't let him be dead! he thought as he squeezed his eyes shut. Forcing them open, he saw familiar Blaster faces, but none was Yang.

"No!" Lee heard an anguished cry behind him. It was a voice he feared he'd never hear again. Turning, he saw his brother leaning against another man who was helping him walk. Yang looked like he'd risen from a grave, completely covered in dirt. His eyes were the only grime-free place on him. Blood seeped from a gash in his head. He held his arm at an awkward angle. "No, no, no!" Yang wailed as he stared at the dead men on the ground, lined up like chopsticks.

Yang didn't even notice when Lee exchanged places with the man who'd been supporting him.

For a while, Lee didn't know what to do. The last time he'd witnessed anguish like this, he'd hidden in a barn. He shuffled them closer to the dead men, as that is what Yang seemed to want. As he did so, he realized that Yang was warm, and he was still breathing.

As his own trembling subsided, he thought about Mother, Mo Chou, and Fu-Chi. Lee regarded the dead men. It seemed like speaking their names out loud was the right thing to do. "Big Buck, Dust Biter, and Poker Face," he said.

This brought about a shift in Yang. His face changed from shock to recognition. He clutched at his brother with his good arm and sobbed. Lee held on, keeping them stable as waves of grief abraded them like sea glass.

※

Ah Get rearranged his team so he could drive a wagon back to Cape Horn Camp. Yang and Rip Snorter rode in the flatbed alongside their fallen blasting mates. Lee sat on the bench seat next to Get; none of the men felt up to exchanging words.

After stopping to drop off the living, Ah Get continued on to deliver the dead to the nearest camp where the Six Companies had a bone recovery area. In his pocket, he carried identification information that the Blue Canyon Chinese supervisor supplied.

The remains would lie in shallow graves until the soft tissue decomposed. After several months, holy men would do a final cleaning, then arrange the bones in a precise order to fit inside pottery jars crafted for this purpose. From there, they'd be shipped to their Six Company headquarters where clerical officials would render a final report. Their names would be added to scrolls in the altar rooms. If affairs were in order, the sad package would ship to China and be forwarded to the home province.

These sojourners were transformed into dry, stick-like material, arranged inside a pitch-black jar, nested in straw, inside a wooden box, returned home, and labeled with the names their parents had given them. In their last resting places, no one would ever know the nicknames bestowed upon them by their friends.

Every sojourning Chinese took comfort in knowing that, one way or another, they would be buried alongside their ancestors. Being remembered and honored by the living is immortality. A fate worse than death would be to become a gui hun, an abandoned and forgotten soul doomed to wander a foreign land for all eternity.

Foshan and their camp doctor greeted the injured party when they arrived. They worked together to bathe Yang and Snort, clean and dress their wounds, reset Yang's dislocated shoulder, and wrap his broken ribs. Snort had a broken arm and stayed with the doctor in the convalescent tent. Foshan helped Lee move Yang to his own tent, even going to locate an extra cot and clean bedding.

Yang's eyes were droopy from the medicinal tea the doctor gave him. As soon as his head hit the pillow, he was out. Lee and Foshan stood, regarding him for a moment. "It's been a hard day," Foshan commented.

As if surprised, Lee asked, "How did lunch AND dinner go?"

Flashing a huge grin, Foshan said, "I'm still intact. No stab wounds."

"Well done," Lee replied. He suddenly felt like he was about to collapse.

Noticing the weariness on the other man's face, Foshan waved a hand toward Lee's bed. "You need rest too, boss. I have the morning meal, from your plan, already prepped. You can sleep late if you want to."

"Good man. Thank you, Foshan."

※

Lee arrived in his kitchen at midmorning. When he'd left his tent, Yang was still asleep, and Lee was relieved to find that he didn't feel feverish. He saw that Foshan was out delivering tea and he'd already started heating water for the next batch. Moving aside a jumble of dirty pots and cooking utensils, Lee made a clear counter space. From his supply shelves, he pulled out dried chamomile, lavender, and lemon balm. He added several scoops of each to the center of cheese cloths squares and tied them up in neat bundles with cotton twine. He dropped the balls into the deep pots with brown oolong simmering. The mixture instantly filled the space with a lovely scent. Both the smell and the chemical plant compounds would be good for spirit calming.

"What is that?" asked Scarred Eye as he approached the counter opposite from where Lee stood. He inhaled to sample the novelty in the air. In his hand, he carried a burlap sack that had sharp white objects poking through the fabric. Before he could reply, the man plopped the heavy object on the counter. It made a dull thud.

Lee made an abbreviated bow to the man as he pulled an apron over his head and began tying it behind his back. "Those are herbs added to promote health."

"Ah ha," commented Scarred Eye. "This here," he pointed at the sack, "is a surprise."

Remembering the rattlesnake, Lee raised an eyebrow. "Do I want to know?"

"Have a look, then you tell me."

Gingerly, Lee approached it and began unraveling the top of the sack. When it was loose enough, he lifted the burlap so he could get a good look inside. He straightened, taking a quick step back. "What is it?"

Scarred Eye flashed a smile. "It's a porcupine, and I plan to eat my next meal in your kitchen so I can see what you've done with it." His expression was smug. Letting the moment settle between them, he moved on to a new topic. "How's your brother? I heard about the accident yesterday."

"He's alright," Lee said, leaning his hands on the counter on either side of the animal. "He's lucky to be alive," he continued, "and will need rest. If you wish, I will send word when he's ready to receive visitors."

"You do that."

※

Foshan arrived in time to see the porcupine displayed on the counter. "Fresh meat. This is wonderful!" he said.

"I'm glad *you* think so," Lee replied. "You butcher it...Cut the meat into bite-sized portions...and save the quills. I will prepare a marinade."

An awkward silence crept up on them. Foshan frowned while bracing his hands on his hips. "What if I *prick* myself?"

"Ah..." Lee started, then stopped. Shrugging his shoulders, he said, "Stop the bleeding, bandage it, then get back to work." Retreating to his work station, he thought he heard Foshan whisper something that sounded like, "Sometimes that's easier said than done."

※

Near the end of the second day of his convalescence, Yang was ready to get some fresh air. Lee had just come in to set a cup of hot tea on his bedside table when Yang groaned. "That smells really good." His voice lowered an octave as he swung a leg to the floor. "I feel like a statue."

Lee offered a hand to help. "Your qi has settled. Let's work on some Qi Gong movements to get it flowing."

"In a minute," Yang said, letting out another groan as he reached for the teacup. After a noisy slurp and a satisfying sound, Yang lifted his gaze to regard his brother. "You've changed since I saw you last," he commented before upending his cup and finishing the drink.

"I wear an apron now."

"If you were a daughter, Mother would be proud."

As fast as lightning, Lee gave his brother's arm a hard poke.

"Ow! That hurts!" Yang complained and laughed, rubbing the area.

"It was supposed to. Now let's walk. I have to get back to work."

As they stepped outside, Foshan was waiting. "How are you feeling, Mr. Manly?" His voice sounded breathless; his cheeks were flushed.

Yang shot Lee a quick, questioning glance. Lee handed Foshan the empty teacup while saying, "He's better. He needs privacy. Shoo!"

As they walked slowly toward the shitting log, Yang casually said, "That friend of yours could wake snakes."

Frowning, Lee replied, "He's not my...well, yes, I guess he is my friend. Wake snakes?"

Grinning, Yang waved it off. "Forget it."

The log could seat ten men comfortably side by side. As one approached it, the ground was level, then it dropped off over the edge. With all the segregated camp areas, it surprised him that no one had given a thought to separate latrines. *Apparently, balls and asses don't matter as much as faces.* Yang thought. As gregarious as he was, he was glad to have the place to himself in this instance.

The big bosses who lived in the train cars eliminated in pots in their living quarters. Yang watched as a servant carrying one of them stopped to speak to his brother. He could tell from Lee's posture that he wished the man would have spoken with him *after* he'd emptied the pot.

When Yang finished, Lee handed over a small box with flat sheets of imported paper used for wiping. "Do you need help?"

"No! You remind me of Mother," he complained testily.

After a quick wash and clothing adjustment, the brothers went to the pen area where they gathered for evening fires. Coals still smoldered in the center of the pit. Logs where men sat stood like empty sentinels. Lee led them through gentle Qi Gong brocades. Bending at the waist, they exhaled, arms outstretched, palms facing out. As they scooped up qi, turning their palms toward their bodies, they inhaled while almost touching the soil. Slowly pulling the Earth's energy into their core, they breathed in while straightening and bringing their hands up to their waists. Flipping their palms upward, they stretched toward the sky, exhaling. In this way, they breathed and moved in slow circles, stretching and healing.

When they finished, Yang was moving easier. His skin had a healthy glow, and he greeted the men who stopped to chat with a welcoming smile.

For Lee, it was a surprise to learn that people in camp wanted to listen to the exploits of Manly, the brave and infamous blaster.

He left his brother to his followers and headed back to his kitchen wearing a smile.

※

Yang's presence in his tent reminded Lee how much he missed family and feeling like a place was home. Their whispered conversations before bed were soothing and intimate.

Their discussions went something like this.

"Do you worry about dying?" Lee asked. He wondered at his brother's thoughts, especially since so many of his own dwelled on that topic.

"Every day." Yang quickly changed the subject. "People are saying you're one of the best camp cooks. You might even be better than Mother."

"Really?"

"I'll never admit to saying that." Yang threw him a wink.

Lee picked at his clothes. "What do you think Father is doing?"

"Ha, there was a time when I'd never have to give that a thought. It's fall, so the harvest is in and he's getting ready for winter. Probably chopping wood, since you aren't there to do it!"

"I've been a disrespectful brother to you," Lee whispered.

"There's room for improvement for me too," Yang said. "Do you love your wife?"

"Deeply."

"I'm sorry," Yang said. He couldn't imagine what it would feel like if he had become deeply attached to Ai. The brothers were silent for a time.

Then Lee asked, "Do you think about Fu-chi?"

"Yes. You?"

"I hope he's one of the ancestors watching over us."

"I hope so too."

"I give you a bad time over the Manly name," Lee said, "but I am very proud of the work you are doing."

"I'm proud of your contributions too, brother."

Lee raised his eyebrows. "You said it was women's work."

"It is...but you are good at it."

Smiling, they nodded to each other.

"Was the accident caused by carelessness?" Lee wanted to know.

"It happened too fast. I couldn't say."

"In the future, will you try to be more careful?"

There was a long pause before a barely audible response came. "If I return home in a bone jar, you'll be a good First Son. It should always have been you, anyway."

Both of them knew better than to bring up Fu-chi's wife and child. Though their names never crossed their lips, neither could completely block them from their thoughts or keep from wondering what happened to them.

※

Two weeks had passed since the tunnel cave-in that killed two men and brought the brothers back together; Lee knew Yang would move back to a blasting crew soon. While his brother looked healthy, Lee knew he wasn't sleeping well. *Yang needs more time,* he thought. Part of him imagined a conversation with Kite To where he made an appeal for Yang to remain here. He could work in the wagon repair shop. But

Lee knew if his brother ever found out he'd had a hand in his demotion or loss of status, their relationship would be in serious trouble. He promised himself he'd be more accepting of Yang's decisions.

The Cape Horn shelf was taking shape. Supervisors were growing tired of Yang's consultations and proclamations about how much more of the soft rock they could move if only they would follow his blasting advice.

For Lee and Foshan, this time was doubly busy. They'd been planning a feast for the men in celebration of a successful meeting of dignitaries. Speaker of the House of Representatives, Schuyler Colfax, along with a short list of San Francisco's elite, had been lavishly entertained by the leaders of the Chinese Six Companies. The event was one that would live on in the history books. While some men bemoaned their monthly membership payments, every worker along the line was proud to have played a part in the favorable, lasting impressions made by their countrymen on one of the top leaders of this nation.

On the afternoon of the camp celebration, Lee and Foshan were in their kitchen supervising the extra cooks who'd arrived to help. Yang appeared at the back of the mess tent with a miserable dog in tow. "Lee, this poor sap needs your help."

Glancing over his shoulder to verify everything inside was continuing to progress, Lee turned to his brother. "What happened?" he asked. His eyebrows drew together as he squatted down for a better look. The dog was a brown mongrel with his tail tucked between his legs. There were multiple puffy welts along the animal's face, neck, and shoulders.

Trying to hide a smile and not quite succeeding, Yang explained, "Rip Snorter found a nest of ground hornets. He tricked one of the Irish into walking right on top of it!" Yang hooted, further frightening the dog. "You should have seen that man holler. It was rambunctious!"

Lee did not find this amusing. "And the dog followed him in?"

"No." Yang sobered. "Snorter chewed up dried meat and made a trail for the dog to follow once the hive had calmed." Seeing his brother's expression, he said, "What? I got him out. Look here." He pointed at two welts on his forearm.

Not saying more, Lee directed Foshan to smash fresh garlic. To each wound, first on the dog, then on his brother, Lee rubbed garlic. He followed this with dollops of used, wet tea leaves on the spots. With the treatment, the dog's tail relaxed and Yang sighed. "Better."

"Whose dog is he?" Lee asked as he ladled chicken soup into a bowl.

Yang reached out to receive it, but Lee squatted and placed it on the ground in front of the four-legged patient.

"I don't know," Yang said. "He'll find his own way home."

※

At the end of the highly satisfying Sunday meal that included special touches of rose wine, fresh fish, and fruit, Lee settled at the campfire to read the news out loud. Most items were from their Chinese newspaper. A few, however, were from the local papers that Foshan was using to tutor Lee in reading English.

Lee also included snippets from letters he exchanged with Mr. Quong Toy. Many men in the audience remembered when he was their camp cook.

—

Alta California | Friday, August 18, 1865
The Grand Complimentary Chinese Dinner to Speaker Colfax,
 The grand complimentary dinner to Hon. Schuyler Colfax and party, tendered by the "Six Chinese Companies in California," which has been in contemplation for some weeks past, took place last evening at the Hang Heong Restaurant, 808 Clay Street.

—

Skipping the formalities, and list of dignitaries, Lee read off the highlights he'd tick-marked. "They served three hundred and thirty-six dishes in one hundred and thirty courses!"

The men, "Ooooed."

"All who partook of the famous 'bird nest soup' pronounced it delicious."

"Ahhhhh," sighed the group.

"And you will note," Lee continued, smiling, "rose-flavored wine was served, from the same stock that you enjoyed with your meal tonight."

At this, the men cheered, got to their feet, and clapped while bowing their appreciation.

Lee got up to go double-check Foshan's kitchen cleaning. He had not relayed the other information he'd recently received from Toy. The cook would remain in San Francisco. He sent Lee an open invitation to come to work with him there.

※

Yang and Rip returned to their blasting crew together. Throughout their convalescence, they avoided talking about what happened. Their fellow workers heaped acclaim on them; they soaked it up.

Catching a ride on the back of a delivery wagon, they talked. "I stopped to blow my nose," Rip said, as his eyes gazed off in the distance. "Then the world went black, and I couldn't breathe."

"We thought it was all clear when Poker Face stopped to light his lantern." Yang was silent for a few beats before continuing. "Maybe if the lantern was lit before we went inside, we might have seen the weak spot."

"When it was collapsing, did you know what was happening?"

Yang nodded. "It felt like the world was coming down. After that, I don't remember anything until Lee was there, and I saw Buck, Biter, and Face laid out." He bit his lower lip and wrapped his arms across his middle. "I've been having nightmares."

"Me too, Manly." Snort rubbed a hand over Yang's shoulder. As he spoke, his eyes got wider and wider. "What if they've become gui hun? What if their souls are stuck inside and waiting for us to come back? I'm thinking we should make a run for it."

Seeing his friend near panic, Yang needed to do something. "Sacred Mother of Tudiye, we aren't pussies who run. We're Blasters!"

"Yeah." Snorter started rocking. When he spoke next, it was as if he were only parroting what he'd heard. "We are Blasters. Nothing spooks us."

"Right. Nothing spooks us. We need a signal. Something we can do or say that will clear our minds if we hesitate."

They worked out a set of hand signals that involved pussies, strength, and cursing sinister ghosts.

※

They checked and rechecked their gear. Their lanterns were lit well ahead of time, and they spat out anything they'd been chewing that could be a distraction. Yang had even gone so far as lighting incense at the camp altar, something he'd stopped doing long ago.

When they joined the team for the next round of charge setting, they noted sorrowfully the unfamiliar faces that replaced their fallen friends. As they approached the maw of the black hole in the mountain's side, Rip saw the mouth of a mighty dragon waiting to skewer them with sharp teeth. Yang thought about the foul language and ear-splitting screams that the bosses yelled at tunnel men who'd lost their nerve.

Noticing the change in himself and in Snort, he jabbed his friend with an elbow. He made their hand signal then shouted, "Blasters Shangpu!"

Swinging his head in Yang's direction, Rip's eyes cleared. He made fists and echoed, "Blasters Shangpu!'

In they went. Their muscles remembered what came next.

News:

Sacramento Daily Union | September 4, 1865
City Intelligence
Railroad Extension to Colfax
The track of the Pacific Railroad has been completed to the new town of Colfax, the track-layers having reached that point at about 6 o'clock on Friday evening. This addition adds twelve more miles to the road and makes its entire present length from Front street fifty-five miles, leaving some seventy miles yet to build before reaching the eastern boundary of the State.

THE KNIFE
Winter
Alta Camp, California
1865
—

As the rain came, Lee and some of the other cooks moved to Alta Camp. The best of the Chinese camp cooks were set up near the big bosses. Since the Colfax event in San Francisco, the bosses requested meal catering for visiting guests. While the Six Company managers did not pay for the extra work, they rewarded the cooks with larger-than-ordered quantities and a wider array of spices and ingredients at no extra cost. To their way of thinking, the goodwill was worth the expense. It also gave the crews bragging rights as their chefs advanced in stature.

Railroad gangs shifted to tasks that involved clearing frequent mudslides. Tunnel crews worked on tunnels regardless of the weather.

Lee opened a box with little what-nots from home. He unpacked dried herbs from Mother's garden and four sacks of rice from the fall harvest. Bringing it to his nose, he could pick out the unique essence of their soil. Smiling and nodding, he could tell that Father was still making compost the way Grandfather had taught them. Packages of dried shrimp and chili powder came next, followed by scented oil that Wèi An had made to soothe tired muscles. Finally, he held up scribbly paintings by the children.

Mother's letter was very short. *Congratulations on becoming head cook. Has Yang completely recovered from the accident? Why have you stopped sending letters together and why has the share of Yang's money been so drastically reduced?*

That last sentence started a headache. Lee suspected that was Yang's plan. Now Mother wanted him to sort it out. *We're too old for this.* Lee thought. *I do not need to babysit my older brother!*

He slipped Mother's letter into a pocket and turned his attention to the letter from his wife.

Her missive was filled with love and longing, remembrances she shared about their time together sharing a pillow.

Wèi An also wrote that their son was starting to walk, and he laughed at everything. He was the joy of the Gee household.

Lee held the fragile paper to his nose trying to smell her. He longed to run his hands over her soft skin and kiss her lips. He tried to see his son through her eyes. He re-read the letter by candlelight every night for weeks.

Her words left him feeling cold loneliness and simultaneously on fire with desire. It was an impossible situation that caused him to lash out at those closest to him. Namely, at Foshan.

Troubling also was Wèi An's note about his mother's behavior. At first, he'd shrugged it off. *At least they have enough to eat. My family will never know starvation again.*

The realization that he'd missed something came to him in the early hours of the morning during a lull between blasting. *Has an owl flown over my tent?* His mother had sent him a pair of chopsticks and wood splinters tied together with twine. He'd been too busy to wonder why she'd wasted money sending him something so ordinary.

Wèi An's comments came back to him. *Your mother's been making secretive visits to the village. I found out that she commissioned woodworkers to build a shipping box with an extra-strong bottom. Mother Gee says, 'bottom' so much that I wonder if her mind is slipping.*

Lee jolted up in bed. Who had he given the crate to? Had it already been taken apart and burned? Mother was clever, sending the wood shavings. Too clever!

Lighting a lantern, he donned layers of clothing. With stiff, cold fingers, he laced up his boots. He stopped in his kitchen, making a pretense of starting the cooking fires early, then he went back outside and crunched over frozen earth, visiting refuse piles and looking for the box from home.

When he found it, he breathed a sigh of relief. Hefting it, he noticed its weight was slightly heavier than expected. *How did I miss that?*

Hurrying back to the kitchen, he nodded to Foshan, who had arrived to start heating the huge vat for today's tea. Picking up a mallet and chisel he used for animal butchering, he pointedly ignored Foshan's questioning glance.

Back in his tent, Lee placed the box on his bed and put on his leather gloves. It made no noise when he jostled it. Setting his lantern down inside of it, he followed all the joints with his fingers and still discovered nothing out of the ordinary.

Perhaps I am mistaken? Removing the lantern, he turned it upside down, setting it on the rough wooden floor. Pressing the chisel's flat blade along a long seam, he hammered with the mallet. It was solidly constructed.

Repositioning the chisel, he whacked it again. A small crack appeared near a nail. Bracing the box next to his boots, he gave it another go. Another crack appeared.

This time, his neighbors started complaining, "Shut up! Stop making a racket!"

Ignoring them, he gave the box five more hard hits. When he saw earth spilling out of the hole, his heart fluttered. Kneeling beside it, he pulled the lantern in close. The morning light was almost bright enough to see without it, but Lee was so excited he didn't want to miss a thing.

Pulling off his gloves, he picked up a small dirt clod. With shaking hands, he brought it to his nose and inhaled. It still retained the loamy richness of the banks of the Shiqiao River. Tears gathered in his eyes. *Home, sweet home!*

He reverently scooped up the dirt, placing it in a wooden bowl. Returning to his task, he continued to crack apart the planks.

Lee was as excited about this mystery as he'd been as a boy when dressing in his finest, preparing to visit neighbors during the New Year celebration.

As he peeled away the wood, the soil continued to spill out. A small red cloth became visible. It was tied tightly into a tiny packet with the same twine that bound the chopsticks. Holding his breath, Lee tugged at the string. It was so tight he needed to pull at an end with his teeth. When it came loose, three brass rivets landed in his palm.

Smiling, he knew there was more to come. Setting them carefully on his small table, he returned to the box. Next came two pieces of wood, rounded and dark on one side, flat on the other, with holes drilled through. Lee was beginning to understand what his mother had in mind. Sitting back on his heels, he thought, *Oh, Mother please don't have done what I'm thinking!*

Fear began to replace excitement. The giving of a knife is taboo. To send one to your sojourning son is to risk losing all that is important to the family. It could—permanently—cut off the relationship! Lee knew how his mother thought; if she gave it to him in parts, it wouldn't hold "severing" energy.

The evil spirits will curse us! Why Mother? Why would you do this?

As he lifted the box, more earth spilled out and a metal blade flashed into view, its cloth wrapping having come partially undone. Hopping as if a rattlesnake had appeared, Lee jumped away.

"No!" His eyes grew wide. He couldn't catch his breath. "No! No! Foolish Hai!"

Acting quickly, he put on his gloves. He picked up the metal and wooden pieces and shoved them under his mattress. Collecting the rivets, he dropped them into the bowl of dirt and slid it roughly under his bed.

Stepping outside, he glanced in both directions, hoping no one had seen. Men were starting to rise; he didn't have much time! Hurrying to the refuse pile, he threw the remains of the crate away with all his might. It cracked again. He didn't notice that something else was poking out from the false bottom.

※

For three nights, Mother visited him in dreams. "Food is love," she said while reminding him how to cut paper-thin slices of meat. "Metal is stronger than wood." "A sharp knife is a cook's most important tool."

Mother-guilt finally won over piety, and the more he thought about it, the more he liked the idea of wielding a special chef's knife. Lee found a food box large enough to hide everything. He took it all over to blacksmith Baldy. Baldy has been in California a long time. What was unusual about the man was that he'd shaved the hair completely from his head.

Lee had asked him about this when he served him lunch.

"I don't plan to go back."

Lee leaned in and lowered his voice. "What about the Company men?"

"They can report it…but what are they going to do? The Emperor has no enforcers in this land. I'm not worried about losing my head over it." He chuckled.

"What about the gods? Are you worried about displeasing them?"

Baldy smiled and looked to either side of him. Raising his hands and shoulders he said, "They don't care. Look," he said. "I need the work. I don't need burns, which could stop the work. Eliminating a risk is the right decision for me."

Lee trusted Baldy. If anyone could help him with his knife dilemma, it was him.

When Lee placed the naked blade in Baldy's hands, he felt as if the man's gaze could drill holes through his head. Baldy rubbed a thumb over the hardened steel. "I know its maker," he said quietly. "The quality is among the best. But your mother…"

Lee dropped his eyes and nodded. "I know."

"If she was a man, I'd say she has steel balls."

Lee's cheeks burned. "No balls, Lotus feet."

Baldy nodded. "Strong women, the ones who endure." He regarded the items in the box. "You're asking if I can complete the knife without risking damage to your family?"

"Yes," Lee nodded, "that is what I am asking."

"Very well," Baldy frowned. "This is what must be done. Everything but the blade must be destroyed and multiple appeasements to the gods must be observed." Rattling the rivets in his hand, Baldy asked, "You're sure?"

"Shì de." Lee nodded.

Baldy turned and tossed them on the coals. They made a little hiss, like droplets of water in a hot wok, and disappeared.

"You must go into the woods to find a good hardwood—oak or madrone," he said. "Fashion it to fit your grip. Keep the shavings. Over at the mill, ask someone to make a clean cut down the center. Bring it here, so I can mark the places where the drill holes must be made. Once the holes are drilled, I'll make new rivets, attach the handle, and use the scrap wood to smoke evil spirits out from the blade."

"Got it."

"Right now," Baldy held out the wooden handle sections Mother had sent, "you must light incense at your altar and declare your intentions. Tell the gods this is part of your offering. Cut these into small pieces and add them to special fires and do a lot of kowtowing!"

"Thank you!" Lee exclaimed.

After Lee left, Baldy's shop assistant came around the corner from where he'd been eavesdropping. He folded his arms saying, "That doesn't sound like any ritual I've ever heard of."

Baldy sent him a wink. "He's a good kid. If he thinks it will work, it will."

News:

Sacramento Daily Union | October 21, 1865

The Tunnel Commenced. — S.S. Montague, Engineer of the Pacific Railroad, has just returned from the summit of the Sierras, which point he visited for the purpose of starting the work on the summit tunnel. This tunnel will be 1,750 feet, or about the third of a mile long, twenty-six feet wide and twenty feet high. The excavation will be sufficiently wide for a double track. The entire work runs through solid granite. It is expected that a year and a half will be required to complete it. The work was started by Montague at both ends. This tunnel is not level but descends to the east at the rate of ninety feet to the mile. The summit is about fifty miles east of Colfax. Thirteen miles of the road between Colfax and Dutch Flat will be graded by the first of January. It is expected that the summit will be reached before the tunnel is completed, and that a temporary track will be laid over it for the purpose of facilitating the work on the eastern slope.

[Grass Valley] ***Morning Union*** | February 1, 1866

A San Francisco telegram to the Bee says four hundred and sixty Chinese left for Hongkong a few days since, on the ship Terese, taking with them half a million dollars.

WOOD HUNTING
Winter
Alta Camp, California
1865
—

It was a clear day when Lee set out to search for the perfect piece of wood. The camp was quiet. Many of the workers on his thirty-man crew had been called down to Colfax to work on repairing a roadbed that had sunk under the tracks after the last bout of heavy rain.

When Yang was here last, they'd had a conversation about his brother's knowledge of events that were happening up and down the hill line. "Lee, Lee, Lee." Yang shook his head while laying a heavy hand on his shoulder. "You don't know?"

Whenever Yang started mimicking their father, Lee could almost guess what was coming.

"Look at this wagon road," Yang swept his hand on a horizontal line, "and tell me what you see."

Lee sighed. "Wagons, horses, people."

"That's all? Father wasn't wrong when he was trying to get you to pull your head out from your—peach."

Lee shrugged Yang's hand off.

"Let me tell you what I see. I see teamsters, and metal workers, and bosses, and line workers, and delivery men."

"So?"

"Every one of them is carrying information about their jobs, the people they work with, and where they just came from. But you'd have to talk to them to know that."

Lee quickly learned that Yang was right. This was how he found out that Yang's blaster crew had begun work at tunnel #6. He'd also learned that Yang had been reprimanded for inviting too many of his own men down for meals at Lee's table. It might explain why Lee hadn't seen him for some time. They still had not had the conversation about the money Mother was missing.

※

Lee was enjoying the muffled peacefulness of the forest, the pine smell crisp in the air, and the twinkle of sunlight reflected in droplets suspended from branch tips. If he looked closely at a drop, he could see an upside-down reflection in it. He laughed at the images of his finger, pinecones, and pebbles he created by bringing them near the looking-glass droplets.

He carried a basket with a saw and a digging tool. The saw was for the branch and the digging tool was in case he found mushrooms. It was on days like this when he didn't have to feed so many mouths and keep large quantities of tea brewing that he was able to experiment and expand his cooking skills.

He'd left Yow Foshan in charge of their kitchen and mess tent to serve whoever required it. Another bit of interesting news was that Foshan had been offered a head chef position at another camp. The man was certainly capable, but Lee would be sorry to see him go. They'd worked out an efficient rhythm between them that would be difficult to replace.

He noticed a large raven that appeared to be following him. It flew from tree to tree, watching and cocking its head. Every so often, it made a burbling sound. Lee tried not to worry about being spied on by a spirit inhabiting the bird. "*It is just an animal*," he said to himself.

The forest mushrooms were plentiful. It amazed him to find them pushing up through the soil, creating gopher-like mounds. Their caps protected gills as they emerged into the open air from beneath leaf litter, camouflaged to mimic decaying redbud leaves, small white stones, or golden clumps as large as pie plates. He uttered thanks with each cluster found. Of course, not every mushroom made it into Lee's basket. Only those he knew for certain were safe to eat would he serve to his men.

His basket was almost full, and he had just finished sawing a small branch with a length of wood that fit his hand as if it were made for him. He was tying up the cloth he'd laid down to capture the sawdust when he heard someone walking. Standing up, he looked in the direction from which the sound had come.

"There you are!" a relieved voice called out.

Lee relaxed. "Foshan, what are you doing out here?"

"I needed to see you," he said, glancing down into the basket. "Mmmmm, Chanterelles. Nice!"

"Yes," Lee smiled, "and look at this!" He held up the wood section for the knife handle, showing Foshan the indentations that fit his fingers.

Foshan nodded. His eyes began to dart, and his smile looked more like a grimace. "I…ah…" he started.

"I think I know," Lee said. His previous enthusiasm drained away. "It's about your new job."

Foshan's eyes flew to meet Lee's. They lingered there, then moved to his hair, to his lips, then to his chest.

Lee could see warmth infusing his friend's face as his skin changed color. Something about the intense regard made him feel as if he were returning that gaze through a raindrop.

Foshan was about four inches taller than Lee and slightly heavier. His queue was thick, and his skin was clear. He wasn't classically handsome, but nice looking. Lee knew he was not married. He would make a good husband and father one day.

As intensely charged as that moment became, Foshan changed it abruptly. His eyes narrowed, zeroing in on something beyond Lee's shoulder. "Morels!" he pointed. Side-stepping Lee, he took long strides toward the treasure.

Lee shook himself and hurried to pick up his basket. Squatting beside Foshan, he said, "There's not much room left."

"It doesn't matter," Foshan enthused. He placed a few in the pile with the others then pulled out his shirt to cradle the excess. "These are so fresh." He brought one to his nose and inhaled. Leaning over so his shoulder touched Lee's, he held it so Lee could catch the scent too. "Doesn't it make your mouth water just imaging how they'll taste?"

Inhaling slowly, Lee nodded as he gulped saliva that began filling his mouth. He held his breath and watched Foshan glide a gentle finger along the lacy gills, tracing the trilateral shape of the head.

"They'd be good if we dried them," Foshan said, "but it can't compare to right-from-the-ground sweet and soft." Foshan adjusted his arm, so it contacted Lee's from shoulder to elbow.

The man radiated heat as if he were enflamed embers. Lee swallowed again, not sure what to do.

Common Raven,
Corvus corax

FEET & WINGS: Flutter, hopping from branch to branch, the raven follows the man carrying a basket.

I recognize his face; he is a frequent visitor in my forest.
He forages for plants and small animals. I know his shelter.

She also watched for his proximity to the smoking firepit.

When he is here, he tosses pieces of fat.
Humans who feed me are endearing pets!

WINGS: Launching into the blue, above the treetops, she circled, watching.

Something about the other human makes him move in unusual ways.
Is he mate-displaying?
If they have chicks, maybe they will teach them to Raven feed!

That night, Lee served a delicate shrimp and coconut dish featuring fresh mushrooms. Mother had known how many men he had to feed. She'd included a note in her package. *Remember Auntie Liu's soup from your wedding? Make that for them.* He'd used the dried shrimp and spices she'd sent and found the rest of what he needed in his supplies and in the forest. The results were astonishing.

The scent and flavors created a pleasant tug on his heart and a hollow ache in his loins.

In the kitchen, Foshan behaved as he always had—chopping, washing, wiping up, and cracking jokes with their patrons. Lee began to question if he'd imagined their earlier encounter.

Back at his tent and settling in for the night, Lee was restless. He frequently glanced at the empty cot where Yang had slept. No one had come to take it away and Lee hadn't offered it up. He stretched out on his bed, reaching under it to touch the tin, but didn't open it. He tossed and turned a long time before sleep came. When it did, his dreams took him to shadowy, wet places that both aroused and terrified him.

PRIVATE ENTERPRISE
Winter
Dutch Flat, California
1865
—

Rip and Manly accepted Yeehaw and Charming Chalie into their cohort. When they left tunnel #6, Charlie suggested they spend time at Dutch Flat. Yang had money saved. He'd set some aside for Mother, but he didn't feel guilty about spending it on pleasures. When one lived on the edge, delights were a necessity. Since he could no longer treat his friends to free food at Lee's, he figured, *why not?*

He and Rip invested in a box of dominoes. "I studied the game runners on the ship," Yang said. "We need someone who is good at distracting the audience. I'll be the dealer. I know how to keep the house winning. We can make some good money!"

Their first stop in Dutch Flat was the Chinese brothel. It was Yang's initiation to such an establishment. The girls were unlike any he'd ever encountered. He remembered the group they'd seen when they first arrived in San Francisco. Those looked like frightened rabbits. These were sleek foxes, aggressive, cunning, and bold. *All of these women want me!* His lips expanded into a slow grin.

The madam, a tall busty woman, came to his rescue. "Off with you!" she scolded. "He's mine, first." The girls scattered. She smiled as she placed a hand on his chest, leaning so close he could smell the peppermint on her breath. "My name's Lizzie. You ever lie down with a white woman?"

"No, ma'am," Yang said.

"Ma'am!" Lizzie belly laughed. "You'll soon see I'm no lady." She slid her hand down his body, then laced her fingers through his. "There's a premium for me; you got enough money?"

Her caress sent sparks shooting off everywhere her fingers touched. Yang wasn't completely sure what she was saying, but he knew enough. "Hoo-ow m-much?" he said, drawing the words out, enunciating with care.

She whispered in his ear. The amount was in gold, he knew. At her raised eyebrows, he nodded. She tugged him into a bedroom. Pushing him to sit on the bed, Lizzie began showing him things. She was a large-busted goddess with nipples the size of medallions. Her movements hypnotized him. Her bottom and thighs were luscious and curvy. He yearned to run his hands over every surface, but he kept them at his sides, unsure if it was allowed.

Noticing this, Lizzie paused. Taking a step back, she placed an index finger over her lips as if she would shush him. Opening her mouth, she pressed her tongue against the finger. Yang's gaze locked on as if it were magnetized. She opened her mouth further so her finger could go in up to the first knuckle. As she did so, her eyes lowered and followed the length of his erection like a touch, making it waver.

Lizzie's eyes narrowed with her smile as she leaned in, running her wet finger along his length from base to head. Yang's back arched with surprise and pleasure. A sound, like one would make when handling hot coals, erupted from him.

"Honey," she said, nuzzling his neck, "you're free to do anything you want."

Yang was agog, he wanted to dive in and locomote in her ocean. Guiding his hands and placing them on her hips, she showed him what she meant. After a raucous learning session, he lay against the headboard wearing a goofy grin.

Lizzie asked, "Are you done in, or do you have anything left in you, Manly Blaster?"

"Yes," Yang responded.

Wrapping a sheet around her, she went to the door, opened it, and called, "Lin Fee!"

To Yang's astonishment, another beautiful woman entered. At something Lizzie said, she dropped her wrap and peeled away her silky negligee. Naked, she stood there with her chin held high and her eyes blazing. Lizzie dropped her sheet, approached Lin Fee, and started making love to her.

"What!" Yang laughed, leaning forward. It wasn't long before the three of them became a warm, writhing octopus-like animal on the bed.

When there was time for talking, Yang asked Fee if she'd help negotiate a deal with Lizzie. She agreed to translate. He quickly understood that she inserted more into the dialogue than he spoke. Lizzie agreed to let Yang and Rip Snorter run dice games several days a week in a corner of their parlor for a cut of the profits. If her husband, the saloon keeper, became upset with the arrangement, Lizzie agreed to intervene before Manly or Rip got shot.

Lizzie also wanted Yang as an exclusive lover. Lin Fee pouted at this negotiation point. "Don't worry, honey," Lizzie said, "you'll get your share."

Yang would pay a room fee. Once Lizzie gave the all-clear for the other girls, sex with him would be a side benefit to all willing parties.

"One last thing, Manly," Fee said as her eyes darted to Lizzie and back. "People here do not like Asian men going with white women. They'll murder you if they find out you were sticking it to that cow."

This was sobering, but the inherent danger made Yang feel more alive than he had since first setting foot on this foreign land.

VOLATILITY
Spring
Dutch Flat, California
1866
—

In Dutch Flat, sizable multi-racial communities lived alongside each other. Tempers could explode like dry barrels of black powder. A group called America for Americans took umbrage at any slight provocation.

While Yang congratulated himself on his good fortune, Rip, Yeehaw, and Charming Chalie found lodging at the Joss House.

Yang assumed that staying at the brothel might be like being home. The household would run efficiently, and the women would always think first of—and cater to—the men. Plus, sharing a pillow with Lizzie would give him a lifetime of bragging rights.

A peak behind the "shop curtain" revealed how far his fantasy was from reality. The women slept late and were slovenly until right before the doors opened for customers. New girls cooked and cleaned until they advanced to work on their backs and between their legs.

Lizzie fought against religious leaders who wanted her establishment gone, greedy landlords, and proper wives who slandered her behind her back. She kept a notebook of dirty secrets and proclivities to keep her clients, with certain reputations to protect, in line.

It was on the second night that Rip Snorter set up his domino game that Lizzie's world crumbled. When it did, it went down fast. It never registered with the common folk of Dutch Flat that a regime change had occurred.

Not long after the brothel opened, Randy, Lizzie's husband, flung open the front door with such force it ricocheted off the wall. His eyes were bloodshot, and his step wavered. He carried a loaded pistol with his finger resting on the trigger. Charming Charlie and Yeehaw had just started a game with Rip Snorter and two new fellows from the Joss House. Lizzie nestled on Manly's lap while Lin Fee sat next to them, filing a fingernail.

"I heard my woman was cavorting with a Celestial!" Randy shouted.

Lizzie sprang out of her seat as if a roasting-ready branding iron had prodded her. "Now, now, Snookum." She walked straight toward Randy, deftly placing her hand on the gun barrel, redirecting its aim to the floor. As she did, she cast a warning glance in Fee's direction. "You're a little drunk," she said, petting Randy's chest, "and you know what we do here. It's all for show. There's no one but you."

Yang stood immediately after Lizzie; fear sent a cold wave coursing through his midsection. The armed man blocked the exit. He shared a panic-stricken look with the domino players. Fee skirted the room and whispered to a kitchen girl, who turned and ran.

"That may be," Randy seemed to settle. Then he puffed up again and screamed, "But that ain't!" His gun came up and aimed at the players. "We had an agreement, Liz, no side hustles!"

The room exploded to a boil. Bodies scrambled and collided. A shot was fired. Yang felt a blinding pain in his foot and slumped forward. He could hear yelling and see feet shuffling. Yeehaw carried Yang over his shoulder like a flour sack.

Yang could see Rip and Charlie trotting alongside them. When he raised his head, he saw three Chinese men hustling to load the house girls into a waiting wagon.

At the Joss House, there was only enough time to hastily bandage Yang's wound. The manager moved efficiently but scowled and ground his teeth, "You have to leave. No time to waste. I don't want your kind of trouble in this place."

Almost as if by divine timing, a mule packer arrived. From the back door, the blasters loaded up and moved into the forest on a deer trail. It was almost too dark to see. The animal handler walked with the lead mule and insisted on maintaining complete silence.

※

After some time passed, they stopped in a clearing. A full moon hung low in the sky while flossy clouds drifted across its face. Tall pine trees made a whooshing sound while raining down dry needles. The blasters hugged themselves tightly and shivered.

"My name's Tom," the driver commented to no one in particular. "If you have to talk, keep it low. I prefer it if you speak as little as possible." Unlike the others, Tom wore a coat, hat, and scarf, but he stomped his feet as if they were cold. "I will build a small fire over there." He pointed. "You'd do well to gather leaves and brush to crawl under. It's warmer that way." He hobbled the mules before moving to search for firewood. Tom constructed his wood stack with care, clearing needles and leaves away from the ember zone. As he squatted to light the kindling, the others could see his rugged features. There were scars across his brow and on his chin. In the tie holding the end of his queue were bird feathers.

Yang missed out on these observations. His brain felt like it was scrambled with cotton. The waistband of his pants had grown tight, and he shuddered.

"We leave before first light," Tom said as he stood with his back to the crackling fire. He left briefly to do something with the mules. When he returned, he carried a canteen. Handing it to Charlie, he said, "Take turns making him drink. Try to get some sleep."

He left them alone to crawl under their brush mounds and wonder if Manly would die.

"Where do you think he's taking us?" Charlie whispered.

"When we fall asleep, I think Tom is going to take the mules and leave us here," Yeehaw said.

"No—" Charlie replied, "if they were going to do that, they could have killed us back in town."

"Then why is Tom not sleeping near the fire?" asked Yeehaw.

No one had an answer.

"We could ask him to take us to Nevada City," Charlie suggested.

Rip Snorter had taken the canteen and moved over to Manly. He supported his neck as he dribbled water into his mouth. Snort was thinking Manly's eyes were going glassy. He was feverish. These were not good signs. It startled him when Yang roused enough to say, "Alta Camp. My brother is there."

※

Lee fought against the shaking that was insisting on taking him out of his resplendent dream.

"Mr. Gee!" Rip Snorter growled next to his ear. "It's Man...Yang. He's got a bullet in him."

Lee sat up, rumpled and groggy. Rip held open the tent flap and whispered to someone outside. "Bring him in. There's a cot there."

Standing, Lee grabbed Rip's arm. "What happened?"

"Doesn't matter," he said, shrugging him off. "He took a bullet in the foot. He's running a fever."

"How long?"

"Last night."

Lee put a flame to the lantern wick as the men shuffled inside. He pulled on a flannel shirt over his long underwear. As the two men carrying Yang set him down and then stood up, Lee took inventory of them. "You all look ragged, but first things first." As he leaned over to lay his hand on Yang's forehead, he called out a directive, "Snort, get Foshan."

"I don't know this camp layout."

"Wáng bā dàn!" Lee exclaimed. "Straight across, two to the right." Lee poured water onto a cloth and placed it over Yang's face. "You two," he directed, "help me get him out of these filthy clothes."

Foshan arrived with his tent mate, Jung Foo, another assistant cook. While Foshan seamlessly traded places with Yeehaw and Charlie, he said to Foo, "Bring the doctor, then feed these men. Heat bath water. After they've bathed, send them to sleep in your tent."

Seeing the terrible state Yang was in, Lee felt jiggly. Foshan's calm presence steadied his nerves. They'd taken his pants off and were removing the bandaging when the doctor entered through the tent flap. "It's putrid," he said.

"We knew that from the smell," Lee snapped.

"Let me see," said the doctor, taking command. He dragged a stool over to the end of the bed and draped an apron over his head. "I'll need better light." He nodded to the lantern. "And a bowl. Foshan, open my bag and lay out the knives."

Foshan gave Lee a nudge toward the exit. "It might be best if you wait outside."

Once he was through the flap, Foshan turned back inside to grab Lee's pants, boots, and coat. Shoving them into Lee's arms, he said, "Go make tea." As he turned to go, Foshan stalled him with a hand on his shoulder. "Doctor knows what he's doing, Yang will be alright."

Lee nodded vacantly. He knew there could be no certainty in a statement like that, but it was good to hear. He turned to walk toward the familiar.

※

It had been an exhausting week and a half since Yang had been shot. His fever had raged for the better part of the week, which caused feelings of despair in Lee. Thanks to Foshan, he'd been able to spend all his time nursing his brother. As the first snows set in, Lee was laundering sheets and hanging Yang's long underwear out to dry.

Foshan filled in as head cook in Lee's kitchen, and Foo became his assistant.

When Yang started asking for food and cracking sarcastic jokes, Lee knew he was going to be alright.

Lee's longing to go home had reached a new level that was painful and prickly all the time. Perhaps it was being away from the kitchen, or thinking about telling Mother that Yang had died, or that they'd recently paid off their travel debt, but Lee was ready to go—right now.

When he mentioned this to Yang, the response was a swift and definitive, "No."

"What do you mean, no?" Lee sputtered.

"I'm not ready to leave, and you can't go without me."

In consternation, Lee propped his fists on his hips. "Actually, I could," he declared.

Yang, who'd been lounging on his cot laying out cards for solitaire, raised his eyes and smiled. "That's cute, but you don't mean it. How would it go, explaining that to our parents?" He rolled his eyes, "and to Ting Ai." He chuckled. "She'd probably drop everything to come fetch me. How embarrassing!"

Pacing and holding his head, Lee whined, "I don't understand. Why do you want to stay?"

A mood came over Yang that bunched up Lee's skin like an underwear wedgie. "It's that tunnel," he said in a strange voice. "Lucky number six. She spoke to me when I was in there. I will return in the spring, and I must be there when she sucks in the mountain air from the other side." Yang blinked slowly. Whatever had possessed him had gone. With a soft laugh, he flashed his brother a six of clubs and said, "That's when we can go home, Lee, not before."

SHAVE
Alta Camp, California
1866
—

Lee wasn't sure if he wanted to laugh, cry, or rage. He stomped out of their tent, going straight to the altar to pray. After a long walk, he ended up at his kitchen. Foo was gone and Foshan was working on final cleaning. The linemen were laughing and telling stories around the campfire.

Foshan filled a cup of tea and set it near Lee's elbow as he sat at their serving counter. "Tell me," he said, "I can see you've got something simmering."

Lee hesitated. He wasn't sure he should tell Foshan he was thinking about leaving. Shrugging his shoulders, he let it rip. "I'm tired, Foshan. Being away from my family feels like I'm missing limbs," he sighed. "I just told Yang that I want us to go home."

Foshan staggered slightly as if he'd been struck. Recovering quickly, he folded his arms and took a wide stance. "I see," he said tightly.

Taking a sip of tea, Lee let his eyes roam over the man. *Have his shoulders gotten wider?* "We're not going," he continued. "Yang said we can't go until Six is finished."

"I see," Foshan repeated. This time his voice sounded softer.

Just then, the men at the fire quieted. A new arrival had come with an erhu. As the first strains of its sweetly haunting sound drifted over to them, Lee felt as if he'd been shot, straight in the heart. He placed one hand on the counter and clutched his chest while lowering his face and doing everything possible to keep from cracking open.

Watching that anguish damaged something inside Foshan. It hurt to fight against the urge to soothe. Instead, he leaned his elbows on the counter, near Lee's hand. While their heads were close, Foshan spoke softly, confident that his voice would not carry. "Look Lee, you've been working long hours taking care of your brother. I know you miss your wife, children, and parents. You probably haven't gotten enough sleep and you're frustrated." He smiled a little as he saw Lee nod. Glancing behind him he said, "I've got enough hot water left for a shampoo and a shave. How about we get you cleaned up? It might help you sleep."

Raising his face, Lee rubbed his head. Nubs of hair bristled where it should be smooth. His chin felt scratchy. For a dismayed moment, he looked startled that he'd let himself go. He glanced over at the steaming water and imagined how nice it would be to say yes. Taking in a long breath, he let it out. "OK," he said. "That would be nice."

Foshan fastened up the mess tent for the night so they wouldn't be disturbed and brought the hot water and towels over to the bench seat. He had Lee lean back on his elbows.

As Foshan draped the first warm towel over his face, winding it around to leave a hole for his nose, Lee let out a thankful sigh. Still hearing the erhu, he pictured Wèi An on that last night. He made love to her with ferocity, and he was convinced that her song was responsible for the conception of their son. Breathing steadily to keep from constricting into a miserable ball, he let tears flow unchecked into the towel.

Straddling the bench behind Lee, Foshan began loosening his long hair, running his fingers through to release tangles. As he knew it would, his erection lifted the fabric of his apron. He poured warm water over Lee's head and began a soapy massage, spending time at the pressure points to release accumulated tension. Foshan allowed himself to feel the joy of giving and touching and being in this moment with someone so dear, even if this was all that ever transpired between them.

At this point, Lee's tears had stopped. He reclined in silence, an empty vessel, receptive to the warm water and the ministration of kind hands. He may have fallen asleep.

From behind, Foshan replaced the face towel with a fresh warm one and began rinsing Lee's hair. Another sigh of contentment from him made Foshan smile. When Lee's hair was clean and towel dried, Foshan replaced another face towel and began mixing shaving cream for the Manchu-style head shave. Spreading the slick, smooth soap on Lee's scalp felt like a mixture of delight and anguish. He spoke for the first time. "The blade is in my hand and I'm ready to cut. Hold still."

"Mmmmmm hmmmm."

Foshan made efficient work of scraping and cleaning the razor edge on a cloth, holding Lee's head steady as he did so. His final step was wiping the shave tracks with a discarded face towel.

"Looks good. Straight lines," Foshan commented as he mixed another batch of shaving cream. The brush handle clinked against the bowl cupped in his hand.

"No doubt," Lee's response was muffled.

They adjusted Lee's seating position so his back rested against the table. Foshan came round front and took a deep breath. His erection had been firm the entire time but now, knowing Lee would see it, it tightened and enflamed like a fervid coal receiving a burst of fresh air.

Pulling the towel away, Foshan stood erect and honest, letting the passion in his heart shine through his eyes.

Lee knew this moment was coming. He held the anxiety surrounding it at bay as he relaxed into the treatment. Barely cracking his eyes, he gazed at Foshan through clouded vision. A twitch between his legs astonished him. He was not repulsed by it or by the sight of Foshan's boldness. His mouth watered as sensory images flooded his mind. Foshan with his shirt off, sweat glistened as he bent over a wash tub. The curve of his lips. The shape of his collarbone. *What does his skin feel like? How does he smell?* Remaining still, he opened his eyes completely and cleared his throat. Lee said, "You are splendid, Foshan."

Receiving this like a gift, Foshan blinked and whispered, "Xièxiè." Taking a slight step back, he raised the bowl along with his eyebrows. At Lee's nod, Foshan began swirling the soft brush over the planes of his jaw.

Although the nervous tension had faded, Lee's heart was beating fast. His nostrils flared. Shutting his eyes, he raised his chin as blade met skin. For a moment, he pictured Humbug rolling on his back, exposing vital organs to trusted friends who were likely to give belly rubs. It was over all too soon, and Foshan was running the clean-up towel over his face.

Lee let out a groan as he got to his feet. Foshan gave him more space. They maintained eye contact as Lee unbuttoned his shirt. He hoped his long underwear wasn't stained. Slowly, he draped the shirt over his arm and held it in front of him to hide his arousal.

Foshan's glance dropped, following the motion. The corners of his mouth twitched up.

"Do you want help straightening up?" Lee asked.

Stifling a laugh, Foshan shook his head. His voice sounded froggy when he replied, "No. Sleep well."

Making a formal bow, Lee said, "I will. Thank you."

THE BUILDER
February
Dutch Flat & Nevada City, California
1866
—

As soon as he was ambulatory, Yang began making shelves, small tables, and stools from salvaged wood in the camp refuse pile. He bartered some of his pieces, but what he really needed was money.

Wood Mouse,
Apodemys sylvaticus

Material above her clattered and shifted.
Light shown through where it was dark before.

She'd lost the dwelling inherited from her mother when the trees left.

WHISKERS: Raised, sensing the edges of her hiding space.

She was a new builder, figuring it out as instinct prodded.

Another seismic pile shift.

FEET: Scurrying out from under.

EYES: From a safe distance, she watched the giant two-leg remove pieces of her home.

"I've been robbed," Yang said to Lee. "I only have five dollars to send to Mother."

Lee was irate. "How can that be? Who would dare trespass on a blaster? Did you report it? Mother needs the money. Haven't you been reading her letters?"

Frowning, Yang wouldn't meet Lee's eyes. His brother made him feel small. Crossing his arms over his chest, he huffed, hoping the scolding would be over soon and that no one he cared about was listening. He also hated the scorn he felt for himself when he recognized part of what Lee was saying was correct.

Lee stopped. *Are those my words mine or Mother's?* Since he had been spending time with the other camp cooks and their assistants, he'd started noticing different communication styles. Foshan—though he might not realize he was teaching—had been pointing out better ways for delivering orders. Lee changed the conversation so abruptly it took Yang a moment to catch up.

"We should leave the camp for a while. We could go to Dutch Flat and stay through the New Year," he said, referring to the February celebration.

Shaking his head, Yang tried to clear his thoughts.

"The doctor says you should be walking," Lee continued. "Why don't we walk over there to see if there are places we could stay? Plus, you've filled my tent and Foshan's with furniture. We could ask about reserving a place on the parade route to sell them."

"Really?" Yang sat up straighter.

※

Lee carried the package he had for shipping. He'd convinced Yang to at least scribble his name at the bottom of his letter for Mother. "They've been asking if you're alright," Lee mumbled as he folded the paper and tied it securely.

"I'll make it up to them next month," Yang grumbled.

As they walked, they stayed clear of the road. It had become a quagmire of clingy mud that even the mules didn't want to traverse.

Yang was worried about showing his face in Dutch Flat. He'd never told Lee details about the night he was shot. The Joss House manager might recognize him, but it was unlikely that anyone else in the Chinese community would.

As they came into Dutch Flat, they saw a full Chinese funeral procession making its way down the main street. The mourners wore white, which meant the deceased was young. As they walked, before and behind the horse-drawn wagon carrying the body inside a plain pine box, they clashed symbols, rang bells, and beat on drums. Knowing that the commotion would drive away evil spirits was comforting to the Gee brothers.

Scattered among the assemblage were Chinese women. The site of them was a rarity. Their lard-slicked hair glinted in the sunlight. They wore traditional clothing and comported themselves with solemn dignity befitting their station and the occasion. They carried familiar food dishes that the brothers could smell. Their mouths watered. The food would be arranged around the gravesite. These were ancestor offerings.

A strange sight was several white boys following in the group's wake, as if they were part of the procedure.

While it was a relief to be in an established town with permanent buildings that housed banking, laundry, livery, and marketing activities, they couldn't help but notice the unwelcoming behavior of the townsfolk. They stood on the wooden walkways, watching the funeral with mean expressions. Most surprising was the sight of an unkempt woman trotting on unsteady feet, trailing after the schoolboys. She was yelling and waving a fist in the air.

When Yang saw her, he frowned and leaned forward, as if attempting to get a closer look. Immediately he turned in the opposite direction, appearing to take great interest in window shopping.

The apothecary smelled like Chinese herb shops everywhere. Invigorating hints of clove and orange peel mingled with traces of dust along with the robust scents of cinnamon, sandalwood, and camphor, ingredients commonly found in incense.

"Who died? Why are those kids there?" Yang asked the man behind the counter. He referenced the group with his thumb, pointing back over his shoulder.

"Mrs. Hoy, wife of the soap root mattress maker. The boys are curious, I suspect," replied the bespectacled older fellow. "When the mourners have gone, they'll be eating the offerings."

Yang and Lee made a face.

As Lee handed over their bundled package containing money and letters for the family, he asked, "And the woman in the street?"

Accepting it, the merchant placed it on a scale. Expertly, he chose three weights for the opposite plate. When the weights were equal and the indicator came to a rest, he began sliding abacus beads along wires to calculate the cost. "She's a hundred man's wife." He glanced at them over the top of his glasses. "She's parroting what her customers say."

"And what is that?" Yang asked.

"That the Chinese are taking the jobs that should go to white men and that the capitalist Crocker is making it worse by having them shipped in from China."

Lee's worried eyes locked with the merchant. "Do they all think this way?"

"Not all of them, but enough…They call themselves America for Americans. I have a Chinese newspaper from San Francisco if you want to follow the developments."

Yang shook his head. "No thanks, my brother already takes it. We're good."

※

On their way back to camp, Lee and Yang reconsidered spending any more time in Dutch Flat.

"If we are going to travel, we should go somewhere we haven't been." Yang brightened, tapping Lee's arm with the back of his hand. "I hear Nevada City has a cooking contest with cash prizes. You could win!"

He nodded thoughtfully. "The cooks have been talking about it."

"It's settled then!" Yang enthused. "When do we leave?"

"Let's go next week."

News:
Morning Union | January 7, 1866
...the President of the Company [Leland Stanford] proceeds to offer an excuse for the employment of Chinese to the almost entire exclusion of white men..." The greater portion of the laborers employed by us are Chinese, who constitute a large element in the population of California. Without them, it would be impossible to complete the western portion [of] this great national enterprise, within the time required by the Acts of Congress."

CHINESE NEW YEAR
February
Nevada City, California
1866
—

In the week it had taken to prepare for their adventure, things had gotten complicated. Yang's friends wanted to go, and he invited Scarred Eye. Foshan, Foo, and his boss, Won Shuck, were going. Rather than taking the stagecoach, as Lee had imagined, they'd pooled their resources to hire a teamster to transport them and their gear.

※

The night before their departure, Baldy showed up at Lee's mess tent. He reverently carried the original box Lee had brought with him in both hands.

"It is finished," Lee said under his breath.

Baldy nodded and with great care, set the box on the counter, bowed, and slid it across to Lee. As tradition dictated, Lee fished in his pocket for a coin. He set one on the counter, bowed, and slid it to Baldy.

Foshan, Won Shuck, and several late-evening patrons gathered around to watch. Yang must have heard what was happening. He quietly slipped in to join the others.

Lee carefully opened the box. Resting inside was a glorious tool. It was a work of fine craftsmanship. Glints of lantern light reflected off the metal surface.

"It's a five-pin construction," Baldy explained. "Durable. Very strong."

The weight and the fit in Lee's hand were perfection. Made of madrone, the wood felt warm. The finish brought out the red tones. When Lee turned it over, he noticed something unusual, a thin yellow line between the handle pieces. He ran a finger over it.

Coughing into his hand, Baldy glanced at the onlookers. "It's gold," he said.

The audience exclaimed, "Ahhh!"

His face flushed. "It is an illusion. Looks like a lot more than it is."

Lee's expression turned from relaxed and smiling to wide-eyed and distressed. He laid it down in the box and slid it back. "I cannot afford this with such a precious metal."

Baldy shook his head. "No, no. Our agreed-upon price has not changed. These," he waved a hand over the box, "flourishes are my own contributions. A gift. At your table, I remember my aunties and my sister. Your meals bring back loved ones I may never see again. I had to make it exceptional—for them. Don't you see?"

Lee raised sad eyes to Baldy and moved from person to person around the circle. Yang stepped forward, laying a hand at the back of Lee's neck. "This chef knife must belong to you. It would not accomplish greatness under any hand but yours, brother."

Nodding, Baldy took a handkerchief from his pocket. He wiped at the perspiration on his forehead, dabbed at his eyes, and then blew his nose.

Inflating his chest, Lee picked up the knife, laying it flat across all of his fingers. He bowed formally to Baldy, saying, "I thank you. I will use it to prepare many more meals you will enjoy."

The small group clapped their approval. Foshan added, "You can use it to win the contest!"

"We shall see," Cook Shuck said.

※

When they were getting ready for bed, Lee pulled back his top cover and saw a belt. "What's this?" he asked.

Yang flashed a wide grin. "It's for your new knife and other chef-related things." He lifted it and showed Lee a snap pouch on one side and a sheath on the other, complete with a security strap for holding the handle secure."

"When? How—?" Lee started saying.

Rolling his eyes, Yang waved the questions away. "You're going to have to sleep with that thing when we're in Nevada City."

Lee nodded as he slid the knife into the tight leather casing.

Yang stood close, watching. Their shoulders touched. Feeling sentimental, he commented, "The cutting blade is metal, like Mother's personality—sharp, strong, and focused on accomplishment. Wood is for the East and the Azure Dragon. Gold is for the West and gathering your power inward. You must never lose it—" Yangs' eyebrows raised as he leaned back to face his brother. "Sautee Sam!"

Tossing the belt to the bed, Lee went after Yang. "No! No nicknames."

"Too late." Yang laughed, fending off the play slaps. "First Brother has awarded it. It's going to stick."

※

As the teamster approached their meeting place, Lee noticed he was developing a new habit. He wore the knife belt under his loose shirt. Every few minutes, he patted the area to verify the knife was in place. He spotted a familiar face undulating with mules. Grinning, he hurried forward. "Jumpin, is that you?"

She twiddled her ears and looked as if she were smiling. Jumpin was second in line on a string of six.

Lee waited for the teamster to stop before he got closer to greet her properly. "Oh, look at you," he cooed while scratching between her eyes. "You've got a new job and friends to do it with. You must be so pleased. I hope your handler is treating you well."

"Is that animal talking to you?" the mule man asked as he shuffled a toothpick from one corner of his mouth to the other.

"In her own fashion," Lee replied, smiling. He patted her flank as he continued. "We were on a grading team together near Newcastle."

"Ayuh," the man responded. "I wondered if she was talking because she told me her name is Jane."

"Jane!" Lee laughed as he bent down to give her a closer look. He could have sworn she winked.

Mr. Strobridge came striding down the middle of the street. His clothing and eye patch were slightly askew as if he'd dressed in a hurry. He pulled a young girl along with him, who appeared to be about eight or nine. Clearly, he was making a direct path to the traveling party, and he looked anything but happy.

"Jiānchí zhù! Nǐ juédé nǐ yào qù nǎlǐ?" he hollered, botching it so badly the men tried not to laugh.

Spotting Scarred Eye, Strobridge switched to English, all the while waving his arms and growing red, like a summer cherry. The men continued loading the wagon as Scarred Eye sorted it out.

Lee was searching through his special food supplies for something to give Jumpin when Foshan approached.

"The boss isn't happy we are leaving," he commented.

Lee pulled back, sending him a frown, "You understand English?"

"Of course," Foshan replied. "I attended a Christian missionary school."

"What's he saying now?" Lee asked as he pulled out a small apple.

"He's complaining about labor shortages up and down the line. We're not the only ones leaving for New Year's." Foshan glanced at the fruit. "You're not planning to give that to the mule?"

"I am. Why?"

"Hang on," he said, rooting around in his own supplies. He brought out carrots that he began snapping into smaller pieces. "They're a team. You can't give something to one and not the others."

※

The hour-long drive to Nevada City was pleasant as the team wound down the canyon, over the Bear River bridge, and up the other side. They only had to stop once to help push the wagon out from a mud bog.

Lee and Foshan sat with the mule driver. They challenged each other to remember the words of songs they knew. Sometimes the men from the back would join in and other times they'd be off in their own conversations. Lee noticed that Scarred Eye was relaxing after the dressing-down he'd gotten from Strobridge.

Last year, Lee might have been worried about one of the big bosses flying off the handle that way. By now, he had confidence in the Six Companies and their labor negotiation skills. He'd also read about the court cases that were going before magistrates as their representatives fought for equity. The white men struggling to form labor unions could learn much from the Six Companies if only they knew how to listen.

※

The freight wagon muleskinner was familiar with Nevada City and the preparations that were being made for the upcoming celebrations. "You can check with the Joss House to see if there are beds. All the Chinese livery stables are ready for visitors. They've got fresh straw in their lofts and are charging reasonable rates."

"What about my merchandise?" Yang called out from the back. "Where should I try to sell it?"

Din laughed. "Depending on your prices, you will probably sell out on the first day. Take everything to my stable, which is in the center of town. Ah Tow might even trade with you for lodging."

"All right!" Yang laughed. "I know where I'm going."

They all ended up taking loft space at the livery. Yang traded several of his furniture pieces for reduced rates for the group. Ah Tow suggested he set out his wares the following morning right outside the stable doors. He also pointed out places where they could take their meals. Scarred Eye, Yang, and the blasters ate at the cheapest place.

When their bellies were full, Scarred Eye took his leave, mentioning something about sluice work down on Deer Creek.

"Let's find a game—" Yeehaw started, "at the brothel?"

"Uh—yes!" said Rip Snorter.

Yang couldn't let his friends go without him.

※

The railroad cooks sat together at a table in the back, where they enjoyed each course of their meal. With the Wonton Soup, they critiqued the saltiness levels and discussed the balance between the chicken livers and mushrooms, along with the Chinese mustard garnish on top. They splurged by ordering Leong Bon Faw Opp Peen, lychee pineapple roast duck. No one said words about this dish beyond "Yum!"

When their Chow Dow Don, eggs with garden peas arrived, Lee got a good look in the kitchen. He saw what was making the constant knocking sound he'd been hearing. It was knife work on butcher blocks, incredibly fast, cutting along with intervals where the cooks twirled their blades. "Did you see that?" he pointed out with excitement.

Won Shuck smiled. "It takes a long time to learn."

"I want to do that," Lee said quietly as he returned to a proper sitting position and looked down at his hands.

"I know some of those moves," Shuck said. "I will teach you when we are back and camp if you like."

"I would," Lee smiled. "Thank you."

They were sipping tea and nibbling on Hung Ngon Beang, almond cookies, when a commotion from the kitchen attracted their attention. Someone had arrived that everyone was happy to see. Not too long after that, a man burst through the kitchen doors, heading for their table. "I heard my railroaders are here!"

Greeting the men, he bowed while saying each person's name. When he reached Foshan, warmth glowed in his eyes. Foshan seemed to return the sentiment as he introduced Mr. Heong to the people he did not know. "You look well, Heong Hang," he said. "What brings you here?"

"I own a restaurant now. It's called Hang Heong!"

Finding humor in his switching the places of his sur and given names, as the Westerners did, the men erupted in laughter. After the excitement calmed, he pulled up a chair. "To answer your question, Foshan, my restaurant is a sponsor of the competition. I'm a judge and we're recruiting." He regarded him. "Given the company you're keeping, I assume you're still with the railroad. I thought you were planning to leave."

Nodding while turning his teacup in a clockwise rotation, Foshan said, "I am."

Lee noticed Foshan was making a point of not meeting the direct looks Heong was sending his way. He didn't understand the undercurrents passing between them, but he knew he did not like it.

As their evening concluded, the table mates were ready to move in different directions. Shuck stayed back to continue talking with Mr. Heong. Foo joined Lee and Foshan for a walk but took his leave when their livery stable was in sight. Lee and Foshan continued for a time without speaking. They arrived at the end of Broad Street and were turning to walk along the next block when Lee blurted, "You didn't tell me you were leaving."

"Nope."

"But I thought…"

"What? What did you think, Lee?"

"I thought we were good." He shoved his hands in his pockets and scuffed the toe of his shoe on the boardwalk.

Foshan sighed and would have spoken, but laughter and ruckus interrupted them. It came from a group of men on the street who moved toward the brothel. A shaft of light beamed out of the open door, illuminating Yang.

Lee moved to take a step in that direction. Foshan grabbed his forearm, stopping him. "What are you going to do?"

He released Lee when he felt his weight shift to his back foot. Scanning their surroundings, Foshan spotted one of the narrow, dark alleyways that ran along some of the row-like buildings. He took hold of Lee's wrist and tugged him into the shadows. Turning, he directed Lee back against the wall. Leaning in, Foshan flattened his hands on the brick siding above his shoulders. He shifted, eliminating the space between them. Their erections pressed alongside one another. Foshan held this intimacy, allowing them time to notice their hearts beating and the heat they generated. He moved his face nearer, so the side of his nose brushed against Lee's. "When I want to do this," Foshan whispered, "and I can't. It hurts. That is why I'm leaving."

Lee had heard stories of opossum hunters freezing their prey by lantern light. *This must be what freezing feels like,* he thought. Storming within him was a riot of conflict. His hunger for touch and intimacy was powerful. All it would take for his lips to touch Foshan's was to move his chin a fraction of an inch. But he could not. Lee squeezed his eyes and made no movement other than the heaving of his chest.

"You are honorable and naive." Foshan sighed. That is why I care for you." He did not dare shift beyond this swirl of heaven and hell. "If I could show you a way to…release tension…without violating your marriage vows, would you?"

When Lee remained silent, Foshan sighed again. "We cannot stay in This Now forever, Lee, though I wish otherwise. You don't have to say it—*no*—but if you remain as you are, that is the only answer left." Foshan held his position for several more heartbeats. Each one felt like tortuous cracks widening in his soul. Resigning himself, he pushed against the wall, pulling away.

Lee didn't know what he was going to do until he did it. When he felt the frigid night air thieving Foshan's warmth, his hands shot up beneath his loose shirt. Skin met skin. Desperate, he pulled Foshan toward him and lifted his chin. Their lips collided; they opened their mouths, tongues mingling. The tempest inside Lee broke like a tornado. His hands were in Foshan's hair, grasping, pulling him in tighter. Lee inhaled his scent. He wanted more.

Foshan bent his knees, then raised up, sliding the length of his body along Lee's in a caress ardent lovers cherish. Like a symbol clash in a parade, Lee convulsed. His seed erupted with the force of a log jam breaking in a storm surge. When he would have cried out, Foshan covered his mouth. Lee convulsed a second time. Foshan's body tightened, then shuddered, and relaxed.

Lee's terrified gaze locked with Foshan's unruffled one. They blinked. Unable to control himself, Lee started crying.

Foshan traded places, sliding his back down the wall until they were sitting on the ground, Lee in his lap. Bushes on both sides concealed them.

Foshan cradled Lee. One arm held him against his chest. The opposite hand stroked his hair.

Sometime later, Lee pulled away. With his index and middle fingertips, he traced the line of Foshan's jaw from ear to chin. Watching Foshan close his eyes stirred up another jumble of discordant emotions. Almost questioning himself, he said, "I kissed you. And you kissed me. And we…"

Cracking his eyes open, a corner of Foshan's mouth lifted. "This is true." He guided Lee's hand to his lips and placed a kiss on his palm.

"What happens now?" Lee asked.

"I don't know." Foshan shrugged. "Maybe nothing."

Lee frowned.

Foshan became alert, assessing their surroundings. "You'll have to think about this, no doubt. We can't stay here, Lee. It's not safe. We need to get cleaned up before we go sleep in the stable."

※

Yang saw a goddess that night. She crossed his path for only a brief moment, but it was one he would never forget. He caught sight of movement in the hallway, a dark tunnel with many doors lining its corridor. Sounds drifting in from behind her were laughter and moans. She scanned the space; their eyes met and locked. Pouring into him, the kingdom of the stars filled crevices inside that he just now realized had been empty and waiting for—*her*. Then she was gone.

Yang was to learn her name was Susi.

LOST AND FOUND
February
Nevada City, California
1866
—

In the weeks leading up to the festivities, all the railroad men were busy. As predicted, Yang's furniture sold out. Scarred Eye came back from Deer Creek with an offer of work in the diggings. They might even find small nuggets the mining company would let them keep. The pay was less than the CPRR, but it was better than lounging about and drinking the time away.

The cooks rotated through all the Chinese restaurants in Nevada City and Grass Valley; mining towns only four miles apart. Judges networked in the restaurants and with the patrons. Local merchants used the opportunity to invite business leaders in for elaborate feasts.

Food-preparation learning and recipe-sharing were intense. Since their schedules varied and they worked long hours, the Alta Camp cooks saw little of each other.

Yang was enjoying the mining work. Physically, it was less demanding than tunneling. It kept him in the sunshine and along the water. He liked imagining Uncle Lung doing the same activities. *Could he have been in the very place?* Yang laughed. When they were little and listening to Uncle's stories, they did not know about the size and scale of Gold Mountain. He felt sad knowing that he couldn't share his experiences with Uncle once they returned.

He also liked his surroundings. The nearest trading post was in a wide-open valley. Farmers raised cattle and grew fruit trees. Rumor had it that it had been an important gathering place for the Nisenan People.

Supplies and merchandise were available in Rough and Ready on Randolph Flat. Grass Valley had saloons and nightlife. It was where the blasters went to gamble and pay for women. Yang alone made the longer trek back to Nevada City.

Nevada City Road was usually busy. Yang felt safe enough. He walked to save money.

On a return trip, when the road was empty, three masked men jumped out of the bushes as he came close to their hiding spot. "Stop right there, Chinaman!" the tallest man shouted. "We have you surrounded. Give us all your money and we'll spare your life."

Crouching and spreading his arms wide, Yang took time to inhale calming breaths while assessing his adversaries. He was relieved to see they were not threatening him with guns or knives. If it was to be hand-to-hand combat, Yang knew he could dispatch all three.

Squeezing his hands into hard fists, Yang shouted, "Lái ba, húndàn." *Bring it on, assholes!*

They were on him like angry hornets dive-bombing a howling dog. Keeping his eye on the large one, Yang swung a hammer blow to the side of his head. Spittle, blood, and a tooth flew from his mouth as he went down.

Yang weathered some hits, moving his body to avoid punches to his gut and face. A side kick to a knee sent number two out of commission. Number three lost enthusiasm once his compatriots stopped moving. He turned and ran.

Cursing, Yang used his handkerchief to mop his face and dab his wounds. Nothing appeared broken. He checked to verify he had lost none of his valuables. His downed opponents squealed like stuck pigs as he approached. He reached into their pockets to see what was there.

They were empty. "Nǐ lián chénggōng de qiángdào dōu suàn bù shàng." *You're not even successful robbers,* he said. Fishing in his change purse, he pulled out two coins. Each one had a square hole in the center. Characters marked the horizontal and vertical sides. The thieves would never know that the writing represented the city and state from which the coin was made. Yang dropped one in each of their hands, shaking his head. "Húndàn," he said, spitting onto the road.

From then on, Yang paid for a stagecoach, hitched a ride on the back of delivery wagons, or spent the entire night at the brothel.

He'd been after Susi for some time, mystified why his magnetism seemed to work on everyone but her. Arriving before the doors opened, Yang paced up and down the street. He wore a wide-brimmed hat and kept his eyes on his feet. Lee could be anywhere; he didn't want to have to explain himself to his brother. As soon as they opened, Yang went straight to the madam and paid extra for Susi and a full night with her. She came to him soft-voiced and smiling, smelling as if she'd just come from a bath.

Susi was a professional, well-versed in the vices of men. Since this John paid more, she played fancy tricks. From his responses, she knew he was satisfied with the service.

From the moment he saw her glowing, naked skin, her perky, palm-sized breasts, and he inhaled her sweet body nectar, Yang entered the star kingdom. Susi's small hands and mouth launched him through the galaxy to burn like a comet blazing a bright path across the crystal clear night sky.

As she often did, Susi observed her actions from an altered state, somewhere up in a corner of the ceiling. While it registered that this man was more effusive than most, she'd heard too many emotional declarations to believe in words. She was always a stand-in for someone else; a semen receptacle for strangled balls, backed up like angry boils. All-nighters like this were tiring, but she kept up her performance until the end.

When the first rays of delicate pink shifted the light in the room, a sharp pinch jolted Yang awake. "Ouch!" he yelped, instinctively scooting away from the source of pain.

"Time's up," Susi said harshly, speaking around a smoldering cigar clamped between her teeth. "Out!"

"Wait!" Yang scrambled into his clothes. *What is wrong with her? Last night, our dragon and phoenix met in the heavens and serenaded the gods.* "This can't be happening! I..."

Susi regarded him with her head cocked. She leaned against the open door jamb while sucking on a cigar held between her thumb and forefinger. Letting out a puff that looked like a steam engine warming up, she said, "What? Are you going to profess undying love? Ask me to run away with you?" She cackled. "Like I haven't already heard that a thousand times. You want me? Buy me a house." She eyed the length of him. "We can talk when you give me keys. Maybe I'll consider marrying you." Stepping clear of the door, she waved the cigar. "Out!"

Hastening to do as directed, Susi increased his momentum by giving him a shove as he went by. He collided with another body just outside the door. The person was small. The mop and bucket she carried went sprawling.

"Get that cleaned up!" Yang heard Susi shout before she slammed her door.

Unwinding from the entanglement, Yang muttered, "Sorry." Righting the mop and offering a hand, Yang saw for the first time the face of the person he'd knocked over. It was a face he knew, older but unmistakable, especially with the scar on her eyebrow. "Duck!" he exclaimed.

The girl's eyes grew wide. She scuttled away, glancing up and down the hall. She was obviously pregnant, four or five months. An open weeping sore crusted the edge of her mouth.

"N…" he started.

But she swept it away with a furious whisper. "Don't say it! They'll kill me." She rushed at him, pushing him toward the exit. "Leave and never come back." When they reached the stoop, Yang checked if there was anyone on the street. It was early; no one was about. He turned and clamped a hand on top of hers as it rested on the rail, holding her there. She tugged, like a panicked bird flapping senseless wings. Tears coursed down her face; she brought up a trembling hand to press against the wetness. With her face tilted toward the ground, she begged, "Please go. I cannot bear to have you look at me."

"Listen!" he hissed. "We are working on the railroad, east of here."

Miserable eyes raised to meet Yang's. "We?" she squeaked.

He nodded, frowning. "Lee is in town." He glanced over his shoulder. "He's with the cooks. We're here for New Year's."

"Uncle Yang, you mustn't…" Ngon's shoulders caved inward.

He gave her hand a squeeze. "I won't," he whispered. "He'll never see you if you stay inside." He leaned in so his mouth was next to her ear. "I'll get you out of here."

"Too dangerous," she said. "The triad won't let me go." She pulled her hand away and hurried back inside, firmly closing the door behind her.

※

Seeing his niece sent Yang into turmoil. In his nightmares, devils pricked at his skin. As he usually did when times were tough, he visited an altar. Lighting incense, he prayed for forgiveness and asked for guidance.

It happened so often, Scarred Eye showing up when there were problems to solve. Yang stopped feeling gobsmacked. He wondered if the man was an immortal.

"I can tell you've had a bur up your ass for days," Scarred Eye commented.

Yang nodded, not entirely sure if this matter could be openly discussed. It took some time for him to explain. "Once my oldest brother and his wife were—gone." He hesitated.

Scarred Eye regarded him without comment.

"My mother—sold their daughter—so she could send me and Lee on this sojourn."

"I see." Scarred Eye wore a serious expression. He nodded and dropped his eyes, allowing Yang the freedom to continue.

"I thought Ngon would become a house servant—" Yang's voice cracked. The powerful emotions threatening to dismantle his composure dumbfounded him. "I found her here two days ago." His chest shuddered as he took his next breath. He squeezed his eyes shut while pinching the bridge of his nose. "She's a—"

"Hundred man's wife." Scarred Eye completed the sentence, compressing his lips.

Yang nodded with vigor. "But that's not the worst part. She's with child!" He detailed their meeting and hurried conversation at the brothel.

"The way I see it," Scarred Eye began, "you have three options." He held up fingers, bending them over as he ticked off choices.

"You can do what she says. Leave her be. Your family can hold on to the mystery, imagine something better. She'll die young, of course. Either of disease or childbirth. If she and the babe live, they'll sell the baby and put her back to work."

"You speak of her like she's a farm animal," Yang complained.

"Manly, we're all farm animals." Scarred Eye continued, bending a second finger. "You could offer to buy her back. If you do that, they'll know you want her. They'll go straight for you if she disappears and target your brother if you're not available." He glanced at Yang. "I do not recommend this option. These guys are known for torture. They've had centuries to perfect their methods."

"Third," Scarred Eye said, folding his last finger. "You could find her a husband, change her name, hide her away."

"Number three is the only reasonable option," Yang said. "But I don't know any husbands or hiding places."

Scarred Eye grinned. "Then it's good that I do." He patted Yang's back. "You'll need money, about $200." Watching Yang's expression, he continued. "I know it's a lot. If you can get it, I can do the rest. Think on it and let me know."

※

Yang did think on it, and he'd asked around. The Six Companies could provide a loan. If he got back to blasting and continued making and selling furniture, he might be able to make it work.

During calm, solitary moments, waist deep in the creek, shoveling gravel into a sluice box, Yang fantasized about Susi. He pictured a two-story Victorian house on five sunny acres. They'd grow apples and pears, much easier crops to manage than rice. Maybe they'd have sheep and a few pigs. Living in the house, he saw his parents, Lee, Wèi An, and their children. In place of Ai and Ming, Susi was there with three little Gee boys.

Most Chinese in California were not landowners. Yang reasoned that, since the mining company he worked with had managed it, maybe he could, too.

His bubble burst when Ngon's tearful, diseased face broke into his thoughts.

I could pretend I never saw her. Susi wouldn't tell, he thought.

Yang tried to shake the feeling that ancestors were arriving, a tickle between his shoulder blades, beyond the reach of a back scratch. To his right, he imagined Fu-chi standing on the bank, glaring at him, holding his arms crossed over his chest. In front of him would be Grandfather shaking his head, and to his left would be Uncle Lung.

"Why are you looking at me like that?" Yang yelled. "We don't care about females!"

His outburst sent them away, but he scooped up three creek rocks and threw them through the spaces where they'd been standing.

If he committed to this rescue, he could never buy land or build Susi's house.

※

Yang was sitting in the Six Company field office in Grass Valley making a loan application. Two hundred dollars was significant. When asked what the money was for, he said it was to buy a mining claim, land, and to build a house.

Accepting this, the agent wrote it down. "Do you have family or title to offer as security?"

Yang squirmed, not knowing how to reply. *Does this office correlate information with San Francisco?*

When he failed to respond, the agent continued. "If there is no collateral, the transaction can be made, but at a much higher interest rate."

"How much more?" Yang asked.

When the clerk said the amount, Yang felt his stomach seize up as if it wanted to turn inside out. While the agent commenced writing their binding agreement, Yang saw faces flashing before him, Ngon's, his mother's, and Mo Chou. Even Ai and Ming made a brief appearance. Saying "no" was not an option. He nodded as he reached for the pen to sign the documents.

※

"I arranged it," Yang told Scarred Eye when he saw him.

Nodding, Scarred Eye said, "Good, we'll make the extraction on New Year's. The crowds will provide cover. Do you have the cash? We'll need it on February 14th."

"I'll have it." Yang nodded and bowed. "Xièxiè nǐ!"

SUNFLOWERS
February
Nevada City, California
1866

—

It was late when Foshan returned to the livery stable. He thought everyone would be asleep but was glad to find Lee awake and brushing Jumpin Jane. "Hello," he greeted him happily.

"It's good to see you," Lee said. "It seems like it has been a long time."

"An eternity." Foshan stepped closer, giving Jumpin Jane a scratch.

"Are you glad the contest is over?" Lee asked.

"Uh-huh." Foshan nodded. "How did you do?"

"Second."

"I got one too!"

They smiled. Second prizes got $50 each.

"We're rich!" Lee leaned close to whisper.

"Do you want to celebrate?" Foshan asked, feeling the air between them electrify.

Jumpin must have felt it too. She let out a fart and stomped a foot.

Lee had been thinking about this nonstop. The intensity of the competition had blocked his internal debate, but only in short stretches. Standing here now, feeling his heart race, Lee realized his body already knew the answer. "I do," he said.

"I know a place."

"Where?"

"The brothel has a back room," said Foshan.

"It's private?"

Foshan nodded.

"Secure?" asked Lee.

He nodded again. "I'll go in first," Foshan whispered. "You'll come in about ten minutes later. Tell the doorman you've got an appointment in the blue room."

"Blue room," Lee repeated, nodding.

Stepping next to him, carefully verifying they were in the shadows, Foshan hooked a pinky finger through Lee's. "You're sure?"

"I'll see you in ten."

※

Lee's heart was in his throat as he approached the entrance. He'd never set foot in a place like this. The idea of being alone with Foshan made him tremble. *What are you doing?* He mentally screamed. *You don't like men! You have a wife who loves you! Mother warned about vices!*

Separation from his family had created a desolate loneliness he lived with daily. He couldn't catch his breath when he realized he couldn't remember what Wèi An and Song looked like. It was like a death. He imagined his face overlying Fu-chi's when the priests had delivered his body. If his outward appearance resembled how he felt on the inside, it was that.

The alley experience with Foshan resurrected him. And while he didn't feel attracted to men, there was an undeniable draw to that one person. *Can a moth resist the pull of the moon?* When he tried picturing the mechanics of how they'd be together, he was perplexed. But the memory of Foshan's warmth, skin, and lips propelled Lee forward.

Telling the doorman "blue room" had been easy. He hadn't received a disgusted look.

"This way," was the practical response.

Glancing into the main salon, Lee's step faltered. *Yang!* His brother was sitting at the end of a plush couch, feet planted, legs open. His head rested against the high back. He was laughing as a woman standing behind it leaned in to start tongue-kissing with him. Another woman sitting beside Yang ran her hand along his thigh and began massaging his crotch stuff. The spectacle flooded Lee's system with outrage that made his ears ring. *How could you?! Húndàn!*

The doorman tapped Lee on the shoulder. "Improper to stare."

"Right!" Lee muttered. "Sorry." He stumbled blindly in the direction the man indicated, almost forgetting his destination.

Hustling to the room, Lee saw Foshan was standing at the far end. It was so small, that it could have been a converted broom closet.

Foshan had been inspecting a picture hanging on the wall. Turning at the sound, he smiled. "You made it." His tone sounded unsure.

Lee stepped in and closed the door behind him, leaning against it. He looked spooked.

"What's wrong?"

"Yang's out there!"

"Did he see you?" Foshan asked, crossing to him. He stopped in front of Lee, his toe even with his instep.

"Uh…" Lee began. "I don't think so." He blinked as his mind lost the ability to hold a thought. "There's heat radiating off of you."

"Really?" Foshan asked. He cocked his head and moved in as if he were about to kiss him, then stopped. "Why that would be?"

Lee enjoyed the close-up view of Foshan's eyelashes. "You are a tease, Foshan."

"Am I?"

"I want to touch you, but I don't know what to do."

Foshan's eyes changed; his irises dilated. "Did you think about it last time?"

"I didn't think at all," Lee said.

"That worked."

"I…" Lee gave him a pleading look. "I want to do so many things, all at once!" He pushed the words out in a rush.

"Shhhhh." Foshan pressed a finger to his lips. "Pick one. Tell me."

Lee opened his mouth, gently nipping the finger before Foshan pulled it away.

"Tell me," he repeated.

Lee took a deep breath. "I want to hold your hands."

Foshan held his hands open near his hips.

Lee grasped them, lacing their fingers. Foshan's grip was firm.

"Now what?" Foshan asked.

"I want to bite your bottom lip." Lee raised up on the balls of his feet, so their mouths were even. He reached for what he wanted. It was like stepping off a cliff and screaming on the ride down.

Their clothing came off. Words were unnecessary. Lee noticed rough patches on Foshan's back and torso. Scars. Each one a story for another time.

Together, they found boundaries that were acknowledged and honored. Without pause, they flowed around them like rocks in a stream, seeking alternating ways to give and receive pleasure.

For most of the night, they were busy. A sense of urgency permeated the room. Neither knew when nor if another opportunity like this might come again. In the early morning hours, tangled in bedsheets and body parts, they were warm and smiling when they finally slept.

Lee dreamed he was home. He could hear Ngon in the main room with Mother and her aunts. A rapid knock sounded at the door. "Ten minutes."

Lee awoke to see Foshan leaning on an elbow, staring down at him. "I like watching you dream," he said.

Grinning, Lee felt like his heart was a sunflower with petals reaching for warming light rays. He pulled his lover to him. Their mouths welcomed each other into a new day.

At the five-minute warning, they hurried through sponge baths and dressing. Lee was just buckling his knife belt when a loud, insistent knock pounded on the door.

"Gee Lee! I know you are in there!" It sounded like Father! Ice suddenly replaced the liquid sunshine infusing Lee's veins. Frowning, he yanked open the door.

His brother stood there; face mottled in fury. He pushed his way inside, slamming the door. "What the fuck do you think you are doing?" Yang shouted.

For a stunned moment, all eyes darted here and there as threat assessments were made. Lee was the first to recover. He crossed his arms over his chest, saying, "I would think that is obvious."

Yang looked like a crazed bull, huffing and pawing at the ground before a charge. "You're gay now?" he screamed, lunging at his brother.

Foshan, attempting to intervene, stepped between them.

Interrupted, Yang raised a fist, aiming right for Foshan. A savage snarl twisted his face into an ugly mask.

Lee threw his arm out in front of him, knocking him from his path. "Don't you even think about it!" he warned. His free hand rested firmly on his knife handle.

"You wouldn't dare," Yang ground out.

Lee had never heard his brother so angry. All their lives, they'd played power and duty games. He had always been the one to kotow and bow, to apologize and retreat. Giving way to First Brother was correct. In this, he would not. With a voice that sounded deadly, he said, "If I were you, Yang, I would not try to find out."

Just then, Susi stood in the doorway. She knocked against the jamb, saying, "Room's got to get cleaned gents. If you are planning to stay longer, we're charging for another night."

"We'd better go," Foshan said, shouldering his way out. Lee followed on his heels.

When Yang focused on Susi, he felt like he'd run a hundred miles. To him, she was the embodiment of the goddess Ma-Tsu, daughter of the Dragon and Empress of Heaven, fulfiller of love in one's life. She revived him. "Susi," he sighed.

"Oh, it's you," she said, sounding indifferent. "How're you coming on my house?"

PARADE PLAN
February
Nevada City, California
1866
—

Chinese New Year in California may have been more of a rambunctious affair than it was in China. Sojourners were extra exuberant about gaining the gods' favorable attentions. They had to be louder and more colorful so they wouldn't be missed. And there were many more evil spirits that needed to be frightened away.

Scarred Eye's plan was to separate Ngon from the brothel girls at the height of the festivities during the Dragon Dance.

Yang had been at the brothel the night before to apprise Ngon of the forthcoming plan. Today, he'd made a show of asking for her and a private room. When the other girls ridiculed his choice, he said, "My lovelies, you're all some pumpkins, but sometimes a man has tastes that are unusual. Tonight, I want foul. The diseased, pregnant one is the only one who will do." Saying those things made him feel filthy, but there was no other way. A sour taste filled his mouth as he entered the Blue Room.

He outlined the plan and made her repeat it so he was sure she remembered. When he brought out the money she would need to hide on her, she kneeled before him, kowtowing deeply with her head on the floor. "Thank you." Her voice hitched in time with her sobs. "Thank you, Uncle Yang."

He let her carry on until a time warning knock sounded at the door. "Look," he said. "There's fresh water and soap on the washstand. How about if you use it? There's no telling when you'll be able to bathe next."

Ngon nodded and went behind the privacy screen to follow directions. "I'll have dancer clothes for you to wear tomorrow and another change once we get where we're going.

"Thank you, Uncle."

"When you're finished there, we'll secure the money around your waist. We have to do it tonight because there might not be time to do it tomorrow. You'll be able to keep it safe?"

"Yes. Thank you, Uncle."

As they completed their task, Yang asked Ngon to repeat the plan one more time. She did so without fault.

Fishing inside his pocket, he pulled out a tin of salve he'd picked up at the herbal shop. "I almost forgot," he muttered, handing it across to her. While there, he'd also asked for a remedy for himself. His urine felt combustible.

Taking it, Ngon pried open the lid and sniffed. It was lovely: lemon balm, tea tree, and Chinese rhubarb.

For the first time since they'd reunited, Yang glimpsed the solid young woman he remembered. He would never—ever—want her parents to know what she'd gone through. He hated imagining the parts of it he knew, but admiration grew inside him for her fortitude. She was a survivor!

"It's for the…" he pointed at the corner of his mouth. "Apply as needed."

Ngon nodded, dipping a finger into the ointment. She slathered some of the medicine over the infected area.

DRAGON DANCE
February
Nevada City, California
1866
—

Nevada City was bursting at its seams with Asian visitors and every other curiosity and fun seeker for miles around. Horses and buggies crowded the liveries and side streets. Incense and delectables were everywhere. Merchants brought their wares outside, famous plays were performed, and they mixed songs and music between eruptions of fireworks and the shooting off of rockets.

The grand finale was the Dragon Dance at the end of the parade. Ngon wore black pants, a long-sleeved tunic, and black cloth shoes. She braided her hair like a queue. Inside her pocket, she carried a small cloth cap she would slip on when she got the signal.

In a cacophony of unmistakable sounds, symbols crashing, drums beating, and bells ringing, the red and gold dragon came to life. Twenty men dressed like Ngon lifted the long cloth. Two men operated the animal's massive head, bobbing it, swinging it, and opening its mouth. Men, undulating and side-winding the mid-section and tail, followed behind in single file. Shimmering fabric that made up the dragon's body covered the men, only showing their feet. The dragon started its journey on Commercial Street, close to where the brothel women stood on the stoop, dressed in their Sunday best.

Ngon positioned herself at the far edge of the of the group, closest to where the dragon would first appear, and next to the triad guard. Nervously, she watched for the man with the scarred face to weave through the crowd and approach her location.

The dragon advanced, shaking and wagging its head. Clamorous merry makers walked before it and at its side. Onlookers clapped and cheered. If Ngon wasn't gripping the cap in her pocket so tightly, she'd have covered her ears. *There he is!* The scarred man, wobbling with an unsteady gait as if he were drunk. In his hand, he held a rocket firework on a long pole. Catching her eye for a split second, he nodded. The dragon's mid-section was going by. Inside, men were running back and forth across the length of the narrow street.

The drunkard cheered as he stopped next to the guard. "Lookie! Here comes the tail!" Holding a light to the rocket fuse, he watched it catch then planted the pole in a knothole in the boardwalk.

Ngon pulled on her cap and watched for the dragon's tail to arc across the road.

People around the scarred man shouted and scrambled in all directions.

"Madman!"

"What are you doing?"

"You'll burn the town down!"

As the tail reached its closest point to her position, Ngon bent low and shuffled out into the street. She was worried she'd get caught in the moving fabric rather than making it under. The scarred man swept a hooked ankle under the guard's foot, toppling his balance in one swift motion.

The dragon's tail man saw her coming and lifted the edge of the cloth, enveloping her in the interior of the splendid beast. She had to run in time with the others so as not to trip them. As they rounded South Pine Street, Ngon believed that this plan might work! The dragon paused in the middle of the block while the frontmen played theatrics. As the focal point of the dragon dance, the tail wagged. The man behind Ngon gave her cues for which direction they would move next.

It was hot inside and smelled of sweaty men. The dragon started moving forward again and Ngon picked up her pace, jogging in line as the noble beast rounded the corner onto Broad Street. She could hear the crowd laughing and clapping as the head puppeteers performed comical movements. The tail wove toward the little park at the bottom of the hill.

"Get ready," her accomplice warned.

A pair of feet raced up beside them. Ngon crouched low again as the section of cloth to her left lifted. Strong hands grabbed her by the shoulders and led her into the crowd. Releasing her, Yang took her hand and pulled her along behind him. They wove through five layers of parade watchers before making their way into a tiny park. It held one large redwood tree and a dozen evergreen bushes.

Yang led her into the brush and next to a two-story building. Deep shade gave them some cover. Stopping, he squatted to remove a loose grate at the foot of the structure. Looking up at her, he said, "I'll go down first. You follow. I'll catch you."

She nodded. In no time, they were in. Yang dragged a crate over to the wall. He climbed up to pull the grate back over the hole.

He hopped off and let himself plop down on top of it. "Sit." He indicated the space next to him. "Take a moment to catch your breath." He handed her a canteen. As she unscrewed the cap, he said, "You did well, niece. That was the hard part. I think we're safe."

Ngon nodded. She didn't know what to say.

Slapping his thigh, Yang stood. "We've got to keep moving. We have a way to go yet." He handed her a lantern and lifted his own. "Follow me."

The path ahead got oppressively dark. Ngon heard drips splashing in puddles, her cloth shoes quickly became saturated. Her teeth chattered.

"Sorry about that," Yang commented as he glanced over his shoulder. He stopped to remove his jacket and drape it over her shoulders. He buttoned the top two buttons to keep it in place. "I make these things." He pointed to the tunnel walls. Grimacing awkwardly, he continued, "and I forgot about the water. I'll carry you if you get too cold, but it will be best if you walk as far as you can."

"I'm alright," she said. "It reminds me of the last time we had to hike with Grandmother up into the hills."

Yang nodded. He glanced down at her belly, thinking, *Ai was pregnant then.*

They continued for what seemed like hours. The quality of light shifted as they neared the mine exit hole. They'd walked under the entire length of Nevada City and came out above it near American Hill.

At the roadside, a man waited, leaning next to a tree. With him was a two-mule wagon cart. Yang strode ahead. "You are Kilkenny?"

"Yes sir, I am." The man straightened, tipping his hat.

"I am Gee Yang." He nodded then turned, waving a hand back to Ngon. "This is my niece, Gee Ngon." Although he knew the rest of the plan, Yang was at a loss. He'd already used all the English words he knew!

Ngon stepped forward. "Do you have the package?" she asked the man.

"Yes ma'am. Right here." The young man moved to the back of the wagon, pulled back a cloth, and handed her a paper-wrapped parcel.

"If you'll excuse me," Ngon said. She turned toward the tunnel to change. On her way, she removed Yang's coat and handed it back to him.

The men stood in place, ill at ease, not knowing where to look. Yang started digging in his coat pockets. Pulling out an envelope, he handed it over. Inside was the amount of money Scarred Eye had said to include.

"Thank you," Kilkenny said. "You don't know how much this opportunity means to me. I know you might not understand what all I am saying, so I hope you'll understand by my meaning. My name is Cornelius. I'm seventeen. My mother's a widow with a bunch of little kids." He removed his hat and fiddled with it as he continued, "I know how to look after young ones, and I am a hard worker."

When Ngon came out of the cave, she looked completely different. She wore a voluminous skirt and a long-sleeved blouse with a high collar. A blue knit shawl and a matching wide-brimmed bonnet completed the outfit.

Yang almost laughed out loud when he saw her expression as she hefted the heavy skirt while walking. Dropping it when she reached them, Ngon placed her hands on her hips.

She is her mother's daughter, Yang thought.

Glancing at the two, Ngon correctly assessed the situation. "You're to take me down the Champion Mine Road to Newtown where we'll go to Rough and Ready," she said to Kilkenny. "There's a justice of the peace there who will marry us, then we'll go to Marysville, take the boat to Sacramento, and another one to San Francisco. From there, we'll go to Seattle. Is that your understanding?"

"Yes ma'am," Kilkenny nodded.

"Alright then," Ngon said. "Let's get going."

Cornelius walked the mules to the road. Ngon repeated to her uncle what she'd said, and that Kilkenny had agreed. Yang blinked rapidly. "You still have the money I gave you?"

"Yes."

"Don't tell him you have it. I gave him some too, enough to get you where you're going and make a fresh start."

"Ready when you are." Kilkenny came around to her side of the wagon offering her hand up onto the bench seat.

From behind, Yang thought, *You'd never know she was Chinese.* Yang stepped next to her. "That's Fu-chi's grandchild in there." He nodded to her mid-section. Reaching out tentatively, he hesitated. Ngon took his hand and laid it there.

"You tell her—or him," he said, "stories of our homeland?"

She nodded, then added, "And about my two uncles. One who taught me to think, and one who saved us."

Yang leaned out to make eye contact with Kilkenny. He stepped back and bowed. He watched until they were out of sight around a curve, then turned to make his way back into town.

He'd visit Susi. He had enough money for an hour. He'd pretend like nothing had changed.

※

Foshan was up late reading by lantern light. He planned to report local news to the men, along with Lee. Foshan subscribed to the *Dutch Flat Enquirer* and the *Sacramento Bee* because he could read English. Tonight, however, he was reading *Prince of Denmark* by William Shakespeare. He probably would have been a scholar if his parents hadn't died.

In their loft sleeping arrangement, Foshan had chosen a spot near Yang because, when they first arrived, he wanted to increase their chances for conversation. Tonight, he was wary about how that might go. He was hoping Yang would stay over at the brothel.

Hearing heavy steps on the ladder, Foshan glanced over the top of his small, round reading spectacles. It was Yang. *Shit!* When their eyes met, they nodded. Foshan quickly returned his gaze to the book, keeping Yang visible in his peripheral vision.

Something in the way Yang moved struck Foshan as unusual. He looked older, defeated.

Is that from finding out about me and Lee?

Just then, Lee, who'd been sound asleep, jerked upright into a sitting position. His vacant gaze scanned the area. "Fosh!"

Startled, Foshan looked over but didn't reply.

Working at pulling his arms out from his coat sleeves, Yang whispered, "He's sleep-talking. If you don't answer, he might start walking."

"Fosh!" Lee called again. This time, worry tinged his voice.

"Yea?" Foshan responded, trying to keep quiet so as not to disturb the others.

Lee's head stopped moving. "You're going back to railroad camp, aren't you?"

"Yes, Lee." Foshan dropped his chin, attempting to hide the smile that spread across his face. "I'm coming back to railroad camp."

When Foshan glanced back toward Yang, the man was already under his blankets, snoring.

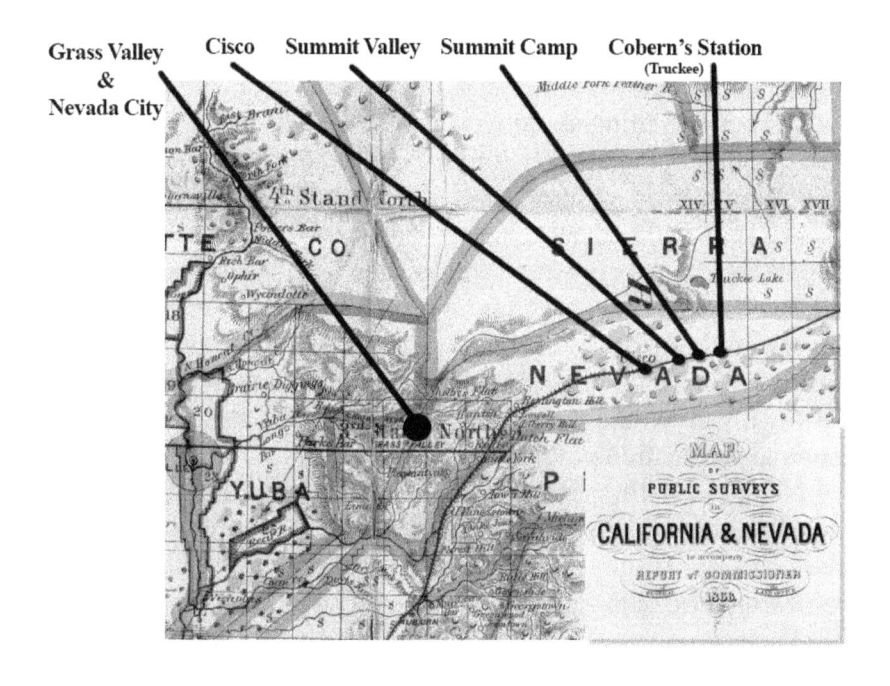

MAP | The Hill (Upper) Railroad Camps
Cisco | Summit Valley | Summit Camp | Coburn's Station (Truckee)

SLEET & CHICKEN HEAT
Winter
Dutch Flat Donner Lake Wagon Road
1866
—

The freight wagon muleskinner clicked his tongue at the girls to get them to pick up the pace. A biting wind had started icy fingers crawling around his collar and between his coat sleeves and gloves. If he knew anything about working in the Sierra Nevadas, it was that the weather could quickly turn from a fair maiden to a Zhong Shigui, the Winter God of Pestilence. He glanced at his passengers and hoped they had heavier clothing than what they were wearing. They were the railroad crew he'd transported a few weeks ago. The tunnel blaster—Manly was his name—had brought a load of small furniture over with him. He'd made a nice commission off the batch Ah Tow sold in front of the livery. Din told Manly that they knew a merchant in town who would take everything if he built more. He hoped their mutual association would be profitable.

Yang sat jostling in the back of the wagon, hugging himself. He eyed the heavy tarp covering a load of chickens being delivered to Lee's camp. If the temperature dropped any more, he was going to crawl under it.

Their group was smaller as they headed back to "The Hill." Yeehaw had joined the Deer Creek Mining Company. Won Shuck and Jung Foo, the cooks, had moved on to San Francisco. Yang had not seen Scarred Eye since Ngon's rescue. With the secretive nature of their operation, he couldn't even ask around. This left Charlie and Snorter from his blasters and Lee and Foshan. Yang was too tired to think much about that problem.

Ominous clouds roiled above. Thunder cracked and echoed in the distance, reminding everyone how nice it had been not to hear black powder blasting for a few days. Yang watched light-weight hail twirl in air whirlpools as they floated down. A few pieces bounced off his long-sleeved shirt. "Shit," he mumbled. He lifted the tarp and crawled under. The strong ammonia stench caused a gag. He mushed a section of the covering against his eyes and nose and worked out a balance between wedging his face in a gap and clamping it down to keep in the heat.

The blasters didn't have to think twice about following Manly's lead. They wedged themselves in, head to toe, backs pressed against chicken crates. Foshan and Lee eyed the activities of the others. Foshan's distasteful expression kept Lee in place as he shivered. When hail soon turned into sleet, Lee glanced over at Din. "Smart," he commented, glancing in the back. Lee went in.

Foshan held out longer, and then he succumbed too.

They lost track of time, riding that way. The skies opened up and pelted the covering with a mixture of ice and wet while the mules forged steadily onward. Harness rattled in time with trotting steps. Lee wondered if it bothered the mules when water got in their eyes. Every now and then, investigating textures within reach, the feathered travelers pecked at their backs.

Thoughts of Zhong Shigui were on many minds as the verdant Sierra Nevada forest crystalized and hardened. The railroaders wondered if the American White Witch was blasting fury at them in retaliation for altering a landscape she'd spent forever sculpting.

CRICKETS IN A BARREL
Winter
Summit Camp, California
1866
—

Human bodies raised in tropical climates experienced shock and sickness in response to extreme cold weather. Fingers, toes, and noses were frostbitten and ruined. Many men left the Sierra Nevada railroad crews, but many more came until they were 10,000 strong.

Those who would survive adapted. They fortified protective clothing, set their minds on things other than the pervasive cold, and were vigilant about keeping dry. They built wooden structures to house animals, people, and supplies. When warm rain melted snow drifts, the Dutch Flat Donner Lake Wagon Road became a mud morass. Some wheeled vehicles became so entrenched they were abandoned, waiting for the following season to dry out. When snow covered the muck, traffic on the freight road resumed with sleighs pulled by oxen and mules.

Yang and the blasters were living at Summit Camp, perched on a granite shelf near the eastern tunnel mouth. While the tunnel's length wasn't great yet, he knew it would continue getting deeper, even if only by inches a day. He had conquered his fear of entering dark space by focusing on the blackness being temporary. Lantern light would paint their faces and the jagged granite surfaces with a flickering orange and yellow glow. Beautiful in its own way, the light was crisp and clear at the beginning of the shift. At the end, with dust congesting the air, the light would diffuse, creating distorted shadows.

Inside, they were just out of reach of the winter eddies that deposited snow drifts near the entrance. Once the muscle work got going, body heat melted the cold, replacing it with a steamy, testosterone sauna. On most days, their coats came off in the first thirty minutes. After that, there were only seven hours and thirty minutes remaining of the shift.

At this worksite, they were the drillers, blast setters, and rock haulers. It took a three-man team all day to hammer and twist-turn hand drills to create one borehole. It had to be deep enough to hold the amount of black powder required to break the hard granite into slabs small enough to carry and dump over the mountainside. The men used a double jack method—two men, grasping eight-pound jacks (hammers) with both hands, alternated swings at the steel (drill bit) held by a shaker. Within the group of three, men alternated jobs when muscle and grip fatigue endangered accuracy. *Pound, pound, quarter turn. Pound, pound, quarter turn.*

To keep their minds focused, they played sound games. Sometimes their hammer strokes synchronized, creating a single crescendo. At other times, one team would start, and the others would join in at specific intervals until echoes ricocheted around the space like crickets in a barrel. Along with the sledge strikes, sometimes they sang and sometimes they shouted.

Yang still got a thrill after the fuses were lit and everyone ran for cover. The blast boom made his heart beat faster, and it continued as he walked through the dust cloud to survey the results. He also enjoyed debris hauling. It engaged different muscle groups. His thighs seemed less prone to fatigue than his biceps. When they lifted, the men enjoyed imitated cries they remembered from watching Shang Pu Ying wrestlers during exhibitions.

※

A recent activity that no one liked was excavating snow tunnels. It was impossible to walk on top of fresh thirty-foot drifts. The weather gods delivered these regularly, with brief breaks in between. To keep their railroad work progressing, the men followed the way of the mouse, hollowing out passageways through it from food sources to den.

Rip Snorter was standing tiptoed on a crate, using a long-handled shovel to push away an additional layer of snowfall from a vent hole. Yang and Charlie were working about fifteen feet behind, smoothing the ceiling to eliminate drip sources. They heard a whoosh and turned to find a large hole, open to the sky, above where Snorter had been.

"Rip!" Charlie cried in alarm.

Both men raced to the mound and began scooping snow like frantic dogs digging for a savory bone in sand. They screamed his name as they worked. Yang started worrying that their rescue efforts were taking too long.

"A finger!" Charming Charlie shouted. "Here's his hand."

Yang dove forward to clear the area where his face should be. As Rip Snorter's head, chest, and arms came free, it wasn't looking good. The man was pale and unmoving.

"Help pull!" Yang directed as he gained leverage under an armpit. It took several tries, but eventually, the body was free.

Charlie pulled Snorter's face into his lap and began slapping and rubbing. "Wake up! Rip, wake up."

Yang squatted next to them and began rubbing Rip's arms and legs. When help arrived, they loaded him onto a stretcher.

Rip Snorter had come around, but he shivered uncontrollably. Charming Charlie and Manly sat with him in Johnny Bird's mess tent, drinking hot tea. Rip still had a thick blanket wrapped around his shoulders and head. He kept pulling at the edges near his throat to keep it close. "I felt the ceiling give way—took quickly—like I hit a soft spot." His voice wavered.

"When it buried me, I thought I'd be able to brush it off or push my way out. But I was stuck!" he said. His voice sounded hoarse. "My arms were stuck over my head. It felt like I'd plunged into hardening concrete."

"It's OK, buddy," Charlie soothed. "We got to you in time."

"It was in my nose and mouth…" Snorter blew his nose then spit into a handkerchief.

Yang hung his head, nodding in sympathy.

"I imagined going out in a blaze, you know?" Rip said. His expression looked lost. "Like in a colossal blast with fireworks. Back there, I thought that was it. Taken out in a snow dump."

Yang reached over, placing a hand along his forearm, squeezing. "Why don't we take the day off tomorrow?" He spoke. "Go find someplace to get drunk?"

Rip Snorter eyed him in silence. "I'd like that, Manly," he said, then cracked a small smile.

News:

Placer Herald | January 13, 1866

The Railroad. — The Sac. Union says the Pacific Railroad Company has purchased from Louis McLane, of the house of Wells Fargo & Co., 800 tons of railroad iron, sufficient to extend the track from Colfax to within four miles of Dutch Flat, and that the iron will be laid down immediately. — Other iron is on the way from the States, and some will be due by the time the above amount is laid in track. The graded track between Colfax and Dutch Flat is understood to be nearly ready for the rails.

Placer Herald | February 10, 1866

The Santa Cruz Powder Works 5,555 kegs of blasting powder during month of January just past, beside a quantity of sporting powder.

UPGRADES
Winter
Alta Camp, California
1866
—

When Lee and Foshan first arrived back at Alta Camp from Nevada City, the camp layout was completely different. Incensed, they fumed across the compound to Kite To's area. He was their Six Company representative, labor contract negotiator, and paymaster. Kite To was round in both his face and mid-section. He was missing a front tooth, which made his "s" enunciations sound like "th."

Pulling up short, they found a small wooden building in the place where his tent had been. It had a front door with a small pane of glass. Foshan peeked inside. There was a cozy woodstove with a fire burning. Kite To's long fur coat hung in a corner, and the man was focused on something at his desk.

"He's in there," Foshan said, glancing back.

"Good!" Lee said, taking hold of the door handle and marching in.

Turning at the sound, Mr. Kite swiveled. "Well. Good evening Mr. Gee, Mr. Yow." He nodded but remained seated. "It ith nice to thee you again."

"There are strangers in our tents," Lee stated.

Foshan added. "Where's our stuff?"

"Ath you will dithcover, the camp hath gone through thignificant changeth thince you've been gone. You've been reathigned."

"Reassigned?" Foshan repeated the last word. "You know that we both," he pointed at himself and Lee, "scored well in the Nevada City contest?"

Catching onto Foshan's thinking, Lee added, "And that we could have gone to work in the city."

Regarding them, the pudgy man nodded. He crossed his arms while leaning back in his chair. "I know all of that."

"Then why would you reassign us?" Foshan asked.

"I've reathigned your living quarterth, not where you are working."

"To where?" Lee said.

"Directly behind your meth tent, next to the embankment, you'll find a new bunk houthe. Attached ith a new guest quarterth. Besides your camp cook dutieth, you and the other cookth will provide visiting guetht therviceth. Your belongingth have been moved there."

"Hold on a minute!" Lee raised a hand. "I've had my own space since I became a head cook. Now, you're expecting me to share *and* do more work? Is there a pay raise?"

"You think a wooden building ith not a pay raithe?" Kite To replied.

Lee opened his mouth but didn't know what else to say.

The boss raised an eyebrow at this. Spinning back toward his desk, he commented over his shoulder, "Be glad you have a job to come back to. I can't afford to have my cookth taking time off when thereth tho much line work that needth to be done. Goodnight, gentleman."

As they were walking out, Kit To half-turned in this chair. "Watch yourthelf, Yow. If you think no one ith watching, you're wrong," he warned.

※

Foshan and Lee eyed each other, not daring to speak. Creating greater distance between them, they walked in stunned silence to the structure Kite To had directed. It was similar in construction to Kite To's office. A large great room contained a series of bunks, stacked three high, arranged around a wood stove. It was dark inside. The fire had burned to embers. Men occupied four of the nine bunks. They spotted their belongings stacked neatly against a side wall.

Getting their bearings, they stood near the stove, warming their hands. Foshan added logs to the fire.

Not wanting to disturb the others, they climbed onto empty beds and fell asleep fully clothed.

※

Baldy had asked about the knife's performance in Nevada City. When Lee reported its excellence, the two men made plans for an excursion to Verdi, where Baldy would introduce Lee to woodsman and charcoal maker, Su Ne.

CHARCOAL
Verdi, Nevada
1866

The camp they planned to visit was twenty miles away. Travel would take at least two days. They rode mules Baldy supplied. Lee prepared food for the trip and brought along empty baskets. He was eager to buy charcoal for cooking purposes!

Baldy's mule hauled a small cart. The coal he planned to buy was for his forge. He'd also packed tarps and snowshoes in case they hit the weather.

"I've seen men making those," Lee commented as he pointed at the leather-laced foot contraptions.

"If you have them, now's the time of year to make repairs," Baldy said.

"What are they for?"

"Walking on the snow."

"I don't understand; your boots don't work?" Lee said.

"They strap on to the boots," Baldy said, chuckling, "for weight distribution."

At Lee's continued look of confusion, he attempted to explain. "Not all snow is the same. When it's been on the ground for a while, it compacts. It becomes solid, like ice. When it's newly fallen, it's light. You'll sink right through it if you walk through fresh, light snow. If it is only four inches deep, that's not a problem. If it's over your head, it can be serious."

At the halfway point, they took a lunch break. So far, the sun was still out and there was a gentle breeze. Lee had been thinking about snowshoes. He eyed the puffy clouds building on the horizon and hoped they wouldn't need to use them.

He found a flat rock and put down a blanket, upon which he laid out their spread; dried Chinese sausage, rosemary and thyme herb biscuits, and bean cake with meat sauce, along with plenty of warm tea.

Groaning with pleasure, Baldy consumed his food with gusto. Lee smiled, enjoying watching the other man's gastronomic appreciation, including his atrocious manners.

Lee handed him a napkin.

"This brings me back, Mr. Gee," Baldy commented, around a loud slurp of tea.

As Lee was fastening the straps over his saddlebags for the second half of their journey, Baldy came near to pat the mule's back. "There's a delicate matter that I need to talk about."

Lee glanced at the man.

"It's Yow Foshan," said Baldy.

Lee's mouth turned dry. "What about him?"

"In some camp circles, he's—known."

Lee's heart started pounding. "I don't know what you mean."

Baldy took a wide stance, frowning. He stroked sausage-like fingers along his chin as he thought. "Look," he said, "I can see that you care for his welfare."

"Of course," Lee responded. A suspicious tone crept into his voice. "Why?"

Baldy took a deep breath, propping hands on his hips. "In those circles, we look after our own. He's been warned. Now I'm warning you."

With wide eyes, Lee said, "I don't...."

Baldy held up and hand, shaking his head. "What's between you is not my business. You're a married man and, as far as I can tell, you've never had to concern yourself with people who'd punish you for—something you were born with. Be very careful."

They rode the rest of the way to the lumber mill without speaking. Lee's mind buzzed with questions. *Yang would not have talked about me and Foshan. Would he? What does 'certain circles' mean? Is Foshan in danger? Am I? Shangdi, what have I done?*

Lee noticed Baldy checking on him from time to time. When the man turned back in his saddle, Lee tried to arrange his face in a neutral expression. He was not sure if he'd succeeded.

Once they got to the Verdi Lumber Camp, Lee's worries began fading as he engaged with learning about how the charcoal-making process worked there. Instead of the small oven they built at home, this one was a rectangular building constructed of bricks. The amount of wood it held was forty times more than their earthen oven. The airflow process was the same, just spaced differently for the building's thirty-foot height and seventy-five-foot width. Where their home kiln took two or three days to burn, this one would go for one to two weeks!

They'd taken a tour around the lumber mill, watching the procedure of moving logs along the ground using a wooden trough that resembled a water ditch. Horsepower transported them from one place to the next. A giant blade, set in a flat table, spinning faster than the eye could see, was run by a large steam boiler engine, similar to the Black Goose.

From the opposite side of the blade, flat boards emerged where two men received them, adding to a neat stack.

Lee was excited that Su Ne had given him free sawdust that he loaded at the bottom of his baskets before covering it with charcoal. He imagined the tender meat he would cook as he watched Baldy tucking the tarp carefully around his cartload, tying it down securely at each corner.

After a hearty meal, they spent the night in the bunkhouse with the lumbermen. There was no shortage of stories about working in the forest, animal encounters, and felling trees.

※

As they readied for their return trip, Lee could feel himself growing anxious. He wasn't keen on talking about his relationship with Foshan. "You think it's going to rain?" Lee asked.

"Maybe," Baldy said.

Flurries started when they were within five miles of Alta Camp. Lee secured his coat, remembering that uncomfortable chicken trip with the freight wagon muleskinner. When the snowfall grew steady, the mules struggled. Baldy said, "We have to walk this last stretch. You look worried Gee Lee. Snow walking will be easy."

"It's not that," Lee said, as he watched Baldy preparing their snowshoes.

"Well, then?"

Lee couldn't help himself. He had to ask. "Are you a Tóngxìngliàn? *Homosexual.*"

Straightening up from securing a strap over his boot, Baldy regarded him. His mouth opened to say something, then he closed it. "Are you?"

Wide-eyed, Lee shook his head. "No!"

"If my answer to your question is 'yes,' will you seek to kill me?"

"Absolutely not!"

Baldy crossed his arms, frowning. "Then you are not a typical man, Mr. Gee. I don't know if we can say the same for your brother and his associates."

A chill swept through Lee that had nothing to do with the weather.

When Baldy checked the strap tightness on Lee's boots, he said, "A word of advice?"

Lee grunted in response.

"Foshan would not admit that his association with you could put him in danger. It does. Walk away."

※

Snowshoeing was a tiring and sweaty business. Lee was grateful that the exertion kept him behind Baldy. His heavy breathing and running nose masked the churning emotions that welled up after the warning.

The last leg of their journey was slow going. It gave him time to process. It was frightening to think that something that caused such joy could also bring destruction. Lee's heart twisted painfully when he thought about Foshan being hurt. *My love will keep him safe,* he thought.

And there it was. His feelings lay bare, as if he were a turtle on his back under a scorching sun.

SKILLS & NETWORKS
Winter
Moving to Donner Summit Camp, California
1866
—

The winter of 1866 felt like one never-ending storm. Sleet and wind came in from the southwest. Warm rains gummed up supply roads. Fresh snowfall, high drifts, and continually repairing manmade snow warrens kept everyone exhausted. In this bitterly inhospitable environment, in the sticky, sucking mud, iron rails were laid between Colfax and Dutch Flat, a distance of about twelve miles. Crushed gravel was animal-hauled and hand-shoveled into place. Cross ties were placed, then rails that were attached with pounded-in spikes.

Foshan, Lee, and other cooks transferred to Donner Summit Camp. Wooden buildings had already been constructed and were move-in ready. Railroad bosses were relocating all available laborers to the summit...their tolerance for defectors was at an all-time low. In addition to food prep and serving meals, the cooks labored to keep their gangs clean, dry, and well-informed.

Collecting solid water was never a problem. Wood was also plentiful between the mill discards and shipping containers.

To increase and maintain immunity, Lee and Foshan made large quantities of tea that included crushed ginger, ginseng, turmeric, garlic, basil, cayenne and licorice root, and mint. When they could buy local honey, they offered it along with freshly sliced lemons. This was something Lee thought was miraculous. Surrounded by deep snow, there were places in the state that were warm and producing citrus!

The cooks composed stimulating flavors by combining items they brought in from fishing ports such as oysters and abalone, along with items shipped from China: dried bamboo sprouts, dried seaweed, and salted cabbage. Where locally-sourced produce was available, they added that too: dried fruit, pork, poultry, and mushrooms.

Chinese all up and down the West were working to establish the variety of food abundance they knew was possible. Railroad cooks and farmers created networks to support each other.

For Lee, being back in the same camp as his brother was reassuring and worrisome. He liked seeing his Yang, even if from afar. Living closely with him was how life always was and should always be. However, Baldy's warning about Foshan introduced new anxieties and planted seeds of uncertainty over Yang being a trustworthy secret keeper.

A letter had gotten through from home, which put Lee in a very good mood. Mother had received his Nevada City contest winnings. She was gratified that he liked his chef's knife. He was using it now to julienne carrots and water chestnuts. Learning complex knife skills had grown into a sport once he'd grown completely familiar with the basics.

Foshan was excelling in dough making. Requests for his dumplings and potstickers were constant. They'd recently prepared a special meal for the Strobridge family, Mr. Crocker, and engineers Gilliss, Metzler, and McCloud.

Loon Tong Chung, Mr. Crocker's man who traveled with him, came along to serve the meal. He kept the cooks entertained with stories about the Strobridge children and their reactions to the new foods they were tasting.

It was here that the Chinese first heard about the new blasting method the bosses were considering: nitroglycerine. While the children horsed around, keeping their mother occupied by trying to get them to behave like adults, the men were discussing increased blasting power, dust clouds, and the increased accident risks.

News:

Dutch Flat Enquirer | March 3, 1866

The C.P.R. Co. have about sixty men, aided by several hundred inches of water, engaged in sluicing out the deep cut just below Gold Run, that was filled up by a huge slide during the late stormy weather.

Dutch Flat Enquirer | April 14, 1866

SERIOUS ACCIDENT. —On Saturday last, Mr. N. Fellows, a foreman in the employ of the C. P. R. Company, above this place, while engaged in charging a blast, was seriously, though not fatally, burned by the accidental explosion of a keg of powder.

San Francisco Chronicle | April 8, 1866

EXPLOSION AT COLFAX – Six Men Killed – Colfax. A terrible explosion occurred at Camp 9, near Gold Run, on the line of the Pacific Railroad. Six men were killed – three white men and three Chinese. The foreman … was blown to bits … One man was thrown fifty feet in the air and one hundred feet from the blast. The blast had been set off, and while reloading for a seam blast, an explosion took place. No further particulars.

UNDER SNOW
Spring
Donner Summit Camp, California
1866
—

Beneath twenty feet of snow, inside a translucent, wet cave, the kitchens remained functional. A fire burned in the center of a large carved-out room with a chimney hole. It provided space for gathering, eating, and warming, jackets and clothing draped every chair, bench, and table. Drying lines crisscrossed, sloping with the weight of pants, jackets, and boots hanging from laces. Only those items closest to the flames had a decent chance of drying all the way. It smelled of damp cloth, cooked food, sweat, wood smoke, opium, and candle wax. A series of tunnels led to the bunkhouses, the latrine, the blacksmith sheds, and up to the surface where the brightness of daylight would jolt the system.

As sun-warmed tree sap quickened in the forest and hibernating creatures began stirring, ice warrens cracked open, forming deep channels directing swift flows of run-off. Wet feet caused rotted skin, becoming a health hazard. Many toes were lost. Tweezers were used to pluck away black flesh.

Their first avalanche started on a morning when sunlight winked across the embankment face, heating the snowpack. An unusual roar sounded; it was not at all like road blasting. Loud cracks and groans accompanied an earth-shaking rumble. The snow moles, as they called themselves, wondered what new terror was about to unfold.

When silence returned, wide eyes searched around the dim cave, making tenuous reconnections. Slowly and carefully, they moved toward daylight. The sight that met them was mind-numbing.

Half of the camp was swept away by a wave of snow, as efficiently as wiping a crumb from a table. Churned-up debris remained in its wake. Trees snapped like twigs. It reduced wooden buildings to splinters, entire avenues, corrals, and telegraph offices…gone.

Swarming out of their hole like ants, they strapped on snowshoes and grabbed long implements to use as probes. Spreading out, shoulder to shoulder in a line, they searched for buried survivors. After about an hour, their efforts turned into a recovery operation.

Never was Lee more aware of the value of his work than when survivors emerged with bluish skin and bone-rattling chills. Dry clothing and hot soup, spiced with ginseng and a hint of cinnamon, gave them a chance at living another hour, another day. On these days, it did not matter if you were yellow, white, or black. The cooks kept the warming fires burning and tea simmering for everyone in need.

Late that afternoon, a misshapen man appeared in the distance, coming out of the forest, moving awkwardly toward camp. As he got closer, a cheer went up when the men recognized him. It was Scarred Eye, hauling something over his shoulders and pulling a sled. He'd hunted two deer and was bringing them to Lee and Foshan so they could feed the men fresh venison.

It felt traitorous, rebuilding camp, and filling it with fresh faces so soon after the tragedy.

There was never time to grieve. Road building took priority over every aspect of life.

News:
   Stockton Independent | April 17, 1866
Fourth Dispatch— Full Details of the Calamity.
…At 1:14 P.M. an [nitroglycerine] explosion took place, either in a storeroom of Well, Fargo & Co.'s building, or in G.W. Bell's assay office adjoining on California street, which demolished everything within a circuit of forty or fifty feet, including the whole interior of Bell's assay building…The explosion was so powerful as to shake the earth like an earthquake for a circuit of a quarter of a mile. Every window in California street, between Montgomery and Kearny, was demolished…Eight bodies have been taken from the ruins. Most of them were so badly mutilated that they have not yet been identified.
   Daily Alta California | April 18, 1866,
BY STATE TELEGRAPH
EXPLOSION AT COLFAX—SIX MEN KILLED
Three white men and three Chinamen were killed, several of them being blown to pieces.
   Placer Herald | April 21, 1866
SERIOUS BURNED. —Mr. N. Fellows, a foreman on the Pacific Railroad, was seriously burned by the explosion of a keg of powder, while charging a blast, on last Saturday.
   Dutch Flat Enquirer | April 21, 1866
LAND SLIDE. —A huge landslide occurred a few days since near Buckley's ranch, just above this place, on the line of the C. P. Railroad, damaging the ditches of the Dutch Flat Water Company to the amount of several thousand dollars, and rendering a change of the railroad bed necessary, which will also cost an immense sum. Nearly a quarter section, extending along a heavy fill of the railroad several hundred yards, suddenly gave way and moved off in a solid body, taking with it ditches, flumes, and everything else that obstructed its course, and making a change from the original survey of the railroad at that point imperative. The material that gave way, it seems, was of a soapy or pipe clay formation, and the pressure from the railroad fill is assigned as the cause.
   Auburn Stars and Stripes | May 28, 1866
Petrified tree found in the Hydraulic works on Home Ticket Mining claim at Gold Run. Eight feet wide and forty feet long - trees this large don't exist here. How can it be found so far down in the earth? Fossilized turtle also found.

CORNUCOPIA
Late Spring
Dutch Flat & Summit Valley
1866
—

The other men in Foshan and Lee's bunk house were two head cooks, two assistants, and two servers. They took turns entertaining visitors who came to stay in the guest quarters. These were suppliers and Six Company men. The cooks were eager to make connections and exhibit their importance.

As Lee and Foshan went about stoking fires, steaming rice, stirring soup, chopping and stir-frying vegetables, Foshan kept up a steady stream of conversation.

"They remind me of grouse, standing on the tallest log and puffing out air sacks."

"Did you see Keet gushing over the cabbage farmer?"

"Lung Hee was slipping notes to Khing Fong."

"That makes sense," Lee responded solemnly. "He's cultivating work opportunities after he's done with the railroad. Khing Fong has San Francisco connections."

Since his discourse with Baldy, Lee had taken to talking and smiling less around Foshan. He didn't want anyone to suspect their relationship was more than friendship.

They'd had heated discussions about this when they found fleeting moments of privacy. Foshan didn't like Lee changing his behavior. Lee was worried Foshan's relaxed nature would get them both in trouble.

"You don't even know what it is you are worried about." Foshan huffed. "I'm well aware of how I can and cannot conduct myself."

"But someone saw us in Nevada City, and they talked to someone in camp," Lee said, explaining as if Foshan were a child.

"People do that sometimes," Foshan said. "You can't control all people everywhere."

"Maybe not you, but I…"

"There's a simple solution, Lee." Frustration in Foshan's voice was evident. "We look each other in the eye and agree it's over."

Lee massaged his temples. His feelings for Foshan intensified daily. He made this place bearable. He also loved Wèi An; that would never change.

※

Lee was assigned to a visiting guest. His charge would be Mr. Hang Coy, the San Francisco herbalist who had treated his and Yang's bed bug problem. The man was a medicinal plant expert and would make a map of plant communities in the high country.

While Lee was excited by the prospect of learning from Mr. Hang, he was worried about leaving Foshan alone all day.

They had been washing up the last dishes. The mess tent was closed. Tomorrow, Lee would be away.

"I don't know why you are worrying so much, Lee. I've been in these camps longer than you and I survived. I'll be fine."

"What about Yang?"

"He already knows about us," said Foshan.

"I know that!" Lee said testily.

To ensure no shadows escaped, Lee blew out the last lanterns. He stepped close behind Foshan, leaning his front against his back. They were aroused.

"Your brother had his chance to beat me," Foshan whispered as he bent his head toward where their hands clasped. "He didn't."

"Because I prevented it." Lee tightened his grip, kissing the back of Foshan's neck.

"He'll be blasting in the tunnel the entire time you'll be gone." Foshan shifted his weight, accepting, welcoming.

Lee groaned and reached up to Foshan's shoulders to pivot him around. As their lips came together in a hungry kiss, they folded to the floor.

When tranquility returned, they straightened their clothes and exited separately, as if nothing had happened.

※

Kite To had rented a small cart for Lee to use. If the herbalist found plants he could sell in his shop, The Company would set up a supply contract. The cart was similar to the one Lee had used while grading in Newcastle. A single donkey or horse could pull it and the bench seat was just wide enough for two people. The freight wagon muleskinner was kind enough to give them Jumpin.

"Wonderful!" Lee exclaimed when he arrived to collect the conveyance.

When Jumpin saw Lee, she gave a perky little hop, nuzzling his hand.

"We'll have a lovely day, my beautiful girl." He gave her a hug.

"She does like you," Din said.

"Has she been well?" Lee asked. "She and all your animals."

"It was a tough winter. We worked till we almost had nothing left," said the muleskinner. "She's like the rest of us." He patted Jumpin's hind end. "When the sun comes out, it makes everyone a little more cheerful."

"Indeed." Lee nodded.

※

The road was firm but moist enough to prevent dust. For the next ten miles, they stopped when Mr. Hang spotted a fungus or lichen he wanted to inspect. Mostly, they kept to the road, flowing along with the constant stream of supply line traffic. For a time, they traveled behind a large prairie schooner with a dog in the back who barked greetings at them every now and then. Lee wondered if it could be the same dog who'd been stung by the ground wasps.

Mr. Hang's company was amicable. He told Lee that his wife and daughters had recently arrived. His trip was possible now because he had someone who could mind the store while he was gone. "We may open a second shop in Sacramento or Dutch Flat. Have you visited the herbalists in either town?"

"Oh, yes, the one in Dutch Flat. His shop isn't as large as yours, but he seems knowledgeable and well supplied."

"Now that you've been in the country for a while, what have you found surprising?"

Lee's first thought was Foshan. He smiled as he considered the question. "Living the daylight hours by this thing." He reached into a pocket to pull out a watch. "Everything is on railroad time, when we wake, sleep, when work starts, mealtimes, shipments, passenger schedules—it feels as if the entire world hinges off the rotation of its gears."

"Changes for the modern world. That aspect moves us away from following the sunlight, stars, and listening to the sound of water."

"Chop! Chop!" Lee laughed at his own joke.

"How are you finding the railroad work?"

"It is hard, but it pays more than laundryman wages. The money is good for my wife and mother."

Hang chuckled and nodded. "Of course. I remember you had a tall brother."

"Yang, yes. He is working at Summit Camp, blasting in the tunnel."

"I hear they are thinking about bringing in nitroglycerine."

"We have heard this too," Lee said.

"Nasty, stuff, that. There was a box that came off a ship in the city. It was in the Wells Fargo storage yard. It went up unexpectedly, taking half a block and killing at least six people."

Lee nodded; he had heard the story. "We have concerns. The Company is considering our options."

Passing several small lakes, Lee directed Jumpin off the main road so they could take a lunch break. He found them a peaceful glade near the water's edge. Coming back from visiting a tree, Mr. Hang was enthusiastic about a patch of wild tobacco plants he'd spotted.

Jumpin was happy to have her harnesses removed and given a long lead. She moved her head and back in several vigorous shakes to work out the kinks. Her adoration for Lee increased when he offered her a crisp green apple. She also enjoyed the gratitude he gave her for the challenging work she did and the long hours she kept.

The picnic Lee unpacked included Foshan's famous pork steamed buns, spring rolls, and pickled vegetables. During their meal, Lee learned how medicinal herbs could expand his culinary repertoire. He knew some of the basics, like ginseng, ginger, and cinnamon in tea. Mr. Hang showed him wild oregano and thyme within arm's reach of where they sat. Both held immunity and healing properties.

Refreshed after their break, they hooked Jumpin back up to the vehicle and resumed their journey. Turning a corner on a rise, the sunlight seemed to brighten and expand. Before them was a lovely meadow: Summit Valley. When Mr. Hang would have stood in his excitement, Lee cautioned him against it. "Too dangerous, Mr. Hang, to stand while we're moving. I'll stop so you can explore on foot."

The valley was about a mile long and a half mile wide. The wagon road skirted the eastern edge. Near its center, a sparkling watercourse meandered a snake path through willow thickets and wild roses. Both of which, Mr. Hang pointed out, Lee could cook with.

A plethora of birds of varying species dipped and glided over the water and into tree cover. Lee heard a crow call, followed by its deep-throated burble. *Could it be?* Sparkling springs provided baths with which to dip and flutter. Turtles left sunning rocks in favor of underwater camouflage. Red and green dragonflies patrolled territories, landing on long-stalked sentry stations. In the distance, a group of deer twitched tails and raised noses to sample the air. A male quail with a comma-shaped crest, startled by their nearness, peeped out a high-pitched warning before the entire group took flight in a wing-flapping whoosh.

"Magnificent!" Mr. Hang exclaimed, clapping his hands. "It's a cornucopia! I could stay all day."

Lee smiled in agreement. Reluctantly, he pulled out his watch to note the time. "We can only stay for an hour and a half before I have to get you back to the stagecoach stop."

Once Mr. Hang completed his notes, they continued the last miles to Summit Camp. On the way, Lee noted several hotels and a sheep pen that looked to have been newly built. It reminded him of a conversation he had with Foshan about mutton meals. Lee and Yang had never tasted sheep. It might be time to change that.

BLAST SICKNESS
Summer
Central Shaft, Donner Summit
1866
—

Yang and his team had been excavating the east face. Today, the supervisor told them they'd be moving to work on the opposite side. "Faster progress is needed there," he said. "I know I can count on you."

As they hiked across the hill crest, they could see activity. A borehole, established at the midway point of the tunnel, looked like a bottomless well. Black Goose, the hulking engine they had seen inching along the wagon road, was already hissing and chuffing sooty steam. Crews were busy hauling buckets in and out of the hole.

Yang's gang established a name for itself with their track record for blasts that dislodged exceptionally large slabs.

She Bang, Charming Charlie, and Yang sat on rocks drinking tea as they watched five wagon loads carrying ten kegs of blasting powder each make their way up the rocky road. Once a sizable slab was removed, the next blast would be double-packed.

Teamsters cajoled and encouraged the mule teams, tentatively finding footholds up and across the slick and uneven surfaces. When they could go no further, men hand-carried barrels to the blast coordinates.

The blasters carried extra-long ignition cords wrapped in a thick coil slung across their shoulders. Yang fingered a pack of matches inside his pocket as they set to work going through the steps that would accomplish their attack plan. Mr. Gilliss, the head tunnel engineer, had been in their way more than usual. Other headmen were gathering to watch.

Yang had told the east face crew leader to keep the white bosses and spectators away. They could not afford distractions. When he observed the portly Crocker and his eye-patch-wearing Strobridge friend standing directly where he planned to fly the seventy-ton boulder, he smiled grimly but said nothing.

Men were finishing up pouring powder into boreholes. Yang knew both Crocker and Stro were calculating the expenditure in their heads. At $15 per keg, this blast alone would cost $750. Attempting to hide his grin, Yang called over to the supervisor. "I have a good feeling about this one. We should add another barrel." He bit the inside of his cheek to keep from laughing as he watched their exchange.

As they were preparing the last step, She Bang elbowed Yang and nodded toward the bosses. Again, Yang signaled to the supervisor. "Those bosses are going to get squished like bugs if they don't move!" The blasters chuckled as they watched Strobridge clamp a hand on Crocker's elbow, even before Yang's words were completely translated, and begin pulling the man away.

The three blasters approached their target, securing the ends of their fuse cords into the powder. They began uncoiling the length from around their bodies. Gilliss, through the east face supervisor, had told them that they would begin working night shifts tomorrow. Production would continue around the clock from this point forward. The other two did not know that Yang had been asked to set charges inside the borehole. He agreed because the increased risk came with a slight pay raise. He was concerned, however, about not having complete control over where his body was when the charge went off. Even with this monster, he knew where he needed to be and how long it would take to get there. Inside the hole, he would have to trust the bucket operator to goose him up before the blast ignited.

To dissipate his nervous energy, Yang started singing under his breath. "Blasting yo ho. Big bang, here we go. Fly, rocks, fly!"

Once they lit the fuses, it was a quick hop over a large rock to their cover place. Their hands trembled as they pulled out the matches. "Sing it loud and clear," Charlie requested.

"Please!" She Bang agreed.

"Blasting yo ho," Yang sang. Together, they drew match heads along the strike paper. "Big bang, here we go." They lowered their flames, "Fly, rocks, fly!" They touched the cords and held their breath as the sparks bit in.

Tossing the matches to the side, they scrambled over the boulder, where they crouched and laced their fingers over their heads. Yang counted the seconds he knew it would take for the fuse to engage with its fiery lover. One second before contact, he stood, pressing the palms of his hands tightly to his ears. He would not miss seeing this for anything.

Lodgepole Chipmunk,
Neotamias speciosus

TESTICLES: Turned black and relaxed for once-a-year mating.

VOICE & BODY: Chirps, whistles, and postures.

I am ready! Come here lovelies!

Ka Boom!!!!!!

Stunned, laying belly-up.
He watches as a red-tailed hawk,
circling above, folds its wings to dive.

The colossal blast jolted the earth. If there was a sleeping dragon at its core, it would be awake now. In place of Yang's hearing was white noise and a high-pitched squeal. Bracing a knee against the protective boulder to counteract dizziness, he watched the granite slab propel through space, shredding full-grown trees. It landed precisely where he'd intended with a jolting thud almost as mighty as the explosion.

His head was pounding, his vision slightly blurred, and his steps were unsteady as people crowded around to pat his back, congratulating him. No matter what the clock said, Yang's shift was over. He was making tracks to his bunk.

Lee was there when he arrived, smiling at first, congratulatory like everyone else, until he realized something was wrong. He frowned and tried pushing tea at him. Yang turned away, slapping it out of his hands. She Bang and Charming Charlie were behaving strangely too.

"They can't hear!" Lee said, alarmed. "We must call the doctor."

"Doctor can't help this, neither can tea," said Rip Snorter. "It's blast sickness. They have splitting headaches, and their vision might be messed up. I have what they need," he said, patting his coat pocket.

Lee watched in revulsion as the man pulled out an opium pipe, placing it in Charlie's unsteady grasp. He loaded the bowl with pea-sized white crystals from a tin he carried in his pocket. Rip lit a flame for them, holding it steady while Charlie leaned forward to inhale. A sickly sweet stench filled the space. A few puffs later, Charlie's pinched expression relaxed. His body transformed from what looked like a brittle eighty-year-old man to an after-sex Doufu Hua.

Lee observed an identical transformation take place with She Bang. When Snorter approached Yang, Lee tugged against his arm. "No! You must not!"

Rip Snorter turned on him, snarling. He gave Lee a hard shove. "Kitchen man, you have it easy. You do this job for a day, THEN you can have an opinion. Yang will not suffer for your ignorance."

In distress, Lee watched Yang suck on the pipe. Only a small part of him relaxed when his brother did. A greater part wanted to puke.

Rip Snorter turned to Lee. His voice and demeanor were controlled. "He'll be alright in the morning. What he needs is sleep."

Lee nodded and left. As he was walking back to his bunkhouse with his hands shoved deep in his pockets, he realized Rip had used his brother's real name.

NIGHT SHIFT
Summer
Central Shaft, Donner Summit
1866
—

In the following days, Lee was still stinging from Rip Snorter's comment about his ignorance. As Yang was preparing to return to tunneling, Lee asked, "Can I join your work gang for a day?"

Yang looked surprised. "Why would you want to?"

"To better understand what you do."

Blinking and frowning, Yang thought about it. "The white supervisors would never notice. It wouldn't be difficult to sneak you past the crew boss." He grinned. "Once we're in the tunnel, it could work…" His grin widened even more. "Whoever I pick to give up their spot will owe me big! Would you expect blaster pay for that day?"

Lee shook his head. "No, I…"

"It's settled, then!" Yang enthused.

※

On the night shift they selected, Charming Charlie and Yang used their bodies to block Lee from the supervisor's view. As they approached the tunnel, Yang slowed his pace. He was even with his brother when they reached this point. When Lee's step faltered, as he knew it would, he urged him forward with the slight pressure of a hand on his back. "I know it's strange that you can't see in front of you, but keep going," Yang coaxed in a low voice. "The way is kept clear of stumbling rocks."

Soon, the stark blackness was illuminated by a river of moving lantern lights. If he didn't know better, Lee could imagine being in a forest at home, watching lightning bugs hovering over tall grass. As his eyes grew used to the new environment, he noticed Yang motioning for silence from the crewmen who recognized Lee.

Yang led them to their workstation, running his hand along a cut on the wall. "This is mine from yesterday," he stated matter-of-factly. Holding his lantern close to the rock, Yang scrutinized the surface, poking here, rubbing there. Once he found what he was looking for, he licked his thumb. "Right there, Charlie," he said, marking it with moisture.

"If we're going to get caught," Yang looked at Lee, "it will be now. They'll know by the hammering if something's off. Do you trust me, Lee?"

He nodded.

Charlie handed Lee a drill bit. It was cold, heavy, and about a foot-and-a-half long. "Put the point to the spot Manly marked, hold it straight, and keep it steady."

Suddenly, Lee wasn't so sure about this. A miss could mutilate. Before Lee could change his mind, Yang stepped in, guiding his hands to the angle needed. "After each of us strikes, you make a quarter turn, like this," he showed. "Keep the tilt steady, and we'll hit it every time."

In a swift motion, Yang stepped back, positioned his grip, inhaled deeply, bunched his muscles, and moved.

Lee watched this, along with Charming Charlie's similar actions, as if in slow motion. The first strikes hit the bit. Ringing stung the insides of his ears. Reverberations rippled into his bones and up his arms. He turned it on the quarter turn. *Pound, pound, quarter turn. Pound, pound, quarter turn.*

When they took their first tea break, Lee's arms felt like they'd vibrate off his shoulders. His fingers had trouble uncurling. A headache wanted to split his head in half.

Before returning to their positions, Yang guided Lee's fingers inside the small hole they'd made. It was about a quarter inch deep. While Lee couldn't hear what his brother was saying, he understood the look on his face. They were doing well so far. Now they had to keep going.

It took discipline to keep his mind focused on holding and turning. As the hours ticked by, exhaustion kicked in, making that task more challenging. Honestly, Lee didn't see how the men did this day after day.

At some point, Charlie asked Lee if he wanted to take a turn sledging. He slid the handle of his hammer into Lee's hand. It dropped to the ground with a heavy thunk. Lee shook his head, "Can't grip it," he said, using as few words as possible.

Pound, pound, quarter turn. Pound, pound, quarter turn. This is torture, Lee thought.

When Lee could barely remain standing on wobbly legs, Yang put his hammer down and stepped near his brother. He pried the bit out of his claw-like grip, pulling it out from the hole. Smiling, he pushed a finger inside, checking the depth. He helped Lee straighten his index finger so he could feel it too.

Charlie and Yang supported Lee between them as they walked out. "You did better than I thought you would," Yang commented.

"After a day like this," Charlie said. "You can see how much we value the taste of a good meal."

※

Lee was fast asleep on his bunk when the blast reports began bombarding the section of tunnel they'd drilled.

In his dreams, Lee's mind replayed, *pound, pound, quarter turn. Pound, pound, quarter turn.*

News:

Morning Union | February 24, 1866

Yesterday we saw from fifty to seventy-five of our Chinese population pulling up stakes, with baggage ready —a huge quantity of it, —and about starting for Dutch Flat, where their services have been secured, to help "diggee" for the Pacific Railroad, says the Transcript.

Placer Herald | July 21, 1866

The Nevada Transcript says that a cave-in occurred in the tunnel on the line of the Pacific Railroad, above Dutch Flat, on Friday, and six Chinamen were killed. The tunnel runs through soft slate and sliding rock in which caves frequently occur.

Dutch Flat Enquirer | August 18, 1866

The Railroad Company are now working day and night shifts on the line of their road above here, and it is stated that the night shifts accomplish more, with far less discomfort, than those that are compelled to work and swelter in the sunshine, which is hot enough just about now to give a thick beefsteak a decent broil.

Letters

Dear Yang,
Thank you for sojourning and working for your family. You bring us great honor.
We have not received a letter from you in many months!
Lee sends news that he sees you sometimes. At least there's that.
Don't you want to know about your daughter? About me?
I hope you remain well, Husband.
Ting Ai

—

To our dear sons Yang and Lee,
May Guan Gong and Guan Yin watch over you and keep you safe until your return.
We are in good health. Father has hired workers to make roof repairs, and he is thinking he will try raising catfish again. He says to remind Lee about their hardiness. "They can survive almost anywhere," he says.
We are worried about Yang. Has he forgotten he is First Son?
As his brother, it is up to you, Lee, to remind him of his obligations. We rely on you to guard over his virtues.
You are a dutiful son.
Mother and Father, Shao Pei, and Gee Fong

—

Dear Father and Mother,
Your sons are both alive and well. Yang has difficult and dangerous work. He is a head blaster, and the bosses keep him very busy. I convey his apologies for not writing and his good wishes for your continued excellent health.
As First Son, Yang has decided that we will correspond separately. I must honor and respect his decision.
I will keep trying to remind Yang to write.
Please tell Father that I am thinking about growing catfish here too!
Your Son, Gee Lee

—

Dear Lee,

Since the weather has been warm, the children have been enjoying playing in the creek. I have been teaching them to float and stay close to the bank.

Your Father and I have been talking about making a new batch of charcoal. We have enough wood! He thinks his grandchildren are old enough to be the mud makers.

I am well and in good health. I just miss you! I miss working at your side during the day and I especially miss sharing a pillow with you at night.

I hope, sometime soon, we will know when you will come home.
All Love,
An
P.S. I have enclosed two seeds from my wedding purse. The tree we planted is growing so well! I thought it might be like a sister tree.

—

To My Dear Wife,

Thank you for sending the tangerine tree seeds! I look forward to seeing how our tree has grown.

The camp where I work is high in the mountains. It can freeze at night and there is winter snow that carries over into spring. Sadly, a sister tree would never grow here, but I will keep the seeds safe and warm in my pocket until I can plant them in hospitable soil.

I enjoy imagining Song, Ming, and Luck packing mud the way their fathers used to!

As summer approaches, I have been watching for the Weaver Girl and Cowherd constellations. If the skies are clear when they align, I will cross the Magpie Bridge to you, my love.

I dream, frequently, of holding you and listening to our hearts beat together. We should make another child when I return.

Thank you for all you do, caring for our loved ones. Your work is important, An. You are a star in my constellation.

With Much Love,
Lee

—

MAGPIE BRIDGE
August
Maiden's Retreat, Donner Summit
1866
—

During his free time, Lee had been hiking up and down the mountains around Summit Camp, scouting for places to grow catfish. Everyone would value fresh fish! The location had to be far enough away from the waterworks overseen by the railroad bosses and Irish so that people would not steal them, but close enough to harvest for a meal.

The search and thinking about fish farming reminded Lee of his father's planning. He felt close to Father when he "walked in his steps" like this.

It also made Lee think about their dismay when the Taiping rebels came through, damaging levees, taking their stock, and leading Fuchi to his death. While yearning for his loved ones was painful, he didn't miss the civil unrest and persistent hunger. His parents had been right. Sending him and Yang to sojourn solved one of the family problems.

On the wide-open granite slabs to the northeast of the tunnel site, he'd found a small pool that looked deep enough for the fish. It was about a hundred feet wide by seventy-five feet long. One end butted up against a small granite cliff and the other offered gently sloping water access. It was an ideal location for the fish, and it would also be the perfect place to access the Magpie Bridge!

Legend says there is one day a year when separated lovers can meet. When the Cowherd and Weaver Girl constellations reach their zenith, a flock of magical magpies forms a bridge.

Lee had never seen a magical magpie, but he hoped they were real.

※

Kite To had been talking to Lee about working in the Company office to manage the camp food budget. There'd been more grumbling lately about the pay discrepancy between the Irish workers and the Chinese. Lee's job would be to see if they could change their food purchases so that they could increase worker pay while also continuing to provide satisfactory meals.

Lee would only agree to this if Kite To promoted Foshan to head cook. Bringing in a new chef's assistant was part of the deal. This gave Lee more time to work on his catfish idea.

Since he and Foshan weren't spending so much time together, Lee found it easier to create distance in their relationship. It wasn't what he wanted, but he thought it necessary for safety.

As the Magpie time approached, Lee was troubled. While he had a deep yearning to reunite with his wife, he was apprehensive she might notice differences in him. No matter—if he had one chance to see Wèi An this year, he would take it!

When the bunkhouse was empty, Lee packed his camp gear along with food and tea. He fashioned a backpack to carry it all and was about to set out when he had a moment of uncertainty. Looking in the little wall mirror, he verified his shave was close and neat. He'd bathed last night. Pulling back his lips, he inspected his teeth. All was well there. *I should have brought a gift.* Shaking his head to clear those thoughts, he ventured forth on his trek.

It wasn't a long hike to get to his little lake. He wound through several shallow crevasses and did a few scrambles over large boulders; in no time, he was out in the open enjoying the expansive views of the sky. Approaching the cliff drop-off, he reveled in the long-range views of Donner Lake and the state of Nevada.

※

Laying out his bedroll, Lee unpacked his dinner and teapot. He walked around, gathering firewood while studying the craggy Juniper trees eking out life in rock cracks. They were taller than he was, but they reminded him of the Penzai, miniature trees, grown by generations of ornamental horticulturists. Picking up a dry branch, he could tell by the weight that the wood was dense. It was another creature that survived the harsh weather of the Sierra Nevadas. Just standing near it, he knew it was old. *Maybe it has been here for thousands of years.* He bent down to pick up several tiny cones then bowed, thinking, *These trees are standing at Heaven's gate.* Lee noticed more than a few dotted this landscape. *They would know how the Magpie Bridge works.*

He finished gathering wood and started a small fire, then filled his pot with lake water and set it to boil. He'd prepared egg foo young thinking it was something Wèi An would like. With a start, he realized she knew very little about his work. He wished he could prepare a luxurious meal for her, like the Colfax feast.

A raven landed with a smooth glide about twenty feet away. He was sure it was the same one who'd been following him since Alta. "Are ravens related to magpies?"

Lee pinched an egg bit and tossed it between them. The animal cocked its head, considering. It hippity hopped over to gobble the morsel.

"Do you want more?"

The bird eyed him up and down. It looked like it was nodding "yes" to the question.

Smiling, Lee tossed the remnants of his bowl, then took it to the lake's edge to rinse. The water in the teapot was steaming when he returned. He sprinkled dry tea into it and removed it from the heat to steep.

The sun was setting, layering the horizon with lovely shades of pink and purple. In his peripheral vision, Lee saw the raven lifting a wing and rubbing its head under it.

"Am I supposed to pray or light incense? Should I sing?"

The bird stopped to regard him.

When he felt worry stirring, the bird took flight. It circled overhead, cawing. There were answering calls that echoed in the canyon. Three more ravens joined the first, and they vocalized together. It may have been a trick of the mind, but Lee thought he heard a word he understood. Sleep.

Crawling under his blankets, Lee adjusted his head so he could monitor the constellation's zenith. "I pray this works!"

※

Lee jerked awake with a start. It took him a moment to remember where he was. Looking around, the night was clear, but along the rocks, a fine mist swirled. Moonlight reflecting on the glassy surface of the water pointed a tapering finger in his direction. He blinked as a structure began taking shape on the opposite bank. It was a Peony Pavilion! Inside was a woman; her back was to him. She was standing at the rail, gazing up.

Lee stood, taking a few steps forward. "Wèi An?"

She turned. Her hair was arranged in a bun, showing the graceful line of her jaw and neck. She wore her wedding gown. Her face was powdered. "Gee Lee?"

He ran.

Because Wèi An was wearing traditional wooden shoes, she hustled to the edge of her Pavilion where Lee scooped her up.

"You're here! You are really here!" He slid a hand up and down her arm, making sure he wasn't dreaming.

"I can't believe it!" she marveled with sparkling eyes. "You feel like you," she leaned in, "and you smell like you!"

When Lee set her back on her feet, she looked around. He kept his hands on her, just looking down and grinning.

"What is this place?"

At her question, he looked up, distracted. "This," he said, "is Maiden Lake. I just named it that for you." He bent down then to claim a ravenous kiss he'd been holding since the day he left.

They were lost in each other for a while, running hands over backs and along arms, fingers tracing. Her hair came down. He shook the sticks out of it that she'd used to hold it in place. They clattered to the rock, unnoticed. Lips tasted and touched. Tongues mingled. Ears welcomed breathy endearments. Remembering. Remembering.

Hushed, she pressed flat palms against his chest, laying her cheek on top of her fingers. His head was bent, curled on top of hers. His arms encircled her.

She shivered. He pulled back. His expression was serious, "Annie I…"

At the unfamiliar use of her name, a perplexed expression appeared on her face.

When he continued speaking, it sounded like he'd changed tracks. "Missing you feels like a wound that doesn't heal."

"It does." She nodded.

When she shivered again, he carried her over to his bedding. She knelt on it, sitting back on her heels. When he went to pull the tie at her waist, she covered his hand. "Wait," she said. "I need to look at you."

In the faint red glow of his cooking fire, she peered at his face, tracing a finger over his brows. "You haven't been getting enough sleep." She drew his braid through her fingers. "Your hair's longer." Cupping her hands along his jaw, touching the corners of his eyes, a sad look crossed her face; then she smiled.

Lee took an inventory too, noticing similarities, but he said nothing. When she leaned back, arching slightly, he finished pulling the tie. Her robe fell away. She was naked. Her skin glowed like silver over delicate, rounded curves. His inhale was audible. With tears pooling at the corners of his eyes, he whispered, "So beautiful." Leaning forward, he suckled.

Wèi An maneuvered so she straddled his lap, gripping him tightly with her legs, pressing her fingers into his scalp. She understood he wanted her as much as she wanted him. Dropping her arms, she reached down to tug at his shirt. He helped, and as soon as the fabric was gone, he closed the space between them.

Keeping her pressed against him, he laid back. They kissed again for a very long time. She raised up, reaching for the fastening on his pants.

His whole body jolted as if burned. "Wait!" He stayed her hands.

"What's wrong?" Wèi An blinked rapidly.

"I…I…" He searched for words. "I read that if lovers consummate…fully…on the bridge, it will disappear. Immediately."

"That can't be right!"

"It isn't right," he sighed, gliding his hands around to cup her breasts, "It is not at all. But I will make it right." Pulling her back to him, he drew her into a sensual kiss. He encouraged her to rock on him. If she left a snail trail, he vowed to never wash these pants. Pleasuring her with his mouth, his fingertips, and with his breath, he absorbed her satisfied cries as if they were stars that landed on earth.

Wèi An, always a quick learner and an exquisite lover, reciprocated.

They played this sweet song in a loop, singing words that never grew tired. When they came to rest, they were stiff and sore, and completely drained. He cradled her close, smiling when he noticed that her hair was tangled like seaweed around his arms. As he'd known when they'd first become lovers, he confirmed that Wèi An was his home, the one place in the world he belonged more than any other. He made a silent promise. *Even if I am tattered and broken, someday, I will return to you, Wèi An!*

He noticed a Juniper cone lying on the ground next to them. He picked it up. Dropping it in her palm; he curled her fingers around it. They slept.

※

Lee awoke to a tinkling sound, like chopsticks dropping on a tabletop. Opening his eyes, he watched the raven picking up a limb and letting it go. He breathed in slowly and out even slower until he realized he was, once again, alone. He didn't want to move a muscle. Tears traced the contours of his face, leaving cold tracks for the morning breeze to enhance.

The raven picked up the stick again, taking three steps toward him. It dropped it near his nose. Lee frowned. *That's Wèi An's.* "Hey! Give me that!" He snatched it. The bird took to wing. Looking around frantically, Lee scrambled over to the second one. Gripping them in a fist, he returned to his blanket, kneeling. He pressed his lips to them and rocked, trying mightily to hold in the harsh, raw sounds of his heartache.

※

When Lee returned to camp, slow-moving and looking strung-out, he could tell people were wondering about him. If they wanted to think he had been off drinking into oblivion, let them.

"Where have you been?" Foshan would not be put off. "I've been searching all over!"

Lee continued walking, waving him away as if he were an annoying fly. "Scouting."

"Look at me, damn it!" Foshan grabbed his elbow. "Are you sick?"

Lee turned; his eyes squinted. "Take your hands off me!" he yelled. Not waiting to see Foshan's reaction, Lee spun on his heel. He needed a hot bath, and he needed to think.

MEASUREMENTS
August
Central Shaft, Donner Summit
1866
—

When Yang joined the shaft crew, the men working there nodded to him. Everyone knew Manly.

A hoisting device hung over the formidable hole in the ground. A thick cable on track wheels lowered and raised a wooden bucket carrying excavation debris. Cast iron containers transported men.

Forty-five days into the project, they were averaging less than a foot of progress on the tunnel.

A fifty-foot by fifty-foot building was being constructed over the Central Shaft hole. Employees pounded nails and sawed cross beams. When finished, it would contain the pit crew and all the machinery. Its purpose was to protect the site from winter weather. This year, the big bosses would not let any amount of snow stop the work.

Supplies that would eventually end up inside the building were also nearby: forges for tool sharpening, stacks of wood for the steam engine, and barrels of blasting powder.

As Yang observed the comings and goings of men in buckets, he felt a quiver in his core. He did not want to go down in there, but he knew that was precisely what they wanted him to do.

He eyed the pit critically, approached it and squatted, making rough estimate measurements. Walking back to the Central Shaft supervisor, he said, "I believe you have enough room there to frame two squares. With two frames and two buckets, you can move twice as much material."

Frowning, the supervisor planted his hands on his hips.

"Yeh, yeh, I know," Yang said. He held himself back from rolling his eyes. "I'm rude. Disrespectful. But did you hear what I said?" Yang watched as Mr. Lim looked over the hole. He saw the moment that the man understood.

Lim's spine straightened. "Wait here," he said as he carried the information to the engineer.

Yang observed their hand gestures. They turned to look in his direction. Mr. Lim nodded and pointed. Gilliss handed something to Lim before he walked away.

Mr. Lim waved Yang over. "It's a decent idea," he said without preamble. "Do you know how to write?"

Yang's chin lifted; he regarded Lim as if he were nothing more than a bug. He slowly raised a hand.

Lim's eyes followed it. Yang extended his middle finger, bringing it up to scratch the side of his nose. "Yes, sir," he said. His tone dripped with sarcasm. "I know how to write, AND I can do math." He smiled with tight lips.

Growling, Lim shoved a fist into Yang's solar plexus, wiping away the smile. "Good," he said, opening his hand to reveal a measuring tape. "Take measurements and draw up a plan. Mr. Gillis has graph paper on his desk. Take it to him when you're done. He says if it's good, you can supervise the work." Lim stomped away, leaving Yang in a daze.

He snapped out of it quickly and hustled to the east face tunnel mouth where Mr. Gillis kept a desk. As he hesitated, his eyes lit on something familiar. A small pencil holder sitting in a far corner. It was one that Yang had made. Smiling a genuine smile, he found the paper he needed and set out for a mess hall.

※

This afternoon, Lee was working in the kitchen over a large pot of lamb stew. He needed a break from numbers and analysis. Returning to the kitchen always brought him back into balance. Leaning over the cook pot, he waved a hand toward his face, sampling savory aromas. He dipped a spoon below the surface to taste the broth. As he did this, he remembered the afternoon he'd gone over to Summit Valley to meet the Basque sheepherder. His English was getting better, and they'd completed a sales transaction for two ewes. As cooks, they spoke a universal language. Mr. Strambini had been more than happy to feed Lee a bowl of the lamb stew he had simmering over his cooking fire. They'd talked about ingredients, spices, and cooking times. Strambini was thrilled with a packet of dried ginger Lee gave him. He gifted Lee oregano he'd collected on his mountain treks with his herd. *That's it!* Lee remembered; he'd forgotten to add oregano.

Before he left Strambini that day, the two men lingered near the sheep pens to watch an astonishing number of orange butterflies flowing past them on the breeze. One landed on Lee's arm, opening and closing its wings. When folded closed, the animal resembled a dry leaf. When it was fully open and horizontal, it showed a dominant bright orange color, black spots, and a thin, blue crescent at the wing tips. "What this?" Lee asked, pointing. "Very many!"

"Beautiful, aren't they?" Strambini chuckled. "We see late hatches following years with heavy snow. The Natives say witnessing a kaleidoscope—that's my word, not theirs—is lucky. It means big changes are coming."

Lee contemplated the butterfly kaleidoscope on his way back to his kitchen.

※

"Something smells great, Lee!" Yang called from the doorway. He deposited his papers and pencils down on the counter as Lee waved him into the kitchen.

"You must try this," Lee said, returning the oregano container to the shelf. "It's mutton." He ladled soup into a bowl and handed it over.

Yang smelled it, then sipped it. He looked perplexed. "I don't know about this one."

"Give it a chance."

He sampled it again. "OK, maybe it's a taste that grows on you."

Lee listened as Yang described his new project. He was pleased to see his brother looking so gratified. Lee watched him set up a workstation at a table near a window. Lee had been needing to talk to Yang. If he could time it before the dinner crowd started arriving, this would work.

Puttering around his kitchen, Lee was glad that Foshan was busy elsewhere. He took a pot of hot water out to warm the cups of the other two men using the space. Lee could tell by Yang's body language and his expression when he'd finished his design. He poured two cups of tea and brought them over, setting Yang's far away from his papers. Lee went to stand behind him so he could look over his shoulder. Yang happily paged through his work, pointing out intricacies.

"I'm glad you are out of the tunnel," Lee said. "I presume that's not permanent?"

"It is good," Yang agreed. "I'm sure they'll send me back in." He winked. "I'm too good at what I do."

"You know, don't you, that Mother made me promise to see you home safe?"

Yang chuckled. "I didn't know, but it's not surprising."

"You make it difficult sometimes."

Yang looked down, fiddling with a pencil. "I know," he sighed. "Our parents didn't know when they sent us that no place is safe."

"There were a few times I was afraid I'd failed. That time the tunnel collapsed."

Yang's response was uncharacteristically kind. He nodded, placing a calloused hand on Lee's arm. "That tunnel was in soft earth. Where we are now is solid rock. Nothing comes down inside unless we force it."

Lee pulled his arm away and began tapping a fingernail on the tabletop. "There's something we need to talk about."

Yang cocked his head. "You're pregnant."

Lee punched his arm. "Stop. I'm trying to be serious."

"I am," Yang said, under his breath.

"I saw Wèi An," Lee whispered, leaning closer.

Yang sat up straight, clicking his tongue. "You're losing your marbles, little brother."

"I'm not." Lee placed a hand over one of Yang's. "I have proof."

"Show me," Yang said.

Lee continued as if he hadn't heard. "It was the Magpie Bridge; it brought us together! We must go home, Yang." He squeezed his hand, hard. "We need to go right away!"

Yang shook his head. "I can't. I…"

"Mother has already told me you've stopped sending money. I don't know what you're doing with it, and I don't care. If only one of us is supporting the family, we've done enough. We need to go."

Yang yanked away, standing. He covered his mouth, gripping his chin, and paced. "Are you going to tell your wife." He eyed the other men across the room, then mouthed, "about your lover?"

Lee blanched. "I…"

"You'll have to, Lee. You're not a good liar."

Lee's mouth formed an "O." He frowned, then snapped it shut. "Are planning to tell Ting Ai? I saw you in that whorehouse!"

"Right!" Angrily, Yang gathered his papers. "I told you already! We aren't going until Six is open." He stormed out, leaving the door open in his wake. As he marched back to his bunkhouse, Yang thought, *I am such an asshole! I stir up his juices about lying when I'm lying to his face. I couldn't go home if I wanted to.*

Tortoiseshell Butterfly, *Nymphalis*

When hormones signal, transformed animals emerge from cocoons.

EYES: See a world of color with a honeycomb-like vision.

ANTENNAE & FEET: Chemoreceptors, like a sense of smell, guide the way to mates and food.

Taking flight, pair-seeking in a swarm. Stopping, briefly, to recharge on sips of nectar and salt.

Ideal mate awaits! Keep going.

WATER DRAGON
Fall
Coburn's Station (Truckee), California
1866
—

Coburn's Station was an energetic town. The Chinese had already been there for a decade, attracted by mining and establishing a lumber industry. As the work on the railroad progressed, a forward camp grew. It was closer than both Dutch Flat and Nevada City; plus, it offered a nice variety of goods, services, and recreational activities.

Yang discovered it before Lee. He preferred spending time at the gambling houses, but he noted other things to do there as well. Briefly flush with money after receiving a bonus for his Central Shaft double bucket plan, Yang invited his brother and Foshan to join him for a night on the town.

He wished he could tell Lee about Ngon and the loan, but he'd made a promise. Also, keeping him silent were mixed-up feelings about Fu-chi.

Lee's claim that he'd seen Wèi An had shaken Yang. He'd seen enough of their relationship to understand their devotion. *I wish I could send him home tomorrow!*

He also knew there'd been a schism between him and Foshan. He didn't think his brother was gay. Neither could he wrap his head around finding pleasure with someone of the same sex. Part of his anger on the night he discovered them together was Lee stepping out of line. He was the brother who *always* followed Mother's rules! Lee's wellbeing wasn't something Yang thought much about. He was thinking, *Lee has been no fun to annoy lately. He was better when he and Foshan were...*

If patching things up with Foshan could return Lee to the fucked-up normal of this railroad life, he was all for it.

※

All three felt good to be freshly groomed and in clean clothes as they mingled with the multicultural people of the town. Their meal was good. Yang found it amusing to listen to the chefs' sample and critique the food, and then conspire to recreate what they liked in their own kitchen.

Strolling along the boardwalk with their boot heels clicking on the planks, they bought bags of warm peanuts and sat to watch people rolling kite strings.

"The butterfly kite, with the wings that move, is a nice one," said Yang.

"I liked the dragon," commented Lee. "Its coloring made me think it was a water dragon."

"You see water dragons everywhere," Foshan said, chuckling. "The bird with the long tail was my favorite."

The Chinese opera, *The Heavenly Maid Scatters Blossoms*, a story about the Buddha's test of faith, transported them to a familiar place. It kept a dreamy grip on them for most of the evening. As they walked more after the show, Yang sang some songs he'd heard.

Surprised by his voice, Foshan encouraged him to continue. Their amble took them by barber shops, grocery stores, and tea shops. They read a store sign for a French Canadian Chinese doctor.

Yang paused in front of a brothel to comment, "They have a back room." He pointed with his thumb.

CATFISH
Fall
Maiden's Retreat, Donner Summit
1866
—

The barrels of catfish arrived!

Lee and Foshan moved slowly, grasping pine poles in both hands. Braced at hip height, elbows bent and palms chaffed as the heavy wooden barrels suspended between them sloshed and shifted.

When water splashed over the side, Lee yelled, "A curse on your whole family, Foshan!" He stopped, setting down his end.

Having no choice but to follow, Foshan did the same.

"On the count of three, match your steps with mine," Lee said.

"If you wanted to dance, Lee, all you had to do was say so." Foshan grinned.

Across the wagon road, through the staging area abuzz with activity; sawing, construction, and supply loading, they made their way to the opposite side. When a boulder needed to be scaled, they stopped, handing up the barrels individually.

Moving along in their awkward gait, they made their way to the small, out-of-the-way pool Lee had selected for this purpose. Setting their burden down, they adjusted the barrels so they sat near the water's edge. As he tipped the container, the whiskered, black fish rode the wave into their new home. He nodded to Foshan, signaling him to tip his barrel.

Lee settled into a squatting position, watching the fish. Foshan joined him, dropping onto his seat. For the first few moments, the catfish remained in place, as if the icy mountain water were an affront.

"Come on," Lee urged.

Fins engaged, slowly. The young fish propelled forward, gills pumping double-time.

Reaching in his pocket, Foshan came up with a handful of dry breadcrumbs. Tossing them across the surface, they floated like cotton seeds. The fish congregated around them, opening their mouths, eagerly sucking down the treat. Lee and Foshan laughed.

"They made it." Lee smiled, patting Foshan's shoulder. He rested his hand there.

Foshan reached up to cover it with his own. "They made it," he echoed. Taking his hand away, he drew up his knees, rested folded arms along them, and leaned his chin on top. "Are we going to talk?"

Inhaling a heavy breath, Lee said, "I saw Wèi An." He pointed across the water. "Right over there."

"But she's in Panyu." Foshan frowned. "You dreamed you saw her."

Closing his eyes, Lee continued, "The Magpie Bridge brought us together." He pressed his thumb and forefinger against his eyelids. "I made love to her right there!" He pointed to an area next to where they were sitting. His voice sounded on the edge of hysteria. "I… I…" Lee started sobbing.

Alarmed, Foshan moved close so their hips were touching. He wrapped a comforting arm around him and held on. "It's alright," he crooned.

Lee rocked as he desperately tried to get words past his weeping.

Foshan squeezed tighter, making shushing sounds. "Don't talk. Let it out. There's no hurry."

Eventually, the storm blew itself out. Lee sputtering between hiccups. He used his sleeve to mop up the snot on his face, then rested his forehead against Foshan's neck. Looking over the water, he said, "I can't talk to you about Wèi An."

"Too late, Lee." Foshan patted his arm. "You're already talking about her. I'm strong enough to listen to anything you have to say. If you trust me, maybe I can help."

"I…I…I had her in my arms, Foshan, this woman I love, who is my wife, and I…"

Foshan held his breath, not at all sure he meant what he just said.

"She wanted to be with me as in clouds and rain. And I wanted her too, but I could not be a man with my wife—because of what I have done with you. I want to go home, but I am afraid I am ruined."

"I see," Foshan said. His mouth compressed into a thin line. They sat quietly for a time. Foshan moved his arm away and created space between them. "Will you be leaving tomorrow?" he asked.

Lee shook his head. "Yang says we can't go till Six is open."

"You're still following what Yang says?"

Lee looked over at him, blinking. "That would be strange, wouldn't it? To do something on my own."

Foshan raised an eyebrow. "Would it? There's nothing stopping you."

"But I'm ruined, Foshan."

"Ruined because you've loved a man?" Foshan's voice sounded hard. "Or ruined because you were intimate with someone who was not your wife?"

Lee shifted to face him. His mouth turned down as he regarded Foshan. "Yes—to both. But it's not only that."

Foshan raised his eyebrows, waiting.

"When I made vows to Wèi An before a priest, I did not know her. The promises were wooden. But as I grew to love her, they became true." He groaned, scrubbing his hands across his face. "But you, Foshan—" He dropped them to his lap. As he gazed deeply into Foshan's eyes, he slowly blinked. His voice was raspy. "You make the moon hide behind the clouds."

Dropping his head so Lee would not see the shine at the edges of his lashes, he whispered, "Thank you." Clearing his throat, he raised his chin. "You are not ruined, Lee." He paused, releasing pent-up breath. "When you see Wèi An again, you'll have to tell her who you are, who you've become."

Lee jolted as if slapped. Twisting, he heaved to his feet, looking anywhere but at Foshan. He strode toward a Juniper tree, resting a palm along its trunk. He willed some of its stalwart steadfastness to bleed over onto him.

"We should go before it gets too dark to see," Foshan called across the distance.

Acknowledging that he heard, Lee dropped his hand and returned reaching down to lift an empty barrel, saying, "It is not my intention to hurt you."

"I know," Foshan said. "I don't want to hurt you either." His expression seemed to say he didn't think that was possible.

NOT YET
September
Summit Camp
1866
—

The first snow of the season blanketed the ground. Hard edges were rounded, varied rooftop colors became monochromatic, and road ruts were softened as if a giant pencil eraser rubbed them over. With the weather change, undercurrents of tension began vibrating throughout camp. After last winter, everyone was eyeing wood piles, questioning if they had enough fuel. They inventoried clothing and snowshoes, patched roof leaks, and stuffed padding into cracks.

Lee was hard at work in the Company office running through numbers and double-checking supply quantities. Kite To had left three days ago to attend a meeting at the San Francisco Huiguan house. Lee hoped the man would return soon. He didn't want to get pulled into filling in for his job!

The sun had set and the temperature inside the office dropped with it. Lee had just replenished the woodstove. He was securing the window covering when he heard footsteps crunching outside. A rapid knock sounded at the door. Opening it, he wasn't sure who was standing there. The person wore a thick coat with a deep hood pulled over his face. Fresh snow dusted the shoulders of the jacket. Immediately obvious were the scintillating food aromas wafting up from the box in the man's hands.

The smell triggered Lee's hunger, and his stomach rumbled like a grumbling tiger. "I must have forgotten to eat!" Lee said, pulling the door open wide, making way. "Thank you! This must be Foshan's doing."

Setting the box down on a small table, the currier threw back his hood, revealing that it was Foshan. "Sorry I couldn't get here sooner; the mess hall was extra busy tonight."

"Thank you for coming at all!" Lee said, taking the cup of hot tea Foshan poured. Lee watched as he removed other items from the box and filled a plate with Yuke Beong, pork meat patty, and long beans and mushrooms with plum sauce. Finally, he ladled a bowl of chicken soup with mustard greens and bamboo shoots.

Foshan poured himself a cup of tea and took a seat. They remained in companionable silence as Lee ate, making appreciative noises. When he picked up the soup bowl and took a sip, Lee commented, "You've already started serving cold remedies. Smart man."

Foshan nodded, then dropped his eyes to his cup of tea.

Both men had given considerable thought to their conversation by the catfish pond. On Lee's part, he'd experienced a significant shift in feelings. As Foshan aptly pointed out, he *could* leave tomorrow. While the family's disappointment about that decision would make him uncomfortable, it no longer held the power to crush him. A recent letter from Mother let him know that they continued to benefit from his work, even if Yang was failing on that count.

A revelation had been the emotions that surfaced when he thought about saying goodbye to Foshan. His advanced level of selfishness was a cause of dismay.

Foshan was always clear about Lee and his priorities. He knew full well that he was married, in love with his wife, and committed to providing for his family. Foshan's problem was that he'd allowed himself to fantasize that he was a member of their family. Even now, as he glanced across the space that separated them, his heart softened as his eyes roamed over the planes and surfaces of Lee's face. A face he longed to caress.

In his adult life, Foshan had cultivated an expertise in "This Now" moments, diving in and teasing out every aspect of joy they contained. But permanence was not established with "This Nows." The duality of desires had begun causing more pain than delight. His parting with Lee would be agonizing. Was there a choice he could make now to minimize it? *I could leave tomorrow.*

Breaking into Foshan's ruminations, Lee asked, "Where were you before we met?"

Blinking, Foshan shook his head. "I'd been working with Mr. Quong for a few weeks when you arrived. Before that, I was mining in El Dorado."

"Mining!" Lee smiled, leaning forward. "You never said."

"You never asked."

They stared at each other for a few moments before Lee dropped his voice, saying, "I'm asking now."

Foshan drained his teacup, set it down, and rubbed his chin. "I answered an advertisement nailed to a tree. The railroad was hiring miners."

"Were you part of a mining company?"

"I was."

"Did other members of your company come to work on the railroad, too?" Lee asked.

Foshan's expression closed in. "No." He started biting a thumbnail. "The ones who survived fled to San Francisco. I don't know what happened to them after that."

Since Foshan did not seem to want to elaborate, Lee changed the subject. "What brought you to California in the first place?"

Foshan regarded him out of the corners of his eyes. "What's going on, Lee?"

With a heavy sigh, Lee set down his teacup. "I've been thinking about what you said about leaving."

Foshan nodded. "So have I."

"There's something beyond Yang keeping me here," Lee said.

"Hmmm?" Foshan mumbled.

"You." Lee reached over to take Foshan's hand. "I'll have to go some time, but I'm not ready—yet."

Foshan's grip tightened; his eyes turned glassy. "I don't know if I can stay, because if I do, when that day comes, it might be the end of me."

Lee released Foshan's hand, blinking back the moisture that clouded his vision. "I understand," he said. "Have you decided what you're going to do?"

Foshan shook his head "no" and began picking at his cuticle. "I came to California to search for my father." His eyes had taken on a faraway look. "I may continue searching."

"I thought you said your parents were dead."

"My mother is. We assume my father is too since he never returned from Gold Mountain."

News:

Morning Union | November 15, 1866
CENTRAL PACIFIC RAILROAD.
The Central Pacific Railroad will be in running order to Cisco, ninety-three miles from Sacramento, in about a week. This point is but a short distance on this side of the summit and is at an elevation of about six thousand feet. Being so high in the mountains, we shall have an opportunity this winter to see what effect the deep snows will have upon its usefulness. Its elevation is nearly the same as that of Meadow Lake, from which place it is but ten miles distant. The work has actively commenced on the other slope beyond the summit, and will be prosecuted with vigor through the winter, below the snow line. It is not too much, perhaps to anticipate that a year hence, the cars will run to Crystal Peak, on the Truckee River, just at the boundary between California and Nevada, a distance of 140 miles from Sacramento. The building of railroads on the side of the mountain is not so difficult or expensive as generally supposed. The contractors are said to be making a large profit on their contracts for construction.

INTO THE PIT
Late Fall
Central Shaft, Donner Summit
1866
—

It had taken nearly three months to excavate the Central Shaft down to floor level. Gilliss had been one of the first bosses to descend into the pit. He'd taken a lantern and measuring instruments with him. His slight build seemed a benefit in the tight space.

The men working the steam engine took bets on how long people would last in the pit before they lost their wits. Gillis took it in stride, ascending with a determined expression. When he came up, he proclaimed how much farther they had to go.

They'd reached the floor at a seventy-two-foot depth. Their next step was to work on the east and west sides, expanding them toward the bores. The proof in the pudding would be when each side met and how close they'd be when they did.

It was with a mixture of satisfaction and terror that Yang stood inside the metal bucket with his grip firmly clasped around the thick metal cord. The chuffing sound of the Goose changed as the surface left his sight. Surrounding him, with only fractions of an inch to spare, were the planks of the square shaft he'd helped construct. They soon winked out of sight as total darkness consumed him. A temperature drop raised goosebumps on his skin. His quaking innards caused the bucket to rattle against the sides.

He screamed then, high-pitched and panic-stricken, like a little girl. "Stop! Stop! Let me out!" But there was no response beyond the continued, steady movement, down, down, down.

This gang didn't give themselves nicknames, make jokes, or sing. Yang had elected to take on drill bit turning, only sledging when someone needed a break. From missed hammer strikes, he'd gotten a crushed knuckle, and a severely bruised wrist, and aside from cursing when the injuries happened, he mostly kept his mouth shut.

As the pit transformed into a cave, the men laid narrow gauge tracks for ore carts. These made moving blast debris rocks to the buckets easier.

Yang's skill at fuse setting and explosion timing remained undiminished. Every time he made it out of the bucket before the blast ignited, he whispered under his breath. "Thank you, Nezha, for giving me another day."

Inside the pit, they'd already lost three men. Pockets of undetonated powder exploded when someone brushed against one or tapped a drill bit too close. The resulting blast instantly turned a man into blood spray, bone slivers, and meat chunks. *Whose finger was that?*

Feeling like his mind was numb and his feet were made of wood, Yang dropped a foot and a patch of scalp with a long queue into the haul bucket. At the end of the braid was a leather strap with a turquoise bead. It belonged to Simi, a man Yang had laughed with this morning when they shared different versions of the joke, "What do you call a Chinese man with one leg?"

Yang had to let his mind do what it wanted to keep from spinning out of control. He fantasized about Susi and Ting Ai merging into one. His daughter, Ming, was picking apples in their orchard where pears and grapes grew on the same tree. Her room was at the top of the Victorian house he'd built.

The sons Susi had born were teenagers. They laughed and hollered from atop steeds as they herded cattle. In Yang's mind, they moved in slow motion. Long, unbound hair flowed in the wind. They had strong smiles with good teeth, and their skin was sun-kissed to a deep brown. They reminded him of the Native worriers he heard about that had once roamed free across the planes.

For his coming-of-age ceremony, his youngest son wanted to be branded. A Buddhist priest held an iron in the fire. He came at the boy with the end glowing red under a starlit sky. His son removed his shirt and knelt, waiting, anticipating. He laughed and cried as the dragon's design seared into the flesh of his pectoral muscle. Yang wanted to be branded, too. The priest obliged.

Susi loved him. She wore palace clothes made of fine silk and shuffle-walked on diminutive dancer feet. She brought platters of lychee to hand feed him as he lounged on their bed, which was on a dais in the center of a fountain inside an elaborate garden.

In a moment of clarity, Yang made the connection between Susi and the fishmonger's wife, the woman who'd inflamed his adoration as a young man. Susi's jawline was similar, as were the tilt of her eyes. Even the timber of her voice was familiar. Of course, his feelings for the fishmonger's wife were only reflections of his attachment to Mo Chou. When *she* came to mind, he immediately shut those thoughts down.

He and Lee were eagles flying above the Sierra Nevadas, then speeding over the ocean and circling their farm. They could see Father and Mother and the family shrine. Yang saw his own name written on the record wall. He blocked Lee's view so he couldn't read it.

Immortals were hidden in pine trees near their tunnel worksite. Scarred Eye had transformed into a raven and was one of them. They mourned for the over-harvested forest. They were singing to the dragon inside the mountain, and she was awake and listening.

His mother was a young woman holding him when he was a baby. All the family gathered behind her, smiling down at him, their dear boy.

EMOTIONAL CAGES
Winter
Summit Camp
1866
—

Violent November winds coming out of the south and west hammered Summit Valley and the surrounding railroad camps. Relentless and ferocious, it was almost as if the gales were showing what it felt like to be pounded and drilled upon.

Heavy and cold snow fell steadily all month. It wasn't deep enough to excavate tunnels through yet, but the clearing of it took considerable time and effort.

Lee stood on the porch of the Company office taking in the night. The weather seemed to have broken, and stars were twinkling above. Pine branches, white and heavy, leaned against tree trunks that remained ramrod straight, pointing toward the towering cliffs above.

Orange glowing fires that appeared to be about the size of his thumb dotted the road course at the mouths of the tunnels under construction. The only sounds in the muffled gloam were metallic sledge strikes and powder blasts.

Camp-bound and frustrated, Lee was climbing out of his skin. He wondered if Mother felt this way, tied to her house. *Do those feelings subside when you've had them for a long time?*

His mother had been trained to project acceptance and tranquility. His father seemed proud to have a wife behave so. *But is any of it real? Does Mother feel like a caged animal?*

Lee bundled up and headed across the compound to his bunk. If tomorrow was sunny, he needed to get out! Foshan had been complaining about running low on salt and some other spices. Coburn's Station was only four miles away. Lee was sure he could pick up the needed supplies there.

※

In the mess hall the next morning, Rip Snorter solved Lee's transportation problem. "When the weather's clear, I've been running a small delivery service for the freight wagon muleskinner. Passengers are welcome if there's room. You can have today's seat if you want it."

"Thank you." Lee bowed. He met Rip in the stable as he was finishing the harness and sleigh hook-up. Inside was warm and smelled of hay and dung. The man didn't look good. His eyes were bloodshot and his hands trembled.

"Is everything alright?" Lee asked.

"Sure, sure." Rip nodded. "Nothing sleep won't fix."

Lee had not ridden in a sleigh before. It looked like a donkey cart with rails instead of wheels. There was a bench seat up front where the driver and passenger sat and a small walled bed in the back for sundries and packages.

Approaching from behind, Lee dropped the extra blankets he carried in the back.

"Good thinking." Snorter nodded. "We're almost ready." As he picked up the reins and was about to call the command to move, Lee stopped him with a hand on his arm.

"Hold up." He walked around to the front with a grin breaking across his face. "I thought I recognized those ears wiggling!" He patted his old friend. "We have another day to spend together. If only you knew how often I think about buying you and taking you home." He searched in his pockets for something sweet.

Jumpin helped by nudging her soft nose toward his pockets. Lee's eyes lit up when his fingers touched a piece of hard candy. It probably wasn't healthy for her, but he knew she'd like it. Unwrapping it so no one could see, he dropped it in the palm of his hand and lowered it so she could snuffle it up. He stroked her forehead as he said, "You might like my home, but I don't think you would like the boat ride."

Snorter walked Jumpin and the sled outside and into the snow. They loaded up and tucked blankets around them. As they set off, Lee let out a "Whoo hooo!" thinking it felt like they were flying.

Rip smirked. "She's performing for you. When it's just her and me, she doesn't do that hop step."

Jane was smiling. It was a resplendent day, and she enjoyed the easy exercise. The sleigh wasn't heavy. She didn't have to concentrate on picking her way through rocks. The snowpack was hard; no need for those dismaying mule snowshoes. She liked the man she frequently worked with. *I LOVE Lee, Apple Man!* she thought.

The sky was blue, the sun was shining, and they were pleasantly gliding along. For a time, they took it all in, not saying a word. As the day warmed, large chunks of snow sloughed off branches, making sliding and plopping sounds. Light rays refracting through the ice crystals twinkled.

"I haven't talked to you since..." Lee said. He didn't want to bring up the opium issue. He suspected Yang was still using it. "How've you been?"

"Hunky-dory," Rip said. "Still working. I'll keep at it as long as I don't have to worry about being buried again."

"By earth or snow?"

"Either."

"Are you staying through winter?" asked Lee.

"Heck, no! I'll be moving to Coburn's Station once the big snows hit."

"Do you think the weather will hold for today?"

Rip eyed the sky. "I think so. Just the same, I want us to head back no later than 3:00 p.m."

"No problem. I only have a few items I need. I'm very glad to be out."

They separated once they got to town, agreeing to meet at the livery stable at the appointed time. Lee visited the apothecary and the grocery store, quickly purchasing the items he wanted. With time to spare, he visited the bookstore, picking up a book for himself and one for Foshan. He went to the tea shop for a leisurely beverage and some reading time.

Lee was feeling rested and rejuvenated by the time he made it back to visit with Jumpin Jane. He'd brought her a carrot and an apple. She was licking the apple juice off his hand when Rip Snorter returned.

The scowling man reeked of smoke and whisky. His arms were full of packages. He dropped them in the sled without ceremony. "Good, you're here," he ground out. "I was going to leave if you were late."

Lee stepped away, folding his arms. "Did something happen?"

"None of your business!" Rip yanked at the leads, making the animal nervous. He jerked Jumpin and the sleigh out and onto the road. Motioning Lee to get in, he did the same.

They launched into a run. Lee had to hold on to the bench seat to keep from being knocked in the back. "What in hell are you doing?" he shouted.

Rip Snorter did not respond, but he cracked the lead lines, commanding Jumpin to go faster. They flew along the road. The trees became a blur. They passed a man on foot and a four-horse team, all of them yelling at them to slow down. Lee could see the driver of the hose team struggling to keep them in line.

They'd gone just over half the distance back to camp when Lee saw foam forming in Jumpin's mouth. "You're hurting her!" He yelled at Rip and fought to take control.

Rip elbowed him in the mouth, nearly sending him over the side. But Lee caught himself and came back swinging. The sleigh zigzagged across the road, the reins came loose and streamed behind the mule-like ribbons in the wind.

The men clawed at each other and struggled against falling or being thrown out of the sled. Lee heard a distant crack. Not the report of a powder blast, but something as powerful. The ground beneath them rumbled. Snorter stood and threw his weight against Lee, sending them over the side. Their fall pulled against the sled, causing it to overturn and swing around to the side of the frantic mule.

The men tumbled together, thrown across the road. A tree put a sudden stop to their motion. Rip took the brunt of the force with his back. Stunned, Lee came back to awareness, listening to Jumpin's terrified screams. Checking to see if he could move, he crawled to his hands and knees, noticing blood and blurred vision. The trembling of the ground under him grew stronger.

Lee had to get to Jumpin. "Jane!" he called. She was stopped about a quarter mile up the road, the sled and harness gear tangled behind her. Scrambling toward her, he spread his hands wide while talking to her in as soothing a tone. "It's alright, girl. I'm going to help."

Behaving as if she understood, Jumpin stood still, her great round belly expanding and compressing. "There, there," Lee crooned, taking hold of the strap near her jaw. From this vantage point, he could see there was only one strap left connecting the overturned sled to the mule. If he could unbuckle it, she'd be free. Running a gentle hand along her spine, Lee moved slowly. "It's OK. We can do this." He just had the pin piece pushed out when Jumpin rolled her eyes and went wild. She reared, catching him in the chest. The contact sent him flying. Hot pain exploded around his heart. Lightning bolted up his shoulder. He couldn't feel his left hand.

Freed of her constraints, Jumpin took off, racing back the way they'd come.

Gasping on the ground, looking like a fish trying to breathe air, Lee saw what was coming. A wave of snow broke free from the cliff above, picking up speed and spreading out. Jumpin was running straight into the path of the avalanche. Instinctively, he brought his left elbow up while cupping his nose and mouth with his right hand. He braced for impact.

It swept Jumpin Jane off her feet in an instant, rolling her around like an insignificant toy. She didn't know which way was up or down. The panic that drove her moments before switched to confusion. Everything was in a crazy motion until it stopped. When she tried to breathe, the material surrounding her locked in place, blocking her nose. She was encased in solid ice. Panic returned. A final herculean effort to move made no difference.

As her vision faded to black, everything became warm and calm. The darkness had a welcoming quality. Jane's last thought was of Apple Man and how soft his hand felt when she licked it.

※

In the still silence, the fact that he was breathing surprised him. There was a light just above him. With a wiggle of his head and shoulders, he broke the surface. Through a haze, he noticed his left hand was misshapen and that the entire side of his body hurt. Yet, he managed to squirm and push free. He heard shouting and could make out shadows moving among the trees.

※

The first time he woke, he was in a fiery underworld. Frightful, distorted faces floated around him, stabbing him with sharp weapons and forcing acid down his throat.

The second time, he was struggling against constraints binding him. "Mommy! Mommy!" he called out. Fat tears dripped from the corners of his eyes.

On his third awakening, Lee groaned from a headache that felt like spikes pounding into his skull. He heard voices across the room. Recognizing the doctor's quarters, he thought, *It must be bad if I'm here.* Images of Rip Snorter's horrendous behavior began flashing through his mind.

Kite To came into view, carrying a steaming mug. "Willow bark tea for the pain," he said as he set the mug on a side table.

As Lee always did in Kite To's presence, he wondered about the man. He wore a queue like most Chinese, but this was where their similarities ended. He wore chunky diamond rings on the fingers of both hands and his clothing was expensive. If To and Mr. Crocker were standing side by side, one might think the Asian was wealthier, but Lee thought this unlikely. He was surprised when he reached over to help Lee move into a sitting position, fluffing a pillow behind his back.

"Thank you, sir." Lee would have bowed if he could. He lowered his chin and dropped his eyes.

"No, no," Kite To said. "Unnecessary. You mutht dismith formalitieth until you've recovered."

Lee's eyes wandered behind the man.

"They've been here." He smiled. "Your brother, the cookth, your line crew, and the freight wagon muleskinner. You're very popular."

At the mention of the muleskinner, Lee's mind went to Jumpin. "J...the mule, is she alright?"

"I'm thorry." Kite To shook his head. "You're the only thurvivor. You were lucky being at the outer edge of the thlide."

Lee closed his eyes, leaning his head back. He sighed heavily. "Thank you, Mr. Kite, for coming by. I'd like to be alone now, if you don't mind."

"I understand." Kite To bowed. "I am pleathed to thee your improvement."

※

Lee was up hobbling on his feet when Yang came by. His brother wore a look that reminded him of Fu-chi. Yang crossed the floor in wide strides and held onto him in a tight grip, not releasing him until Lee complained.

"I was worried, little brother!" Yang looked down and appeared to brush something from his pants. "I started a speech for our parents...It wasn't going well." He looked up. "Don't do that to me again!"

Lee smiled. "I can't make any promises." His eyes dropped.

When they sat next together on his cot, Lee whispered, "Kite To was here."

Yang nodded like he knew something. He shook his head slightly while throwing a glance in the doctor's direction.

Lee understood he couldn't speak freely. "I am going to have to get back to work soon," he said. "Otherwise, they'll send me back to Sam Yap."

"Are you up to it, office or kitchen?"

"I think so. Mr. Kite said the kitchens need the most help now. I need to get the qui flowing better so I can move without groaning. Would you help me move through the eight brocades?"

The doctor smiled and nodded his approval as he watched them begin their slow-motion exercises.

DANCING ON THE MOUNTAIN
Winter
Summit Camp
1866
—

As winter deepened, the days grew shorter. Virile Pacific winds pushed dense, water-leaden clouds over the Cascade Mountains. It shoved them down and through the Sacramento Valley, where they dropped a rain payload. Wind continued, whipping the clouds into motion, higher in altitude, until they formed foreboding cumulonimbus columns, capable of electricity and thunder that rumbled like war gods.

As their ferocity increased, they released delicate, uniquely designed ice crystals that drift, swirl, float, clump, and plop to the ground, blanketing the peaks in a stunningly magnificent, transformative covering that can bring both life and death.

Visitors to the region rarely arrive with due respect. Nature teaches them harsh, unforgiving lessons. If they are lucky, they live to tell their stories.

Animals adapted to the environment enter a twilight sleep, a time when minds and bodies are less active and accumulated body fat sustains them.

Outliers are rare individuals who successfully inhabit their environment when others struggle. One of these was a fellow from the Telemark region of Norway. He was an emigrant who answered a U.S. Government call to deliver mail to "The Lost People of the World."

Because Charles Crocker and other railroad bosses spent so much time at the summit, they established a telegraph system ahead of the iron road. This was how the linemen knew to come out and watch a spectacle, one that they'd likely never see again.

A special delivery was due, carried on the back of the infamous character, Jon Torsteinson–Rue, aka Snowshoe Thompson, who was traveling between Meadow Lake and Coburn's Station. The men gathered at the base of Lee's Magpie Bridge mountain to watch.

It was said that the man performed Norwegian folk dances on flat rocks when snowstorms were too thick to move through. Today, the sun was shining, scattering diamonds of winking light off a thin crust of ice. At the crest of the mount, the delivery man paused, looking no bigger than a pinky finger.

At the bottom, the audience cheered. The Viking waved and hollered a response before leaping forward and beginning to make a snake trail down the snow-covered slope.

The man's long, golden hair streamed behind him like fine silk. Daylight appeared to glow through the strands. On long wooden ski skates, he glided downward with great velocity, arcing to the right, sending up a scattering of spray, and then to the left. In front of him, he balanced a long pole that he held horizontally. It swayed with his turns, looking like a pair of wings. On his back, he carried a heavy pack.

Making way as he came to a shooshing halt, the crowd clapped. "Delivery for Charles Crocker!" he called as he shrugged off his pack and unbuckled the straps. "Who's accepting it?"

Loon Tong Chung shouldered his way through the crowd. "Here!" he called.

Foshan had come in next to Mr. Loon, carrying a package. Where Lee was standing, he couldn't make out what was happening. Within minutes, Thompson was refastened and skate-sliding along the flat road on his way to the next incline. The man raised a hand in farewell as he rounded a corner and went out of sight.

"What did you give him?" Lee asked.

Foshan grinned. "A little something Loon Tong Chung asked me to make. Fortune cookies and hot tea."

※

On Lee's first day back working in the kitchen, Foshan seemed different: sadder, resigned. His step faltered when he saw Lee. Bowing formally, he said, "It is good to have you back, Mr. Gee, sir."

Foshan's neutral expression felt like an arrow piercing Lee's heart. He missed the warm light that so often kindled in those eyes!

Hee Chiu was Foshan's new assistant. He reminded Lee of his niece. The man was wiry and strong. When left unchecked, he talked nonstop.

Lee had an easy job—basting a roasting pig. Foshan worked at the counter, developing a peanut and coconut sauce. Hee Chiu was at the butcher block chopping mountains of carrots, onions, and cabbage.

Frustrated, Lee was tense because he had not been able to talk to Foshan about the revelation he'd had during his recovery. In his own code, he tried reaching him. "I purchased a book for you in Coburn's Station. Unfortunately, it remains buried in the snow."

"Hmmm? What was the book?" Foshan replied. He sounded uninterested.

"*Dream of the Red Chamber* by Cao Xueqin."

"I think I've read it."

※

Later that evening at the waste station, Loon Tong Chung joined Lee sitting on the log.

"I was hoping to see you, Mr. Gee," Loon said. "I've news from the Sam Yap house. There's been some trouble in your village."

"How do you know this?" said Lee. He didn't make eye contact with the man because he did not like talking while pooping.

"Loon Ping Fing, secretary at Sam Yap, is my brother." He tapped Lee on the wrist. "New sojourners come through every day. People talk."

Frowning, Lee moved his hand into his lap and bit his lip. It had been some time since he'd heard from home. "What sort of trouble?"

"All I know is that some families in the Panyu District have been moving."

"Moving?" Lee dared a brief glance over at the man. "Why?"

Mr. Loon shrugged his shoulders. "Perhaps we will know when the next letters arrive or when the next Chinese newspaper is published."

Lee nodded as he went through possibilities. *Floods, famine, war, an earthquake?* To distract himself from spiraling thoughts, he asked, "What was in the delivery that the snowshoe man brought?"

Leaning close so they were shoulder to shoulder, Mr. Loon whispered, "Signed contracts. They've hired a British chemist to produce nitroglycerin here at Summit Camp."

※

On Saturday evening of that week, Yang's crew had to help dig the gang who'd been working in the east-facing tunnel out from the snow that blocked the tunnel mouth. Wind, moving snow in drifts like great sand dunes almost completely covered the gaping tunnel mouth. It had taken hours, even with men inside digging too.

The cooks all knew, even before being told, that the weather would delay their crews. Foshan and Hee Chiu had gone out to help with snow digging and hauling. Lee was alone in the mess hall watching over the food, making sure it didn't burn or dry out. On nights like this, it was important to serve the men with excellence.

While he waited, Lee prepared for himself a bowl of rice and ladled a robust chicken broth over it. It had been steeping for days with bones, skin, and fat. He'd caramelized onions until they were translucent with golden edges. Lee forked a serving of them into his mixture. To top it off, he expertly added oil to a hot pan, making a sizzle that sounded like monsoon rain striking a tin roof. Right-handed, he cracked an egg, separating the halves with his thumb and forefinger until the gooey contents plunked into the pan. With his damaged left hand, he'd learned compensation techniques. Before the egg could set, he plunged his fork into the sunny center, breaking the surface tension. With a flourish, his fork moved like he was painting a language character. If he was writing, his word would be "harmony." Between worrying about what was happening at home, Yang's money problems, and Foshan's behavior, Lee felt his life was anything but.

When the egg was the perfect amount of cooked, yet still soft, he slid it on top of his rice. Lee gave himself over to a hyper-focus on the rice, onion, and egg textures and the recognition of minute details of their flavors. His soup and the careful consumption of it became a form of prayer, an affirmation of his joy for life and a profound sense of gratitude for the people he loved.

While it had taken time to get used to being surrounded by lots of people, really from the moment they boarded the Arracan, Lee realized that their absence, like a beehive going silent, was significant.

Raising his bowl to drink the last drops of liquid, Lee's thoughts landed on Rip Snorter. *What caused his upset?* It bothered Lee that he didn't know the man's family name. When he lit incense for him at the altar, would the gods know where to look for his soul? *Kite To might have it recorded in his employment files. But would "Rip Snorter" be listed too?*

※

Lee could hear voices coming before the men entered the space, filling it with the sounds of relief. He was ready for them, smiling as he placed bowls of warm, life-affirming food in their icy hands. While he remained annoyed with his brother, Lee was thankful to see his familiar face, weary as it was. They nodded to each other as Yang passed through the chow line.

※

Tomorrow, Lee would make sure the cooks had hot bathwater ready early. He planned to enlist some of the junior team members to fill in while he was gone. Most men were happy to be asked to move from line work to the kitchens. Kite To, within reason, allowed enlistment as needed. Lee was going to follow Yang into Coburn's Station.

※

Foshan was not pleased when he saw new kitchen helpers arriving.

"Start the tea," Lee said, handing a box of loose leaves to Foshan. "They are here to tend fires and keep the water hot today. I wrote out a meal plan and precut vegetables." He paused, then continued, "I'm going into Coburn's today to spy on Yang. He's not being truthful, and I need to see what he's up to."

"Yang again," Foshan stated quietly, his voice threaded with sarcasm.

SPY
Winter
Coburn's Station, California
1866
—

The traffic going to Coburn's Station was considerable. It wasn't hard to catch a ride on the back of a wagon, several back from Yang's. His brother was his usual effervescent Sunday self—loud, smiling, and entertaining those drawn into his orbit. As drivers maneuvered around and through muddy puddles, the going was slow. The countryside was mostly covered in white with patches of evergreen pine needles showing through.

Keeping track of Yang was much easier than Lee expected. Two blocks away from where his group disembarked sat the White Crane Saloon. Yang's group entered, looking like hourglass sands bunched at the glass bottle neck. Once they were inside, Lee didn't see any of them come out. He walked past the place multiple times and looked in the doorway. Yang sat at a far table holding a fan of cards in his hands. Everyone was smoking. A cloud hovered above their heads. As Lee watched, he saw Yang toss a hand down and swipe an arm across the table, sweeping in winnings.

Realizing Yang would be busy for a while, Lee visited the barber shop. He smiled under the hot towel as he remembered Foshan's daring during a shave. For a brief moment, he wished he lived in a world where all feelings of love were honorable. There was a fundamental wrongness about shame—or threats—for private, life-affirming experiences.

After the avalanche and Mr. Loon's ominous news, Lee had decided that love could not afford to wait. He needed Foshan and he hoped Foshan felt the same.

※

Returning to the bar where Lee had last seen Yang, he saw one man left, his head on the table, snoring.

Walking over to him, Lee jiggled his shoulder.

"Wha?" He raised his head. His eyes were bloodshot.

"Where's Gee Yang?" Lee asked.

"Who?" Spittle glistened at the corner of his mouth by the lantern light.

"Manly. Do you know where Manly went?"

"Ahya. Bunch of them went to sleep in the barn on Jibboom Street."

※

Lee's breath came out in puffs as he tugged his jacket collar higher. "I should leave him," he muttered. *He's a big boy and can make his own way home.*

"No," Lee mumbled the answer he knew Mother would say. He continued walking without a pause. He found his brother wedged between several others. *They look like a pack of puppies*, he thought. "Stinky ones," Lee said, pulling on Yang's arm to move him into a sitting position.

He managed to move Yang's dead weight over to the livery stable, where he'd rented a Clydesdale to take them back. The stable owner helped get Yang up. Lee mounted behind him, clamping him into place.

The way wasn't far; moonlight illuminated their path. Lee allowed the horse to have its head. It wanted to run. The smooth ride the gigantic beast gave them as he flew across the terrain was the stuff folktales are spun from.

At the stable, Yang roused enough to glance at his brother. "Oh goodie," he said, grinning. "You fetched me home."

Scowling, Lee jabbed Yang under his arm.

"Ow! Why'd you do that?" he whined.

Lee looped his brother's arm behind his neck and gripped his hand to keep him steady.

"Are you gambling all your money away?"

"Naaaah." Yang smiled, giving Lee a bleary-eyed look. He exhaled rotten breath in his brother's face. "I never lose, you know that."

Grimacing, Lee waved a hand to clear the air. "Your mouth smells like you never clean your teeth!" He continued in a sharp tone, "If you aren't losing, then what are you doing!?"

"Can't tell you. I'd have to kill you…or it would kill you. Everything's spinning, Leeeee."

Yang opened his mouth and hot vomit erupted, soaking the front of Lee, and dribbling down inside his pants.

The shock of this disgusting assault caused Lee to release Yang's hand.

Yang maintained a wobbly balance as he regarded his own spoiled clothes. "Drinks drown your sorrows, little brother, but your sorrows always return in the morning."

※

In the morning, both Gee brothers were aghast when they learned that the roof of the Jibboom Street barn had collapsed under the weight of the snow, killing every man who had been sleeping there.

News:

WEATHER

Chinese Historical Society of America | Pg. 4. A.P. Partridge excerpt.
(1867) The snows came early that year, he said, "and drove the crews out of the mountains. There were about 4,000 men…3,000 of them Chinese. Most …came to Truckee and filled up all the old buildings and sheds. An old barn collapsed and killed four Chinese. A good many were frozen to death."

Weekly Butte Record | December 22, 1866
Now that the Central Pacific Railroad is blocked up with snow, and is likely to continue so during the winter, it is proper for the people, who are being burdened with taxes for the construction of that stupendous folly, to inquire into the subject, and ascertain, if possible, whether there is a practical route for a railroad leading into California.

Morning Union | December 29, 1866
CHINAMEN KILLED BY SNOWSLIDE—On Saturday a gang of Chinamen employed on the railroad were covered up by a snow slide, and some four or five of them died before they could be exhumed. Snowstorms, accompanied with high winds, made the stay at the Summit anything but agreeable, the snow being from ten to fifteen feet deep; notwithstanding which the road is kept open, and the sleighs of the Pioneer Company make their regular trips to Cisco. The snow fell to such a depth on Friday that one whole camp of Chinamen was covered up during the bight, and parties were digging them out when our informant left.

Dutch Flat Enquirer | December 25, 1866
…a gang of Chinamen employed by the railroad were covered up by a snow slide and four or five died before they could be exhumed…The snow fell to such a depth that one whole camp of Chinamen was covered up during the night.…

RAILROAD BUILDING PROGRESS

Sacramento Daily Union | December 31, 1866
CENTRAL PACIFIC RAILROAD—This road is now completed and in daily operation from Sacramento to Cisco, a distance of ninety-three miles, reaching within twelve miles of the summit of the Sierra Nevada mountains, and 5,911 feet above the level of the sea—a higher altitude than is attained by any other railroad in America.

Sacramento Union | December 31, 1866
…the completion of the Central Pacific from Sacramento to Cisco, a total of 92 miles. … twelve tunnels ranging from 800 to 1650 ft long are still under construction along the "snow belt" from the summit to Truckee river. … work on the tunnels is progressing 24 hours a day, with three shifts of men working eight hours each, and that the railroad expects completion by the spring of 1867; the sole exception is the 1,650-foot summit tunnel, expected to be ready to receive track by September 1867.

BRAVEST MAN
February
Tunnel Number Six, Donner Summit
1867

—

A flake of snow and a single drop of water are nothing on their own. But a flood that washes villages away in angry roiling torrents, or trillions of ice flakes coming down non-stop for five full days causes conditions few humans relish.

Snow tunnels were reconstructed. Men were digging, patching, and reinforcing passageways and chambers, mostly in darkness. Missing daylight, the Chinese referred to themselves as snow moles.

Edema, where excess fluids pool in the legs, became a widespread problem. It caused the skin to stretch tight, making it hard to bend the knees. The doctor worked tirelessly, using acupuncture to treat it. He didn't have enough needles or time to treat everyone, so he taught the acupressure points and encouraged the men to show the technique to anyone in need.

Feet were always wet and shoes were full of snow. Chilblains, blistering itching patches of skin irritated by small vessels repeatedly exposed to the cold, turned walking into a form of torture. Witch hazel lotion was in constant use.

Where humor still existed, the men joked that this must be what it feels like for women with bound feet. "We're luckier," one man commented. "When spring comes, our wounds will heal." That winter, many silent vows were made to be kinder to the womenfolk.

Iron-rich foods and warming spices—cayenne pepper, turmeric, and ginger—were generously added to the meals. When preparing rice and tea, the cooks included bibhitaka, one of the many specialty items the cooks could order from spice brokers in San Francisco.

※

A stagecoach arrived, carrying the slight English chemist with a beaky nose and a perpetually sour expression. With him, he offloaded boxes containing glycerin and sulfuric acids, ingredients that were deemed safe to transport.

James Howden was hustled into Crocker's office building, where he met with the big bosses for the better part of his first day. Mr.

Loon, drinking coffee in Foshan's mess tent, reported that "They built a new cabin for him to sleep in."

Foshan, Lee, Hee Chiu, and the other men not on shift in the mess hall gathered around to listen.

"The tent they've been building close to the tunnel is where he'll be mixing his blasting oil. I hear he negotiated $300 per month."

With bulging eyes, the group let out a collective exclamation. It would take a year for any one of them to earn that much!

Lee took a sip of the beverage, making a face. Loon had brought coffee grounds and showed Lee how to brew it. "It takes some getting used to," he said, grinning, before taking another sip. "Mr. Crocker requests that you prepare a meal to honor Howden's arrival next Saturday." His comment was directed at Lee. "Mr. and Mrs. Leland Stanford will be coming too."

Lee nodded; he was familiar with the request. They wanted something "exotic," which, according to their definition, meant, "not too spicy." The meal would be served on fine china in Crocker's cabin. At its conclusion, the chefs would be expected to step into view, smile, and bow. Once that was done, they would be excused.

Grinning, Lee turned to Foshan, pointing all five fingers at him. "Chef Yow's doing this one."

Loon crossed his arms over his chest. "Is he as good as you?"

"Better," said Lee.

Shrugging his shoulders, Loon said, "As long as the food is good, it doesn't matter."

Foshan spoke for the first time, crossing his own arms. "Fine," he said without enthusiasm.

"If we entertain an enemy, we do it with a smile." Mr. Loon flashed a wide, toothy grin. "And we learn much."

Chuckling at the exchange, Lee knew that the man was right.

※

Howden's cabin was set up in a flat area close to the east tunnel mouth. Lee had heard rumors that the white men would not touch the stuff that the man made. The Chinese were expected to accept the increased danger. Anger simmered under his skin. The Six Company managers consented to the situation to keep coins flowing. *Men who work with Howden should be paid like Howden! Maybe Howden shouldn't be here at all!*

Lee noticed the Englishmen stalking around the perimeter of his chemical-mixing tent. Dressed in a long apron, Lee watched as the tips of the man's boots appeared and disappeared with each stride. He wore dark, long-sleeve protectors; in his hand, he carried six red flags. Lee, and the rest of the gangs, were briefed about the meaning of the red flags. When Howden was mixing, the perimeter inside the flags must remain clear.

When Howden first started manufacturing the stuff, he had a curious audience, albeit at a distance. Many of them included the chefs. He worked with a huge kettle and a fire. He had measuring and stirring instruments. In some ways, Lee thought Howden's work looked similar to his own.

Nitroglycerine is a clear liquid. It has no smell, yet it tastes sweet. Oily to the touch, it causes severe headaches and sickness if it is absorbed through the skin. It is heavier than water and sinks to the bottom when the two are combined.

In a very pure form, stored in sterile containers, it can be stable. If impurities are introduced, a sneeze could set it off.

Round tin cartridges of the liquid were carefully loaded into a wooden crate. The man who would carry it stood nearby, waiting for the signal. Beyond his sallow skin and rapid blinking, he stood ramrod straight, making no extraneous movements. When the first batch was enroute, Howden placed a white flag near the tent doorway.

"That's what I imagine the lamb looks like, from the Christian Bible stories," Foshan commented behind Lee, "before going to the sacrificial altar."

Frowning, Lee turned. "Zzzzt." He shook his head at Foshan to make him shut up.

Lee didn't know the name of the man who carefully transported the frightful box. After the avalanche, he'd deliberately detached himself from learning names and stories. But, just now, he wished he'd not done so. If the fellow survived, Lee would prepare something extra special for him.

Stiffly, slowly, the carrier disappeared into the tunnel. Foshan repeated something he'd recently learned. "Nitroglycerin freezes at 45 degrees Fahrenheit. Before putting the cartridges into the drill holes, they'll have to warm it with their hands."

"Look!" someone called, pointing to the group of blasters running from the tunnel.

Ka Boom!!

That night, there was a jubilant feeling around Summit Camp. Kite To even made the unusual move of eating with the men.

Everyone was talking about the nitro. The borehole lengths were reduced by half, so the hand drilling took less time. The oil created a uniform blast, blowing all places at once. This broke the rock into smaller pieces, making them easier to carry. The residual smoke wasn't as dense or didn't last as long. Instead of 1.18 inches of progress in the tunnel, today's measurement had been 1.82 inches!

While the men were celebrating, Kite To was thinking about his work contracts and what it might mean if the road progress went faster than expected.

Lee joined Yang at his table. As usual, his brother surrounded himself with friends. Lee recognized the carrier. Yang introduced him as Wong Goon. "He's from Dieshi, down on the southern coast. He's only been in the country for two months. What a day he's had!" Yang slapped him on the back.

Wong Goon looked slightly uncomfortable with the attention, but he was nodding and smiling.

"This is my famous brother." Yang waved a hand at Lee as if he were presenting a gift. "Gee Lee, excellent chef, and occasional cook for Crocker himself."

Lee nodded to Wong Goon and the other new men Yang had not introduced. "We've been asked to prepare a meal for the chemist. Foshan says we should make fish and chips."

Yang raised a dubious eyebrow.

Glancing over his shoulder, Lee made sure Kite To was out of hearing range before saying, "I'd like to make Wong Goon a celebration meal but, unfortunately, Mr. Kite has forbidden such activities."

Wong Goon straightened at this.

Yang tapped Lee's forearm. "Leave it to me. I'll find a place." He glanced at the rest of the men at the table. "None of you are old enough to remember, but back in the day, I used to bring guests to Lee's for parties." He raised and lowered his eyebrows, causing laughter to ripple through their group. Turning back to Lee, he said, "Can you get another Sunday off?"

"You remember?"

"Of course."

※

Yang arranged for Lee and Foshan to commandeer the entire Imperial Dragon restaurant in Coburn's Station. The cooks had all morning to purchase supplies, plan the meal, and start marinades. Yang had also established credit at the shops they visited. The guests would arrive at 4:30 p.m.

Leaving before dawn, Lee and Foshan acquainted themselves with the kitchen layout, did the shopping, and accomplished their other pre-planned activities. They finished by eleven. Without discussing it, they knew how they'd spend their free time. Foshan drew a finger across the top of Lee's hand before they left.

Within half an hour, they were settled in the back room. "I wasn't sure you'd agree to see me like this again," Lee said.

Foshan was sitting on the bed, fully clothed. With hands palm up, he motioned for Lee to come to him. "Before your accident, I almost left."

"I was worried that you would," Lee confessed as he laid the back of his fingers along Foshan's jaw, stroking his cheek with a thumb. "I want you to stay—with me."

Leaning into the caress, Foshan closed his eyes, a tear seeped from a corner. "The longer I stay, the more it will hurt when we part."

"I know," Lee said in a gravel-filled voice.

Looking at Lee, Foshan saw his grimace. Lee's breath hitched against a great force of emotion he was battling. While it was gut-wrenching to see his Love struggle, it filled him with something he'd been missing...hope. A corner of his mouth lifted as he reached up to guide Lee to sit next to him.

"Why do you want me to stay?" Foshan asked. He held Lee's injured hand, gently massaging it.

Lee opened his mouth. Nothing came out. Tears streamed on both sides of his face. His expression became alarmed. Shaking his head, he looked down at their hands. "I can't," he choked out.

Lee was acutely aware when the shift happened. The pressure on his hand let up and warmth receded as Foshan pulled away. If being asked to say words was frightening, this was terrifying. "No! No! No!" he cried, clutching at Foshan. Grabbing his shoulders, he pulled him to his chest, locking his grip over his wrist to keep him in place.

"Wait, Foshan." Lee huffed as if he'd run a mile. "Give me a minute."

Foshan was like a statue in his arms, non-responsive. Lee knew This Now was pivotal. If he couldn't speak the words in his heart, he'd lose Foshan. When he pictured the emptiness that would encompass that void, it looked like hell. Intuitively understanding that Foshan was carefully listening, Lee loosened his grip. He lifted Foshan's queue so he could release the tie securing the braid. Working his fingers in, he freed the woven strands. Stroking the back of his head, he worked to calm his breath. "You know this." Lee nuzzled into Foshan's hair, under his ear. "I'm sorry I've not said it before." He shut his eyes. "It's important to you—to both of us."

This time, when Foshan leaned back, Lee wasn't worried. He let his fingers trail along Foshan's arms, then stilled.

"I need to see your face," Foshan stated simply.

Nodding, Lee used his sleeves to scrub the moisture from his eyes and nose while inhaling deeply. Looking up to engage, he held Foshan's gaze. The light was there, infusing him with strength. "I love you, Foshan."

※

Yang arrived right on time, leading the party. Wong Goon was the nitroglycerine-carrying man of the hour. Jan Hoi and Bee Soy Yang's new blasting buddies, as well as the Central Shaft Supervisor, were there. Unexpected, but welcome, additions were Scared Eye and Animal Boy.

"Look who I found!" Yang laughed, nudging Animal Boy on the shoulder as he placed liquor bottles on the table.

Lee and Foshan came out to greet everyone and ask Animal Boy and Scarred Eye what they'd been doing since they last saw him. "Trestle building mostly." Animal Boy smiled. Scarred Eye was evasive. "This and that."

"Have you encountered more rattlesnakes?" Lee asked Animal Boy. "Oh no. When it gets cold, they're scarce."

Before they began the meal, Yang invited everyone to could come into the kitchen to watch the cooks display their knife skills. They put on a show worthy of a theater performance. As Lee did elaborate knife twirls and tosses, Yang shared the story about Mother sending the blade and Baldy crafting it. The demonstration concluded with applause and smiles.

As everyone pulled chairs up to the table, Lee and Foshan began serving the first course, egg flower soup and fried wontons. They took turns after that so they could both enjoy sitting with the others. A meal for nine was a terrific number as far as Lee was concerned. The pots and pans needed did not have to be gargantuan. The food itself could be delicate and served at the perfect temperature when it was ready. One didn't have to yell to be heard, and everyone shared what was relevant in their lives. When their bellies were full, warm feelings persisted. Yang started making toasts. "To Wong Goon, the bravest man I've ever met, whose name will be etched into history."

"Here! Here!" the group agreed, drinking to that.

"And to my brother," Yang's jovial tone turned serious, "a man I admire in ways he'll never know. If there was ever a person one would want to emulate—aside from the great Confucius," he paused for laughter, "it would be him."

Animal Boy raised his glass and said, "Here!"

Yang held up his hand. "I'm not finished. And to Yow Foshan, a man who has been a good friend to our family, someone who has become like a brother."

"Here! Here!"

At the conclusion of the evening, after fond farewells, Yang stayed back to help the cooks clean and lock up. While the dishes were being washed, he asked Lee for a private moment. Stepping into the restaurant, he indicated they should sit. "I know you know what I've been doing," he started, meaningfully.

When Lee opened his mouth to reply, Yang waved him off. "Hear me out. I have been winning more than losing," he said as he reached into his coat pocket to pull out a fat envelope. Placing it on the table, he slid it across to Lee. "That's how we got this." He arced a finger overhead, indicating the restaurant. "I can't say when I'll have more, and I…"

Lee wondered what he was going to say.

"This is for our parents. Would you send it with your next letter?"

"I thought you—"

Yang laid a hand on his wrist, squeezing. "Will you send it? Please?"

"Yes," Lee agreed, placing a hand on top of Yang's. "I thank you for what you said tonight. I admire you too. You're braver than I could ever be."

Yang looked sad but nodded. "Thank you for tonight. It was flawless."

"It was an evening we can always remember." Lee grinned.

OX TAILS
February
Summit Camp
1867
—

Lee was happy to be back in the kitchen after spending three days in Kite To's office. He'd been writing letters, negotiating a bulk price for rice that would supply the Summit Camp kitchens for the next few months. Dock handling and shipping had to be sorted out next. He was glad not to have to worry about it once he arranged for the delivery to the train station. The Central Pacific Railroad didn't charge them for shipping.

Scarred Eye called a friendly "hello" when he entered the mess hall carrying a burlap sack over his back.

Lee groaned. He could see blood on it and remembered the porcupine. "What do you have for me, sir?" He smiled while wiping his hands on a dishcloth.

Scarred Eye stamped his feet. "It's wicked cold out!" Grinning, he said, "Ox tails!" He dropped the heavy bag onto the serving counter.

Propping hands at his waist, Lee reluctantly asked, "Where did you get a sack full of ox tails?"

Foshan had stepped forward to dump them from out of the bag. They were covered in coarse grey hair with black wispy bobs at the tip. The places where it would have connected to the animal were raw, thawing, and getting drippy.

"Out on the wagon road," Scarred Eye said, winked.

When Lee motioned toward the bubbling pot of sweet and sour soup, Scarred Eye nodded with enthusiasm. "See?" he said. "This is why I bring you the good stuff."

As Lee filled a bowl and added dumplings to it, he listened to the story. Snow accumulating on the tracks between Auburn and Cisco was a major problem. They'd tried keeping them clear, with up to twelve engines pushing at once. But the Sierra Cement proved to be a formidable challenge. Banks of snow were freezing up to thirty feet deep. It wouldn't budge for the engines. They'd resorted to putting teams of Chinese out there with picks and shovels, clearing it as the white stuff came down.

Things on the wagon road weren't much better. Teamsters strapped modified snowshoes to their oxen. They used animals and heavy wagons to push through and keep the way clear. In fresh snow, the oxen sank. In icy snow, they'd pull until they wore out. When they couldn't take it anymore, the beasts lay down. Teamsters could get them up by twisting their tails, but that had its limits.

Foshan and Lee shared a glance. "A soup for tomorrow?" Foshan suggested.

"That's good." Lee nodded at Scarred Eye. "You are welcome to join us if you are still in camp."

※

Snow continued falling through March. Howling winds lifted the new stuff and swirled it around. It accumulated in hefty piles next to places that interrupted it: walls, doorways, and tunnel mouths.

With a few exceptions, everyone had raw, blistered feet. Bouts of acidic diarrhea spread through the men in camp. Not only did it hurt to walk, but now it hurt to sit too.

A steady trickle of workers kept leaving. When departing men stopped by the kitchen to thank the cooks and say goodbye, Lee couldn't help feeling envious. He'd started imagining what his last day in camp would be like.

Most of the railroad workers who remained counted the minutes until they could sleep. The ones who were the most successful sleepers had clean, dry clothes and a warm pile of blankets to crawl under.

Warming fires were essential, though they only heated a front or backside at one time. They also melted the walls and ceilings of the snow shelter. Most were grateful for the protection. Exposure to wind on the surface would cause certain death.

While Yang could perform the functions necessary for blasting and keeping dry, the infernal cold was getting to him. There were three types and all of them were bad; outside, exposed to the raw mountain elements, inside their burrowed passageways, and the extra special quality inside the rock tunnel where runoff formed frozen waterfalls. Mud puddles became slick patches, bone-breakers for men who let their minds wander.

Wong Goon was long gone. He hadn't even made it inside the tunnel mouth when the box of explosives he carried went off. Scraps of his clothing were all that was left of him. They were now on carrier

#3. The men started giving them numbers, and bets were placed on how long they'd last. Yang had won ten dollars in the last pool.

Jan Hoi and Bee Soy were still alive, but convalescing in San Francisco. Jan Hoi only had one foot and Bee Soy had lost his right hand and forearm.

Every time Yang thought about returning to his wife mutilated, it made him ill. These days, the memory of Fung Kee's opium addiction didn't seem that bad. He'd rather waste away on a flower of joy than freeze to death or be blown to bits. The drug provided relaxation; it made one feel warm from the inside out, and it deadened the sex drive. A year or two ago, losing that would have been one of the worst tragedies Yang could imagine. *Funny, how a person changes.* Yang reclined on his bunk, inhaling pungent smoke from a fiery crystal.

Yang had no illusions about his odds of survival. While he put on a good show of confidence for his brother and the other men, he knew it was only a matter of time.

Yang's fantasies, both in his right mind and out of it, rarely featured his niece, Ngon. However, on the edges of sleep, he heard echoes of her voice, "Thank you, Uncle. Thank you."

※

The kitchen crews had their own temperature issues. The first inch of standing water froze everywhere. While the tunnel men hacked away at rock, the cooks hacked at ice. Some of them would have enjoyed experimenting with nitroglycerine.

TROUBLE
March & April
Summit Camp
1867
—

When it happened, Lee had no forewarning of doom. He didn't even know about it until many hours had passed. Realizing it was long past when Foshan should be joining him in the kitchen, he turned preparations over to their assistants and went looking for him.

He wasn't in his bunk, or at the latrine. He wasn't in the supply sheds or at the stables. Beginning to feel alarmed, he jogged over the Kite To's office, yanking the door open without knocking first. To was in a meeting with a visiting Six Company representative. "Sorry to interrupt," Lee said. "I can't find Foshan. Do you know where he went?"

Kite To frowned. He whispered to his guest, got up and walked Lee outside, closing the door firmly behind them. "Unacceptable, Mr. Gee," the manager reprimanded. Lowering his voice, he leaned close. "I warned you to steer clear. Men like Yow Foshan don't last long in places like this."

Turning a shade of green, Lee stumbled backward, "Is he…?"

"I don't know," Kite To said. "Ask Baldy."

Of course! Lee thought. *Why didn't I think of that?* Running at top speed, Lee raced across the compound, leaping over snow patches and weaving through traffic. At the blacksmithy, he wasn't surprised to find the shop doors locked. Hastening to the living quarters at the rear, Lee pounded on the door. "It's Lee! Let me in!"

Like a spring-loaded bull, Baldy burst out. Jamming a flat hand into Lee's chest, he sent him sprawling. Landing in a puddle, he didn't notice the frigid water soaking his clothes. Opening and closing his mouth, Lee ground out, "Is Fosh…?"

Walking into the water and standing over him, Baldy pointed a finger in Lee's face. "He's not dead, but he came close."

Letting his elbows collapse against his sides, Lee made a splash as he laid flat on his back, pressing a trembling hand to his mouth. Lowering it, his miserable eyes met Baldy's. "What happened?"

Sighing, the big man backed up while offering a helping-up hand. "Nobody knows. Somebody dumped him in the rubbish pile over there, leaving him for dead. He was unconscious when I found him."

"I *have* to see him!" Lee said, looking like he had just now realized what a mess he was.

Laying a hand on Lee's shoulder, Baldy squeezed. "That's not a good idea."

"But he must know I'm here! I'll bring him to my cabin and take care of him."

Shaking his head vehemently, Baldy said, "You can't unless you want to give whoever did this to a reason finish him off." He continued, "The best thing you can do is go back to your kitchen, get cleaned, up and act like everything is normal."

"No!" Lee's eyes were wide.

From inside came a noise. Recognizing Foshan's voice, Lee made a lunge toward it. Baldy caught him, holding him in place. Leaning close to his ear, he said, "His jaw and shin are broken. He's clean and bandaged. So far, there's no sign of infection. You can come back after it's dark. Make sure you're not followed. I'll leave a candle in the window."

※

The first night after Foshan's attack, Lee cried when he saw him. That cherished face was swollen, bruised, and unrecognizable, except for the eyes. Lee brought soft, comfort foods loaded with healing herbs and spices.

Foshan couldn't speak for a while, so he wrote letters to Lee, who read them and responded verbally when he came to visit, bringing food, each night. Lee saved each one, keeping it in the box below his bed where he saved letters from home.

It frustrated Lee that Foshan didn't remember anything about that night. It worried him that Baldy and his network were coming up with nothing about who was responsible. Lee wanted to find the person who did it and…do something uncharacteristic for him.

Beyond worrying about Yang, he was now anxious to get Foshan out of the camps too.

※

Foshan gradually healed. While his face cleared and his sense of humor returned to full force, his leg would never be the same. He'd walk with the help of a cane for the rest of his days.

To do as Baldy requested, Lee pretended like nothing was amiss. It took a toll, faking smiles and friendliness when any one of the men passing through his kitchen could have been responsible for hurting Foshan. Most people assumed Foshan had grown tired of the snow and left camp for the city. To this, Lee shrugged his shoulders saying, "I wouldn't know."

※

When there was fifteen feet of snow on the ground, Lee was transporting meal components to Mr. Crocker's cabin. The guest he and Mr. Stanford were entertaining was Authur Brown.

Lee understood English words here and there. In Mandarin, he asked Mr. Foon to explain what he missed.

Brown was a seasoned fieldman specializing in bridge construction. This afternoon, the bosses were discussing building structures to cover the tracks.

"As soon as you're ready," Mr. Crocker said, "and we're finished with the tunnel, we'll move men onto building crews."

With Yang's wood affinity, Lee knew his brother would be interested...if they were staying. Camp gossip said that the tunnel six breakthrough was getting close.

A letter from home arrived.

—

To my dear sons Yang and Lee,
May Guan Gong and Guan Yin watch over you and keep you safe until your return.
Distressing news. Father has died. Bubonic Plague.
Ming had it too. She recovered.
Thanks to you, Father's funeral was honorable.
Come home.
Mother, Shao Pei

News:

Daily Alta California | February 14, 1867
THE DISGRACEFUL ATTACK ON CHINESE.
The disgraceful riot of Tuesday will injure no one so much as the bad men who were engaged in it. They have exposed themselves to the punishment of the law; they have placed on their reputations a stigma that will last so long as they live, in ruthlessly beating and mutilating Chinese laborers and wickedly burning and destroying their house and property. They have blackened their consciences with a stain which they can never wash out and have set at naught the dictates of the religion in which they pretend to believe.

… Mob violence will not succeed. The good citizens of San Francisco, the general sentiment of the community, the interests of the State, the law of the nation, demand that no such mob shall have its way.

BREAK THROUGH
May
Tunnel Number Six, Donner Summit
1867
—

Mother's letter and the crushing news it contained hit the brothers in different ways.

"We must leave today or tomorrow!" Lee exclaimed. He rushed around, pulling items from shelves to pack.

"Hurrying home will not bring him back," said Yang as he laid a hand on Lee's arm, gripping it tightly to hold him steady. "We should finish the month and go at the end of the pay period."

Inside, Yang was sobbing and yanking at his hair. He'd always viewed Mother as the stronger parent, but now that Father was gone, he wasn't sure. By default, he'd become head of the Gee family. It was his duty to stand firm for all of them. Reviewing his behavior since he began this sojourn filled him with something thick and foul-smelling.

Lee spent every free moment burning paper offerings, lighting incense, and praying. His skin lost its healthful glow and dark circles formed below his eyes.

Foshan wished he could hold Lee to comfort him. Unable to do so, he did his best by preparing Lee's favorite foods and encouraging him to eat. It was discouraging to watch him refuse. "You'll be of no use to anyone if you waste away," Foshan said. "Your wives have been working on the farm with your father all the time. They'll know what to do to keep things going."

Yang's debt was a long way from being paid off, in spite of his sending in gambling winnings and submitting much of his monthly pay. The Sam Yap Company would prevent him from leaving.

※

On Saturday morning, Yang was coming off his night shift. Since the roads were clear, he went to Coburn's Station. Before leaving, he had a note delivered to Foshan asking if he'd meet him there, alone.

Yang sat at the bar sipping his third glass of whiskey. He was old enough to remember Uncle Lung's homecoming and his father's enjoyment over listening to the travel stories. All the time they'd been gone, Yang had been thinking that his return to Father would be similar. Wrapping his mind around the idea that no new memories could be made with him, ever, was nearly impossible.

For the first time since he arrived in California, Yang thought about his daughter and what her life had been like since he left. *Is Ming six years old now? Did she get sick before or after Father? Was she afraid when she saw the black boil? Her mother must have been beside herself.*

Foshan limped in, leaning heavily on his cane. He sat next to Yang. Catching the bartender's attention, He pointed at Yang's glass. "It's early for that," he commented.

Yang eyed him. "And you're doing it too," he said wryly.

Foshan sighed. "A death in the family is extenuating circumstances."

When the bartender placed the glass in front of Foshan, he raised it. "To Mr. Gee, a father of fine sons."

"Thank you," Yang said quietly. "I didn't ask you to come here to drink."

"It would be alright if you did."

He nodded. "I have a serious problem." Yang dropped his voice. "I need someone to talk to who knows both my brother and me." He glanced over at Foshan. "Lee must never know about it."

"I see." Foshan blinked. "What makes you think I'd agree to keep a secret from him?"

"Once you hear it, you'll be like me, and you'll want to protect him."

Foshan turned and stood. "He's hurting enough. You're asking me to do something that could add to it? I won't do it."

Yang grabbed his arm. "It's something I've done, Foshan. If he finds out…" His eyes glistened. "I need help. Please?"

※

They met in the back room. When Foshan walked into the place, the doorman eyed him and cracked a smile.

Yang was already inside sitting on the single chair. A bottle of whiskey and two glasses sat on the table. He nodded at the bed; Foshan shook his head. "I prefer to stand."

Groaning, Yang stood. He picked up the table and moved it next to the bed. He took a seat there and offered Foshan the chair. After filling their glasses, he paused. Looking lost, he said, "I don't know where to begin."

"At the beginning is usually best," Foshan said curtly. "Look, Yang, I have to get back to work the breakfast shift. Maybe we should pick another time?"

"No! It has to be now." He shook his head. "Has Lee spoken to you about our older brother?"

"Fu-chi?"

Yang nodded.

"He has. And about his wife, Mo Chou, and their daughter, Ngon." As he listed each person, Foshan extended a finger, counting. He continued, "Your parents, your wife, Ting Ai, and your daughter, Ming, Wèi An, Song, and little Luck."

"OK," Yang said with a sigh, "that's a good start." He took a sip, nodding to Foshan to do the same.

Foshan shook his head and raised his eyebrows.

A hard glint came into Yang's eyes. "Did he tell you what happened to Fu-chi…and the rest of his family?"

Foshan gave a curt nod.

"Here it is then." Yang spoke quickly, as if he were in a rush to get the words out. "I found Ngon in the brothel in Nevada City. She was a hundred men's wife, with child."

"What!" Foshan leaned forward.

"She doesn't want Lee to know she's here—ever. I don't want him to know either. If he found out, Foshan, it would be worse than Father's death."

Foshan sat back, scratching the back of his neck. "Flying dragon shit."

"Yes, flying dragon shit," Yang agreed. "Here's the rest. I couldn't leave her there. Scarred Eye arranged to steal her away from the Triad. I needed money for his plan. Six Companies made a loan."

Yang slouched, letting out a pent-up breath as he finished. "I still owe them money and I can't leave the country until it's paid."

Foshan nodded. "How much?" Hearing the amount, Foshan stood abruptly, putting both hands on his forehead. "Lee's got to leave today!" he exclaimed.

"What do you mean?"

"Don't you know how those contracts are written?"

At Yang's blank look, Foshan stopped, glaring. "Lee remains unencumbered as long as you are making money. If something happens to you, your debt transfers to him."

Yang knocked back the rest of the liquid in the glass, setting it down with a clink. "That can't be right. I made the loan in Grass Valley. I didn't tell anyone I have a brother."

Exasperated, Foshan threw up his hands. "Everything gets back to San Francisco. Everything!"

Yang's hands shook as he poured another splash into his glass. "This isn't helping."

Angrily, Foshan grabbed his cane and strode to the door. With his hand on the knob, he paused.

Yang asked, "What are we going to do?"

Foshan's shoulders dropped. He leaned his forehead on the wood. "I don't know yet." Turning back to face Yang, he pointed at the bottle. "Stop that. And stop doing anything else that clouds your thinking. You need to be careful!"

Yang hung his head. He regarded his feet. "Nothing's going to happen today." He raised his eyes. "I paid for the room. I might as well stay in it."

"I don't know what to say." Foshan's eyes went watery. "Yang, you're an idiot, a bastard, and a hero."

After the door closed, Yang poured more whiskey and raised a glass. "Here! Here!"

※

Yang tried following Foshan's directive. He swiftly discovered the painful consequences of withdrawal. To keep his mind clear, he had to continue with his vices, if only to maintain stability.

Excitement was increasing on all four sets of tunneling crews. If Mr. Gilliss' measurements were correct, they'd be breaking through any day. With every fuse Yang lit, he hoped this would be the one.

Lee took direction. He was grateful Foshan was there to remind him what to do next. He assumed they'd be working till the end of May before leaving for home. He moved as if he were in a thick fog where time lost meaning.

Of the three of them, Foshan had the most intact reasoning abilities. However, the complexity of the puzzle he was attempting to solve bogged him down. He agreed Lee should not know about his niece. If he packed Lee's bags and took him to San Francisco to put him on a boat, he'd have to explain why Yang wasn't going with him. *Maybe Yang could pretend to go until the passengers were boarding? But then Lee would feel like we both lied. Yang must tell Lee about the loan,* Foshan concluded.

Friday, May 3—it was 12:30 p.m. Yang and his crew were finishing their tea break. As the rocks were cleared from the previous blast, word quickly spread that the east-end gangs had broken the last barrier. The pressure was on for Yang and the west-end crews to finish the task. They were watching #7, carrying a load of blasting oil into the tunnel. By the way the tins clinked against one another, Yang was guessing he'd win the current betting pool. If the man made it to the end, he'd set the box on the ground and the crew responsible for tin placement, fuse setting, and lighting would go back in.

Yang could hear the familiar squeal of the hoist and Goose chugging as it pulled men out of the pit for an identical exercise. He didn't place bets on the pit carriers who rode down in the buckets. That transport mechanism added elements of risk that made predicting success or failure more difficult.

He tried, mightily, to keep his mind from wondering about Foshan and Lee. Nitro carrier #7 was leaving, wearing a relieved expression.

Next, the pit and east blasters needed to clock it so their explosions went off together. Since lowering in a bucket took longer than walking into the tunnel, the supervisors tracked time on their pocket watches. They blew a whistle for the bucket blasters to begin, and another for the tunnel blasters.

At his whistle signal, Yang moved. "Gotta go," he said to no one in particular. It was an unspoken rule not to make eye contact with anyone before setting a fuse. Keeping his head down, Yang waved to the bucket operator when he was in and ready to go. In his peripheral vision, he noted the second bucket lowering his partner.

Once inside, with flickering lantern light giving his movements a ghostly appearance, Yang's grip tightened on the fuse line looped over his shoulder. On the gravel, he was alert for shiny areas. He'd slipped on an ice patch earlier in the week and his back was still aching.

Their steps sounded loud as they approached the hole. Yang secured the fuse line to an anchor rock he'd selected earlier. He stuffed the other end into the drill hole while his partner rolled the tin vial of nitroglycerin between his hands. He could tell by the way the oil moved when it was ready. At his partner's nod, Yang began uncoiling the line, moving back from the drill hole.

Yang heard the whispered prayer the crewman spoke before upending the tin container. He knew from experience, that if the volatile liquid went off by accident, there would be nothing recoverable from either of them. Yang said his own prayer.

His partner walked past Yang as if he were leaving after a temple service. Yang stood by the end of his fuse line, waiting for the man to signal the bucket operator. When he was halfway up, the man rapped his knuckles three times on his bucket. Yang squatted and struck a match. His hands were shaking so much that he failed at it three times. On the fourth try, he lowered it to the line and watched as sparks began flying. Quickly jumping to his feet, Yang ran.

Standing in the bucket, Yang signaled to the top. The seconds between his motion, before the hoist engaged, were utter terror. Into the blackness, he watched the fuse hurrying toward its target. He couldn't remember what he usually thought about. Today, Foshan's words came up, *If something happens to you, Lee can't go home.* Feeling the bucket lifting, Yang gripped the line and closed his eyes, opening them when he smelled Goose oil. Even the Central Shaft crew ran for cover before detonation. In this case, they left the building. Breathing heavily, Yang leaned against an outer wall, ritualistically patting his thighs. This accomplished two things. It helped to stop his legs from shaking and it verified that he hadn't peed his pants.

※

The east face report boomed, followed within seconds by the pit blast. The men waited for the wave of rock rain to pass before going back in. Limping slightly, Yang was at the tail end of the group, heading back down. Up ahead, he heard a cry. Had they missed someone inside? But then the surrounding men were jumping up and down, clapping each other on shoulders and backs. "Breakthrough!" they cried.

※

Word spread like wildfire through Summit Camp. Even those who were sleeping were awakened and given the news.

Lee thought he was dreaming when Foshan jiggled him. "They did it, Lee!"

Only half awake, Lee frowned. "Is someone hurt?"

"I don't think so," Foshan said. "They broke through. Six is open!"

※

One week later, the entire camp came out to watch as torchbearers spaced themselves out every twelve inches inside the 1,650-foot-long tunnel. Mr. Gilliss was taking final measurements to evaluate the results of the last two years' worth of work.

Calculation mistakes were highly likely. Visibility inside the tunnel was always an issue, as were moisture and condensation. The uneven floor as well as working four faces, along with a required slight rise, descent, and curve, were all areas where something could have gone wrong. Every error would cost the Central Pacific Railroad more time and money—resources they could not afford to waste.

Collectively, the camp held its breath as they watched Gilliss appear and disappear, writing numbers and geometric equations on a notepad on his dusty desk. Finally, after what felt like ages, the man stood tall, facing the onlookers. His face remained inscrutable as his gaze passed over the waiting faces. Finally, he cracked a smile and raised his voice so everyone could hear. "Less than two inches error! All four bores fit! We've made fine work of it, lads!"

※

The Chinese railroad men asked the cooks to prepare a celebration feast. Some wondered if the catfish had survived the winter. "Fresh fish would taste good!"

But the railroad bosses vetoed a break; they had track to go down, the task that resulted in their government writing payment checks.

Resentment was trickling through the camp like the melting snow, building into streams that were picking up momentum.

※

After the tunnel breakthrough, Yang approached the Central Shaft supervisor to request a transfer. "I'd like to work on the snow sheds. I'm good with wood."

The supervisor eyed him, raising an eyebrow. "I'll be sorry to lose you," he said, extending a hand for a western-style shake.

Yang clasped it firmly, flashing his famous smile.

"You've done fine work here, Mr. Gee. I wish you well."

"Thank you, sir!" Yang bowed over their hands.

News & Quotes:

"It is a big job of itself to get several thousand men property camped, proper foremen selected, and each to his peculiar duties so that all goes off right." - Charles Crocker

"We had hard work last summer and fall to get Chinamen to work in this hard rock and they kept leaving rather than do it. What men we have now are trained to hard rockwork and we can depend on them. But we cannot rely on new men to stick to it." - Charles Crocker

AUBURN STARS AND STRIPES | October 30, 1867
Democracy created a 'white man's government.' We expect a moral, social and political purification of the State. As Democracy is responsible for the advent of the Asiatic race that curses the Pacific Coast, we expect that party to provide fully and speedily for its exodus. (Large gathering 1,000 people or more with flags and drums, meeting in Dutch Flat to demonstrate about the Mongolian problem). People were pissed about the Chinese labor force. They wanted to wait at the Summit, with a lash, and drive them out and let the railroad crumble and rust. Wash-houses of California are to be emptied of disgusting Asiatics. The great mission of Democracy is to crush out the last vestige of Republicanism.

COVERING TRACKS
May
Donner Summit
1867
—

Snow types vary. Some are fluffy, gentle fairy dust that clings to the eyelashes and evaporates on the tongue. Some are clumpy and wretched. If it splats on your skin, clinging and dripping, it can cause shivers and misery. Some snow is like sharp, cutting blades, dashing in gale-force winds. It feels as if it could shred your skin.

The Sierra Nevada mountains have a type of snow called Sierra Cement. This condition occurs when snow near a body of water in this case the Pacific Ocean, becomes laden with moisture. When the flakes conclude their descent, they constellate, often freezing in solid blocks when night temperatures dip below freezing.

Sierra Cement was a blight for the railroad builders. In lower elevations, where tracks were complete, their first thought was to send the steam engines barreling through, armed with pointed prows like an ocean liner. In other places in the world, where snow remained soft, this worked brilliantly. It did not hold true in the Sierras. Their next thought was, if one engine didn't do the job, surely more horsepower would. Multiple coupled engines, steaming away, rammed the stuff at full force. The cement held.

At considerable company cost, hand crews were employed, starting at the outset of each storm. Men with picks and shovels attempted to tame a frigid beast that refused to cooperate.

Charles Crocker and Arthur Brown were devising a plan to cover their tracks.

※

It was a Monday, and Yang was feeling upbeat. Maybe it was from the sun warming his back. Maybe it was from the ankle-deep fluffy snow that had dusted the ground the night before. Maybe he was feeling better because he was sleeping at night now and awake during the day.

Wood had always been Yang's choice material. He loved the sharp smell of sap. Especially now, he appreciated the slow, steady motions of hand sawing. He enjoyed watching steam engines powering massive saw blades in the mills, cutting beams heavier than a man could lift. Working out grain direction for strength and piecing together cuts to form something new were also satisfying activities.

After selling his small scrap-constructed furniture in Nevada City, Yang started imagining developing a side business. He could earn daily wages on the railroad and continue making designs from the waste products. He already had a dealer ready to take whatever he built.

He grinned as he imagined paying off his loan and becoming his own boss. Maybe his Penn Valley dream could become a reality! He counted himself fortunate to be at this juncture. It had been unnerving to live knowing that every day in the tunnel could be his last.

Yang's mood was so buoyant that he thought about breaking his opium habit and admitting the truth to Lee so they could strategize, together, over ways they could dig him out of his financial hole.

Shifting gears, he reflected for a moment on a conversation he'd had with his new crew boss, Mr. Nun Ho, on his first day. The man explained the plan to build barns—extraordinarily strong ones that could withstand tons of snow weight and avalanches. Watching as he brought out the specification pages, Yang allowed himself to be drawn into the place in his mind where he could envision the thing already built. Returning to the present, he pointed out where the joists met, suggesting a modification that would increase load capacity.

Mr. Nun Ho frowned at the interruption, then took a closer look. "I heard you were good," he said. "Now I see why."

Yang smiled, reveling in it.

As they continued the discourse, Yang pointed out another design flaw. "Aren't they selling nature views?"

Mr. Nun Ho regarded him with a questioning expression.

"If we build these barns," Yang said, "passengers will be riding in the dark."

Mr. Nun Ho cracked a smile, but it wasn't one of glee. "Since we are going to make lots of money on this job, I don't think we say anything about that, do you?"

※

Yang took a moment to stretch as the sun reached its zenith. A stiff wind was picking up, racing down the slope in his direction. He arched his back, bending to the right and then to the left. He smiled as he squinted, watching the trees above sway, sloughing accumulated snow from their branches. Digging in his pocket for nails, Yang allowed himself to imagine returning home to the warm nights and humid days, to the familiar sites on the farm.

He clamped six nails tightly between his lips and braced the edge of his left hand on the support beam. Pinning a nail between his fingers, he pulled back his hammer to strike a blow.

That powerful stance and those uplifting thoughts would be Yang's last.

News:
Marysville Daily Appeal | March 14, 1867
A TERRIBLE AVALANCHE NEAR DONNER LAKE. —We are informed by Mr. Hamilton, telegraph operator at Cisco, that a fearful avalanche fell on Thursday night last, overwhelming a collection of Chinese shanties situated some distance below the Summit tunnel, and down the grade toward the lake. The shanties were either crushed in or swept away, and over 60 Celestials buried in the snow. Some were exhumed shortly after the disaster, but others were so long buried that at time it was supposed that no less than 30 had perished. Forty hours elapsed before all were dug out, when it was found that only 17 were dead—enough in all conscience. The last man found was alive, although 40 hours under the snow. He was in bed and the roof of his shanty had been crushed down in such a manner as to confine him there without, inflicting bodily injury. When dug out he got up and shook himself, exclaiming, "Ugh! too much hot!"

Marysville Daily Appeal | September 18, 1867
SNOW AND SNOW SHEDS - The Bee says between three and four inches fell at Cisco on Saturday but towards evening the temperature moderated, rain supervening, carrying off the snow which had fallen. The Railroad Company which are actively engaged with covering the cuts, with sheds, to prevent the snow from encumbering the track during the coming Winter. Their operations in this respect are extensive, involving a large outlay of money.

CLEAN SWEEP
May
Donner Summit
1867
—

"You must come, Mr. Gee," said the messenger.

Foshan glanced up at the man standing beyond their serving counter picking nervously at the hat in his hands. His expression made Foshan feel as if his intestines were liquified on the spot.

Lee nodded, still only half functioning with his hazy, grief-muddled mind. He started to follow when Foshan stopped him.

"Here, Lee." Foshan held out his coat. When Lee reached for it, Foshan asked, "Do you want to take off your apron?"

Looking down, Lee seemed surprised to see he was still wearing it. Nodding, he reached for the tie, but his fingers weren't working properly.

"Allow me." Foshan stepped closer, tugging at the knot. He pulled the apron over Lee's head. As he started folding it, he felt something in a pocket. Pulling it out, Foshan saw it was half a carrot. A food scrap Lee had saved to feed the animals. Not knowing what else to do with it, he shoved it into his pocket.

Foshan made eye contact with the messenger. He knew what was coming. The man's terse chin movement confirmed it.

As the messenger began leading Lee away, Foshan called to him, "Give me a moment and I'll join you." He motioned to Hee Chiu to take over the kitchen and grabbed his cane to shuffle out for a brief stop in Kite To's office.

※

With a set face, Lee followed the man up through the snow shaft, arising into the afternoon light. Unaccustomed to the brightness, his eyes streamed like a woman in mourning. Shouts from a distance drew his attention.

At the base of Donner Peak, Lee saw the hillside swept clean. Stacks of lumber, wagons, mules, wooden tunnel frames, and cabins were gone. Splintered beams poked through the drastically reshaped landscape. It looked like a massive dump of chefs' knives poking through cotton blanket stuffing. Silence, where there should have been hubbub, made Lee's breath hitch. If it wasn't for the color, it resembled his village after that devastating flood.

When the messenger stopped suddenly, Lee collided with the man's back, almost knocking them both over. As Lee was apologizing, Foshan joined them.

"You have to see this, Mr. Gee. I am sorry," the messenger said. "You would never believe it otherwise."

Feeling panic constricting his windpipe, Foshan was sure he didn't want to see. Pulling the carrot out of his pocket, he placed it in Lee's hand, curling his fingers around it. Leaning close, he whispered so only Lee could hear. "I'm with you. Dig your thumbnail in. It will give you strength."

Lee nodded, looking down at their hands. Foshan stepped away quickly, glancing at the messenger. "OK, we're ready."

As they approached, Lee saw hands shaped like claws and bloody legs separated from torsos, jewel-colored sparkles winking across a sugar-dusted expanse, contrasting with Lee's memory of being buried by the stuff.

Arriving at the place where the messenger was leading, Lee saw his brother standing where they'd uncovered him. A hammer, clutched in his right hand, was raised above his head while his left supported a beam.

"No!" Lee moaned. "Not Yang. It can't be."

Standing next to a perpendicular snowshed frame beam, Yang's eyes were open. Concentration lines creased between his brows. He was holding extra nails in his mouth. If his skin was not gray, if his eyes were not cloudy and his clothes were not sopping, Lee could believe Yang would continue his next action.

When Lee's legs gave out, Foshan was there to catch him. Gripping his shoulders, he kept him upright. Pressing his cheek against Lee's ear, he didn't care who saw them. Fiercely, he ground out his next words. "You're not alone. I'm here. You mustn't fall apart. Your mother needs you, and Yang's wife and daughter need you."

※

There was a wagon waiting to transport bodies. Lee refused to be separated from his brother and would allow no one to touch him. Foshan helped sort out that they'd make room in the wagon bed for

Lee to ride with Yang. The others were piled on the opposite side, covered by a tarp.

Lee sat with his back against the driver's bench with Yang's head in his lap. Foshan took the space next to him, leaning against the tarp pile. Before the driver climbed onto his bench, he handed Foshan an extra covering. He took it from him and wrapped it over Lee like a blanket, leaving an opening for his face and making an allowance for the raised hammer arm.

Yang's body thawed as they rode. When his arm lowered and his grip loosened, Lee took the hammer. He gently pulled the nails out of his brother's mouth. Lee held his warm hands over Yang's eyes to close the lids. He clenched his teeth to keep from wailing.

While Lee's focus was on his brother, Foshan was paying attention to where they were going and to the other things that were happening in the wagon. A hand had become separated from a body. He pushed at it with his toe to keep it contained under the tarp. They were heading steadily downhill. They passed Auburn and Newcastle, leaving the snow and sticky mud behind. Near the Rocklin stone quarry, the driver turned on a remote road that led to an open field. He could see two small buildings in the distance. As they approached, Foshan started seeing mounds—hundreds and hundreds lined up like mahjong tiles. A series of open holes had already been dug.

An old man with a stooped back came out of a building followed by another man. The undertaker carried a clipboard. With a start, Foshan recognized the second man as Scarred Eye.

A moment later, it was obvious that Scarred Eye recognized them too.

While the cart driver and the undertaker worked together to identify men in the body pile, Scarred Eye came round to the other side of the wagon. Bracing his hands on the lip of the wagon wall, he sighed as he took in the sight of Manly, dead. Leaning over so his face wasn't visible, he shook his head saying, "Damit! He made it out of that god dammed tunnel didn't he?" Raising back into a standing position, he wiped his nose with his sleeve.

Nodding, Lee began to shake. "He did!" No longer able to hold his emotions in, he cracked open. While he was sobbing, Scarred Eye helped Foshan scooch him to the end and get his feet under him on the ground.

At a break in Lee's emotional storm, Scarred Eye squeezed his shoulder, leaning close to speak softly. "I've been working here for a while, and I respect everyone who comes here. You know I cared about Manly."

Lee nodded.

Scarred Eye continued. "I'm going to take good care of him. Do you believe that?"

Again, Lee nodded.

"You're going to have to leave soon so I can do my job. Is there anything Yang might have been carrying that you'll want?"

Confused, Lee looked to Foshan. Clearing his throat, Foshan met Lee's gaze when he said, "Would Yang have been carrying anything special? Like a coin or medallion that you'd want to keep or take to his family?"

Blowing his nose, Lee said, "I don't think so, but we should check if he has money. We'll need that."

※

Foshan wrapped an arm around Lee's shoulders. He steered them toward the road, keeping a tight grip to prevent Lee from turning around. Foshan nodded when he heard the driver say he'd pick them up in a little while and give them a ride to the Auburn Joss House.

Overhead, a raven swooped down before them, gliding low, almost as if it was leading the way.

※

Yang's bigger-than-life, magnetic personality was an element of life Lee expected to remain constant.

The memory of watching Ging Cui's canvas-wrapped body plunging under the Pacific waves kept replaying in his mind. The goals Lee had been striving toward, the plans and machinations that usually occupied a hefty chunk of his waking hours, had been completely swept away, leaving something that felt like a rain of granite rubble littering the steep slopes of iron road cuts.

Similar to the Black Goose, Lee moved when a lever turned. His heart was still beating, and he ate when Foshan put food in front of him. Inside, he was vacant. The blackness there swallowed everything. It reduced to a single pinprick of illumination—the bone jar he must place in Mother's hands. A piece of fired earth that would shatter her heart.

News:

Sacramento Daily Union | March 7, 1867

Messrs. Editors: I give you a brief journal of my trip from Virginia (Nev.), across the Sierra Nevada Mountains....Tuesday—All up early, and started about 10 o'clock; snowing very fast, wind flowing hard; walked; broke road and assisted the sleighs up to the top of the summit. There we were all able to ride down to Summit Valley, where the road was very, very bad—15 feet deep...Next day (Wednesday) the roads were better—snow still falling. By walking and working hard most of the time, we arrived at Cisco about half-past seven o'clock in the evening. Next morning we were informed that the sleighs could go no further, but if we would walk down eight miles to Emigrant Gap, we could meet the cars and go through...going round a point we suddenly came in sight of Governor Stanford and Charles Crocker, bundled up in their large coats and comforters, mounted on top of the famous snow plow—four locomotives behind them, snow to the north, south, east and west, under, above and all round them. In fact they were snowed in, and could not, get home to vote at the primary election. We were then compelled to walk on to Alta, sixteen miles from where we started In the morning.

Marysville Daily Appeal | April 11, 1867

A TRIP OVER THE MOUNTAINS. —The Grass Valley Union, April 9th, says: Mr. S.P. Dorsey, agent for Wells, Fargo & Co. at this place, gives us an interesting account of his rather adventurous trip over the mountains. Mr. Dorsey left here last Monday for Virginia and found the storm still raging on the mountains. He says that the railroad, in many places, runs between banks of snow 15 or 20 feet high. Near Cisco they met with an obstacle in the shape of a snow slide and were compelled to take sleighs from Crystal Lake station. The ride from there to the Summit he describes as bring particularly rough and stormy. When near the Summit they encountered another snow slide right on the stage road and were forced to slide down the mountain at an angle of about forty-five degrees to get around it. The snow at this point, on account of the slide, was some seventy-five feet deep...

FOSHAN
Danzao, China & California
1850s & 1867

—

*It is more shameful to distrust our friends
than to be deceived by them.* – Confucius

—

Foshan understood the powerful emotions that buffeted Lee. He also knew that, while it seemed like those feelings would last forever, the great wave of bleakness would recede, funneling effluent through grains of wet sand where the sun would warm them, making them lighter.

※

Foshan's father had sent him to the missionary school to gain status with British and government officials. When he came home from school repeating the Christian teachings, Father had taken a belt to him. The buckle end forged scars across his back.

This taught Foshan how to navigate multiple worlds, to put on a good show. Outwardly, he appeared confident, stoic, and cultured. Depending on the situation, he could blend in with the British, missionaries, and the Chinese.

As he grew older, his father began noticing faults in his character.

"What are you doing?" Yow Doo screamed after catching his son pleasuring himself in their woodshed. He slapped Foshan until his ears rang when a priest at school reported that they caught him in a compromising situation with two boys.

"You must *behave*," Father growled, spraying spittle on Foshan's face while his hand twisted the material across his shirt, cutting off his air.

Every utterance of that word caused Foshan's body to recoil; his scalp prickled and his vision narrowed. What Father really meant was comply.

His secret that he was attracted to men felt like an invisible boil on the tip of his nose—a growing volcano of skin teeming with infection, stretching tight, cooking with fever, screaming for release. *See me!* He wanted to shout. *Smell the puss pouring forth. Taste its sourness.*

Until his father left for Gold Mountain, all that was good and healthy in him submerged below replicating boils. He behaved.

※

Hi Sonee, a younger brother of his sister's new husband, was the first to show him that there could be goodness in men. He taught Foshan how to unwind and experience sexual joy.

Before Foshan left for the United States, Hi Sonee asked, "Why are you going searching for him? You're better off without him."

Foshan shrugged. "Perhaps I will kill him. What I really want to do is see him man to man to understand why someone would treat a child the way he did."

※

California

Unlike most of the Six Company labor contract managers, Foshan kept his knowledge of English to himself. He didn't actively gather and trade information as Scarred Eye did. But he understood that certain knowledge, delivered to the right person, had significant uses.

Flitting through his mind were the months of intelligence he'd been gathering for an elaborate strike. Labor issues were making headlines across the country. Worker strikes highlighted dreadful, unsafe working conditions and low pay.

A concern of the planners were capitalist bosses retaliating with clubs and guns. Those men worried if they gave in to unified labor voices, unions would spread like cancer.

The time was quickly approaching when executing their plan would hurt the railroad bosses where they lived, in their money bags. The Chinese understood their critical contribution to the railroad building project. Simply, it would go lame without them. They calculated that the way they planned to do it, and in such numbers, would lower the probability of the bosses committing violence.

It was an important stand, one that Foshan did not want to miss.

※

Foshan believed his affinity with Lee was as close as he'd ever get to a stable, loving relationship. There were times when he had been completely open and honest with the man, and astonishingly, it hadn't shattered their relationship. He was acutely aware that the harsh working conditions, deprivations, and the environment in which they struggled to live produced cravings that would not survive outside the railroad camps.

After his conversation with Yang at the bar, a new internal struggle took hold.. If handled in a certain way, Foshan could maneuver his lover into a position that fulfilled his own long-held desires.

Lee had become the sole supporter and protector of two women: his mother and three children. *Am I a person capable of placing my own interests ahead of so many?* Even harboring the question made Foshan feel vulgar.

Foshan knew they couldn't last. Only a substantial force of will kept that hurricane of broken heartedness at bay. It would come for him eventually, and he would give himself over to it, but not today.

※

When the messenger had first come for Lee, Foshan knew immediately that he needed to go too. He'd dashed to Kite To's office and went in without knocking or bowing.

"It's Gee Yang," he stated, not needing to explain further. "They're taking Lee to him now. I've assigned men to take over our kitchen. I'm going with Lee to accompany the remains."

Kite To twisted in his squeaky office chair. "I'm lothing boyth fathter than water from a broken cup." With a deepening frown, his eyes narrowed. "You are not going anywhere! You are not family and I need you working in the kitchen."

"Fire me," Foshan said flippantly, "because I am going. After losing his father and now his brother, the fight's gone out of Lee. He won't want to come back."

Kite To considered this with his mouth open.

Foshan watched the man's tongue moving in and out of his empty tooth space.

Then Mr. Kite said, "Fuck it! I can't loothe cooks too. There'll be work for you both if you return."

※

Tossing and turning on his Joss House bunk, giving up on sleep, Foshan slipped on his pants and boots and went out for a walk. He'd only gone a block when he heard his name.

"Fosh."

Squinting and peering into the shadows, Foshan searched for the person attached to the voice.

Lee stepped into the glow of a flickering streetlight. "Only me."

"You couldn't sleep?"

"No," Lee said, shoving his hands in his pockets and looking down at his feet. "Thank you for…everything. I don't know how I would have got through yesterday without you."

"Well—" Foshan stopped himself from saying, *That's what I'm here for.* Instead, he asked, "What are you thinking?"

"I think I'm stuck, for a while at least," Lee said. "Did you know Yang said he thought he'd return home in a bone jar?"

"I never heard him say that."

"I can't," Lee inhaled a shuddering breath, "write it to Mother and Ting Ai."

Foshan nodded while thinking, *Your mother wrote to you.*

"I have to wait for the bone jar so I can be the one putting it in Mother's hands. That's when I'll tell her when we're in person."

"That could take a while, Lee. What will you do in the meantime?"

"Me?" He looked at Foshan hopefully. "Don't you mean we?"

Shaking his head, Foshan bit down on his tongue to keep himself from speaking.

"Mr. Toy invited us to work in San Francisco. If we went there, maybe we could find—" Lee's words trailed off.

Foshan added more pressure on his tongue.

"Can we go home, Foshan? I'd like to be surrounded by our friends."

Foshan coughed. He'd never considered the railroad camps a home. Lee was his home. "Yeah, let's go."

Wolverine,
Gulo luscus

A master of survival, he pads silently in predawn hours.

SMELL: Attracted by grease aroma, he raises his nose.

From under a densely-branched bush, he regards the human carrying a cooking pot.

Others have caught the scent and have come.

VOICE: His low growl warns them he is ready to fight for this one.

In a long brown arc, the contents of the pot go flying.

As the man turns to leave, he is already running forward.

STRIKE
June 24
Summit Camp
1867
—

Immediately following summer solstice, when radiant, active yang energy was at its yearly apex, at the precise time the big bosses were sweating losses of their personal fortunes, and the value of Chinese labor was being recognized in broader society, the Chinese workers at Summit Camp did something unexpected. They did not show up for work.

During the first fifteen minutes of the Monday shift, the crew supervisors consulted their pocket watches and looked at each other questioning, "Where are they?"

At thirty minutes past, James Strobridge marched into their camp, eyeing the men moving about as if nothing unusual were happening. Some were washing clothes and mending canvases, and others strolling about smoking.

He curled his hands into fists, his eye compressed into a slit. "What the fuck is going on?" he yelled.

The Central Shaft supervisor stepped forward, bowing formally. In a firm but hushed voice that Mr. Strobridge had to strain to hear, he spoke. Their interaction was brief. Strobridge's reaction was at first shocked, then hurried as he sprinted toward the telegraph office.

The Chinese made valiant efforts to maintain composed expressions. Not all of them succeeded.

Howden was in his cabin watching as Strobridge hurried by. "What am I supposed to do?" he shouted at the man. Howden did not receive a reply.

Forty minutes later, a currier knocked at the door of Mr. Crocker's lavish San Francisco mansion. A servant delivered a scrap of paper to his home office suite on an ornate silver tray.

He'd just taken a drink of coffee when he reached for it. As Charles Crocker read Stro's telegram, an explosive spray of dark brew stained his 200-dollar oriental rug.

The telegram read: *Chinamen have all struck for $40 and time to be reduced from 11 to 10 hours a day.*

※

Daily chores that Foshan, Lee, and the other cooks performed changed little that week. They kept the fires burning, the tea warm, and the food coming.

In the hours between mealtimes, Foshan brought Hee Chiu and two other recruits into the kitchen. He began teaching them to run it on their own. He could tell by watching Lee that the two of them wouldn't be staying long.

When Foshan first started working with the railroad, he'd assumed he would stay with it indefinitely. Opportunities abounded in every direction. The predominantly male environment worked in his favor. He'd hoped he could find a partner, or partners, who would keep him amused. Nothing had prepared him for falling in love with a married man dedicated to his wife and children.

※

People in camp occasionally pulled Lee into moments of forgetfulness. But bitter reality was a bitch who never let up. She plunged him under the icy waters of this unwelcome new life every chance she got.

Foshan noticed when Animal Boy slipped into camp. He watched as Boy followed Lee at a distance, attempted to approach him, then changed his mind.

What on earth? Foshan wondered. He called to the boy, inviting him to sit at the serving counter. Pouring a cup of tea, Foshan said, "Do you want to talk to Lee?"

Animal Boy's cheeks pinked. He nodded, dropping his eyes. "I heard about what happened to his brother."

"It's a difficult time," Foshan said.

"I brought something for him, but I'm not sure…"

"What is it?"

Animal Boy checked over both shoulders to make sure they weren't being observed. Carefully reaching into his pocket, he scooped his hand in and pulled out his gift. Foshan looked at it for a few tender moments, then said, "This is a good idea. Why don't you take it into our bunkhouse, and I'll send Lee in to meet you."

A grin broke out on the boy's face. He bowed as he returned it to his pocket. "Thank you, Mr. Yow."

※

Lee liked Animal Boy. He nodded when Foshan told him the boy was waiting for him. Lee hoped he would not embarrass himself with a display of emotion. Kindness often made this difficult.

When Lee entered, they shared a friendly smile and cordial greeting bows. "I brought you something," Animal Boy began uncertainly, "because I am sorry for your loss."

"Gifts are unnecessary," Lee replied woodenly.

"Well—" Boy rolled his eyes toward the ceiling and lifted up on his toes. "It's not exactly a gift, but more of a friend."

Lee frowned.

"If we could sit, I'll show you."

Waving a hand at his bunk, Lee invited Boy to sit. Joining him there, Lee folded his hands in his lap. He watched as Animal Boy lifted out of his pocket a fuzzy baby gray squirrel. It curled in a spiral, asleep.

Lee couldn't stop his mouth from dropping open and letting out a soft exclamation, "Ohhh."

Animal Boy glanced up, smiling. "She's precious."

"It's a girl?"

He nodded. "I haven't given her a name. I thought you might like to—"

"I don't know!" Lee leaned back.

"She's no trouble." Boy took Lee's hand, turned it up, and gently slid the warm baby into it. The dreaming animal stirred twitching whiskers, then her moist, pink nose. Delicate lashed eyelids fluttered, opening to reveal a pair of large, soulful eyes. Noticing the unfamiliar surroundings, she startled. "It's OK," Boy soothed as she uncoiled and stood on scratchy little feet. Her flossy tail waved vertically, then swished from side to side.

"She's a little nervous," said Animal Boy.

Lee blinked, feeling a little nervous himself. "Does it bite?"

"She's pretty small," Animal Boy said. "If she did bite, it wouldn't hurt much." He leaned over, holding out a finger. "Huh, girl?" Much like a cat, the squirrel pushed her head up against Boy's finger. She closed her eyes as he stroked her head.

"Where did she come from?"

"Her nest was destroyed when the tree it was in was cut." Animal Boy frowned. "When I checked it, she was the only survivor."

Lee held out a finger to see what the animal would do. To his surprise, she nudged her head against it. Her fur was warm and soft. She made a friendly chittering sound.

"She likes you!" Animal Boy grinned.

"She is beautiful," Lee said. "What does she eat?"

"Almost anything. If you give her vegetable scraps and nuts, she'll be quite happy."

Lee's chin dimpled and trembled. His next words were raspy. "Are you sure you want to give her away?"

Animal Boy's eyes went wide. He became fidgety. "I'm sure," he replied tightly.

"I thank you, then." Lee bowed as tears began leaking from his eyes.

Animal Boy stood up like he'd been shot. "Welcome!" he said while bolting for the door.

The squirrel jumped and chirped at the absence of her caretaker. Her tail waved in circles.

Lee held out a finger. "It's OK," Lee whispered. "I think we'll be able to take care of each other."

※

It had been nearly a week since the Summit Camp Chinese ceased working. They'd received word that multiple camps on The Hill had also laid down their tools and stopped grading and tunneling.

Thousands of Chinese were making an important point. They showed their collective power to stop the work in its tracks in order to be heard and treated fairly.

Armed white men arrived, surrounding the camp. At first, the Chinese reacted with alarm. Most of them did not carry weapons. They feared a massacre.

Foshan began second-guessing their decision to return. Poor Lee had spent years worrying about the dangers of his brother working with black powder, then with nitroglycerine. To have witnessed Yang's flash freezing was beyond what a person could be expected to bear.

The guns in their midst could easily add to their trauma and end their lives.

Foshan let Hee Chiu completely run the kitchen while he secretly followed Lee. More precisely, JJ—that's what the squirrel was named. If anyone was likely to cause a surprise that would trigger a mow down, it was going to be that animal! *What was I thinking to encourage Animal Boy to give us that thing?*

※

When the Nevada County sheriff arrived, he asked for an interpreter. "Tell your men that Mr. Crocker sent his own guards, and me, to ensure that there is no fighting. No fighting in your camp. And we're here to make sure the box car men don't attack you."

The Central Shaft supervisor nodded his understanding. "I will tell them."

The Sherrif ran his forefinger and thumb along his jaw. "You might also mention that your food's about to be cut off. The butchers have stopped butchering and shipments are being held at Cisco."

※

Word of food deprivation traveled like wildfire through the strikers. It was Foshan who discovered who was behind it. From across the compound, he watched Kite To sneaking into the stable. Coming upon him inside, he saw the man loading saddle bags onto a horse. "Where do you think you are going?" Foshan asked.

"Hello, Mr. Yow." Kite To smiled while behaving as if nothing was wrong.

Foshan stepped close, looping his cane handle into the horse tack. "I asked where you're going. You know the camp is surrounded by armed guards."

"I know."

"No one can leave."

"No, no. Only thrikerth cannot leave," Kite To said.

"But you're Chinese."

"I am not on thrike. My buthineth is the buthineth of work. If my workerth refuse to work, I'm not thaying to tharve."

"Tharve? What are you saying?" Foshan frowned. His eyes narrowed as understanding dawned. "You weasel! You told them to cut food supplies to end the strike!"

Leaning forward, close to Foshan's face, Kite To smiled. "And it will work!"

Foshan's mouth twisted in a snarl. He released the horse and raised balled fists. "I should beat the shit out of you!"

Intimidation flickered briefly across To's face before he altered his expression, grinning a toothy smile. "But you won't. Now then, move away."

Once Kite To mounted, he turned in the saddle. Raising a hand in farewell, he said, "Enjoy your thrike."

※

As the news was settling in about their supply line cutoff, the men began joking about survival techniques. Meditation, Qi Gong, and opium smoking were suggestions for fending off hunger. "I know," the Central Shaft Supervisor said. "We could do what the Donner pioneers did…Kite To might be one to consider for that."

"Sorry guys," Foshan said, "that bird has already flown the coop."

Western Gray Squirrel,
Sciurus griseus

WHISKERS & NOSE: Twitching

So much to see! So much to do!

BEHAVIOR: Jumping, running, hopping.

If I do this…

TAIL: Waving and caressing.

They give food.

Lee named the squirrel after Jumping Jane, JJ. She became the camp star performer, hide-and-seek partner, and endearing child. She cuddled, jumped, begged, and vocalized. Sometimes she leaped from a height and landed squarely in the middle of a mahjong or domino game, scattering tiles like they were shooting from the nozzle of a hydraulic mining monitor. An uproarious cry followed this, and statements such as, "Shoo JJ!" "Naughty squirrel!" "Dam rodent!"

Lee worried if the men got hungry enough, they'd start eyeing JJ. Mostly, they couldn't get enough of the squirrels' antics. She made them laugh and forget their concerns. Even when she ripped holes in mattresses or peed on pillows, they responded with chagrin.

Returning her to Lee, they said something like, "Take JJ, she's behaving mischievously today."

It wasn't long before JJ understood Lee was her touchstone. If she was afraid or hungry, she scampered back to him. At night, she slept curled in the crook of his elbow and woke him early by standing on his forehead and licking an eyebrow. Lee's habit was to keep treats in his pocket so she'd know it was safe to go in there.

When he scolded her, she stood on her haunches, holding her front paws before her like Snowshoe Thompson's balance bar. When he pointed, JJ focused her eyes on his fingertip as it moved. Her head motions looked like she was agreeing with his every word. Inevitably, this transformed Lee's ire into a smile. As if waiting for this signal, JJ jumped onto his arm, scrabbled onto his shoulder, and wrapped her tail around his neck as if she was giving a hug.

Foshan was relieved to see that the animal stayed close to Lee and that he was keeping a distance from the armed guards.

※

On day six of the strike, the workers observed Mr. Crocker approaching. He was wearing his suit with the gold pocket watch chain swinging across his pendulous belly. The chain swayed in time with his stride. With him were bossy man Strobridge, John Gilliss, and Loon Tong Chung. Mr. Loon was not wearing his usual white gentleman's attire. He was in donkey clothes.

A tight clutch of men gathered behind the Central Shaft supervisor to listen to the exchange. Few of them, like Foshan, could understand all the words, but they wanted to have front-row seats to watch the expressions. This historic meeting would be story fodder for generations!

Lee stood at the outer edges, struggling to contain JJ. When he noticed several men sending warning glances at him for "Shhhh-ing" her, he took her back behind the kitchen. He'd let Foshan fill him in later.

The Central Shaft supervisor stood boldly before the big boss. In his hand, he held the paper listing their demands. After a terse greeting. Mr. Lim read them aloud, first in English and then in Mandarin. He raised his voice so everyone could hear.

- Equal wages with white workers, an increase in pay to $40 per month.
- Reduced work hours, from 11 hours to 10 hours out in the open air.
- Reduced workdays.
- Shorter tunnel shifts.
- Howden must go, and blasting must return to black powder.

From where Lee sat, he could see color rising in Crocker's neck and creeping up into his face. If he didn't know better, he'd think that he'd soon see puffs of steam chuffing from the man's ears. Crocker gripped and released his hands and shifted his weight between feet.

Another peculiar sight was Mr. Loon stepping away from the back of his group. Seeking cover behind a work shed, he then crossed the line of armed guards—unchallenged. A short while later, he casually joined the rear of the group gathered around the Central Shaft supervisor. *Curious,* Lee thought. *Is he joining the strike or is this something else?*

Once the Central Shaft supervisor finished reading the list, Mr. Crocker delivered a speech he had obviously prepared. "I make the rules here and I will not be dictated to. Only I decide how blasting is done. I will pay $30 per month, but not $40. There will be no reduction of work hours. If you return to work, I won't dock your wages for striking. If you refuse, I won't pay for June at all. You have until 6:00 a.m. on Monday to make your choice."

Not long after Mr. Crocker departed, Lee discovered Mr. Loon's purpose. Before he could engage with Mr. Loon, he had to provide JJ with an afternoon digging project.

Lee gathered a basket of acorn nuts. Clicking his tongue as he walked, he encouraged JJ to follow. The squirrel did this with hops and zig-zaggy scampers.

As they approached the barrier where a guard stood, Lee tipped the basket so the man could see what was inside. He attempted to explain his purpose in English. "Squirrel," he pointed at JJ. "She go trees. You let her out."

The guard looked uncertain.

Lee raised the basket along with his eyebrows.

Glancing to either side of him, the guard seemed to consider it.

"I take nuts." Lee motioned to himself, the basket, and the squirrel. "I come back. You no shoot."

Comprehension appeared on the man's face. He nodded.

Lee and JJ passed. He took the nut basket near the tree line in an area where the soil was soft. Placing the container on the ground, he smiled when JJ ran in a straight line to it. She raised up on her haunches, resting her front paws along the rim. He knew she was excited when she flashed her tail. Lee stroked her head a few times and left her to get to work.

On his way back, he stopped near the guard, pointing at the man's firearm. "You no shoot squirrel, understand?"

His face remained blank.

"You shoot squirrel. I curse you for life. Chinese gods very fierce. Torture you with bad luck. No sleep. Drive you mad."

The guard's eyes widened; his skin color paled.

"No shoot squirrel, understand?"

He nodded. "No shoot squirrel."

※

Back at camp, his mess hall was filling up. The tension was palpable. Lee prepared coffee, listening to the conversational buzz gaining volume.

He served Mr. Loon first, then poured a cup for himself. He offered it to others, but few accepted. Every time Lee sipped, he made a face like he was drinking bitter medicine prescribed by a pharmacist.

"Why are you drinking that filth?" Foshan asked.

"Because all Yankees drink coffee."

Central Shaft supervisor came back with, "Like all Chinese eat rats?"

Laughter in response to the sarcasm broke the ice. The men listened as Mr. Loon explained Crocker's requirement to save face with capitalists all across America. This was a concept they understood. The big boss valued their contributions. His actions, recruiting them from China, encouraged other California employers to try them, depleting Crocker's workforce.

If they returned to work as requested, Crocker would quietly and incrementally raise their pay. He'd already been thinking about eliminating the use of nitroglycerine. And their food supplies, sitting in Cisco, would be here by nightfall.

The armed guards remained in place until Monday morning when the Chinese began crossing their line to go to their worksites.

Foshan breathed a sigh of relief as he watched the guards leave.

※

Central Shaft supervisor reported the Chinese had impressed Crocker and the other big bosses with their razor-sharp timing and nonviolent protest.

They blazed a labor relations trail others could follow.

Foshan's stress over squirrel tracking, eavesdropping, and gun butchery made him more than ready to make tracks for new horizons.

News:
Daily Alta California | June 29, 1867
The Anti-Chinese Excitement.
...I have been told by farmers, miners and politicians, of both parties that so long as the anti-Chinse movement is mere matter of buncombe and political clap-trap, the men of all parties in the mountains are willing to let the affair take its course; but that so soon as it looks as if the Mongolians are really to be expelled then the people generally will be found taking a very decided stand in favor of the yellow men. Whether that prediction is correct I cannot really say; but I know that many persons have lamented in my hearing about the departure of the Celestials for Idaho, Montana and the Pacific Railroad, and not one has rejoiced. Calaveras, Tuolumne, Mariposa and Amador have lost half their Chinese population, and there is in many districts a very serious reduction in the gold yield. The attraction of #1 per month, offered by Charley Crocker, is too much for men most of whom have not averaged more than $25, and even that very uncertain. Those to remain give as a reason for not going, that the work is too hard and is dangerous—very few miners say they can do better.

Daily Alta California | July 3, 1867
End of the Chinese Laborers Strike
The Movement Instigated by Designing White Men.
SACRAMENTO. Charles Crocker, Superintendent of the Central Pacific Railroad, who returned last night from the work at Summit and Truckee River, reports that with exception of one of two gangs, all the Chinamen have resumed work. No increase of pay, except an increase made before the strike or decrease in time, has been allowed them. We have not learned whether this resumption of work by Chinamen will stop orders sent East for several thousand freedmen, but presume not, as the Company can put on any number of hands they may be able to procure. The foundation of this strike appears to have been a circular, printed in the Chinese language, sent among them by designing persons for the purpose of destroying their efficiency as laborers.

Daily Alta California | August 22, 1867
IDAHO
...The Chinese are as thick here as blackbirds, and more coming. There about six thousand in Boise County now.

RIDING A TIGER
June
Summit Camp
1867
—

Lee bounced the bag of coins in his palm. It was his pay for the month of June—including the slight increase Crocker promised. He sat in another state of shock after Kite To updated him on the current status of Sam Yap's record keeping."

"Your brother, Yang, took out a thizable loan last year."

"He did? What for?" Lee asked. His skin was turning clammy.

"I do not know. You can vithit the Company office in Grath Valley to read the original documenths."

Lee shook his head, not fully comprehending.

"To continue," Kite To proceeded, "Gee Yang'th latht pay hath been applied toward hith debt and ath hith only known relative, it now fallth to you to finith paying it."

Lee leaned forward. His bulging eyes darted to the left and right. "But there's no way!"

"Ath per the conditionth of the contract, you will be prevented from leaving the country and collecting your brotherth boneth until the matter is thettled."

Springing out of his seat, Lee paced. "But that means…"

Shrugging his shoulders, To said, "You are welcome to remain ath cook at Thummit Camp, or you are free to theek work elthewhere. The choice is yourth, either way you mutht continue making payments."

Bursting out of the space, Lee yanked open the door, it crashed against the wall. He didn't stop to check if he'd broken the glass. He practically raced the entire way up the mountain to his catfish pond. Reaching it, he threw the coin bag down with such force it burst, scattering gold coins along the granite plateau. Sinking to his knees, he screamed in frustration, pulling at his hair. "Yang! You imbecile! What have you done? You've set me to riding a tiger and I can't get off."

Curling into a ball, Lee let his emotions flow unchecked.

Foshan and JJ found him a few hours later. "Fuck!" yelled Foshan when he spotted Lee on the ground. Racing to him as fast as his limp would allow, he shook him. "Lee, are you alive?"

When Lee cracked open his eyes, Foshan sat back on his heels, letting out the breath he'd been holding.

Rolling onto his side, Lee groaned. Slowly, he got to his knees, spitting several times to clear the dirt from his mouth. Moving into a sitting position, he scrubbed his hands over his face. It felt gritty and sunburned. "I am nothing, Fosh." His voice sounded raspy and despondent. When JJ jumped onto him, he swept her off. "Yang made sure of that."

Carefully arranging his face, Foshan asked, "What do you mean?"

As Lee relayed the story about Yang's loan and his ongoing obligations, Foshan listened and nodded. At one point, he reached over to hold Lee's hand.

Foshan always filled his pockets with breadcrumbs whenever he hiked to the pond. He was pretty sure he'd find Lee there and thought fish feeding would be soothing. He tossed some in, watching the black-whiskered faces appear from below. Foshan shared some with JJ and let her crawl over him, comforting her.

Spent, Lee rinsed his face in the water then began collecting coins. Foshan helped. "What are you thinking, Love?'

Clearing his throat, Lee said, "Not a lot at the moment. If you'll still have me, I'd like to spend the night with you."

Foshan smiled sadly. "I'll always have you, Lee. Never question that." He reached over to squeeze one of his hands. "What do we do about this one?" He glanced over to JJ. "They will not allow her the back room."

※

On their way down, Lee told Foshan that he wanted to pack their bags and leave Summit Camp today, and never show his face there again.

"That's not right," Foshan said. "Your name is Gee Lee and your reputation in this place is the one you built. You cannot slink away because of something Yang did. The men you've been feeding all these years would feel betrayed if you left without saying goodbye."

Lee did not reply. He picked up a rock and tossed it. "Maybe," he mumbled.

"It's settled," Foshan proclaimed. "You find a minder for JJ, and I will tell the assistants they have the kitchen. I will also let people know that we'll be leaving tomorrow."

Lee's forehead furrowed, and his eyes filled. "Thank you," he mumbled before he covered his face and sobs overcame him. Foshan held out his arms, bringing Lee into his embrace. He rested his chin on Lee's head.

"Ow, ow ow!" Foshan complained as the little beast ascended up his clothes.

Lee, knowing exactly what this meant, let loose a laugh that mixed with his sobs.

Settled, JJ looked out on the world from the highest human vantage point, Foshan's head.

※

While Lee was planning for Hee Chiu to squirrel-sit, he thought through his possible next steps. Most every option included going to a city. *Should I leave her in camp? Set her free? Or return her to Animal Boy?* None of those ideas felt right. He wondered if he could find a parrot cage for her in Coburn's Station.

Since it would take Foshan longer to complete the items on his to-do list, Lee visited the bathhouse and barber shop. Soaking in the warm tub, memories arose about the first bathhouse he and Yang visited in San Francisco and the treatments Mr. Hang provided. A shave always reminded him of Foshan. *I need JJ to keep my mind out of rabbit holes!*

※

Lee walked to the brothel, paid for the back room, and went in. Sitting on the edge of the bed, he realized how exhausted he'd become. His eyelids felt heavy and his body droopy. He wilted onto the bed, falling asleep where he landed.

Foshan found him that way. He untied and slipped off Lee's shoes. Foshan pushed and nudged to arrange him on the bed more comfortably. He draped a cover over him and watched Lee's even breaths as he snacked on dumplings and sipped wine. When he finished, he removed his own shoes, stripped to his underwear, and settled in. Foshan pulled his knees up behind Lee's, draped an arm over his chest, and closed the gaps left between them. What the future would bring, he didn't know—though he had a few ideas. He was sorry that Lee had such a traumatic day, but he was relieved that he now knew the layout of the landscape he had to deal with. And he was very glad that Lee seemed to want Foshan to be part of the next part of his journey.

Foshan drifted off, thinking how fortunate he was to be spooning the person he loved most in this world.

※

Lee woke at the usual time, confused by the absence of whistles. *Where's JJ gotten off to?* The heavy hand on his chest and the warm form against his back reminded him where he was. He laced his fingers with Foshan's and smiled when, even in his sleep, Fosh returned the caress. Lee kissed the back of Foshan's hand. What a rare and wonderful feeling it was, waking up together.

Then, the memory of recent occurrences slashed at the heels of his comfy morning mist, chasing it away so only stark emptiness remained. He turned to Foshan, placing a hand behind his neck, and began kissing him. The kiss wasn't tentative or questioning, but direct, almost brutal. Foshan came awake then, pulling away at the unexpected onslaught. Then he shifted, his hands grasping, and he returned Lee's ardor in kind. Their movements could be likened to a hard-boiled wrestling match with teeth, grunts, sweat, and bruises. At some level, both were aware they were working to release monstrous forces of pent-up energy. If someone cried out for it to stop, it would immediately. But they did not. They kept at it until a different type of fatigue depleted them.

When next they woke, it was to a knock at their door and a time reminder for when the room needed to be vacated. They didn't speak as they freshened and dressed. Lee scarfed down leftover dumplings and finished the wine. When Foshan reached for the doorknob, Lee stopped him, pulling him back for a kiss, a reverential one this time. "Thank you for that." He breathed against Foshan's lips, "You possess a gift for eliminating my thoughts."

Foshan pulled back, rubbing a thumb along Lee's lower lip. "We are well matched."

Lee would think about those words for the rest of today and into the next several weeks.

※

Foshan must have read Lee's mind because he'd already asked Baldy to construct a containment unit for JJ. She was not happy about being put in there and she said so, loudly. She also did not like being inside it when it was in the back of a wagon holding all of Lee and Foshan's belongings. As soon as straps were wrapped around it, she got to work gnawing at them. "That might keep her occupied when we're travelling," Foshan said. "We'll have to keep checking to make sure she doesn't chew all the way through."

Lee agreed. "I think she'll calm down once we get going. This is new for her."

The cooks attended breakfast in their mess hall as guests. After all the goodbyes, thank yous, and well wishes, Lee was glad he'd listened to Foshan. Learning how he'd affected so many lives in a good way lifted his spirits. He was also happy that Foshan received gratitude for his work there.

Leaving Foshan's circle of friends, Baldy approached Lee. Reaching out a hand, he gave him a firm, western, handshake. "In many ways, you surprised me, Mr. Gee."

"That is good, I think," he responded. "I must thank you for the incredible knife craftsmanship. It is a tool I will always cherish; you will be in my thoughts every time I use it. Also, I am grateful for removing the bad spirits from it!" Lee bowed deeply.

Scratching his bare scalp, Baldy nodded. "Your chef skills are fine. They'll serve you wherever you go. That blade will show anyone watching that its maker believed in you." Clearing his throat, he added, "Foshan is a valued friend…to many of us." Leaning in close, he whispered, "Watching how you cared for him after his beating, I know you'll watch out for him."

Blinking rapidly, Lee broke eye contact and shook his head up and down.

※

Lee was backing out of the crowd, thinking it was time to leave, when he bumped into someone. "Pardon!" he said, turning around. It was Scarred Eye. "Oh, it's you." Lee nodded. "I haven't seen you since…"

"Rocklin." He nodded. "A bird told me you were leaving. I had to come to say farewell."

Lee regarded the man with a thoughtful expression. He'd been his first work partner when he started with the railroad. Yang had liked him. His presence always made Lee feel a little strange. "I should show you my catfish before I go." Lee couldn't believe those words came out of his mouth. He never offered to show people Maiden Lake. *Why have I invited a hunter there?*

"I'd like that," Scarred Eye said.

Lee pondered the mystery of himself as they climbed the steep path. *I hope I haven't doomed them all.*

When they arrived at the pond, the fish gathered at the surface. It flabbergasted Lee to see their numbers and size. "I hope you won't take them all at once and deliver them to the next chef."

Scarred Eye threw his head back, laughing. It echoed louder than expected. "Not to worry. You were the only chef I killed for." He placed a warm hand on Lee's back, at the base of his neck. "And these fine fellows," he grinned, "will be here for a long time. Hundreds of years from now, their descendants will still be here, looking back at other seekers who come to peer in your lake."

Lee sidestepped away, out of arms reach. Frowning, he studied this odd man.

"You have been one of the most interesting of the Gee brothers." Scarred Eye said. His voice was whisper soft; his gaze remained focused on the fish. "Your father was like that too, a single grape of a different color than the bunch."

"But…?"

Scarred Eye shook his head, showing he would not respond. "Before we part, I must tell you about a location." He squatted. Reaching out, he dipped a fingertip into the water. One fish, the largest, swam over, giving it a bump. "It's in the delta, where the Sacramento River blends with the waters of the Golden Gate. Crayfish are plentiful there. It's a place that can feel like a home—if you decide to make it so."

About to say something, Lee opened his mouth, but then his nose tingled. The sneeze reflex took over, causing him to inhale, close his eyes, and forcefully expel. When he opened his eyes, the man was gone.

Looking in every direction, Lee called, "Scarred Eye? Where'd you go?" He walked around, wondering if his mind had been playing tricks.

Before returning to the path down the hill, he waved to the fish and approached one of the old Juniper trees. Laying a hand along its rough bark, he said, "Thank you for the Magpie Bridge."

Channel Catfish,
Ictalurus punctatus

BARBELS (whiskers): Waving, tasting!

Food man here! He brings friend.

MOUTHS: Opening and closing. Ready.

Treats men toss taste better than algae.

New home good. We only fish in pond.

Little ones safe if they stay at bottom.

NEW ROAD
June
Dutch Flat Donner Lake Wagon Road
1867
—

Foshan and Lee had been rolling along on the Dutch Flat Donner Lake Wagon road for some time when Lee glanced over to watch Foshan on the bench seat of their two-horse team. To be doing something new without Yang made his heart physically ache. But something inside Lee warmed too. Foshan was at his side, and they were adventuring together.

"Where're we headed, pardner?" Foshan said in English, affecting a cowboy accent. "Dutch Flat?"

"No," Lee said, trying not to smile. "Too close. Too many Democrats."

"Agreed," Foshan said. They could head for Sacramento or San Francisco, but he wasn't keen on Lee driving past the bone yard. "How about going back to Nevada City and Grass Valley? I hear they're preparing for a Hungry Ghost Festival that will rival any in the state."

Lee thought about this. "It is Ghost Month," he sighed. "I need to honor Father properly. "And I…" he gulped, "cursed my brother, many times."

Foshan nodded, deep in thought. "It is past time that I honor my father," he said.

JJ had all four feet clamped to the side of the cage door. She pulled and pushed her weight against it, causing the metal to clank like a prisoner banging a metal cup against bars.

※

Foshan was twitchy. He had several loaded handguns hidden for quick access. Two on the road together was better than one, but they could still become targets. He wore a wide-brimmed hat, pinning his queue up so it didn't hang down his back. He asked Lee to do the same. Lee had never traveled outside the protection of the Six Company or the railroad. In some ways, he was a virgin in this country. He suspected Lee did not own weapons. "Have you—battle experience?"

"Not much," Lee said. "There were conflicts on our ship. My brothers used their brawn more than me." He tapped his temple. "My instincts draw me to philosophy."

Foshan attempted to contain his grin. "We had conflicts on my ship too," he said. "You do have brawn, Gee Lee. You proved that this morning."

Feeling heat flaming in his face, Lee looked away. "Before today, what was your long-term plan?" he asked.

Lifting an eyebrow, Foshan said, "Sticking with the railroad. If not the CPRR, then another one."

"We were going home, as you know. Yang blew that up as surely as if he'd packed powder under it and lit the fuse. You could go back—to the railroad—you know? Because I am lost does not mean you need to be."

"I'm good," Foshan replied.

"You are like a shiny pearl in the palm of my hand." Lee's voice cracked. "And I do not know what to do with you."

Patting his leg, Foshan bumped their shoulders. "I know. But Lee?"

Their eyes met.

"Sometimes you know *exactly* what to do with me."

HUNGRY GHOSTS
Grass Valley, California
1867
—

Like their visit to Nevada City for the Chinese New Year, they set out to locate the livery stable where they would return their horses and wagon. Grass Valley's Chinatown was on the southwestern side of the city, bookended by the downtown and a quartz mill. Small shanty buildings lined up like teeth along the banks of Wolf Creek. The North Star Mine, a Cornish stronghold, housed the world's largest Pelton water wheel that powered mining equipment deep underground. A stamp mill, thumping at all hours of the day, pounded gold dust from quartz rocks.

Once at the stable, they stored their gear and planned to sleep in the loft. JJ had not calmed on the journey as Lee had hoped. If anything, he was worried she'd gone insane. They'd stopped multiple times, attempting to soothe her. The only thing that seemed to work was covering her cage, leaving her in the darkness. As he pulled away the tarp, JJ began racing around in circles. *Is the stamping making it worse?*

On their way in, Lee had noticed multiple large oak trees shading sections of Chinatown. In sun patches around them were multiple gardens, lush with root vegetables, greens, and flowers. He wondered if the plant life and surroundings would soothe her. With Foshan's help, Lee wove fresh rope through the bars. They hefted the cage to the base of one of the oak trees. Occupied by their task, they didn't notice they were being watched.

JJ's behavior settled as the tree came into view. Her nose lifted in the air, catching hints of things the men couldn't understand. Her whiskers twitched, and her tail did too. Setting her down gently, the men bent over, hands on knees, watching.

When the hem of a woman's skirt brushed the tips of his boots, Lee jumped. He stumbled into Foshan while he scrambled out of the way.

"I am sorry!" the woman reached out, her fingertips brushing Lee's sleeve. "I did not mean to startle you. I was curious to see what you had in that cage."

"Is OK," Lee said, righting himself.

"It is a squirrel," Foshan indicated, "as you can see."

"An unhappy one," the woman commented.

"It is her first time in a cage; she's been riding with us from Coburn's," said Foshan.

As Foshan and the woman talked, Lee took in details. She wore a long-sleeved blouse with a high collar. Ruffles fringed the neck and wrist lines. More ruffles dusted the ground at the bottom of a skirt that, if the bunched material were straightened, could stretch a long distance. Lace gloves covered her hands, except for the fingertips, and a bonnet cloaked her hair. Her voice was soft, and her eyes twinkled with intelligence. Freckles dotted her cheeks like dried thyme flavoring a sweet and sour soup.

"Allow me to introduce myself," the woman said. "I am Jennie Carter." She reached out, taking each of their hands in a friendly, straight-forward grip. "I used to live on School Street, two blocks over," she released them and pointed up the hill. "Now I live in Nevada City and I'm here to help with celebration preparations. You're here to participate?"

"Yes." Foshan smiled and bowed. "It is a favorable time to worship the ancestors."

She nodded, then continued. "Very good. You must let me know if you or your friend," she said, glancing at the cage, "need assistance. What are you going to do with that animal?"

"Not for eat!" Lee shouted, wagging his index finger.

The woman's eyes widened. "I should hope not!" She took a step back, placing a hand over her heart.

"Lee's English is limited," Foshan used English in a tone meant to calm. We have recently come from a railroad camp where Lee had to protect her from men who wanted to shoot her." Foshan's expression became alarmed. "Not Chinese men! Chinese do not eat rodents." Distressed, Foshan continued, "JJ is a pet. He loves her, ma'am."

"Oh." Mrs. Carter let out her breath. Her expression softened. "Why, JJ?"

"Jane," Lee interjected. "Her name Jane."

Giving them a tentative smile, Jennie said, "Jane is my name, too. My mother named me Mary Jane."

"Jane is good name." Lee nodded.

Foshan turned to Lee, reverting to Cantonese, "JJ can't stay in there and we can't watch her all the time."

"I know. Why do you think we brought her to this tree?"

Foshan looked up, noting the many high branches. Mrs. Carter arched her neck to look up, too.

"If you make room, I will see if this is acceptable to JJ," Lee said.

"Right," Foshan replied. Turning to the woman, he switched to English. "We must watch from a distance."

They walked to the edge of a raised cabbage bed and took seats along the top. Lee appeared to be having a long conversation with JJ, one that included hand gestures. He knelt down and unlatched the cage door, opening it as wide as it would go.

The squirrel leaned her front paws at the foot of the door and poked her nose outside. "That's it!" they heard Lee say. He stepped back and kneeled next to the container, settling back onto his heels.

JJ exited like a shot, coming to a standstill on top of the cage. Stretching up on her hind legs, she gazed into the branches above. Her front feet pawed like she was waving. Another blast of movement landed her on Lee's lap, where she stilled, allowing him to stroke her. Then she scampered onto his head, causing him to cringe. "JJ, that hurts."

Finally, she jumped onto his shoulder, circled his neck, and curled her tail around it like usual. Lightning quick, she bit his earlobe, leapt for the tree, scuttled up, and disappeared from sight.

"Aaaayiiiii!" Lee yelled, pressing his hands to his ear.

"Oh, dear!" Jennie called, racing after Foshan while digging in her purse for a handkerchief.

※

Day one of the festival took place took place on Mill Street, right outside the livery's doors. Lee couldn't help thinking about Yang and his furniture sales. He had to stop to hide his face multiple times as waves of grief overcame him. He was grateful for the concealment that the wide-brimmed hat afforded.

Foshan and Lee walked up and down the road and watched while performers and salesmen set up displays. Even with the hat, the bandage he wore, looped around his head and neck, made Lee feel conspicuous. A thick piece of gauze over his ear made it worse.

Noticing his struggles, Foshan said, "Let's look for a spirit mask, one that rides on your shoulders."

Considering this, Lee nodded. They found a booth featuring a variety of colorfully painted papier-mâché masks. After debating between the white tiger, a dragon turtle, and a carp, he selected the fish. "Symbology of strength and power is always good," Lee commented. "The wide mouth allows for nose blowing."

When Lee suggested Foshan pick one too, his firm response, "No!" ended further discussion.

As the streets grew crowded and the sights became more engaging, Lee enjoyed his persona as a tearful carp.

Loud, raucous music, meant to frighten ghosts, drowned out the stamp mill. Clanging, high and low vocalizations helped console hearts encumbered with soul-eating concerns.

If departed loved ones were suffering from tragic deaths and being stranded in the netherworld, they'd recognize the music and join the festival.

Long tables, set out at intervals along the street, fed whoever was hungry: no payment required. Roast pig, succulent chicken, and other Chinese specialties such as jai, a mixture of vegetables that included bok choy, lotus root, wood ear and shiitake mushrooms, bean thread noodles and dried lily flowers, and chuen guen, spring rolls, adorned them.

In a curtained booth, a ghoul held court alongside a powerful white horse. Street performers wearing elaborate silk costumes contorted themselves into smaller and smaller boxes, while juggling fans and balancing spinning plates.

A delicate female sitting in a throne-like chair sat silently, staring straight ahead with eyes that did not see. Her jet-black hair was clean and worn long. Her clothing was pure white. Silk slippers on her feet curled up at the toes. Most striking was the thick pancake makeup on her face and neck. Blood tears dripped from her eyes. At this display, Lee was dumbstruck. His mouth opened and his breath hitched. He felt as if his feet had grown roots.

Foshan spotted a band of musicians playing stringed instruments and horns at the end of the Chinese section. They were an American band. Mrs. Carter was there, tapping her toe in time with the rhythm. He wanted to go greet the woman and listen, but Lee was behaving oddly. "Is something wrong?" he whispered into the fish's gaping mouth.

"I'm going to the temple," Lee replied, not taking his eyes from the weeping woman. "Don't wait for me. I have to stay for a while."

In the building, the altar room had been prepared with care. New tapestries and calligraphy with poetry and folklore hung on the walls. Lee left his fish head near the entrance and removed his shoes. It was blissfully cool inside. The sights and the smells transported him to faraway places. A handful of men joined him in quiet contemplation.

It was dark by the time Lee left the holy building and walked back toward the livery stable. He carried the carp mask under his arm. He'd spent hours meditating, chanting, and holding the image of the weeping woman in his mind.

Candlelight illuminated the streets and shop windows. Oil lamps further added to the illusion of living light. Paper gods, swaying and flickering, were pinned to walls and posts. They hung from awnings. Wild animals, devils, and unhappy ghosts were also on display. Offerings of thin paper cut into red squares were available in abundant quantities. Every ten steps, one could find a table holding offering papers. Lee took a handful and fed small fires along his path. As each contribution transformed into smoke, Lee felt something heavy inside shifting.

He paused at the base of JJ's tree, calling to her softly. There was no response.

※

Day two began with a parade.

Lee's ear had scabbed over. He no longer needed the bandages. He wore his hat but continued carrying his spirit mask, just in case.

Deities in bright colors, some as tall as ten feet, marched down the street on legs operated by puppeteers dressed in black. Symbols crashing, ringing bells, and rattles accompanied them. Following the parade, observers made their way to the water's edge to set aflame miniature boats that would travel to the netherworld.

Lee and Foshan's fire boats floated separately in the eddies, then flared up and collided when the wind directed their movements.

The marching gods then led them to an open field where enormous dragon and butterfly kites flew. Mrs. Carter spotted them in the field and made her way over, followed by a distinguished-looking gentleman.

"Mr. Yow Foshan and Mr. Gee Lee, I'd like you to meet my husband, Mr. Dennis Drummond Carter."

Everyone did a combination of bowing and handshaking. Since Foshan seemed eager to act as a cultural guide, Lee excused himself. He wished he felt more sociable.

Lowering the mask onto his shoulders, he returned to the temple. When Lee was lighting his third stick of incense, he recognized a blaster. Yeehaw! Temple etiquette prevented him from disturbing the man. He went outside to pick at the food while he waited for him to come out.

Yeehaw didn't respond to Lee's call. He trotted over, pulling on his sleeve. "Yeehaw, hello."

Pausing and blinking, it took a moment for the fellow's expression to change. "Gee Lee!" He smiled. "How are you? How's Manly?"

Gulping, Lee explained what had happened. As they talked, they walked toward JJ's tree, taking a seat next to the cabbage patch. "I don't go by Yeehaw anymore. I've reverted to my family name—Loy Ju Ye."

Lee nodded, smiling. "It's a good name." He listened intently as Ju Ye described his mining company and what life was like at a lower elevation. "I will never live in the snow again," Lee said. Until he spoke those words, he didn't know he felt this way. "When you were here last year, did you visit Grass Valley with my brother?"

Ju Ye shook his head "no." "He was going around with Scarred Eye."

Lee's hopes raised, if he could locate Scarred Eye, he might find out more. But then Loy Jue Ye dashed that line of thinking. "I heard he was killed recently. A robbery and gunfight on the road or some such."

Sighing heavily, Lee revealed personal information he never would have BYD (before Yang died). "He took out a loan when he was here."

Jue Ye nodded, "I'll show you the Six Company office if you want to ask there."

※

Inside, Lee sat holding the loan document with Yang's signature at the bottom. Looking up at the agent, he said, "It says he was using the loan to purchase a mining claim and land. Where is it?"

"Don't know." The agent pulled a cigar out of his mouth and focused on the glowing end. "Can't say. Wasn't here then. But there are not too many places here where something like that could go down. I'd check around Henness Pass Road."

"And this." Lee frowned, slapping the paper. "The interest rate is indecent."

The agent smirked. "Usually means something fishy." He rolled one end of the cigar around inside his mouth, then pulled it out, spitting tobacco flakes on the floor. Nodding toward the carp mask, he said, "Looks like that runs in the family. Was your brother in some kind of trouble?"

Lee snorted.

"You got problems with anything contractual; take it up with the home office."

※

Day three was the grand finale of the spectacular event. The musicians began before sunrise playing ugly erhu music, full of disharmony. Jumbly. Painful to hear. Spiritual leaders, wearing long white robes and silk hoods made of deep blue fabric, came from everywhere. They stood ten feet apart along both sides of the road, where they began singing incantations—long-winded, deep baritone sound movements. When they reached a certain quickening of their pace, they stepped toward the center of the street. Continuing their song, they moved in twos toward the center until they lined up perfectly in a rectangular shape.

Coming from the far end of the street marched drummers and cymbal players. As they reached the priests, they parted and flowed around them. The priests stopped singing and bowed. As the musicians passed, the holy men began following the musical marchers.

Another group of men, also dressed in white, followed in the same direction. They were singing another type of prayer in high falsetto voices, reminiscent of wailing women. Once they passed, the observers filled the street and followed. Some sang falsetto verses, and others remained silent. The procession was returning to the open field where the giant kites had flown earlier.

Waiting there was a goliath, snarling demon, moving about on puppet master's feet. Long, streaming flags fluttered at his ears and shoulders. He growled and protested as the observers encircled him. His limbs and spine were spikey and menacing. Rockets and fireworks, along with significant quantities of black powder, made up the body of this demonic creature.

When the participants were situated, the priests began chanting in low-throated tones. The puppet masters made efficient work of securing the dragon feet to anchor poles sunk in the ground. As each man finished his job, he stepped back and blended into the crowd like he'd been nothing more than a shadow. The singing priests did the same until only one man stood in the clearing with the beast.

Lee, who'd been watching with a sense of awe and reverence, grew dizzy. He knew this moment was when the ghosts and ancestors were most dense. Feelings showered over him— familiar ones, like people he knew. First Grandfather, then his Uncles, Father, Fu-chi.... then Yang. He loved and missed them so very much!

The priest held a candle aloft, saying a prayer for peace and happiness to go with the ancestors into the heavens, where they would live until the next festival. All the angry, despondent, greedy ghosts responsible for bad luck would catapult away, along with the great demon.

The priest lowered the flame to the tail and stepped away as sparks climbed the fuse.

Booming, smoking, whistling, and whirling. The demon went crazy.

From within the discordant sounds of the cacophony, Lee received a gift. He couldn't speak about it. He needed to live with it for a time.

※

As the festivities wound to a close, Foshan enthusiastically told Lee the Carters had invited them for tea at their house. "Please thank them for the invitation," he said. "You must go, Foshan. Enjoy your new friends. I must return to the temple."

At the temple, Lee gave thanks for the sacred space and the Ghost Festival. He picked up some of the last food from the tables and went to sit beneath the oak tree, searching the branches for JJ.

She never reappeared. An acorn fell from the tree, landing on his head. He hoped that was her way of saying goodbye.

LOCKPORT
Sacramento Delta
1869
—

When they left the mountains, in '68, he worked in the fields, re-establishing his relationship with growing things. Foshan had taken a job with their friend Quong Toy, a noteworthy chef with his own San Francisco restaurant.

It wasn't long before the local proprietors heard of Lee's culinary skill. Bing Hap helped this along by repeating the story of how he came by a chef's knife worthy of an art display. They'd coaxed him away from the soil and pleaded with him to return to working with fire, metal, and food.

He'd begun preparing meals in a restaurant along the river for steamboat travelers and brokered produce deals for Quong Toy. Once a month, he met Foshan in the city to laugh and love.

The loan amount was reduced, but there was still a long way to go. Recently, Lee had been thinking about how much faster it would go if Wèi An, Ting Ai, and the older children contributed to the household income. He missed them terribly. Sending money for their struggling farm was making less sense.

The Sam Yap Company had sent a notice letting him know that Yang's bones were clean, in a jar, and being held in San Francisco. In Chinese culture, it is believed that the soul resides in the bones. Lee questioned this. It is the flesh, with the beating heart, pumping blood, and warm skin that we reach for when seeking comfort.

He'd also been reconsidering land ownership too. When one owns something, one is obligated to defend it, with violence if necessary.

Land and soil are life. From it grows…everything. When a sojourner leaves his birthplace, once he sets foot on foreign ground, it knows he is there. It holds his weight and absorbs his hair strands, fingernail shards, and spilled blood. The plants and animals of that place notice his presence and adjust for their own survival.

Visitors and colonists bring pieces of their homeland with them, beyond their bodies. They transport food, pests, seeds, and livestock. The land accepts them.

If he clung to the idea that Yang's bones had to be buried in the family plot in order for him to find peace, it would make him crazed.

He found a measure of serenity when he burned offerings for his brother. Lee had been thinking that Yang's flesh, melted into the California soil had made both the United States and China home for the Gee family.

※

It was on a weekend in the city, in the tiny apartment Foshan rented, that Lee brought up an idea. "Would you travel to Panyu?"

"What do you mean?" Foshan asked. His forehead flattened, and his eye darted.

"You know I can't go. I want my family here."

Raking a hand through his long, loose hair, Foshan's first thought was that it had been a mistake to keep his queue. If he'd cut, it like many of the men were doing these days, Lee would never have asked the question. A Chinese man in China without a queue would be asking to have his neck chopped in two. Foshan maintained the hairstyle because he needed every guise of conformity.

His next thought was far more devastating. "If Wèi An is here, that means that we…"

Lee scowled. "Listen, Fosh." He grabbed his hand, holding it in both of his, squeezing hard. "Please? You know the contents of my heart, and you know I would give my life to keep you from harm." He dropped their hands to begin pacing. "Together, with Wèi An, we can find solutions to our problems."

"I'm a problem?"

"I didn't say that!"

"You don't have to!"

Sucking in breath, Lee made deliberate, forearm half-circles near his waist. With palms down and fingertips almost touching, he "shhhhushed" energy toward his feet. "Is fear driving you to argue?" he asked. When no reply came, he continued, "I am afraid too, Foshan! But there's one thing I keep coming back to."

Rolling his eyes to the ceiling, Foshan said, "What?"

"The children." Lee dropped heavily into a chair. His voice was clogged with unshed tears. "My daughter was a baby when I left. Her dark hair stood on end and would not relax, no matter what her mother tried. She was a smiley little thing. Song is six now, about to turn seven. My son…." Lee hung his head, covering his face. "He's five years old and I've never met him!" He raised red eyes to meet Foshan's steady gaze. "Worse is that my boy has never known his own father. Since his grandfather died, he only has females to guide him." Lee blew his nose. "Too many years have passed. We can wait no longer."

※

Before Foshan left, Lee presented him with his chef's knife and the belt Yang had made for it. Holding it in two hands and making a formal bow, he said, "Carry this as a symbol of my faith and trust." Straightening, Lee stepped close to wrap the belt around Foshan's waist. As he fastened the buckle, his mouth quirked, and his eyes sparkled. "You may also need it to satisfy Mother."

Their parting kiss was passionate at first, then shifted to slow. Their breathing synchronized. With familiar caresses, they communicated all the things in their hearts that they might never say again.

PILGRIMAGE
Ting Ai, age 30 | Wèi An, age 23
Song, age 7 | Luck, age 6 | Ming, age 8
Panyu District, China
1870

—

Foshan agreed, because love motivates you to attempt the impossible. Since the decision was made, he felt like a twenty-five pound-rock was lodged inside his stomach. Sleep eluded him and his comb came away filled with hair.

In Panyu, Foshan followed Lee's map showing the location of the farm. He'd heard so many stories about this place and these people; it almost felt familiar. When he saw movement in the yard, his mouth dried out. A woman was hanging clothes on a line, and another was weeding a garden.

Confused, he checked his directions. *This can't be right. Those women are pregnant!*

The woman at the clothesline saw him loitering near the gate.

"You, there!" Leaning her basket against a hip, she stomped toward him. "What do you want?"

The gardening woman stood, arching her back, massaging it.

Clearing his throat, he said, "I've come with letters for Mrs. Gee."

"We're both Mrs. Gee," said the gardener, walking over for a closer look.

A coughing fit struck Foshan. *This can't be happening!* He tried again, but his voice came out sounding strangled. "Mrs. Gee Fong, Shao Pei."

"She doesn't get mail," said the laundress, dropping the basket while propping her hands on her hips.

"Unless it's from America!" the gardener said, breathless.

The laundress frowned. "There's been no news from America—in ages."

"There is now," Foshan squeaked. He couldn't control his rapid blinking.

※

He stood near the window, hands clasped behind his back, looking out as the gardener daughter-in-law read Lee's letters to Mother Gee.

—

Dear Mother,

This letter is an introduction to Yow Foshan. He is a good and trustworthy friend.

I have sent him, in my place, to deliver news and to assist with decisions.

On May 6, 1867, Yang died.

A great wave of snow broke away from Donner Mountain. It took Yang and all the men on his crew.

His work here was honorable. Your son was a noteworthy blaster (one who explodes house-sized rocks) in the most difficult tunnel on the Central Pacific Railroad. He wanted to witness when the tunnellers broke through, and he did.

The accident happened when he moved out of the tunnel to work on snowsheds (long barn buildings that protect the rails from deep snow).

Yang made many friends, some of them called him Manly.

I am sorry, Mother. there was nothing I could do to prevent it.

Your Son,

Gee Lee

P.S. His bones are here, with me.

P.S.S. Please give my condolences to Ting Ai and Ming.

—

Dear Mother,

Circumstances beyond my control have made it so that I cannot return. Ideally, I would like you to sell everything and for the entire family to come and live with me in America.

I will not dictate what you must do, Mother. Too many have already done that. If you wish to stay, I will support you.

My wife and children will join me in California. Yow Foshan will cross with them in September. If you decide to travel with them, he will assist with property sales matters.

You Son,

Gee Lee

P.S. If you have doubts about Foshan, ask him to show you my chef's knife and the carrier belt Yang had made to hold it.

Numb silence filled the room. One woman, the gardener, swiped tears from her cheek. Foshan turned. He could not look at the younger women, so he focused on the elder. "Mrs. Gee," he bowed. "I apologize for intruding on personal matters. You have my heartfelt condolences for your loss. I've taken rooms at the Red Rooster Inn and will return there now. In a few days, I will return."

As he barreled out, the three children who'd been spying through a side window made him stop. His heart constricted and his breath caught. He saw unmistakable similarities to Lee and Yang in every one of them.

Bowing, he said, "Good day, children," then turned and made quick steps for the gate. While he was lifting the latch, a small hand slipped into his.

"Are you my father?" asked the little boy.

"No," Foshan said, shaking his head. His heart was beating double-time. "But he is my friend."

"Is he coming to see us?" a girl said. This had to be Song.

"He wishes he could, but that is not possible."

"And my father?" the tallest girl asked. "Is he coming soon?"

"Not today." Foshan dropped his eyes so she wouldn't see the tears filling them. "Best to go speak with your mothers."

※

The next afternoon, there was a knock at Foshan's door. Bleary-eyed, unshaven, and barefoot, he wore loose sleeping pants and a stained undershirt under an unbuttoned tunic. Too many whiskeys and not enough sleep wouldn't show well. Resigning himself, he opened it. When he saw who it was, his back straightened. "Wèi An!" he exclaimed. Correcting himself, he amended. "Pardon. Mrs. Gee." He bowed.

"May I?" She pointed to his room.

Panicked and waving in front of him, he said, "No!" Pointing to an outdoor table under the shade of Maidenhair tree, he continued, "That would be better."

Lowering her chin, she bowed before walking to the table and sitting down.

Glancing behind him, Foshan wondered if there was anything inside that would clean him quickly. *A fresh shirt, a wet washcloth?* Deciding against it, he shut the door and joined Wèi An at the table.

"The letter says you are a friend of my husband."

"Yes, ma'am."

"You've seen him recently?"

"He waved from the dock as my ship left," Foshan said.

"He is well?"

"As well as expected."

"He has work and a place to live?" Wèi An asked.

"Yes, ma'am."

"You shall take the children, but I will remain."

Foshan adjusted his seating position, frowning. "Um, that is not what he asked me to do."

Wèi An sat there in silence, her head bowed. She was trembling.

"I think that…" Foshan started, "while he was away, many unexpected things happened." He saw her nod. "The father—?"

She crumbled then; her face turned red. Wèi An covered it with her hands, pressing fingers against her eyes.

Foshan waited. He searched his pockets for a clean handkerchief. Finding none, he removed his tunic, grimacing while he took a sniff. Reluctantly, he slid it across to her.

Wèi An's shoulders were shaking, yet not a sound came out. When she buried her face in his shirt, he could see her neck was splotchy. After a time, she regained composure.

"Was it consensual?" He whispered, needing to know.

She shook her head, blowing her nose.

"I am so sorry." He blinked back an emotional response while swallowing. "Would he have a claim on—?"

"No!" Her head snapped up, eyes blazing. "No one has a claim on me except my husband!"

Foshan nodded, doing his best to keep his expression neutral. "So, there's nothing preventing you from leaving?"

She stood up, pointing at her belly. "Except for this!"

Letting out a long breath, Foshan asked, "Are you the mother of that child?"

Nodding, Wèi An dropped back into her seat.

"Are you also mother to Lee's children?"

She nodded again, wiping at tears that continued to fall.

"If you send your children to California alone, you'll be depriving them of the only parent they know." Compressing his lips and dropping his gaze, his hands floundered. "Right now, Lee is a stranger to them. Certainly, he will love and raise them, but do you trust Ting Ai and Mother Gee to care for them in your absence?"

Wèi An covered her face again. "I don't know."

"The fold needs to be mended even after the sheep are lost," Foshan whispered, almost as an afterthought. He was thunderstruck that any mission lesson remained in his mind after all this time.

※

The next unfortunate discovery Foshan made was crescent marks on the arms of the children and on Wèi An. He was out in the patty fields with Luck, who was showing off his fishing knowledge.

"I caught one, Mr. Yow!" he happily exclaimed, holding up his net, proudly displaying a flailing catfish. The boy was a competent, dependable helper for the women, stocking wood piles, gardening, and tending to livestock.

"Good man," Foshan said, patting his arm. "Please call me Fosh." Inspecting the bumps, he lifted the boy's wrist, running a finger over them. "How did you get these?"

Luck pulled his hand away, seeming to curl in on himself. "It's a secret," he said with a voice that climbed higher. "She says not to tell."

"She?"

"I can't!" The boy looked stricken; his eyes filled.

Getting down on his knees, Foshan firmly grasped both of the boy's stick-like arms. "You have been the man of this place for a long time, and I can see you've been doing an excellent job. But as of now, I am representing your father. I assure you; he would want to know if someone has been hurting you and the others. As a man, it is your duty to tell me."

The boy gazed hopefully into Foshan's face, then seemed to come to a decision. "I will, but not here." He released the fish and stowed his gear, then led Foshan up into the canyon to the same spot Yang had hidden his mother's geese so many years ago. They sat near the old pen fence, leaning their backs against it.

Luck regarded Foshan again. He wore a look that questioned if he could trust this adult. Fingering the scars, he began, "Auntie Ai makes these."

"How?" Foshan's mouth filled with a metallic taste.

Luck picked up Foshan's hand and pressed a thumbnail into it until it hurt. Then he dropped it and swiped moisture from his eyes.

"Why?"

Luck shrugged his shoulders. "She gets mad sometimes. A lot of times."

"Has your mother tried stopping her?"

"Oh, yes!" he said. "Only she is Second Wife and First Wives do not have to listen."

Foshan squeezed the bridge of his nose. Leaning his head back against the post, he asked, "Do you know what it means that your aunt's husband died?"

"She's a widow, like Grandmother?"

"Yes," Foshan said, dropping his hand and looking sideways at the kid. "It also means that your mother is now First Wife."

"Really?" Luck's smile was radiant.

※

Back at the house, Foshan walked into it, not as a guest, but as a leader. Luck stayed close beside him. Everyone was sitting at the table as Wèi An served bowls of soup.

Pointing at Ting Ai, Foshan said, "Get up, right now."

She frowned, glancing at the other women.

"You are packing your things and I am taking you to stay at my room at the inn. You will not come back here."

"You cannot kick me out of my home. I will not be your concubine!"

"You wish," Foshan muttered under his breath, rolling his eyes. "I did not say you were staying with me. I said you'd be staying in the room."

Ting Ai crossed her arms. "I'm not going!"

"You are," Foshan said forcefully. "You, Ting Ai, are no longer First Wife." He walked around the table, lifting arms and pointing at scars. "I am banishing you from this place until—?"

The color dropped from her face. "You can't! I have nowhere to go—no money." She stood, rushing behind her daughter, wrapping her arms around her. "You can't take my daughter from me."

Foshan's head was throbbing. He wasn't going to admit he had no idea what he was doing, but he wasn't going to allow her to hurt anyone in this family again. "Ming stays. Either you pack your bag, or I'll drag you out of here with only the clothes on your back."

※

This was how Foshan found himself sleeping on the floor in front of the fire at the Gee home. He'd been here two weeks, and he'd assumed by now they'd know what the hell they were doing.

Bending an elbow and covering his face, he could feel tears burning in the back of his eyes. This place—China—was no longer his home. He missed Lee and wanted to be wherever he was. He hadn't expected to fall in love with any of these people, yet he had. Picturing them in California made his heart hurt.

His stress symptoms had changed. Instead of a sick stomach and sleeplessness, now he had a persistent headache and Ting Ai, who was a complete pain in the ass.

※

Mother Gee was a sly woman. While she pretended not to see or hear things sometimes, Foshan didn't buy it. She complained about her health, her age, and her duty to take care of the ancestor's graves.

Part of him had a nagging feeling that the prospect of crossing the ocean was both terrifying and thrilling to her. To date, she had failed to say what she wanted.

※

Ting Ai, at the inn, was a big problem. No longer having farm duties or house chores, she liked it there too much. He'd paid in advance for the room and given her money for food, but now she'd begun demanding more, claiming it was for the sake of the baby. She'd begun reading the Cantonese language books he'd left there, and she wanted to have conversations with him about them.

The last time he went to check on her, she said, "The man who violated me, raped Wèi An too. Ah Yun is old. He's forty."

Foshan hung his head. Hands on hips, he tapped his foot while listening.

Raising her chin, Ting Ai rushed her narrative forward. "He's a regional tax collector and has five children with his wife. He's sired at least twenty-five others in Panyu." Her eyes narrowed. "As long as he delivers money, the government supervisors don't care what he does. He's untouchable."

Foshan's mouth was a grim line. He massaged a clenched fist with his opposite hand. The expression he wore was murderous. "We'll see about that," he whispered under his breath.

※

The Gee children, every one of them, astonished Foshan. Their outspokenness, energy, and curiosity made him want to find more for them: more to read, more places to visit, and more to learn.

In China, if one was born a peasant farmer, one would die a peasant farmer. In California, he and Lee never would have imagined becoming chefs, or that they'd like it. Foshan now understood why it was important to Lee to bring them to their new home.

※

Mother Gee was taking so long to give her answer that Foshan was thinking he'd have to leave her. He couldn't imagine how she'd make it on her own.

He discovered her sitting quietly near the ancestor's graves. She'd been cleaning and leaving food offerings.

"I do not mean to intrude," he said, making a quick bow.

For a moment, her dark eyes peered at him through folded nests of leathery skin. "What is that you are carrying?" she asked.

"This?" he brought out a notepad from under his arm. "I've been copying the family lineage." He pointed at the wall where fourteen generations of Gee ancestors were recorded in vertical pictographs.

Mother Gee sighed and nodded. "That is good," she said. "You will add Yang's name before we leave."

Working to keep his expression neutral, Foshan nodded.

Heaving herself into a standing position and leaning on her cane, Shao Pei began her long tiny-step journey toward the home she'd shared with her husband and sons. Turning before she got too far, she said over her shoulder. "I'd like to see that knife and hear about what he's done with it."

Smiling, Foshan bowed. "Then you shall. You will like it even better when you watch him use it!"

※

After Shao Pei had given her consent to move, Foshan visited Ting Ai.

"Mother Gee has decided to go to America," he said forcefully as a greeting.

The pinched expression she wore whenever he was around fell. "She has?" Ting Ai squeaked.

"Yes. I'm planning to have the property sold and ship out by the end of the month."

Wrapping her arms tightly around her waist, Ting Ai rocked. "Is she going to sell me?"

Foshan's mouth dropped open. "Sell...?" Shaking his head, he said, "Lee included boat fare for you."

Ting Ai blinked as if she did not understand.

Softening his voice, Foshan said, "You are the widow of Gee Yang and mother of Gee Ming. As far as I know, that means you are a member of this family."

"But you banished me," she said, dropping her gaze.

"Because you've been a bitch!"

Her eyes flew to meet his.

"Do you deny it?"

She did not reply, but moved her chin to one side, continuing to hold his stare.

"Can you stop doing that? Is it something you can't control?" Foshan asked.

"I can...stop."

"Good!" He seemed flustered. "Then you may return to the farm. We need your help."

"Ok," she said.

Before Ting Ai could start gathering her things, Foshan tapped her elbow. Glancing at her belly, he said, "If you can hold off on that." He waved his index finger in a circle around her abdomen. "Do. We have a budget and didn't account for extra."

"I'll try my best," she whispered.

"I'll be watching you. Any funny business and we're going to have to make some very unpleasant decisions. Understand?"

"Yes, Mr. Yow," she bowed.

※

Closing up a household that had been in use for generations was no simple task. But the women and their community contacts came through, pitching in to organize sales and ready items to ship.

※

Foshan made a focused effort to maintain his feelings of disdain for Wèi An. But as he watched her and worked with her over the weeks, he came to understand Lee's devotion.

Wèi An's reactions to the situation, a swirling mess of anticipation, love, and shame, endeared her to Foshan. He enjoyed listening to how she kept Lee and Yang fresh in the children's minds with stories of their family life: the planting of the tangerine tree, how Song landed in her father's hands on the day she was born, and about Ngon, Fu-chi, and Mo Chou's daughter, a chatterbox and beloved niece.

Often, when she did this, Mother Gee picked up her erhu and strummed chords matching the tale.

When Wèi An started telling them about America, information that came from Lee's letters, Foshan joined in. "Your father, Ming, was known as Manly Blaster, one of the most famous tunnel men. The gangs wrote songs about him."

Mother Gee thrummed several dramatic notes.

"Song and Luck," Foshan continued, "your father prepares delicious meals that remind the Chinese of their homeland. The big railroad bosses asked him to prepare special meals for important guests."

Strumming a backing, Mother filled the pause.

"When you see him." Foshan's attention returned to the children. "You must ask him about the pet squirrel we had for a time."

The music after this sentence had more life to it. Across the space, Foshan's eyes met Mother's. *What's going on there?* he wondered.

※

At low points, when Foshan had found Wèi An weeping in the barn or some other secluded place, he asked, "Are you sad about leaving China?"

"No," she said, rubbing at her tears. "I'm imagining what my husband will think when he sees me like this. What will I do if he can't forgive me?"

Foshan patted her shoulder. "First, know that you and all of your children will be safe. Next, once you see him, you must learn to know him again. Time didn't stand still for Lee either."

Unbelievably, now and again, Foshan caught himself rooting for Lee and Wèi An.

※

They were waiting on the dock for the passenger signal to board. Their cargo was already loaded in the hold. The children were chattering nonstop, and Mother Gee was watching the quick-moving world flowing around her.

Foshan had a black eye and bandages across his knuckles. His limp was worse than normal as he led the old mule and cart down to the stablemaster, who'd agreed to buy them. He talked to the animal as they walked. "You have served this family well. You probably knew all the Gee brothers. I'm sorry if it feels as if you've been used and cast away. I considered taking you, but the journey would be too hard. I hope this muleskinner has a kind and generous heart; many of them do. And I hope you know love again before it's all over." He stroked the velvet nose. "That's all any of us can ask for."

※

"Children change everything," Foshan remembered Lee saying. "They are hope for the future bundled in small bodies."

Foshan's gaze kept tracking Ting Ai and the baby she'd kept inside until they made it on the ship. *Will it be born at sea? Should I tell her Ah Yun won't be fathering any more babies?*

Ting Ai needed a protector, someone of her own, not just a sympathetic brother-in-law. That baby and Ming needed someone, too. For the first time in his life, Foshan could envision a place he could fit into a family.

SIGHTINGS
Ting Ai, age 30 | Wèi An, age 23
Song, age 7 | Luck, age 6 | Ming, age 9
San Francisco, California – four months later
1870
—

Arriving early at the docks, Lee's skin pricked like bees swarming over honey. Glancing down at what he was wearing, he realized he should have taken more care with dressing. After such a long separation, it would have been appropriate to wear something formal to greet Mother. Since there wasn't time to change, his California work clothes would have to do.

Two weeks ago, a note from Foshan had been delivered saying that Mother had agreed to come. *Be prepared,* he'd written, *there will be more people in our travel party than you're expecting. We'll be sailing on the Satsuma.*

While a sense of relief flooded Lee, he frowned, flicking the paper and speaking out loud, "What do you mean, Foshan? This is vague and unhelpful. What are you trying so hard not to say?"

The changes in the Customs House barely registered when Lee strode past it. The closer he got the to water, the more difficult it was to breathe. His chest felt like a fiery barrel hoop was constricting it. When an onlooker called out, "The Satsuma coming into the harbor," Lee braced his hands on his knees. A cold sweat coated his face and neck.

Focusing on pushing air out and sucking it in, Lee was standing perpendicular, feet in a wide stance, hands on his hips, and wearing what he hoped looked like a smile when his family came into view. They were lined up along the bulwarks. *Mother looks older, resigned,* he thought. A sudden memory—the sour odor of her broken feet—caused the back of his throat to quiver. Next to her was Wèi An, wearing a pinched expression. *She's as pale as rice paper.* With one fist planted on the rail and her other hand covering it, she appeared to be kneading bread dough while frozen in place. Her gaze was downcast. *Look up, Wèi An!*

Ting Ai and her daughter Ming were next. *Sister-in-Law is the only adult who is smiling. What is in that bundle she's carrying like a baby?*

Bobbing up and down like a jumping bean was Song. She waved wildly while shouting, "Daddy! There's my Daddy!" *Oh...she's grown so much,* Lee thought as the nervous conditions he harbored broke away and were replaced by warm, glowing joy. With his feet on the rail next to her, a small boy looked as if he couldn't decide to laugh or cry. From behind, strong arms banded around him, allowing for a sense of risk while also remaining perfectly safe. *That's my boy. That's Luck.* Lee blinked hard against the moisture that threatened to spill. His gaze shifted to Foshan, where it held. The distance between them couldn't stop the calming influence Lee always felt around the man. Formally, he bowed to him saying, "Thank you for bringing the family back together."

ALMOST THE END

Pill Bug,
Armadillidium vulgare

GILLS: Breathing. Catching scents of edibles.

Burrowing through night ground,
the land crustacean moves toward rotting vegetation.
Hemp and cotton that could have been clothing.
It also consumes and contains heavy metals.
Lead and arsenic as such, maybe mercury too.
The pea-sized isopod requires moisture as it works to
recycle and enrich the soil.

EPILOGUE I
Lockport, California
1871
—

Lee clanks his scraper against the griddle edge, dislodging burnt food crumbles. Leaning over and swiping across the hot, round surface, he nods, satisfied. *It is ready.*

Lined up neatly along a side counter are bowls filled with a rainbow array of fresh, expertly sliced vegetables. Marinated meats rest in more bowls. Eggs, ready for cracking, complete the ensemble.

As an added flourish, he makes a display of lightning-fast chop work of a sweet, purple onion and three fat carrots, twirling his beautifully crafted, one-of-a-kind chef's knife between each vegetable. They go from palm size to precision-diced toothpick size. He smiles when he hears his audience clap. When he finishes with the exhibition, he places the knife in a wooden stand that Luck made: a stable rectangle of oak, sanded and oiled, with a saw slice along the center that protects the blade edge.

Taking a deep breath, Lee approaches the griddle as if it were a great steam organ he is about to play. With high beginning notes, he starts with flavored oils, sending them spraying across the hot surface in sizzling readiness. Freshly chopped onions and carrots are tossed on, mingling their natural juices with the slippery oil. Fragrant fingers of delicious steam waft to greedy noses.

Using a long-handled spatula, he tosses and browns the food, adding precooked squiggly noodles. While using his implement to move it, Lee taps out a tune—the same one Wèi An played the last night before he and Yang left.

He adds accoutrements with exact timing for a perfectly cooked presentation. The steam and waves of heat with griddle cooking remind him of the explosion flashes after a day of *pound, pound, quarter turning*. While his knife is not a seven-pound hammer, the laborious prep work consumes an entire day.

He feels a hand resting on his back. Warm and reassuring, between his shoulder blades. No one is there, but he doesn't feel alarm or turn to look. With a tingly feeling that starts from that place, Lee senses Yang standing behind him to his right. Fu-chi has come to stand at his left. Flanking them are Father and Grandfather. Behind them are umpteen generations of Gees.

Lee's gaze loses focus for a moment and a small smile forms. *Yang has found the ancestors and brought them here, or Father followed Mother and called to Yang once they arrived. It doesn't matter. what matters is that we are all here, together.*

In his mind, he thanks them for coming and asks that they acknowledge Foshan and the new babies. *Accept them as your own.*

The Gee family left significant parts of themselves in Panyu, but they've also become part of the California landscape, as it has become a part of them.

Tangerine,
Citrus reticulata

*"Fruits don't fall far from the tree
but their seeds can go places
and wherever they go by their virtues
they leave their traces."*
– Indra Mukhopadhyay

News & Quotes:
Sacramento Daily Union | August 30th, 1867
The summit tunnel on the Central Pacific Railway was opened through from one end to the other yesterday.

—

"Nothing is impossible anymore." - *Daily Alta California* November 10, 1867

—

"The grandest highway created for the march of commerce and civilization around the globe."- *Daily Alta California*, June 20, 1868

Sacramento Union | November 30, 1867
The track on the line of the Central Pacific Railroad was laid to the Summit last evening, and the rails through the tunnel will be in place by an early hour this morning. Thus, has been completed the most difficult portion of the company's labors. As compared to what have been encountered, the rest of the route to Salt Lake has not obstacles worth mentioning. The day the first locomotive passes through the tunnel will be a bright era not only in the history of California, but in that of the United States.

Nevada City Daily Transcript | April 12, 1868
The name 'Coburn's Station' has been discarded by the people of that town and it is now called 'Truckee.' We learn from a correspondent that the post office has been discontinued at Donner Lake and a new one has been established at Truckee.

*California Farmer and Journal of Useful Science*s | May 13, 1869
Glorious Competition of the Pacific Railroad
...now that the mass of our people can stop to reflect upon the Grand results which has caused such vast rejoicings over the State within the past week, we shall all begin to see and feel the full value of our State, to Our Country, and to the World, the boundless good which has been achieved for us all by the Grant, Triumphant and Gloriously successful COMPLETION OF THE PACIFIC RAILROAD.

EPILOGUE II

One hundred and eighty years later, in Seattle, a curious young man would use his mother's DNA to reunite the branches of the Gee Fu-chi, Yang, and Lee family.

Sarah Strong, a five times great-granddaughter of Ngon, daughter of Gee Fu-chi and Mo Chou, found herself spitting into a plastic tube to please her college-age son.

As the Director of the University of Washington's Medical Center, Sarah would never have imagined she'd participate in "fad science," but she and Ronnie were making efforts to revise their fraught relationship.

Since he was a child, Ronnie thought he should be in charge of decisions relating to his education. His mother disagreed. The conflict between them made Ronnie's teenage years a blur of arguments for Sarah.

A recent blowout happened when Ronnie changed his major from Data Analytics to Drama without telling his parents. "You have to have a serious major!" Sarah shouted. "You'll need a job that will support a family if you decide to have one."

"There's nothing *more* serious than Drama, Mother," Ronnie declared calmly as he pushed the band of his headphones from his neck up to the crown of his head. Turning away, he nestled earpad cushions in place, terminating the conversation.

Expanding to blow like Mount Rainier, Sarah started to follow her son when Roger, her husband and father to the headstrong youth, stopped her with a touch. He gave her "the look."

It didn't take words for her to understand what he was saying. Compressing her lips, she shook her head and let her shoulders slump.

※

Two months later, Sarah and Ronnie were sitting shoulder to shoulder staring at a computer screen listing her DNA matches. "Look, Mom, it says you have a bunch of relatives in San Francisco. Do you know any of them?"

"I have no clue," Sarah replied.

A sparkle showed in Ronnie's eyes, something Sarah rarely saw directed at her. "If you make me editor of your account, I'll find out how we're related…if you want," he said.

She had to consider that. *What if there's an embarrassing scandal lurking in our family closet?* Then Sarah remembered, when she was Ronnie's age, asking her father about the family history. He'd said to her what his mother had said to him, "It's best to leave it alone."

Is it best? she wondered.

※

Ronnie started a text conversation with a distant cousin who would turn out to be a descendant of Ming, Yang, and Ting Ai's daughter.

All the branches of the Gee brothers' family would meet at a highly regarded Chinese restaurant in San Francisco still owned and operated by descendants of Luck, Lee, and Wèi An. (After their third child, Catharine, was born, the couple would go on to have six more children.)

Nervous laughter filled the space as relatives compared and contrasted similarities and differences. New bonds were formed during that memorable meal.

※

On a pine-scented July afternoon, bus tires crunched over gravel and spewed low-lying dust clouds as the large vehicle came to a rest in the service parking area across the street from Donner Ski Ranch.

They had arrived at the mouth of Tunnel #6.

When a fourth branch of the family heard about the field trip, they joined in. These were Ming's half-sibling descendants from Ting Ai and Foshan's two children.

During the long drive from the Bay Area, through the Sacramento Valley and up into the Sierra Nevada Mountains, the family listened to presentations from the Stanford Chinese Railroad Workers in North America and 1882 Projects. They leafed through binders that the Donner Sumit Historical Society made for them containing newsletter articles about the building of the Central Pacific Railroad.

Offloading from the bus, they affixed headlamps to their heads and zipped jackets. Reverently approaching the tunnel mouth, they knew this experience would change them.

※

At the entrance, rough-sided walls are marked with contemporary street art—graffiti. Youngsters in the group can't contain uncomfortable giggles when they first see obscenities and depictions of body parts their parents wish were not on display. Always changing and colorful, the messages can be philosophical and make calls for social justice, while also destroying historic patina.

As daylight fades inside, the paintings cease and there is nothing left but darkness. Many footsteps can be heard, continuing the journey. Flashlight flares look like moving stars and there's the heavy feeling of granite above, below, and all around.

"If you're very quiet," the tour guide's voice echoes in the cavern-like space, "maybe you'll hear the ghosts."

EPILOGUE III 2042

The Donner Memorial Culture Park and Outdoor Museum is on 20,000 acres inside the Tahoe National Forest. It includes the summit train tunnels and has ample do-not-disturb zones for wildlife.

The museum features replicas of railroad camps, mess tents, round houses, and snow sheds and even has a cold room display showing snow tunnels. The park includes Indigenous Tribal Washoe and Nisenan displays. Film theaters, self-guided audio, podcasts, docent-led tours, borrowing libraries, and bookstores are sprinkled everywhere a desire for information arises.

There are also tiny eco vacation villages for overnight guests.

A narrow gauge steam train runs continuously during daylight hours. It connects visitors with a clean energy monorail system that goes around Lake Tahoe.

The grand star of the Park is a California Chinese fusion restaurant, The Lucky Tangerine. It serves delicious affordable lunches and dinners. Once a year, to raise support funds, the chefs plan and prepare an elaborate meal—similar to the one the Six Companies served to Skylar Colfax—that is photographed and shared on social media worldwide.

CONCLUSION

Writer's Epilogue Notes:

Epilogues II and III marry the past to the present and link it with the future.

Inspiration for the field trip came from a 2018 "Following Chinese Railroad Workers" tour I joined. It was organized by the Community Asian Theater of the Sierras.

During the COVID pandemic, using DNA genealogy, I found my own lost family who were turn-of-the-century San Francisco orphans.

Epilogue III is a vision that grew from *Crossing* project research and from visiting the Skansen Outdoor Museum in Sweden, and the Hida Folk Village in Japan. While the 2042 epilogue is pure fantasy. The following requests are not!

Requests:

If this story made you want to take action, **consider supporting the following non-profit organizations.**

- Working to preserve Chinese culture, history, and civil rights.

Chinese Historical Society of America

1882 Foundation

- Preserving Railroad History – Donner Pass Route of the Transcontinental Railroad.

Donner Summit Historical Society

Placer Sierra Railroad Heritage Society

Visit LittleMountainPublishing.biz for links to each organizations 'donate' page.

Write a review. Reviews are how readers find books. If you liked *Crossing: A Chinese Family Railroad Novel*, please think about writing one. It can be as simple as choosing stars, a single word title, and one sentence.

Fabrications
Crafted in the author's mind.
- All major characters, their dialogue, and relationships.
- Animal thoughts.
- Catfish cultivation in rice fields.
- Hiding livestock.
- Seeds in wedding ceremony.
- Goose challenge as a marriage test.
- Doufu Hua symbology.
- Unusually high rate of gambling success.
- Railroad policy of allowing family members to tend to the sick or injured.
- Letters going back and forth from China to California.
- There are discrepancies in historical records about pay rates.
- Blasters and their nicknames.
- Pillowcase-style horse blinders.
- Chicken heat.
- Mother Gee shipping a knife to her son.
- Gold leaf in a knife handle.
- Blue rooms and back rooms.
- How Maiden's Retreat (catfish pond) was named. Likely Seth Green, a veteran fish culturist (or his associates), planted catfish there in the 1870s.
- Apolo as the white mule's name. The legendary animal belonged to Lewis M. Clement.
- Lodging in livery stables.
- Work vs. time off schedules.
- More avalanche scenes at Donner Summit than historical records show.
- Nitroglycerine warming method in the tunnels.
- Nitroglycerine use negotiations during the Chinese labor strike.
- More deaths inside Tunnel #6 than shown in historical records.
- Tunnel blasts were alternated, not simultaneous.
- Six Company loan practices.
- Blasting sickness.
- Bone processing yard in Rocklin.
- Chinese settlement in Lockport (Locke) in 1869.
- Spirit visitation.
- Immortal innuendo.
- Epilogues.

Author's scene-writing process

Every scene begins with research, moves into evaluation, continues with judgment calls, and finishes with fitting historical events and imagined filler into a cohesive story arc.

Consider the approximately 60-mile stretch of terrain between Newcastle and Truckee, "The Hill." Railroad enthusiasts and historians are meticulous researchers who enjoy details! Because of this, there is an abundance of material written and recorded about the building of the transcontinental railroad in that area. When there's an event that I want to write a scene around, I consider the source material and ask questions like, *Do multiple sources agree? Is the information coming through trustworthy channels?*

When a writer has characters moving through space or time, but there are no source materials to consult, the author then has to find something in common with the characters. *What perceptions and feelings are their five senses picking up? What is their internal dialogue? How do these experiences filter through their personal history and family relationships?*

An example of blending fact and fiction is the number of accidents and avalanches that I portrayed at Donner Summit. While ALL of them may not have happened there, similar ones happened all up and down The Hill. Drama and tension were added by having our brothers live through life-threatening situations.

Locke is another example. In reality, the town was not established until after Lee's time there. In its earliest days, it was called Lockport. I've been to Locke; I can describe it and it seemed like the perfect setting to begin and end Lee's journey. The farming culture, proximity to the Sacramento River, and because it once hosted a vibrant Chinese community, fit with Lee's skills and addressed his feelings of homesickness. Plus, it allowed for a poetic conclusion.

Many Thanks

This book would not exist, as it is, without—

My husband Gary, who is my exploration partner. During the creation process, he held down the fort, filled in the gaps, and allowed time for research and writing. He is an excellent listener, sounding board, troubleshooter, and occasional editor!

My long-time writing compadre, B. McKeegan, who listened to and read the story as it was emerging and did the same six years later, when it concluded. Her friendship, professional relationship analysis, detailed editing, and pep talks are invaluable.

H. Tjoa, my cultural mentor, cheerleader, Chinese community connector, and fellow author.

E. Mailman, historical authoress, whose Mailstrom Writing Clinic answered the big timeline question—linear vs. switching between past and present.

D. Russo, author and Writing Historical Fiction Instructor who helped improve my resource management techniques.

C. Hedglin, Woolman Writers Retreat Facilitator, and attendees Sara, Alexa, Dorothy, and Theresa, who created a friendly space, provided useful feedback and were active, interested listeners. The final chapters and "The End" were written at Woolman.

The first beta readers, P. & L. Greene, T. Juhl, and K. Thompson, who asked the right questions at the right time and helped flesh out the characters.

L. Vrooman, fellow conference planner, Sierra College English Instructor, and writer who commented, "It's got place interest," and shared her perspective about staying true to a character's growth as a human.

Sierra Writers Conference for workshops, lectures, and critique groups that fine-tuned craft and technique. These teachers and professional writers include; D. Keriotis, C. Bramkamp, S. Hall, C. Nemic, M. Volmer, K. Bateman, P. Houston, G. Noy, and C. Crane. Special kudos to M. Hong Kingston, who in her 2023 presentation [1:05:35] said, "It is the most wonderful miracle on Earth when we are able to understand and walk in the shoes of another person."

Culture, sensitivity, and historical expert readers C.E. Shue, L. Ackert, W. Oudegeest, C. Spinks, C. Raiche.

T. McAteer for teaching OLLI Central Pacific Railroad history classes.

J. Cox, my brave and determined Qi Gong teacher.

M. Belluomini for being the final editor to fine-tune grammar and formatting.

My cousin Marion, who taught me how deeply satisfying it is to reclaim parts of my heart (and family) that I didn't know were missing.

My folks Dianne and Wayne for a lifetime of love and enthusiasm as well as multitudes of engaging history and philosophy conversations.

My son Ben, whose presence in the world continually makes me think about how to leave this place healthier for all life forms.

About the Author

Lisa Redfern began her career as an educator for Sacramento County teaching recycling and composting. In the mid-1990s she joined a portrait studio in Nevada County, California where she worked for 20+ years capturing and commemorating individual families in still imagery. When smartphones came on the scene, Lisa shifted to working on custom creative contracts, writing, art, historical research, and in-depth natural history studies.

Lisa lives about an hour away from Donner Summit with her husband and fur people (aka a dog and two cats who are both annoying and delightful and almost always find their way into her books).

L. Redfern
Donner Summit Tunnel #6.
© Bonnie McKeegan 2017

For history walks and hikes connected to *Crossing*, bonus materials, art, and research resources with links visit
https://LittleMountainPublishing.biz or
https://substack.com/@lisaredfern

Comments about *Crossing*

The Gee family saga started after hiking through Tunnel #6 on Donner Summit. It was summer, but inside the sharp-toothed interior, it was dark, cold, and slightly scary.

I often questioned the powerful compulsion to research and write about Chinese railroad workers because I'm not Chinese, an engineer, or a man. That didn't seem to matter. The story kept churning inside and it had to come out.

A sensitivity editor, C.E. Shue commented, "You were feeling your way into the characters' lives."

She was right. I wanted to understand what it felt like to be a young Chinese man who was far from all that was familiar. Someone who was living in the weather extremes of the Sierra Nevada Mountains and working on a job few wanted. If I did my task well, I took you along with me.

Reminder: While diligence was taken to ensure historical and cultural accuracy, errors are inevitable. As a work of fiction, *Crossing* is presented as an engaging family drama. The bibliography will assist those wishing to further explore known historical facts provided by professionals.

Crossing Reflections

Movement through life is crossing.

Aging is a process of crossing from one phase of life to another.

People cross geographical spaces if there's need, greed, opportunity, or environmental trouble.

When others are crossing near where we live, we can be welcoming and accommodating, territorial and cruel, or somewhere in between.

Depending on how our decisions work out, we may cross into new ways of thinking.

Before crossing through intersections, it is *always* wise to listen first, then look left, right, and behind before proceeding.

LittleMountainPublishing.biz

BOOKS BY

LISA REDFERN

Historical Fiction
PHINEAS GAGE: AFTER THE ACCIDENT YEARS
aka PHASES OF GAGE: AFTER THE ACCIDENT YEARS

If you've taken a psychology or brain science class, you're familiar with Phineas Gage. In P.T. Barnum's New York freak show, he promoted Gage as "The Man with his Brains Blown Out." Phineas was the first known person to survive a traumatic brain injury. While working as a crew boss on the Rutland & Burlington Railroad in Vermont, a thirteen-pound tamping iron set off a blast that shot the tool through his skull. But there was more to the man than a case study or oddity. In first-person narratives, those closest to him—his sister, brother-in-law, and Phineas himself—describe what life was like adapting to his physical challenges as the family moved from New Hampshire to San Francisco in 1849.

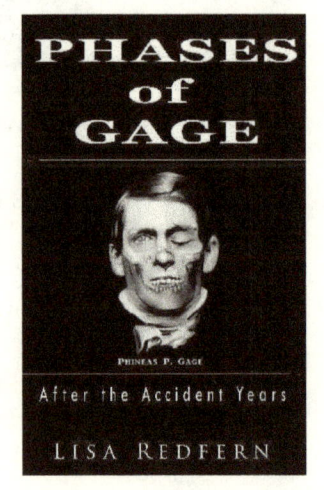

Fiction: Paranormal romance thriller & sci-fi, time travel, contemporary realistic fantasy

Book #1   Book #2

HAYLEE AND THE TRAVELER'S STONE
&
HAYLEE AND THE LAST TRAVELER

Haylee is something beyond a teen with a dead mom and a checked-out dad. She has delayed puberty followed by a dramatic overnight transformation. Delight in her new appearance soon turns to alarm when terrifying, uncontrollable behavior develops. To keep those close to her safe, Haylee distances herself from everyone she loves. Leapfrogging through time, Haylee races to solve her mystery and redeem unforgivable mistakes.

Bibliography

Cookbooks
Chin, Lily (1972) *Your Favorite Recipes* Calico Press
Chung, Su (1965) *Court Dishes of China: The Cuisine of the Ch'ing Dynasty* Charles E. Tuttle Company
Kan, Johnny L (1980) *Eight Immortal Flavors* California Living Books

Books
History: California
Barker, Malcolm E. (1994) *San Francisco Memoirs: 1835 – 1851 Eyewitness accounts of the birth of a city* Londonborn Publications
Barker, Malcolm E. (1996) *San Francisco Memoirs: 1852 – 1899 The ripening years* Londonborn Publications
Benemann, William A. (1999) *Year of Mud & Gold: San Francisco in Letters and Diaries 1849 – 1850* University of Nebraska Press
Huff, Roger (2014) *Tales & Towns Along the Truckee* Truckee Donner Historical Society
Lord, Paul A. (1981) *Fire & Ice: A Portrait of Truckee* Truckee Donner Historical Society
Mann, Ralph (1982) *After the Gold Rush: Society in Grass Valley and Nevada City, California 1849 – 1870* Stanford University Press
Noy, Gary (2014) *Sierra Stories: Tales of Dreamers, Schemers, Bigots, and Rogues* Heyday Books
Speer, William (1870) *The Oldest and the Newest Empire: China and the United States* S.S. Scranton and Company

History: Chinese
Barth, Gunther (1964) *Bitter Strength: A History of the Chinese in the United States 1850 – 1870* Harvard University Press

Chan, Gene O, Low, Russel N, Yee, Andrea (2014) *Voices from the Railroad: Stories by Descendants of Chinese Railroad Workers* Chinese Historical Society of America

Lee, Sue and Yu, Connie Young (2020) *Voices from the Railroad: Stories by Descendants of Chinese Railroad Workers* | 2nd edition | Chinese Historical Society of America

Chang, Gordon H. (2019) *Ghosts of Gold Mountain.* Houghton Mifflin Harcourt

Chang, Iris (2003) *The Chinese in America: A Narrative Story* Penguin Books

Chen, Yong (2000) *Chinese San Francisco 1850-1943: A Trans-Pacific Community* Stanford University Press

Confucius, translated by Dawson, Raymond (1993) *The Analects* Oxford University Press

Dolin, Eric Jay (2012) *When America First Met China: An Exotic History of Tea, Drugs, and Money in the Age of Sail* Liveright Publishing Corporation

Farkas, Lani Ah Tye (1998) *Burry My Bones In America: the Saga of a Chinese Family in California 1852 – 1996 From San Francisco to the Sierra Gold Mines* Carl Mautz Publishing

Harrison, Henrietta (2005) *The Man Awakened from Dreams: One Man's Life in a North China village 1857 – 1942* Stanford University Press

Hom, Marlon K. (1987) *Songs of Gold Mountain: Cantonese Rhymes from San Francisco Chinatown* University of California Press

Lee, Johnathan H.X. (2014) *Auburn's Joss House: The Auburn Chinese Ling Ying Association House* Auburn Joss House Museum and Chinese History Center

Liu, Haiming (1953) *The Transnational History of a Chinese Family: Immigrant Letters, Family business, and Reverse Migration* Rutgers University Press

McCunn, Ruthanne Lum (1988) *Chinese American Portraits* University of Washington Press

Miyazaki, Ichisada translated by Schirokauer (1976) *China's Examination Hell: The Civil Service Examinations of Imperial China* John Weatherhill, Inc.

Ni, Maoshing, PH.D. (1995) *The Yellow Emperor's Classic of Medicine: A New Translation of the Neijing Suwen with Commentary* Shambhala Publishers, Inc.

Qin, Yucheng (2009) *The Diplomacy of Nationalism: The Six Companies and China's Policy Toward Exclusion* University of Hawai'i Press

Sinn, Elizabeth (2013) *Pacific Crossing: California Good, Chinese Migration, and the Making of Hong Kong* Hong Kong University Press

Tjoa, Hock G (2016) *The Battle of Chibi (Red Cliffs): Selected and Translated from the Romance of the Three Kingdoms* Sleeping Dragon Books

Wells, Robert S. (2014) *Voices from the Bottom of the South China Sea: The Untold Story of America's Largest Chinese Emigrant Disaster* Adducent

Zhang Mike and Zhou Limin (2015) *Chinese Railroad Workers Historical Photo Album* 150th Anniversary Celebration Committee

Xueqin,Cao, translated by Hawkes, David (1973) *The Story of the Stone* Penguin Books

History: Donner Summit

Oudegeest, Bill (2015) *Walking Through Donner Summit History* iStreet Press

Signor, John R. (1985) *Donner Pass: Southern Pacific's Sierra Crossing* Golden West Books

Stewart, George R. (1964) *Donner Pass: and those who crossed it* Lane Books

Towle, Russell (1994) *The Dutch Flat Chronicles 1849 – 1906* Giant Gap Press

History: Lumber

Anderson, Cynthia (2019) *From the Woods: True Tales of the Timber Industry* Comstock Bonanza Press

Wilson, Dick (1992) *Sawdust Trails in the Truckee Basin: A History of Lumbering Operations* Nevada County Historical Society

History: Railroad

Ambrose, Stephen E. (2001) *Nothing Like It in the World* Touchstone

Chew, William F. (2004) *Nameless Builders of the Transcontinental Railroad: The Chinese Workers of the Central Pacific Railroad* Trafford Publishing

Deverell, William (1994) *Railroad Crossing: Californians and the Railroad 1850 – 1910* University of California Press

Duncan, Jack E. (2005) *A Study of Cape Horn Construction* RSPress

Galloway, John Debo C.E. (1989) *The First Transcontinental Railroad: Central Pacific Union Pacific* Dorset Press

Kornweibel, Theodore Jr. (2010) *Railroads in the African American Experience: A Photographic Journey* The Johns Hopkins University Press

Kraus, George (1969) *High Road to Promontory: Building the Central Pacific Across the High Sierra American West* Publishing Company

Maniery, Mary L., Allen, Rebecca, and Heffner, Sarah Christing (2016) *Finding Hidden Voices of the Chinese Railroad Workers: An Archaeological and Historical Journey* Chinese Historical Society of America

Mayer, Lynne Rhodes and Vose, Kenneth E (1975) *Makin' Tracks: The Story of the Transcontinental Railroad in the Pictures and Words of the Men Who Were There* Praeger Publishers

Sandler, Martin W. (2015) *Iron Rails, Iron Men, and the Race t Link the Nation: The Story of the Transcontinental Railroad* Candlewick Press

Memoir
Frankel, Victor E. (2006) *Man's Search for Meaning* Beacon Press

Novels
Estes, Kelli (2015) *The Girl Who Wrote in Silk* Sourcebooks Landmark

Ryan, Shawna Yang (2007) *Water Ghosts* (previous title: *Locke 1928*) Penguin Books

Photography & Illustration Sources
Animal and tangerine illustrations, plus Crossing movement through life image – Open AI, Dall-E
David Rumsey Map Collection
Dragon and fish illustration – Pixabay.com
Library of Congress, Lawrence & Houseworth Collection
Library of Congress, Sandborn Fire Maps